Lock, Stock and Peril

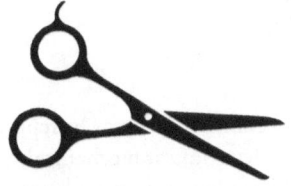

Charlie Cochrane

I0636015

RIPTIDE
PUBLISHING

Riptide Publishing
PO Box 1537
Burnsville, NC 28714
www.riptidepublishing.com

Lock, Stock and Peril

Cover art: L.C. Chase, lcchase.com
Editor: Carole-ann Galloway
Layout: L.C. Chase, lcchase.com

ISBN: 978-1-62649-966-9

First edition
June, 2022

Also available in ebook:
ISBN: 978-1-62649-967-6

Lock, Stock and Peril

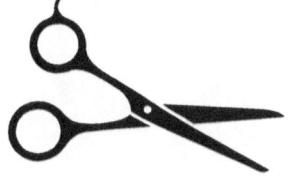

Charlie Cochrane

RIPTIDE PUBLISHING

For my family, who neither murdered me during lockdown nor failed to provide ideas for my writing. Who'd have thought someone saying, "That's a turnip for the books!" would have been so inspirational.

Table of Contents

Chapter One

"No murders allowed, right?"

Robin Bright glanced up from doom-scrolling the news to view the pleasing sight of his husband, Adam Matthews, who'd broken the silence. Hair tousled from where he'd been snuggled up on the sofa having forty winks—with Campbell their Newfoundland providing a useful blanket for his feet—Adam gave the impression of only being half-awake. Perhaps he'd not known what he was saying, still partly in a dream world.

"Eh? No murders allowed when?" Robin asked.

"Now. Anytime, really. I was saying that if we do get away for a holiday this summer, we don't want it being spoiled by you getting called in to a murder case three days before we go." Adam grinned, in a way that could still turn Robin's knees to water. "You weren't listening, were you?"

Robin held up his phone. "Exhibit A. I was trying to keep abreast of the news. If it's possible to keep abreast of it."

What a year 2020 had been, and the start of 2021 wasn't shaping up that great, either. Some activities that had been allowable the previous January were now—in his opinion quite rightly—an offence, and the patterns of crimes had changed. One thing hadn't altered, although it had been emphasized: you were most at risk from those people you knew, friends and family, rather than a homicidal stranger.

"Keeping abreast? We believe him, don't we, boy?" Adam patted the dog's head, getting a yawn in response.

"Pfft. Tell you what, I'll get in contact with all the villains on the patch to ask them to keep their hands to themselves when it's coming up to the school holidays. Maybe a leaflet drop round all the houses would work for the ones who aren't on the radar yet." If only such a thing were possible and, if possible, effective. During every run up to an important family event, like a holiday or their wedding, Robin found himself worrying whether mayhem would break out in Abbotston or any of the local towns. As a result of which, all leave would get cancelled until the culprits were safely locked up.

"We'll help you distribute them." Adam patted the dog again. "I keep thinking that it's been a while since you've had a complicated murder case to deal with and that our luck can't keep going forever."

"You're tempting fate." The last such occasion Robin had dealt with had been off their patch, when he'd been called in by his old boss to cover a team that was short-handed. This part of the world rarely saw killings that weren't easily solved. All in line with his proven belief that you were most likely to be hurt by your nearest and dearest. "May I remind you what has a habit of happening when one of us says something like that?"

"*Don't* remind me. You're too good an officer, so I keep worrying that you'll get whisked away to the other end of the country because the local police can't cope or have all come down with *it*. Maybe when you're handing out these flyers, can you print on them that any crimes that happen have to be within a thirty-mile radius?"

"Shall I start a blog and put my diary on it so the crooks know when they have to behave themselves? Maybe you want to put in a time frame where it would be acceptable for them to commit crimes?" Did other coppers have this kind of conversation with their partners or did his and Adam's quirky sense of humour mean they were unique?

"That's a great idea. Not sure your chief constable would approve, though. Campbell's giving me a look of disapproval. Very law-abiding, this dog." Adam tickled the Newfoundland behind his ear. "Is it wicked to hope that if you *do* have a major case to deal with soon, then it happens during this lockdown period, where it can't get in the way of anything else?"

Not wicked so much as pragmatic. However ... Robin addressed the dog. "Campbell, is your other dad hinting that he's likely to get fed up of having me under his feet again?"

The question didn't need a reply: banter like that had eased them through the previous lockdowns and any other occasions where they'd had no other company but their own. Being lovey-dovey all the time, with no jibes or jokes at your partner's expense wasn't in their repertoire.

The Newfoundland slipped away from his comfy perch on Adam's legs, crossed the room, and rubbed his head against Robin's hand, wagging his tail contentedly.

"He must have heard the magic word *lockdown*." Adam shook his head. "Clearly looking forward to weeks of people being confined to barracks again. He loves it."

Campbell had never been so fit and healthy as over the past year. They'd walked miles with him, singly or together, and when they'd been able to form a bubble with Adam's mum, she'd volunteered to take him out. Ostensibly, this was so the lads could have a break from doggy parental duties and get on with the odds and ends they needed to do on their new home in Cranshaw, but Adam was in little doubt that it was really about being able to spoil the dog rotten. He also suspected the dog formed a useful excuse for her to stop and chat to people, getting the sort of contact that was proving difficult otherwise. Everybody wanted to ask about such a handsome hound, despite the fact they couldn't get close enough to be favoured with his slobbery chops in their hands.

To bubble or not had caused some of their colleagues a lot of angst, but Adam and Robin had escaped lightly on that front. Despite Robin's mum being widowed, they hadn't needed to feel guilty about not choosing her, given that she'd already formed a bubble of her own with his aunt Clare. A more formidable duo than those two women was unimaginable; woe betide anyone who didn't wear a mask or keep their distance when they got on the case. The government had no doubt missed a trick by not employing an army of retired women to make sure that everyone was obeying the rules.

Aunt Clare had a flat over at King's Ashley, which reminded Robin ... "Have you had any further thoughts about that headship at King's Ashley Primary?"

"Yes. And no, I don't think I'll go for it." Adam was still on the young side for taking over a school, and he reckoned the one he'd seen advertised there was going to be a poisoned chalice. It had gone through four headteachers in ten years, a stuck school that needed a big kick up the backside: anybody taking that over would either make their name as the genius who turned it round or be listed as yet another failure.

"I think that's the right answer." Robin hadn't wanted to force the issue, given that he believed Adam would make a bloody great headteacher, even in such a challenging situation, and the school concerned was within easy travelling distance of their new home. But it hadn't felt right, for whatever reason. Maybe his copper's brain had filed away something he'd heard or read about the place, perhaps from Aunt Clare herself, which had left a definite *don't touch this with a bargepole* impression.

"Oh, really? Is that why you've been so noticeably neutral about it?" Adam knew him too well. "Anything you want to share? A murderer on the board?"

"Nothing so concrete. If there had been, I'd have told you. Just a feeling that I've come across the place in the past, like the feeling I had about Aunt Clare's Jeff."

"That sounds ominous, given what your rozzer's nose turned up then."

Jeff had come on the scene the previous summer, his name ringing a worrying bell. It turned out he'd been a suspect in a peculiar burglary case back when Robin was a constable, and the months before Christmas had seen Abbotston's finest—both Robin and his exceptionally efficient sergeant, Pru Davis—solving the cold case and clearing Jeff of suspicion in the process. Satisfying all round and further evidence that if Robin's instinct was that something was worth investigating, it should be done.

"You know what'll happen now, don't you?" Adam continued. "You'll get a case come up at King's Ashley, and it'll turn out to be centred on the school. Some ex-colleague of mine who's the prime suspect, and I'll have to sweet-talk him into giving me the golden nugget of a clue."

Robin rubbed Campbell's ears. "Tell your other dad that I don't deliberately set it up for him to be involved in my cases. They seem to want to draw him in." Too often to be healthy. "He shouldn't have so many useful connections."

"All my useful connections have dwindled to a handful of people with whom I have the occasional Zoom chat. Most of which end up being extremely awkward." Adam stretched out his arms, yawned, then snuggled down.

"Are you having another nap?"

"No. I'm assuming my thinking position. Those Zoom chats had me wondering whether you can murder somebody over the internet. It's been tempting at times."

"Sounds like perfect fodder for one of these noir television series. From Norway or somewhere else on the Baltic." Interesting concept, though. The internet had proved a breeding ground for old crimes in new variants—a con artist's paradise—but Robin had yet to see that taken to its ultimate variation. Except in the hideous case of people being egged into taking their own lives. "Perhaps you should use the new lockdown to start writing a murder mystery. You have plenty of ideas."

"I have my own tame technical advisor too." Adam shook his head. "Nah. I know too much about what cases are really like to put down a made-up version. Too mundane, no *good cop, bad cop* anymore, not as much reliance on forensics as the fictional varieties portray. I could write a light-hearted version, though. A super-intelligent Newfoundland who solves mysteries that leave his owners—a sassy detective and a super-sexy teacher—totally baffled. Campbell the Clever Canine. Dougal the Dog Detective."

"Hamilton the Holmesian Hound. Write it. You'll make a fortune."

Adam gave a contemptuous snort. "Oh yes? In what world do the majority of writers make a fortune? I used to know one through Lindenshaw church, and he always told people who wanted to write a book not to plan on giving up the day job."

"See, you have all the connections. If I end up with a murder case that needs specialist publishing input, I know who to come to."

Adam had provided specialist educational input in the past, along with tales of what it was like serving on a jury. Linking up with old pals, snitching on choir colleagues—Adam's input to solving cases had gone above and beyond on occasions, including the time he'd joined an archaeology club simply to get Robin the information he needed. The bloke was a diamond.

Robin's mobile rang, jolting him out his thoughts, bringing the unpleasant suspicion that they'd tempted fate again and this was indeed the station calling him in for a case that would interrupt the normal running of the Matthews-Bright household.

He suspected wrongly. It *was* work related but nothing worse than his ex-sergeant, Stuart Anderson, picking his brains about a series of armed robberies he was investigating. Now based at Hartwood, some two hours' drive north, he still sought help from his old and—he professed—favourite boss.

"How's he doing on his new patch?" Adam asked, when the call ended.

"He sounds happier than ever. Taken to Hartwood and environs like a duck to water, loving fatherhood, and full of praise for Rukshana Betteridge." If Anderson had a soft spot for Robin, the man himself had a softer one for *his* former superior officer, the woman who had helped form the policeman he'd become.

"She'd have been happier if you'd relocated up there, but I guess she'll find him a chip off the old block. As long as she doesn't have to live with him—I wouldn't wish that on anybody." They'd accommodated Anderson temporarily when he'd had a domestic falling out, and it wasn't an experience they'd hurry to repeat. "I was sure that phone call was the duty officer wanting you to come in and deal with some incident or other. It usually happens when we've been talking about it. Perhaps we should ban the subject."

"Like we've banned Covid clichés? What would there be left to talk about?" A cushion striking Robin's head showed what Adam thought of that.

By the time January was nearing its end, the dreaded major case still hadn't reared its ugly head. Irrespective of them tempting fate. Adam had settled into his new work routine and had started to keep an eye on the primary headships that were being advertised. There were still vacancies around, in this county and over the border into Hampshire, so all he'd need was one within a reasonable travelling distance of their home. If the right one came up, it wouldn't hurt to give it a whirl, despite his not having many years as a deputy under his belt. Good interview practice if he got short-listed, if nothing else, and his experiences when they'd recruited a new headteacher at Lindenshaw would help. Poacher turned gamekeeper and all that. His existing boss, Jim Rashford, would give him a glowing reference, despite the fact he'd told Adam he didn't want to lose him and would do everything he could to give him further responsibility and wider experience while still retaining his services.

They'd had a conversation that very Thursday morning about whether an acting headship for a term might be a good way to tick all the boxes. And if it was within the Culdover cluster of schools, Rashford would still have Adam's brains available to pick. The headteacher had promised he'd get on to the county education department to register Adam's interest, as they were always desperate for good people they could parachute into empty seats. Quite a pleasant prospect to consider as Adam drove home, ready for an evening of cottage pie and football on the telly with the two people he loved most in the world.

Robin's car wasn't there when Adam got home, which wasn't unusual, given that the bloke didn't necessarily keep regular hours, but seeing his usual parking space empty produced a hollow feeling in Adam's stomach. Maybe Robin's copper's nose had rubbed off on him, and now *he* was sniffing something wrong. He pulled out his phone, saw that he'd forgotten to put the sound back on, so had missed Robin messaging him half an hour earlier. Adam decided to go into the house before he read the message. He could pretend it was because Campbell would have heard the car and would be straining to make a fuss over him or be made a fuss of; however, the truth was that he was a touch scared that this would be notification of another case. Worse still, a case that would take Robin halfway across the country again.

Adam got out of his coat, put down the stuff he'd brought home, fussed over the dog, and then gave himself a talking to. Fine bloody headteacher he'd make, not being able to read a text in case it carried bad news. He swallowed hard.

I'll be late home. Have tea without me. We've got word of a murder in Kinechester. Not really our patch but guess what—bloody Covid has hit the team there so we're taking over the case. I'll tell you about it when I do get home.

Kinechester? That was a relief. The main county town—technically a city because of the cathedral, though neither of them were that large—was within easy travelling distance of their house, so Robin wouldn't need to stay away. There'd been nothing about the murder on the local radio news, however, and when Adam checked the BBC site on his phone, the story only appeared as a report of a police incident in the Ramparts ward of the city.

Kinechester was an odd place. As the name suggested, it had been founded by the Romans, although the large Iron Age hill fort a couple of miles south of the city indicated the area had been occupied long before the legions came stomping in. The city centre still based itself on the great east-west and north-south roads, although very little of the original walls and gates now remained.

"Your average Roman would have recognised what's for sale in the local shops," Adam told Campbell, who seemed incredibly interested in his history lesson. Perhaps he was thinking of food, although olive oil, spelt flour, fish sauce and Italian wine were hardly his cup of tea. "A deli-worshipper's paradise. You'd have had to develop a taste for falafels if we'd moved there." The phone ringing interrupted their mutual love fest. "Hi, Mum. How's life?"

"Busy busy. You wait until you're retired. Never a moment to call my own, lockdown or not. What's this I heard on the traffic news about avoiding the Ramparts because of a police incident? Houses prices there are so astronomical you wouldn't have thought they'd have such things."

"Now, why do you think I'd know what this is about?" Adam chuckled. "Or that I'd tell you if I did. Anyway, Kinechester has its rough areas. One of my pupils used to live on the council estate there, although his parents had plenty to say about the prices in the cafés. Arm and a leg for a coffee near the Ramparts. Poshest of the postcodes."

It was an area of Victorian and Edwardian housing taking its name from a much-used, much-loved and much-envied open space that was riddled with humps and bumps. At some point in the past—allegedly during the civil war although nobody was quite sure—earthworks had been set up there and cannon stationed behind them to protect the city.

"It's as well you didn't move there, then."

"Exactly." Adam and Robin had strolled around the area in the run-up to the Christmas before last, when Robin had recently completed investigating a gruelling assault case and needed some fresh air. Somewhere far away from anywhere he'd visited for work. "Nice place to visit, especially the Christmas market and the restaurants, but beyond our means." That had put paid to any idea they'd entertained of moving to the area. "Anyway, your maternal telepathy is spot on. Robin's got the investigation, and that's all I'm saying."

"Isn't that off his patch?"

Adam snorted, always amused when his mum broke into police slang. "It's the bloody 'rona.' Hit the local team so he's got to cover for them." A sudden silence down the line. "Hello? Are you still there?"

"Sorry, dear. I was thinking about Robin. Kinechester's a Covid hotspot, you know. Numbers off the scale. I . . . I hope he takes care of himself."

Ah, so that was what the call was really about. his mum was obsessed with the latest data, able to tell you exactly which local areas had the highest infection rates. Less worried for herself or Aunt Clare than for her son and son-in-law, she said, especially with Culdover usually being another hotspot.

"He'll be fine. The king of hands, face, and space."

After the normal goodbyes, Adam ended the call to find Campbell staring up at him. He rubbed the dog's ear. "Don't you go worrying yourself, as well. Anyway, your other dad's going to be late in, mate. Maybe past your bedtime. Maybe past mine."

However, his partner would be snug at his side in bed in the wee small hours of the morning, alive and well. Which was more than could be said for the poor victim, whoever they were. Naturally, Adam could never help worrying whether Robin would make it through a case intact—hell, the man had been threatened at gunpoint in their old kitchen. But, despite that and other incidents, they'd all three managed to get through unharmed. So far.

His mum's phone call had left Adam feeling strangely uneasy, though. A gun or a knife were visible dangers; you couldn't see this bloody bug. *We'll have to dodge that viral bullet too.*

Chapter Two

Robin, Pru and Ben—their favourite and most reliable constable from the Abbotston team—had headed out to Kinechester as soon as needed. They'd been on standby all day, having heard first thing that the detective inspector at the city station had tested positive and the team members he'd been in close contact with were self-isolating, with at least two of them showing symptoms. Please God they didn't end up with anything serious kicking off on both patches.

Various machinations were going on in the background about ensuring the incoming officers had a safe workspace to operate from in Kinechester, given that Abbotston, at twenty miles away, wouldn't be a practicable base.

"Not as bad as going two hours up the motorway to Hartwood," Pru had said, when they'd been summoned.

Robin couldn't help but agree. "Thank God for that."

Ben hadn't said much at all, although the grin he'd been clearly striving to hide showed how delighted he was to have been chosen for the task over his fellow constables. Robin had been passing word up the chain of command that the lad was ready for promotion and the experience would do him the world of good.

They'd had a briefing over the telephone from the senior officer at Kinechester that dispensed the basic information. A woman's body had been found in a house in Cromwell Road, the street that adjoined the Ramparts green space. She'd been found by a delivery driver, Sam Hoskins, who'd come to drop off a mirror that the deceased had ordered and paid extra to have brought on that particular afternoon. He'd arrived about half past four, got no reply to his ringing the bell, so having a note of a safe space to leave the package in and—perhaps more importantly—not wanting to have to come back another day to somewhere right on the edge of his area, he'd nipped round the back.

The terraced Victorian properties in Cromwell Road were tall, with basements in the bottom where the servants would have worked and attics at the top where they'd have slept. Because there was no side access, a service path ran along the back of all the gardens, separating them from the gardens of the houses in Ireton Avenue.

Hoskins's paperwork said to leave the package in the back garden by the French windows. He'd found the garden gate wouldn't open, but it wasn't that high and he was a tall bloke, so he'd easily climbed up to peer over. He'd been about to shoot the bolt when he'd glanced across at the house and spotted that something was wrong. When he'd found out just *how* wrong things were he'd had a hell of a shock. Well, Robin reflected, he'd had the decency to do his duty and ring 999, despite knowing the inconvenience he'd cause himself. Other folk might have simply walked away and left it for someone else to report.

They found the driver still at the scene, being cared for in the back of an ambulance, where he was clearly in a state of shock. After a brief look inside the house, so that they could get a mental image of the scene—and a horrible one it proved—Robin and Ben took a few moments to compose themselves. Such a sight was bad enough for a case-hardened officer like Robin but, in fact, Ben coped remarkably well, turning green about the gills yet keeping the contents of his stomach intact.

Once the fresh air had worked its magic, they went to interview Hoskins while Pru liaised with the various people already at the crime scene. The local constable who'd been keeping the place secure could then fulfil the important task of seeing off some of the gawpers.

The first thing Hoskins said after Robin had introduced himself was, "You wouldn't pay a delivery premium and then not be there to receive the package, would you?"

It seemed an odd thing to come out with, until Robin reflected that the driver must have been mulling everything over in his van as he waited for them to arrive. "No, I suppose not."

"That's why I wondered if she was out in the garden, so I went round to see. I've delivered here before and knew about the back path." He clasped his hands as they began to shake. "I didn't expect to see her like that."

Robin's team would all sympathise with the man. A body that had apparently been dead for a fair amount of time—in a house where the heating had been on, albeit turned down, according to the first officer on the scene—was a sight to turn the strongest of stomachs. He'd seen plenty of corpses by now, attended autopsies, the whole works, but this instance had made him queasy, not least because of the unique smell of decay.

"I know it's hard, but can you describe what you saw while it's fresh in your mind?" Robin asked, in his most soothing tones.

"I . . . I spotted something on the floor of the lounge, through the French windows. It's not that big a garden, so you get a good view. Too good a view. I saw the shoes, so wondered if the customer had suffered a fall, which could be why she hadn't answered the door. I opened the gate, went up the path and . . ." Hoskins turned green, grabbed a bowl, and vomited into it. After wiping his mouth with a towel the paramedics must have given him, he apologised and continued. "I've never seen a dead body, not in real life. I'll be having nightmares about it. Those flies and things."

"You'll feel better eventually, I promise. If you can tell us everything now, it might help." Hoskins would likely be needed as a witness if the case came to court and have to relive the experience as a result, but Robin wasn't going to mention the fact. "The lounge curtains were open?"

"Yes. Or else I don't suppose I could have seen in. She had nets at the front. I tried to look in there earlier but couldn't."

Many people along Cromwell Road had net curtains or had grown a front hedge tall enough to maintain their privacy. If the curtains were open, why hadn't she been spotted before, though? They'd have to return tomorrow in the daylight to do a proper reconnoitre, but it seemed likely the back of the house would be visible from the windows of those properties that were on the other side of the alley, if not from the neighbouring gardens.

"So, you saw the body and then what did you do?" Ben smiled encouragingly.

"Heaved my stomach contents into her flowerbed. If your CSIs find vomit, it's mine. Then I got my phone and dialled 999 while I legged it back to my van. My mind was going round like a roller coaster and some of it's almost funny. I kept thinking I didn't want to get a parking ticket and would a warden believe me if I said I'd found a dead person and was waiting for the police to come? Would you lot suspect me of having killed her? What was I supposed to do with the mirror? It took me ages to realise I should ring head office and tell them what had happened too. I was doing it when the police car arrived."

"Why did you think she'd been killed?" Robin asked. "She might have died of natural causes and then not been found. It happens with older people."

"Have you seen the state of her?" Hoskins grabbed the bowl again, although he didn't use it. "I may not have seen a body before, but I've watched plenty of stuff on the telly. It seemed like the carpet was stained with blood and—"

Robin and Ben waited while he dry retched, but before they could ask any further questions, the paramedics appeared again and insisted they get some fluids into the bloke as he'd puked so much he was at risk of dehydration. They'd take him to the local hospital where he could be properly cared for—with the unspoken implication that getting him away from prying policemen would be part of the treatment. Robin thanked them for being so conscientious and then thanked Hoskins, saying they'd be taking a proper statement when he felt up to it.

Pru was waiting for them as they emerged from the ambulance. "Victim's name appears to be Ellen Wilkins, sir, according to what's been found in her handbag, although the Photo ID isn't all that useful under the circumstances. She was stabbed, several times, with a weapon that might have been anything from an illegal blade to a large kitchen knife, although there may have been several weapons. At least one of the wounds was either expertly placed or a lucky strike, straight into the heart. The doctor thinks death may have been pretty well instantaneous, given the blood loss. Likely to have splashed onto her attacker, unless he—or she—was very fortunate with that as well. The lounge carpet's probably been cleaned, although the crime-scene lot should be able to find residual evidence. No incriminating bloody footprint on the carpet or even mud in the hallway, like you might expect in the winter. I'd say there's a possibility that the killer had taken off their shoes, so were in their stockinged feet and slipped back into them before leaving."

"Wouldn't that make the victim suspicious, if the visitor took off their shoes?" Ben asked.

"You've clearly not been a guest at a house where they insist on it." Pru shook her head. "I hate it when protecting your carpets takes precedence over making your guests welcome."

"Do you get the impression she was that house proud? She was wearing shoes, herself." Robin wrinkled his nose. Now they were into gathering all the bits of the jigsaw, building up a picture of the victim and what was unique to her.

"Not particularly, but first impressions can be deceiving. Got a puzzle, though. The doctor thinks the victim has been dead for weeks rather than a few days. Initial guess is at least a fortnight and possibly over a month, although they may be able to narrow that down. Which begs the question of how she'd arranged for a delivery this afternoon, unless she did it ages ago."

Odd to pay a premium to fix a particular date so far in advance, though. Braving the wrath of the paramedics, Robin got back into the ambulance. "Sorry about this, Mr. Hoskins. One thing we need to check now. We'd like to know when the order was placed, so have you got any of the delivery paperwork we could see?"

"Placed last week, I think, but I wouldn't swear to it. It's all in my van. Here's the keys." Hoskins shakily fished them from his pocket, then pointed them towards a company-branded van that was occupying the residents-only space outside Ellen Wilkins's house. Given the reputation of the Ramparts, it was probably lucky not to have been given a ticket while the driver was in the back garden.

"I'll go," Ben said. He returned a minute later with some papers. "Have a butcher's at that. It definitely says the order was placed last Wednesday, by Ellen Wilkins herself."

Unless the paperwork was an elaborate piece of forgery—and why anybody should want to do that Robin couldn't think—then the order was genuine. And must have been made by somebody else using the victim's name, address, and possibly bank card. He *could* think of a reason why that had happened, but he'd keep it for the team briefing the next morning as it was exactly the sort of thing that a smart constable should be able to suggest. Doing so would boost their confidence. He didn't know anything about the team at Kinechester, although previous experience had taught him that not every working environment was as good as the ones that he and Cowdrey created.

"Pru," Robin said, "can you take one of the uniformed constables and get a statement from the neighbours at number forty-one while Ben and I tackle number thirty-seven? We'll do a total sweep tomorrow when we have a bigger tranche of information from those who lived closest."

"Will do. I think it's wise not to go out generally until we've got a better handle on things." Pru cast a glance up and down the road. "Lots of people to talk to and I'm not sure at present what the key questions are. This isn't going to be straightforward, is it?"

"That, sergeant, is an understatement."

Alex Carey, the neighbour to the left when viewing the houses from the pavement, had already made herself known to the police, offering hot drinks to anyone who needed them on such a bitter night. Robin, chilled to the bone and regretting not having his base layers on, wished he and Ben could take advantage of the offer while they took the initial statement, but Abbotston policy at present was to refuse any food or drink that might carry an infection risk.

When Robin entered the house, he spotted two girls peeping round the corner of the stairs.

"Over excited," Alex Carey said with what appeared to be a forced grin. She patted her husband's arm. "Can you look after them, Greg?"

"Yeah. Carly, Cerys, how about we watch *Frozen*?"

The offer was greeted with enthusiasm, although no doubt the girls would have preferred being in on the action. It was probably unlikely that the police and CSIs had ever turned up in such numbers in Cromwell Road; no doubt said children would be cross that they couldn't tell their mates all about it in the school playground the next day. If they were old enough to have their own phones, the texting would already have started, misinformation possibly spreading like wildfire.

"She always kept herself to herself, Ellen," Alex Carey said, once they'd settled at the dining room table.

Robin slipped back his mask and took a sip of water from the bottle he'd brought, the iciness of the drink making him curse those Covid protocols. The house seemed full of homely aromas: a spicy tang in the air that must have been their evening meal, a musky aroma of masculine scent that might have been Greg's. Quite a contrast to the awful smell pervading the neighbouring property. Double glazing must have contained it, although wouldn't the person delivering the post have got a whiff through Ellen's open letterbox? The silence, only broken by the occasional sound of buzzing fly, had contrasted to this house, where the telly had been blaring when they entered, fighting the music coming from the kitchen. However, all was calm now, apart from "Into the Unknown" coming from upstairs.

Time to get down to questions. "How long have you lived here?"

"Ooh. I was pregnant with our first, so just over nine years. We love it. Never known anything like this before. It's such a nice area. Nice people." Alex frowned. "What will I tell the girls?"

"The nearest you can to the truth. That Ellen's died and the police are here to find out who killed her. That they'll be safe." Robin smiled reassuringly. "Ben, can you give Mrs. Carey the contact for a family liaison officer before we go? Then you can get some advice if you're worried."

"Oh, thank you."

"That's what we're here for. It's not an easy time for anyone. Still, the sooner we can get answers to our questions, the sooner we can get on the trail. Do you know how long Ellen's lived here? And would you call her a difficult neighbour?" Robin asked.

"I think she moved here a couple of years before we did. And as for being difficult, no, not at all. I'd call her a nice woman, scarily clever." Alex pulled a face, maybe trying to get across how impressed she was. "Greg—my husband—used to get her to help him with his tax return."

Robin picked up on the tense. "Used to?"

"Yes. Last summer, around about the time they usually got together to thrash the figures out, Ellen dropped a note round here saying she wasn't going to be able to help out this time. Said she was very sorry but she'd be too busy. Greg didn't mind, because he'd made plenty of notes from past years and was able to tackle it all on his own, although we felt there might be more behind it than what she'd told us. Maybe she was losing her faculties a bit and didn't want to admit it. Greg's grandmother went that way in her seventies, which might be why he's such a fitness maniac. Wants to keep body and brain active. Ellen used to talk to him about running because she was a great athletics fan. She had tickets for Super Saturday—Greg was so jealous. Sorry, I'm going off on a tangent."

"That's all right. It's probably the shock." Robin gave her an encouraging smile.

"Probably. Like I said, his grandmother never wanted to show any signs of weakness and neither did Ellen. Hated even to be offered help." Ms. Carey thrust a plate of individually wrapped biscuits at them. Ben shot Robin a glance, evidently waiting for him to give the go ahead. They both took one.

"Older people can be like that," Robin said, opening his biscuit and wondering when—if—this evening he'd get a proper meal. "Especially if they've always been independent and used to responsibility. Do you know what job Ellen did before she retired? Accounts?"

"Maybe. I know she worked in a government department, although she wasn't all that forthcoming about which one or what she did there. Rather secretive about herself, but that was her prerogative. Life around here isn't like one of those soap operas where they live in each other's pockets all the time."

Which wasn't helpful for the police. "When did you last see her?"

"To speak to? Last November, a few days after Guy Fawkes's. Lockdown two. I was on the way home from taking the children to school, and she was standing at the front door, arguing with somebody."

"Arguing? Who with and about what?" Robin glanced over to make sure Ben was still making notes, irrespective of his biscuit consumption. Amazing how he could so expertly juggle recording information and filling his face.

"A woman from up the road, Sonia. Don't remember the surname. She's a Facebook friend from my daughters' school, and she normally changes her hair colour each month, so at present she's stuck with fuchsia pink and the roots showing." The witness was clearly enjoying the other woman's discomfiture. "I think, credit where it's due, Mrs. Pink-Hair—sorry, my two girls call her by her latest dye. Sonia. She may have been asking Ellen if she needed any help and was getting an earache for having dared do so. 'I can take care of myself perfectly well, thank you,' Ellen said. Or something like that only not quite as politely. I felt I had to pitch in because I couldn't walk past without saying a word. I smiled, said that if Ellen needed anything, she knew she could come to us, then I ran inside here before I could get a mouthful."

"From Sonia?" Ben asked.

"No, from Ellen. I offered help during the first lockdown, and I'd never be so daft as to do it again. She gave me a right telling-off and told me she could cope perfectly well on her own. She certainly seemed to get on all right. She was going out and about, having grocery deliveries and whatever." Ms. Carey frowned. "I don't think there have been any in the last couple of weeks. I know she stocked up her freezer so it wasn't unusual for her to go a long time in between, but I should have noticed that. Has she been dead a long while?"

"We're not able to say at present. Any idea when the last food delivery was?"

The witness shook her head, pushing forward the plate of biscuits again as she did so. "She definitely had one a few days before Christmas. She normally only used Waitrose, although she swopped to somebody else when it became hard to get a delivery slot last spring. She tried several local companies, so I couldn't tell you for certain who she's been using recently."

"Thanks. And thanks for these too." Robin took another one of the delicious raisin cookies. "And you've not seen Ellen in person since early November? In over two months?"

"As I said, not to speak to, no. But that's not been unusual, especially over the last year. She hunkered down during that first lockdown, like a lot of people did. She hadn't been told to shield—too fit and healthy for that, she said—so when I didn't see her for a week, I was worried something might have happened. Greg said we should check on her, and I told him he could do it, because I'd had my legs smacked only a couple of weeks before, as I told you, for offering help.

He thought I was being daft not wanting to go next door again, but he learned his lesson." She grinned, tipping her head up towards where her partner must be now. "She said she was perfectly all right, wasn't a three-year-old, and asked why a woman couldn't have some peace and quiet without being bothered by do-gooders."

Ellen sounded a right charmer. A highly intelligent, increasingly cranky woman who might have been starting to lose her faculties. Had that combination ultimately contributed to her death? "That must have upset him."

"It did and it didn't. He's pretty tough and, like I said, his granny went the same way, with the aggression and covering up everything. She was always lovely to our girls, though. Every year she gave them an Advent calendar with chocolates in. She said she'd not been allowed such luxuries when she was little, so Carly and Cerys got a bit spoiled." Alex furrowed her brow. "That's another rough date to fix on. Right at the end of November, she was coming home from shopping, because we were putting decorations in the window, the girls and me. I know it's too early, but last year was so miserable, we wanted something to cheer us up."

"My mum's keeping her decorations until Candlemas," Ben said.

"Ours came down on twelfth night. Very traditional around here, you know. You'd be hung if you kept Christmas lights up all year. Anyway, back to that day and Ellen. She waved and clearly wanted to speak. I opened the window, and she asked if the girls could come in to hers and get their Advent calendars. They thought it was such a treat, being allowed out on their own. Maybe it wasn't wise, but I thought, 'Alex, it's only next door and for a few minutes.' I kept an eye on them. Sorry, I'm going on, aren't I?"

"You're helping to build up a picture. I was starting to think Ellen was a bit unpleasant," Robin confessed.

Alex snorted. "Only to people she didn't want to see. She'd put a notice in her window asking people not to call unless invited."

"When was that?" Ben asked, while beavering away to get all this recorded in his usual neat and effective style.

Ms. Carey shrugged. "June, July, maybe? I lose track of time, especially last year, when all the weeks melted into one another. I know it was there in November, probably after pink-hair's visit. I don't think it's there now, although I couldn't swear to it. These things become wallpaper after a while, don't they?"

Robin hadn't noticed any note in the front window, but given the darkness and the focus on both the body and the delivery driver, there might have been fifty notices there. He'd already instructed the CSIs not to move anything that could be seen from the front or rear of the property as he wanted to return the next day to a scene that was as close as possible to how it had been during the previous few weeks. To see the house as others had seen it from outside, note and all. "You weren't suspicious about things like the lights not being on?"

The witness shot both of them a puzzled glance. "But they *have* been on. I've seen them going on and off quite normally. My girls think it's rather pretty where she has that stained glass in the window above the front door, and the hall light shines through it onto the pavement. Ellen likes that window. Sorry. I should say *liked*."

That at least explained part of the puzzle—why nobody had raised concerns about an apparently unoccupied house—but begged the question of who, or what, was operating the lights. "What would you describe as 'going on and off quite normally'?"

"When it's dark, so in the evenings and mornings." Alex Carey addressed him as she might have addressed one of her children who was being obtuse.

"Is it exactly the same time every day? I mean, could they have been operated by a timer?" Ben asked.

She appeared to take a moment to think, then nodded. "Yes, quite possibly. Ellen might have used an app to operate them. Very techno-savvy for someone of her generation."

"Thanks, that's helpful. What about curtains? Open and shutting." Could they be operated via an app? Robin could ask Ben later—he was bound to know.

"She never bothered with closing the front curtains, because she has—had—nets, which were always drawn across. Nobody could see in, and I think she used to sometimes like sitting there, enjoying the view across the green. It gave her a lot of pleasure to see the trees changing with the seasons and the children playing. She liked children." Ms. Carey suddenly burst into tears, the full impact of what had happened no doubt striking home.

Robin told her to take her time, that sudden death was always tricky to deal with and that she was being very helpful. Still, she'd fall into his can't-be-ruled-out category simply because she'd known the victim well, although she'd admittedly given no hint she was experiencing anything but genuine shock and grief.

After a minute and some furious nose-blowing, she said, "Right, Alex, pull yourself together. Lounge windows. Ellen has blinds on all her other windows, but I couldn't tell you about whether they've been open or shut. The hedge between our gardens is pretty high. She grew it like that both this side and the other side, to keep her privacy."

Was this insistence on keeping the world out eccentricity or bordering on the fanatical? "Do the houses in Ireton Avenue overlook these gardens?"

"Mostly, although directly behind us is the Methodist Church, so there's a stretch of houses that have nobody able to see in from the back, including us and Ellen. That's one of the things that appealed to us about this house and, knowing her, I'm sure she'd have felt the same. Liked to get into her garden in the good weather." The witness tapped the table. "She *was* her usual self during the summer though. As soon as we were allowed to travel again, she went away for a holiday. At least we assumed it was a holiday. She went off in a cab and when we got back off our own holiday a few weeks later, she was home again. Cleaning her dining-room windows—those are at the front. We got a wave, which would suggest her lack of help with the taxes wasn't because we'd upset her or anything. We'd actually been talking about inviting her to Greg's fortieth birthday party in the spring, assuming we're allowed parties by then. Extending the olive branch."

Robin looked at his notepad, merely to get thinking time, as he wasn't sure what else they could achieve at present. He was forming a list of questions about other deliveries such as parcels arriving either side of Christmas but he'd hold fire on them for the moment. With any luck, Pru would be able to fill in some of the blanks from the other neighbours' answers. "You never suspected anything was wrong these last few weeks?"

"No. And now I feel terrible about it. I'm sure I saw her in there over the Christmas break, but you know what it's like with the children and presents and getting the groceries in—you don't have time to notice very much. It was extra stressful this year. Almost a punch-up in Waitrose over the last pack of salad."

Robin nodded. He'd been grateful they'd discovered a farm shop locally, which had been both well-stocked and not heaving with customers in the run up to the big day. "So you think she was still alive on Christmas Day?"

"I think so. Although now I'm beginning to doubt myself. If I had to swear that I saw her, I'm not sure I could." The witness sighed. "I've got to confess I'd begun to avoid her. She was clearly becoming a recluse out of choice and having been snubbed before, I didn't want another telling off for saying or doing the wrong thing. But I should have put on my big girl's pants and gone and checked on her. If she'd been taken ill and I'd found her, maybe I could have got help to her in time."

"I wouldn't beat yourself up over that. Without pre-empting what the postmortem turns up, I'd say it's highly unlikely you could have made any difference to her."

On that sombre note and with a few formalities, including a promise for an officer to come back and get a statement from Greg, too, they left.

"What do you make of that, sir?" Ben asked, when they were clear of the property. "Could *you* really not say the last time you saw *your* neighbours?"

"In my case, yes. I'm out all day working and it's dark in the evenings. I notice their lights on but that's about it. I saw them out for a walk a few weeks ago, although I couldn't tell you what day that was and, to be frank, it could have been a month ago. Time flies."

"I guess you're right. If I had to swear to a particular date, I'd be struggling unless there was something to hang it on, like they'd interrupted me watching the big match."

Pru had yet to emerge from the neighbours' house on the other side, so Robin and Ben went back to number thirty-nine. The uniformed officer, PC Brown, had been first to attend the scene and was still present, doing a sterling job of keeping an orderly scene and moving on any rubberneckers.

"I've jotted down the details of anyone who wants to make a statement, sir," he said, tapping his pocket where his notebook must have been. "I said we were very grateful and would be in touch within the next few days."

"Excellent. Any gut feeling about whether they'll turn out to be useful?"

Brown shrugged. "Fifty-fifty, I'd say. I might be wrong but I got the impression that at least one of them saw this as a break from lockdown boredom."

Robin and Ben shared a knowing glance. They'd come across a few of those recently. "Were the lights on in the house when you got here?"

"Yes, which I thought was a bit odd, as she'd clearly been dead awhile. I made sure I didn't touch any switches or anything like that. We had to open the door, but we wore gloves."

"How did you access the property?" That piece of information hadn't yet come across. And who was the other part of the *we*?

"I thought I was going to have to break in. I'd gone round the back with the driver, while Jane—PC Hazel—stayed out front. The bloke next door came out and told her he thought they might have a spare key, so Jane could let us in the front. There's a burglar alarm, which appears to be pretty recently installed, although it wasn't switched on. Doubt it would have been set if the victim was at home."

"Where is PC Hazel now?" Robin wanted to hear more about that key, given that it didn't fit in with the picture he was building up of a reclusive victim.

"She's out on another call. Bit of a busy evening."

"Okay, thanks. I'm going to have a look inside again. Ben, I need your techno-savvy eyes peeled." Although he didn't need them to see that the notice warning people not to call uninvited was still in the window, neatly printed and seeming as though it might have been refreshed relatively recently, given the lack of yellowing on the paper.

They soon spotted a variety of devices that could have been used to control the heating and lighting, although the lounge blinds themselves, while operated by a remote control that they'd found tucked away in a draw, didn't appear to be linked to an electronic system. Ben would need to get into the victim's devices to find out exactly what was programmed and what would need human operation. They found what appeared to be her handbag, which still contained her purse, the contents of which seemed intact, although if something had been taken, only the victim would have said.

Robin gave the kitchen a once-over, but there was no convenient clue like an empty slot in a knife block to show that she might have been attacked with her own implement. The sharp knives were in a drawer among other cooking utensils, although he had no way of knowing if others had been there before Ellen had been killed. Or anything else that could have inflicted a fatal wound. He took a quick gander in the fridge, immediately wishing he hadn't.

"We'll get the CSIs to examine what's in here," Robin said. "They have stronger stomachs, and they can list the dates on the food for us."

Pinning down a date of death surely wasn't going to be easy from the medical side, so any clue would be helpful.

They left the house, at the same time as Pru was coming out of the one next door. Time to compare notes, although the full debrief could wait until the next day, when the Kinechester officers could be involved. They went and sat in Robin's car, masked up and looking a bit like bank robbers, it being too cold for standing around outside.

"Number thirty-seven told me she increasingly kept herself to herself," Robin said. "Seems like she'd created a situation where either nobody noticed anything was amiss or they were too scared to find out."

"Same story from the other side, sir. They said she was highly intelligent, pleasant enough when she wanted to be but fiercely protective of her privacy." Pru checked her notes. "They'd not seen her since early December, although the lights were on and off as normal, so they must be on a timer. Unless someone else is living there secretly."

"They'd have to be tough to live in the same house as that." Ben pointed at the house. "We should check the loft, though. That was in a cop show, wasn't it? Somebody living in a couple's attic and they hadn't realised."

"You can do that now if you can access it. Take Brown with you, in case there's trouble." Not that it was likely, but now they'd had the idea, they'd have to check.

Pru continued. "I asked Trevor—that's the chap next door, lives there with his partner Don—if they'd had a Christmas card from her. I wondered if that might help pin down the date of death if she'd dropped one through the door in December."

"Good call."

Pru grunted. "Not as it turned out. Ellen gave up sending paper cards a couple of years back and used virtual ones, instead. She said it was a waste of paper and stamps and gave the money she saved to a children's charity. The card arrived a week before Christmas, but as they pointed out, you can schedule e-cards months in advance, so as a piece of evidence, it's useless. Not using e-cards myself, so not knowing about them, I was a bit miffed. Thought I'd hit on a clue. Score one for the amateurs."

"He doesn't fancy himself as a Poirot type, does he?" Robin blew out his cheeks. He'd met that sort before, and they didn't usually help the investigation, despite what the cosy mystery books said. Adam was different, of course. He was always a fundamentally reluctant participant in Robin's enquiries, not one to actively seek out a role or pursue his own agenda.

"He didn't come across like that. Genuinely keen to help but knows his boundaries, I'd say."

"Good. What about food deliveries to the victim's house?" The evidence from Ellen's fridge suggested there'd not been any recent ones.

"Trevor reckons there was a delivery sometime around New Year. Not one of the big supermarkets, though. He didn't recognise the name of the business and can't recall it offhand, but he thought maybe it was a local company that had turned their hand to household deliveries during lockdown. That's not been unusual. I asked him to get in touch if he did remember which food supplier it was."

"He didn't see her take it in?"

"No, although he assumes it was her. Not that *we'll* assume anything."

"Quite right. They had a key for her house so the attending officers could let themselves in, I believe. Doesn't quite accord with her being practically a hermit."

"It came with *their* house." Pru consulted her notes again. "They only moved in a couple of years ago and soon realised that while Ellen would be no trouble as a neighbour, she wasn't going to be best buddies with them. They had a small bunch of mystery keys which they found when they took possession, in a drawer with their spare house keys. Once they'd sorted out which were for the shed or the lockable gun cupboard—the previous owners had been into clay pigeon shooting—they were left with two Chubb lock keys which they couldn't identify so put away safely in their desk. You know the principle: if they'd chucked them out, they'd have soon found out what they were for and needed them."

Robin snorted. "Been there, done that. Go on."

"They'd been in a few months when the people at forty-three told them that one of the Chubbs was a spare key for *their* house, which the previous owners had kept for them in case of an emergency. Trevor concluded the other key might be for Ellen's house. Which is why they offered it to Jane Hazel to try, on the off-chance."

"They never asked Ellen if it was her key while she was alive? Or offered to return it once they suspected?"

"They were too scared to. Which seems daft for a couple of doctors, which is what they are by profession. Seems that they were only really nodding acquaintances with her—people had warned them that if Ellen wanted to make friends with them, she'd do the running—but when Covid reared its head, Don popped round to say if she needed anything, then they were happy to help. He felt like he got a straight red card at football."

"They weren't alone. Don't ever turn into a crabby old woman who won't let anyone get close to you."

"I won't. Although isn't that a bit sexist? If it was a man we were discussing, isn't there a chance we'd say he was valuing his independence and not being a burden?"

Before they could debate the point, Ben came back and confirmed that he'd checked the house from attic room to basement and found no obvious evidence of occupation by anyone other than the victim. He hadn't been into the loft, although the space appeared to be so small it probably only held the header tank. Despite the prices on these properties, he reported, they didn't occupy that large a footprint, going up rather than out. They had two decent-sized rooms on the ground, first and second floors, with another pair "below stairs." The kitchen in Ellen's house—and bathroom above it—appeared to be part of a recent extension into what had hardly been a large garden plot to start with.

"Next door were right about her being a silver surfer." Ben was clearly impressed. "She's got an office decked out with her laptop and printer, and there's also at least one iPad in the house. No Alexa that I could see, but I can do a proper sweep when it's not so busy in there."

"You can take all the gear away for examination too. Whatever else we find in her files, they may be some indication of when she last used them."

"To help fix the date of death, sir?"

"Yep. And to establish if there's any truth in the idea she was losing her faculties and trying everything she could to hide it."

Chapter Three

Adam woke to hear Robin pottering around downstairs. To be pedantic, he assumed it was Robin, rather than some cheeky burglar who'd decided to make himself a bit of breakfast and chat to the dog at the same time. The fact Campbell wasn't barking didn't eliminate the intruder option—had said burglar come bearing fillet steak, the Newfoundland would have been his friend for life.

"Did I wake you? Sorry. I *was* trying to be quiet," Robin said as Adam came into the kitchen.

"Nah, you're okay." Adam wouldn't have admitted it, anyway. It was a pleasure to grab even a few minutes with his partner. He slipped his arm round Robin's waist and gave him a kiss. "Early start?"

"Yeah. Straight to the crime scene to see it in the light, then off to liaise with what's left of the Kinechester team. I've got Pru and Ben bolstering the numbers and keeping me sane."

"That's good to know. I see you've managed to keep the details out of the news. Nothing much being said about it last night." Adam, grabbing a bowl and some cereal, had decided he might as well keep Robin company with breakfast, in spite of it being earlier than normal. To hell with routine.

"I've a feeling it's going to be a challenge."

"Keeping the news blackout or solving the case?"

"Both. So far as we know—and it's very early days—the victim, Ellen Wilkins, lived on her own, so that's the normal first suspects eliminated. Then it seems that she managed to place an order last week for a mirror to be delivered yesterday. Despite the fact she must have been lying dead at the time."

"Somebody, perhaps the killer, placed the order for her. They wanted her found at a specific time," Adam said, pouring hot water into his mug.

"That's what I thought. It's possible they also took a series of other steps to delay discovery of the body and unless we can get a fix on when she was definitely last alive—another delivery for which she opened the door, maybe—then the time of death is likely going to be a large window." Robin popped a piece of toast into his mouth. "Thank God we didn't move to the Ramparts. We'd have been right on top of it all."

"Yeah. That case where I met you was close enough to home, thank you." As he chewed his cereal, Adam fondly remembered the time when he'd first met Robin. They'd been recruiting a new headteacher at Lindenshaw primary school and, wearing his school staff governor's hat rather than his teaching one, Adam had been listening to candidates talking about their vision for the school. He'd invented an imaginary bingo card that he'd marked off every time one of them used a buzz word. *Narrowing the gap*, *community cohesion*, all the boys in the Ofsted band. In 2020, he'd made up a Covid-related one to include the latest catchphrases, such as *these strange times* or *the new normal*. Some of those sayings he'd heard so often he was close to screaming. He'd put a Kilner jar in the kitchen cupboard to collect the fines he imposed when he, Robin, or anyone visiting used the banned expressions. The local RSPCA branch had already benefitted.

"Penny for them?"

"I was thinking how if that bloke—I can't even remember his name—hadn't got himself murdered in the school kitchen, there'd have been no *us*."

"Of course there would." Robin, breakfast finished and hands now empty, wound his arm round Adam's shoulders. "I'm sure we'd have found each other somehow. Campbell would have made sure of it, if not fate. He'd have come galumphing over the common and knocked me flying or something."

"You're probably right, you big softy." Adam kissed his partner's cheek, then hastily had to wipe off a tell-tale piece of Alpen. "See you tonight, hopefully."

"Fingers crossed. I'll text you to say when I expect to be in. Assume the worst and you can't be disappointed." Robin gave Adam's shoulders a squeeze, picked up his mug to drain the last of his tea, then stuck his car keys in his pocket. "Feels just like normal times."

"You said 'normal times.' That's a pound for the charity pot!"

"Bugger. No cash on me, though."

"I'll stick another IOU in there, then I'll do a tally up at the end of the month."

Robin gave the dog a pat, told him that he was lucky not to be owing the fund dog biscuits, then headed off. Adam heard the car reverse off the drive as he busied himself with preparing Campbell's breakfast, a nagging thought growing in his mind. All Robin's previous murder cases had managed to pull him in somehow, and he couldn't believe this was going to prove an exception. Still, the name Ellen Wilkins didn't ring any bells, and he wasn't aware that any friends or colleagues lived in the Ramparts area, although that had been the situation when Robin had been temporarily relocated up to Hartwood too. They'd assumed there was no way Adam could become embroiled, and yet the investigation had spread its tentacles far enough to attach themselves to him, via the leader of a choir he'd volunteered to sing in.

"What will it be this time, boy? Do I teach her grandchildren, if she had any? Was she doing jury duty at the same time as me?"

Campbell stared up at him, clearly less interested in the question than in the speed with which his food was being dispensed.

"Keep your thoughts to yourself, then. Only don't you go dipping your doggy paws into things. You've got previous."

The dog's eyes widened, presenting a figure of innocence. *Surely*, he seemed to say, *I'm not the Newfoundland who has recklessly risked his life in protection of his masters, nor have I ever cosied up to gun-wielding villains.*

"Nope. I won't stand for the whole 'Not me, guv'nor!' bit. Eat your breakfast while I have a shower. I don't want the kids complaining about my armpits."

As he drove to Culdover, Adam thought about all the times the pupils who'd still been attending the school had helped to keep him and his colleagues sane over the last year. Watching them run around the school field playing tag or kicking a ball around, while all the rest of the world had been appearing to go to hell in a handcart, had been a real pleasure. A touch of life going on as it always had.

Every time the schools had closed, Adam had still been in work, keeping the facilities open for both vulnerable children and those with keyworkers as parents. His slogan for those times had been "Different and cool!" which might have been corny, but the pupils had loved it. He'd heard on the grapevine that some of the pupils at home had been so envious they'd been trying to persuade their parents to change jobs so *they* could attend Culdover Primary. Strange times indeed when children wanted to go to school.

Damn, that's a pound for the charity pot.

It hadn't been all easy, though. Jim Rashford had come down with *it* during the Easter holidays and, while he couldn't have passed it on to anyone at work, which was a blessing in itself, the poor bloke had been flat on his back for weeks. As a result, Adam had ended up covering *his* job, the most challenging part of which had been making sure that teachers were doing what they were supposed to be doing and that the children were still learning at home, rather than everybody having a huge jolly. He and Rashford had put in place such a good system for home learning, the bigwigs from the county education department were using it as an exemplar for other schools. Another feather in his cap that would help when he did apply for headships or for a deputy's role at a larger school, the other logical career step for someone in Adam's position.

Which brought him back to the matter of King's Ashley and the question of exactly what about the place had set off Robin's alarms.

What transpired when Adam got into the staffroom at the school was maybe inevitable, given his thoughts earlier and the way his life seemed to pan out. Oh, for a murder that had no connection whatsoever to a certain poor, hardworking deputy headteacher.

The Learning Support Assistant based in his class wanted a word. Kelvin Vince was in his early twenties, seeking a change of career from care home work, and using the position to ease his way into teacher training. His performance so far suggested he'd be an asset to any classroom.

"I've got to go over to Kinechester at lunchtime, and I may not be back this afternoon. This will sound mad, but I've got to identify my godmother's body." Distinctly green about the gills, Kelvin looked like he was in need of a run to the school's first-aid room and the use of one of the puke buckets. "I'm sorry to leave you short-handed."

"Don't worry about that." Maybe it would turn out to be a different woman who needed identifying, not the victim whose murder Robin was investigating, although Adam doubted it. He should have known by now that whatever murder Robin had on his plate, no matter where in the country, its tendrils would spread until they reached *him*. "And don't rush to get back here afterwards if you're not feeling up to it."

"That's what Jim said, but I'd rather return to work if I can. It'll take my mind off things. They think she might have been murdered." Kelvin pressed his hands to his mouth and took a deep breath. "Your bloke's a copper. Do they show the whole body to the person doing the identification or only the less gory bits?"

"I genuinely don't know. I think they try to be gentle." They certainly did on the telly, although that was no indication of what happened in real life. If she'd been dead for weeks, she'd be a sight to turn the strongest of stomachs, and poor Kelvin appeared to be a delicate soul. "Did she have any birthmarks or distinguishing features that could help, so you wouldn't need to see everything? Is there a blood relation they could do a DNA comparison with?"

"She had what they call a port wine stain on her leg and a deformed toe on her foot from some old accident—I told the police that when they asked me to come in. You see, she hasn't got any family as far as we know, and my parents live up in Manchester, so it was easier for me to do it." Easier if not pleasant. "She had Mum's phone number printed on a card, pinned up in her kitchen, apparently. If there was a problem, this was the person to ring. It was a hell of a shock when we heard the news last night."

"I bet." Robin hadn't mentioned calling the next of kin, although why should he have done? It was a piece of routine work that he likely hadn't done himself. If he had, he might have recognised

Kelvin's surname, as they'd run into the lad when they'd been out with Campbell last summer. Adam would have to inform Robin of the connection as soon as possible. Not that he thought Kelvin would turn out to have killed his godmother because she'd left him a small fortune in her will or he'd hated her all his life and saw his chance of getting rid of her, but they couldn't entirely discount the possibility of involvement. Feeling guilty for his suspicions, Adam cuffed the bloke's shoulder. "If you need a sympathetic ear when it's all done, then give me a ring later. I'd love to be able to suggest a pint down the pub obviously, but in the circumstance, tea and biscuits here will have to do."

Kelvin forced a smile. "That's okay, Adam. We can arrange a drink when life's nearer normal."

"Deal."

Although if this case turned out *exactly* as normal, some equivalent to a heart-to-heart would no doubt be taking place between them much sooner than that. Time to text Robin and see how he wanted Adam to proceed.

Adam would barely have set off for Culdover when Robin arrived at Cromwell Road. He'd parked round the corner so he could stroll along and get a feel for the area, but at present the only signs of life—apart from the CSIs who were lugging their gear up the road—were the sparrows twittering madly in the hedge that ran along the back of the open space. The delivery van was still there, with a notice on it saying that the police were aware of its presence and would remove it soon, which would hopefully prevent a stream of calls from irate residents about people occupying their parking spots. The driver had been run home from hospital late the previous evening, after being on a drip—in ordinary times they'd have probably kept him in overnight. Hoskins, or someone else from the company, would be able to pick up his vehicle later that day, after it had been given a once-over inside. Robin wasn't sure what they might be trying to find, but if the delivery had only been a ruse to ensure the victim's body was found at a certain time, then who better to be involved than somebody from the delivery business, perhaps the driver himself.

Robin remembered the scene in the ambulance the previous evening with a pang of guilt, given how ill Hoskins had seemed at his discovering the body, but a good officer should never assume the innocence of any party. First to find the victim might have been last to see them alive.

He touched base with the CSIs, who had nothing much to report so far apart from some stomach-churning information about flies and larvae and their usefulness in determining time of death. Luckily Ben came trotting up the road before things became too gruesome.

"Morning, sir! It's going to be a nice day."

Robin gave him a smile; much nicer to talk about weather than postmortem insect infestations. "Shame we'll be stuck indoors for most of it."

They peered down the area steps into what would have been the servants' access when the houses were built. It had occurred to him overnight that somebody might have been able to get into the house from there, but the original doorway was bricked over and now the area itself was used to accommodate plants in tubs. Plants that must have enjoyed low light levels and that appeared to be well tended.

"Let's go round the back first before we go in," Robin said. "I need to see what Hoskins saw."

They kept their eyes peeled as they walked up the road, Robin noting that there were several houses with nets so thick he couldn't see into the front rooms, while others gave a view all the way through to the back garden, where—unlike in Ellen's house—the rooms had been knocked together.

"I'm not sure I'd like a house that's so open to view, sir," Ben said as they strolled along. "Especially as that open area must get busy when the weather's good. From what we've heard of the victim, I'm surprised she didn't choose somewhere down the end of a cul-de-sac."

"Maybe she didn't always want to be so solitary. People change." And maybe she had simply liked to observe without being observed.

They turned the corner into Rupert Drive, where Ben pointed along the road. "The alley must be at the end of this house's garden."

"I doubt they call it an alley in the Ramparts. That's far too common. Access path. Ginnel. Whatever. Here it is."

The path wasn't quite as straight as Robin had anticipated. The backs of the gardens on both sides seemed to bend in and out, shaped like a stream rather than a road. Perhaps that was what might have been here in the past, rather like the roads that could be found in London that wound along the courses of rivers now long enclosed underground. The similarity was enhanced by the vegetation being overgrown in places, especially on the Ireton Avenue side. If somebody wanted to hide from ground-level view, it would be easy to do so.

Robin and Ben headed along, keeping an eye out for anything of note, until they reached the back of Ellen's property, which was easily found due to the police tape across the gate.

Ben was about the same height as Hoskins and couldn't see into the garden until he planted his hands on the top of the wall, wedged his foot on the gatepost, and pulled himself up. "I can see right into the lounge, sir, so that checks out with Hoskins's story. And there's no padlock on the bolt of the gate, so you can easily reach over and open it."

"That also seems a bit odd, given her love of privacy. Unless . . . can you loosen the bolt?"

"Let me get my stuff on." Ben jumped back down, slipped on protective gloves, then swung up again to unbolt the gate.

Robin's idea appeared to be confirmed as he took a look around. "I know gardens don't take a lot of maintenance in the winter, but this one appears to have been kept tidy, like the tubs in the front. No leaves on the paths or other debris, and where we've walked up has plenty."

"If she's been dead for weeks, who's been doing that? Ah." Ben nodded. "The gate being unlocked. She could have had a gardener coming in."

"Yep. We'll have to ask next door if they've seen one around." Robin scanned the back of the house. "Doesn't seem like she's had the windows cleaned in a while, though, so I doubt Wallace the Windows has been here." Robin shared a grin with Ben, who was also a fan of the Nick Park films, then stood with his back against the French windows, peering from left to right. "If I was standing here—or inside—I doubt you could see me from either of the neighbouring gardens, unless you were up a ladder. Same with that church the other side of the back path. There's a window high up that would give you a prize view, but I bet it's intended for light to come in, not worshippers to stare out. Not that there have been many worshippers in churches recently."

Ben scratched his ear. "Almost a perfect storm, isn't it, sir? House location, lockdown, woman who keeps herself to herself. Made it very hard for anyone to have noticed her lying there, blinds or no blinds. Or even to have realised anything was wrong."

"You're reading my mind, Ben. Let's bolt the gate again and go in through the posh entrance."

As they entered the property, Robin noticed the smell wasn't quite as vile as previously, the CSIs having made an effort to air the place once they'd done their bit. He also noticed the small pile of mail stacked neatly on the hall table. "Any idea who did that?"

"PC Hazel, I think. She found it all scattered on the mat when she entered the property and decided it was better off out of the way of muddy boots. In case it already had footprints on."

"Smart woman." Robin flicked through the post before putting it into an evidence bag, adverts and all. "Somebody can go through this. There are some date-stamped envelopes, although nothing that's obviously a bill."

"She'd probably gone paperless, sir."

"Probably. Can you try asking the neighbours about gardeners while I have a look around?"

He started at the top and worked down to the basement. It was a neat house, decorated and furnished in a modern style, more typical décor for a person Robin's age than a woman in her mid-sixties, if that wasn't being patronising. The whole house had been put to good use, with a guest bedroom—when was that last occupied?—a study and a room fitted with both a cross trainer and exercise bike. If Ellen had stayed indoors, she could still have kept herself fit. The attic room was used for storage, with a couple of locked filing cabinets that he would set Pru and one of the local team on to exploring after the briefing.

He noticed a couple of Christmas cards laid on a shelf in the lounge, which he put into another evidence bag after glancing at the names. That might suggest the date of her death was after twelfth night, if she also kept to the tradition of taking everything down then.

No sign of a tree or decorations in the house, but some people who lived on their own didn't bother. That begged the question of whether she'd arranged to spend Christmas with anyone else and if she'd gone through with that. An oil painting of children playing on a beach raised the issue of whether there were any other youngsters among friends or distant family, apart from the Carey girls, that she might have bought presents for at Christmas. He went into the kitchen, avoiding the fridge this time, but the only new thing the daylight revealed were some tiny coloured scraps and a few ancient bits of what might be peelings among the dust on the floor by the kitchen stool. His own kitchen floor would have yielded much the same, although Campbell's hair would have been a major component. Sad, perhaps, that Ellen hadn't kept a pet, like so many people did if they lived on their own. Sad, too, that she only appeared to have received two cards, but maybe she'd thrown the others away.

Deciding there was little else to be learned from a cursory inspection of the ground-floor rooms, he tackled the below-stairs part of the house, which was as gloomy as expected, although the area had been put to good storage use. A wine rack with an impressive array of bottles, a bicycle that didn't seem like it had been used in a while, and a couple of Chinese rugs that must have cost a pretty penny. A well-stocked freezer that would have kept Ellen going for a couple of weeks. There were also tools, along with some spare rolls of wallpaper, paint, and other decorating materials. What might have been called *a man cave* in other circumstances. Further evidence, maybe, of an independent woman—*an independent person*—who could take care of herself.

"Hello?" Ben's voice sounded from the hallway.

"Down here." Robin waited for the constable to join him. "Any luck?"

"Yep. I met Greg. Seems a nice bloke. He said that a bloke comes regularly to tend Ellen's garden. All the year round, although not so often in the winter. Does the tubs in the front and gives the place a once-over at the back. He doesn't know the guy's name but his van says *Man with a Mower*. Greg's seen him letting himself in through the gate in the past, so I guess that's why it's unlocked. He's definitely been here since Christmas."

"Good work. Did Greg mention anybody else who comes regularly?"

Ben chuckled. "Not the window cleaner. He had a dust up with Ellen sometime around October or November. She said he wasn't doing what he should and didn't want him back. Sounds par for the course."

"Greg didn't happen to know who delivered the groceries, did he?"

"I'm afraid not. I did ask about dustbins, though."

Robin resisted saying, *Clever lad!* because it would have sounded patronising. He confined himself to nodding his appreciation of his junior officer thinking of something that he hadn't yet.

"So, all the houses here have wheelie bins, and they get put out the back onto the alley—path—on Mondays. Otherwise they have to be kept inside your garden or else people kick up a fuss. Greg reckons nobody would notice if somebody else's bin hadn't been put out on any particular day."

"How many bins do the properties have?"

"Black for general waste and brown for recycling. They go out alternate weeks and then there are green bags for the garden stuff which get collected the same day as the general waste collection. The garden stuff always gets picked up early but sometimes the bins don't until late afternoon. That path was stinking to high heaven in the summer." Ben paused. "I don't recall seeing any bins or bags anywhere here."

"Neither do I. There's nothing in the house and there's none in the garden, unless they're tucked away. Come on." They climbed the stairs, went through the kitchen, and out into the garden again via the back door. "No. Nothing here. Where the hell have they gone?"

"Beats me, sir. Unless she died on a Monday before she could get the bin back in and some hooligan thought it would be hilarious to steal it and give his mate a ride down the street."

"That could explain one bin going walkabouts but not two if they go out on different weeks." Robin, shrugging, gave the garden another once-over. "Maybe the gardener will be able to help, if he comes regularly. He must have had rubbish to get rid of."

They had a chat with the CSIs about keeping their eyes peeled for dustbins, before leaving them to their job. Out the front, after Ben had set off towards his car, Robin took a final glance up at the house's façade.

What made you hide away, Ellen? Why make yourself so unpopular that nobody noticed you'd gone?

Robin wasn't a bit surprised at seeing a message from Adam when he checked his phone after parking at Kinechester police station.

You won't believe this. The bloke you've got identifying your victim later is my classroom assistant, Kelvin. Go easy on him. He almost spewed just thinking of what he has to do.

Feeling totally justified at spending time to reply—this was case-related—he shot a quick, *Noted. Anything else I need to be aware of?* then realised he wasn't likely to get an answer until lunchtime at the earliest, as the school's safeguarding practice prevented staff having access to their phones during teaching time and lessons would have started by now. *If he happens to mention something about the victim or where she lived previously or whatever that sounds vaguely useful, message me. Sorry, you know that already.*

Robin was about to put his phone down when he realised he was missing an opportunity. *Can you ask him if he knew what her Christmas Day plans were? It makes sense, I promise.*

Albeit not a lot else did at present. He got out of the car, took a deep breath—why did this have to feel like the first day of term at school?—then made his way to the local chief superintendent's office.

Gary Denness could have been a clone of Cowdrey, Robin's boss at Abbotston. Both overweight, giving off the impression they were under stress and possibly heading for a heart attack. And, like Cowdrey, he had a reputation for being honest, efficient, and supportive of his officers.

Robin had met Denness a couple of times at training or liaison events, and Cowdrey would no doubt have briefed the bloke, so the meeting was less awkward than it might have been. After a tricky moment where they had a close shave at avoiding a handshake before remembering the protocol, Denness offered a welcome cup of coffee, then immediately asked Robin for an update on the case.

"We're building up a picture of the victim—intelligent, reclusive almost to the point of obsession—but we've no indication yet of how long she's been dead. Sometime either side of Christmas is as far as the medic will commit herself until there's been a postmortem."

"Stabbed?"

"Yes. As for family, she doesn't appear to have had a partner or children, given that we've needed to get her godson to come and identify her this afternoon." He'd not mention the Adam connection there for the moment.

"And she's lain there for weeks?" Denness raised an eyebrow at such a thing happening.

"So it seems. The blinds were open on the lounge windows, although I don't think you can see in there from anywhere but the garden itself. She had a gardener, so he should have seen her if she was dead when he last visited. If he did it himself, of course, he'd not have reported it. I get the impression he was about the only person who *did* visit the place regularly. She didn't encourage friendships." Robin raised a hand. "Actually, to be accurate, she had been actively discouraging people over the last few months. If she'd wanted to engineer a situation where she could die and not be found, she could hardly have done better. I'm not saying she did, though."

"Old people. Can be stubborn as mules." Denness shook his head. "Got a few in my family. You've decent lines to pursue?"

"Not as many as I hoped, to be honest, but it's early days. Ask me the same question in forty-eight hours' time, and if I haven't got some hypotheses to test, you can have my guts for garters."

Denness broke into a huge grin. "I daren't do that. Cowdrey would have *my* guts if I did anything to harm his best officer."

Robin, both delighted and embarrassed, quickly said, "I'm lucky. I've had good sergeants and constables to help me get results."

"Don't hide your light. You get your killers. If Cowdrey gets fed up with you, give me a bell."

"Don't blame me if I hold you to that." Robin grinned sheepishly, never comfortable with praise. Unless it was from Adam. He rose. "I'm due to see the whole team, in ten minutes."

"Yes. I thought I'd make the introductions and leave you to it. You don't want me hovering about."

"I appreciate the help. I need to get my bearings with them and quickly."

"All the crew will be there, civilian admin team and all. I hope you'll be as lucky with them as you say you've been in the past."

"So do I, sir." And with that heartfelt wish, Robin beat a hasty retreat to the loo before facing the troops.

The large office where the investigation would be based might have been constructed from a build-your-own-investigation-room kit. It was well lit, well equipped, and populated with more people than Robin might have expected, had Denness not pre-warned him. Denness had wanted to introduce the newcomers to as many people as the diary, the room, Zoom, and social distancing would allow. A couple of members of the usual team had wanted to attend virtually but had apparently looked so much like death warmed up that Denness had ordered them straight back to bed.

Pru and Ben were already there, the constable ensconced on a computer while the sergeant had involved herself with getting the incident board sorted. She was working alongside another man and woman, who were all that remained of the Covid-affected team.

"Robin, this is Ashok Mankad and Naomi Reeves," Denness said, with a confidence that suggested he knew his officers, rather than having just memorised their names.

The pair appeared already at ease with their two new colleagues, and each gave Robin a welcoming if tentative smile. Robin had no doubt that Pru and Ben would have put in a good word for him, but it would be understandable if the two Kinechester constables were wary at first. Still, five officers constituted a pretty thin team for what felt like it would turn out to be a tricky investigation.

Once Denness—and some of the people less involved with the case—had departed, Robin got Pru to give everyone a résumé of what they had found out the previous day, then asked Ben to conclude with what had turned up that morning.

"While we wait for the house-to-house enquiries and everything else to come back to us," Robin said, "I'd like Pru and Ashok to get hold of the gardener, then get into those filing cabinets at number thirty-nine."

"Will do, sir," Pru replied, "although I'm due to accompany Kelvin Vince when he comes in to identify the body."

"Can you hand that over to Ben? He's got an appointment with a ton of IT equipment, once the CSIs have done with it."

"*Ton*'s the right word, sir." Ben rolled his eyes. "Mind you, if I were a Ladbrokes addict, I'd have twenty quid on them being encrypted to the max."

Robin feared that was right. "Then you'll be earning your keep. Naomi, you and I can tackle Sonia, Mrs. Pink-Hair."

"I think I have a surname for her, sir," Naomi said. "We had somebody ring the station today to say she'd had an argument with Ellen Wilkins and wanted to tell us before anyone else did."

"Sensible woman."

A voice came from the back of the room. "How did she know the dead woman's name? We've not released it to the media."

"True, but it's not a tricky deduction," Robin said kindly. "If she's local, she couldn't miss the police tape. Naomi, can you make an appointment with her for today? And have we got anything on file for Ellen?"

Ashok raised his hand. "I've been working on that. She used to live the other side of King's Ashley and was one of the witnesses to a fraud case."

"Fraud?" That was it. The reason King's Ashley had stuck in Robin's brain. Not a case he'd been directly involved in but one that he'd discussed with people and that Cowdrey used as an example of how not to conduct an investigation. "Are we talking about the blokes who were duping women out of their money via dating agency link-ups?"

"Yeah. The Miss Lonely Hearts case."

Robin shot a sharp glance round the room, having heard some snickering, and put a stop to it. "And we won't be referring to it as that. Nothing funny in being taken for a ride. None of you would like it if your widowed mother was a victim."

"Sorry, sir. That's what it says in the files." Ashok, eyes fixed on the floor, appeared suitably abashed.

"Okay. Before we discuss it, you all might like to know that it was a classic example of mishandling a case. The investigating team, all from Abbotston, made a right cobblers' of things with the evidence. Some key items ended up being wrongly labelled and stored. Yes, Naomi?"

"Oh, no, sorry, I didn't mean anything by raising my pen." Naomi blushed.

"She always does it when she's thinking," Ashok said.

Robin gave her a smile. "Any thoughts to share?"

"Only that the word is you and your boss went into Abbotston and chucked out the bad apples. Is that true?"

"To an extent. We played a part. This fraud case must have been twenty years ago—is that right, Ashok?"

"Twenty-one, sir."

"Thanks. I think that's when people started to doubt the probity of some of the officers at Abbotston, but it took a long time, perhaps too long, for all those bad apples to be shaken out and disposed of. I suspect they kept their heads down and noses clean until it was time to crawl out from the woodwork again. Anyway, halfway through the fraud investigation, the team was quietly replaced. The new team came in with no preconceived ideas—and no backhanders, Superintendent Cowdrey always says—and made rapid progress towards a successful prosecution. I wish they'd cleared out *all* the Abbotston troublemakers at the same time." Robin waved his hand. "Ashok, I'm stealing your thunder. Talk us through it."

The constable launched into his account of the scam. Money had been obtained by false pretences from wealthy women, middle-aged upwards. The sort of thing that was rife nowadays, he told them, via the wonders of the internet and being able to hide behind an online identity—and photograph—that wasn't necessarily you. But which had also gone on in an era of pens, paper and postage stamps, although the basic principle had been the same. Ashok, who'd have been barely more than a toddler then, made it sound like the Stone Age, although to give credit where it was due, his retelling of the case was clear, concise, and to the point.

"They were befriending women, using false identities and addresses, through lonely hearts clubs and dating agencies. Gaining their confidence, especially with promises of undying love, then plying them with plausible sob-stories, refusing all monetary help on the principle of their pride and then eventually yielding to what was, from the victim's point of view, a genuine offer. Then once the money was in their hands, these blokes said, 'Thank you!' and scarpered. Sometimes quickly, somebody else writing to the women to say that Fred had died, maybe from long-term illness despite the treatment she'd paid for, just like you get in a phishing case. Or the blokes themselves pulled the old 'It's not you, it's me,' stunt. Anyway, in every case the men and the money both disappeared. Six actual frauds, one attempted, and who knows how many that never got reported."

"The victims would have been too ashamed," Pru observed.

"Yeah and maybe some of them still don't realise they'd been taken for a ride. These guys were plausible right to the end." Ashok tapped his notes. "This is almost a textbook on how to play people's feelings. In two cases, when the 'Fred's dead' letter came, it said his last wish was wanting his sweetheart to have a simple token of his affection, something like a cheap but decent piece of jewellery which he said had been his mother's."

Pru narrowed her eyes. "The sods. That would help blindside somebody who would either never consider or not want to consider that they may have been duped. How many men involved?"

"Two doing the dating-scam thing and one acting as their postbox."

That was the connection to King's Ashley school, exactly as Robin's copper's nose had warned him. One of the three men put away had been the site caretaker. Surprising that Adam didn't know about that, given the local schools' grapevine appeared to spread this kind of gossip at warp speed, but maybe the nature of the crime, not connected to either safeguarding or cooking the school books, meant that word hadn't spread. Or maybe the fact it was a caretaker rather than a teacher involved had made it below people's notice.

Ashok explained that Tony Gilzean, the caretaker, had been a relatively minor player in the dirty game, sending the post from King's

Ashley and nearby Tythebarn and providing an address to which incoming mail could be sent.

"Didn't anyone turn up at the door when they realised they'd been diddled?" Naomi asked.

"No. That's another part where they were clever. Gilzean's father had died, and his mother went into a home while the will was still going through probate. There's a theory he got away lightly because the money he made was going towards her bills. They weren't selling the property because the mother wanted it to go to her grandchildren, so the scammers used it as a glorified PO Box, as well as keeping the phone line in case one of those was needed." Ashok consulted his notes again. "The other two, Derek Cavendish and Eric James, didn't get away as lightly. Five years each, which is maybe on the steep side for fraud. The judge was a woman, which may or may not have influenced things."

Pru appeared to be creating some withering remark, then thinking better of it. "So how did Ellen come into this?"

"She was being groomed as a victim. She smelled a rat and started to gather evidence, while playing Cavendish along. Somehow, she managed to get hold of another victim—possibly through one of the people who ran the agency, although that was never really made clear—and then a third. Between them, they built up a dossier, which she brought to us at Abbotston." Ashok snorted. "She'd have been better off coming here. Might have got it sorted quicker."

"What aroused her suspicions in the first place?" Ben had been quiet, taking everything in as usual.

"The address she was writing to. It was standard practice at the agency for clients to use PO boxes rather than their home address, for security obviously. She did the same, so they had no idea she was so local, and she was pretty cagey about giving away personal information. When Cavendish played the 'we know each other well enough for you to write to me at my home address' card, she knew the village and decided to play Miss Marple. It didn't take much for her to realise that the house was probably unoccupied, which is how she got on the trail."

"Thanks. You know," Ben observed, "her involvement, seen in the light of what we already know about her, makes perfect sense. I found out this morning that she worked for the government. Based at GCHQ at one point."

"Was she?" Hopefully, this wouldn't turn out to be espionage or national security related, as that might risk having the case taken over by the cloak-and-dagger boys and girls. While the idea of getting back to home turf appealed, he was intrigued by this case now and wanted to see it through to a conclusion.

"Yes. I'm not sure what she was doing, so I'll work on that. Sorry, Ashok. We keep interrupting you." Ben gave his fellow officer an encouraging smile.

"Not a lot else to say. I'm surprised that she'd signed up to a dating agency in the first place." Ashok must have heard Pru's angry exhalation—frankly, it couldn't be missed. "That's not me making sexist assumptions. According to the case notes, she nearly refused to go into the witness box because she didn't want people to know she'd joined up seeking love. She was worried they'd feel sorry for her. Luckily the officers persuaded her to do her bit, probably by playing the guilt card, talking about all the women who'd been conned so far and others who might be in future if she didn't help put a stop to things."

"I've been told on the quiet that it was likely her work which was pivotal to the successful fraud convictions," Robin said, "as she'd had the sense to make copies of everything and could fill in the gaps where the investigating team had lost the originals. I didn't remember her name so didn't make the connection. Where are Cavendish, James, and Gilzean now?"

"Gilzean died of a heart attack last year. The other two I'm still on the track of."

"Good. You can update us when you know. If either of the others are still in circulation, then that has to be a line of enquiry. One of you can rouse out details about her job, as I want Ben to concentrate on the IT." Robin's gaze swept the team. "Anything else before we set out?"

A hand was raised at the back of the room. One of the admin team, the bloke who'd been snickering earlier and had asked the question earlier about Ellen's name being released.

"Yes, er . . . I can't remember your name, sorry," Robin said.

"Aaron. Doesn't it scream 'dodgy' that people allege they hadn't noticed Ellen Wilkins wasn't around? We're in bloody lockdown. Not like they have far to go."

The reaction to the question—a barrage of snarky responses from the other Kinechester regulars—surprised Robin. It hadn't been an unreasonable question, despite the aggressive phrasing.

"It's not unusual to have a case where nobody's noticed the dead person isn't doing what they normally did," Naomi pointed out, the anger in her voice striking Robin. "It must have been easier to keep tabs on people in the past, given that a greater number of people were about during the day, nineteen fifties housewives in pinnies, going about their shopping and chores."

"Naomi's right," Ashok said. "Where my mum lived when she was little, some old man had died and the first clue they'd got was days' worth of milk deliveries not being taken in. Doors weren't always locked back then, which meant you could go and drop in to check on somebody you were worried about. It's not like that now."

All good points, but something about the manner in which they were being made spoke of tension, maybe a previous argument between the parties. Robin caught Pru's eye, and she responded with a shrug. Time to step in.

"I'm not sure we can read too much into it as yet, Aaron. Yes, more people are at home because of lockdown, but they might be working or helping the kids with schoolwork. By the time you get to the end of the day, it's dark, and if they did go for a walk, they'd have seen the lights going on and off in number thirty-nine." He leaped off the desk where he'd been perched, ready to round things up and get out investigating. "We've made a good start. We need to focus on anything that will pin down the date of death or give us a clue on who's been in contact with her. In person or any other way. Aaron, there's a pile of post we brought in from the house. Can you start with that?"

"Will do." Hardly an enthusiastic response. The sooner Robin found out what was bubbling under the surface between Aaron and the others, the better.

Chapter Four

Robin set off back to Cromwell Road and an interview with Sonia Parsons—Mrs. Pink Hair—with Naomi occupying the seat normally taken by Pru or Ben. He'd been pleased so far with the showing from the Kinechester constables, although the atmosphere at the end of the briefing needed explaining.

"What was going on with that Aaron bloke?" he asked, as soon as they were out of the station car park.

"He's an A1 pain, sir." The degree of honesty was surprising from the young officer. Robin would have expected it from Pru, though, so maybe she'd reassured the Kinechester team that they could risk being frank with him. "You must have heard the way he snickered at the fraud conviction being called 'the Lonely Hearts Club case.' I actually think he had a valid point, questioning why nobody had noticed Ellen wasn't around, but because *he* made it, we jumped on him. He's wound us up so often, I guess we overreact."

"Does he always get jumped on?" Was this a case of someone who was a *bit* of a pain becoming a *hell* of a pain in response to poor treatment?

"Probably." Naomi sighed. "He's always so snarky, sir. Has a dig at everybody and everything. And he pushes the envelope of what's acceptable, but he's never quite sexist or racist enough to make a complaint about. Full of biases and assumptions too."

Clearly Robin had opened up the floodgates. "Go on. I need to know, in case it affects the investigation. As you've admitted, team tensions can get in the way of effective thinking."

"Right, well when the news came in yesterday, he started going on about how you didn't get murders in Cromwell Road, because the worst you get up on the Ramparts is somebody double-parking their Kensington tractor. Anybody else, we might have taken that as banter, but Aaron went on to ask if somebody mixed up the address with Cromwell Close, which is on the council estate where I grew up, the east of Kinechester. Ashok reckons that was mostly a dig at me, but I think he meant it about everyone there. Pig ignorance. Anyway, Ashok went ballistic. Lectured Aaron that he was thick as two short planks if he thought crime only happens on council estates or among people with children on free school meals."

"Ashok's got a point. There's a hell of a lot of nastiness going on behind the twitching net curtains on posh estates." Robin wondered if he should take Aaron to one side and put him straight on a few things, but this wasn't his patch and he had plenty of other stuff to occupy his time. He'd have a word with Denness, though, in case the matter hadn't already been flagged up. "Aaron will have to learn not to make assumptions. Too many investigations lose their way because someone gets a fixed idea in their head."

"Trouble is he wants to get into the force itself and resents not having been successful. He's good at what he does, though."

Would it be wise to ask Denness to swop Aaron for another civilian operative or should they cut the bloke some slack? While Robin didn't have the time to deal with troublemakers, he was always keen to give someone another chance. Better to focus on the case for the moment and air the point about Ellen having lain undiscovered. "That Aaron episode cut short a useful discussion. It may not be your present boss's style but I like to bat ideas about. I don't have the monopoly on right answers."

"That's good to know, sir. Thing is, comparing life under lockdown with life in the past, some parts of it *have* been like what Aaron calls the 'good old days.' Not that they were so good if you were a woman."

"Agreed." Robin also reserved judgement on exactly how great the past had been, for example, if you hadn't fitted into the expectations of sexual orientation. He'd have found himself villain, not hero. Better to stick to how the comparison applied to the case. "Go on."

"There *are* people stuck at home or working from the dining room or whatever. They've been going for local walks instead of hopping in the car and heading out. My mum says she's seen people she's not talked to in years, despite them only living a couple of streets away. Conversations from one pavement across the road to the other." Naomi chuckled. "She also says people are having to find new activities to occupy them and maybe spying on the neighbours is one."

"Checking if they're breaking the rules?" Robin's turn to chuckle. "Your mum might have a point. There's also the nicer flip side of that coin. People are looking out for each other, setting up local groups to pick up medicine or groceries if someone is self-isolating."

"Exactly. You'd have thought that if Ellen lived on her own, somebody would have kept an eye out, even if she'd refused all offers of help."

"Right. I'll be devil's advocate. Item one. A lot of people these days go around with their eyes glued to their mobile phone screen or chatting into it nineteen to the dozen. How many times have you nearly collided with a runner who's so intently listening to music that they're oblivious to everything else? People didn't have those distractions in the past, so they'd have been likelier to notice something amiss than the average person walking down the street now."

"Okay, you can have that one, sir. What's item two?"

"It's slap bang in making-assumptions territory, but is the community spirit as strong in the Ramparts as it is where your mum lives?"

"Hmm." Naomi paused. "You might have a point on that too. My aunt Jo does some cleaning up there, on Ireton Avenue rather than Cromwell Road or I'd have mentioned it before. It's for an older couple, so while she didn't do the cleaning during the first lockdown, she did offer to help them get in anything they needed. They didn't need her, because they were swamped with offers from their neighbours, one of whom they'd put in touch with a woman in Cromwell Road who was struggling to get any help. Mind you, this other woman wasn't a silver surfer, so if there was an online local support group, she'd not have known about it . . ."

"Any chance that they might know Ellen Wilkins?"

"I doubt it. The Reeves grapevine was going like the clappers last night, Mum and Aunt Jo both on the same Facetime call bugging me for information. I didn't give them a name, but they knew it was

Cromwell Road, so Jo said she doubted it was anyone they'd come across. According to the people she cleans for, they're much snootier that side of the back path than they on the Ireton Avenue side." Naomi sighed. "Seems like we might have argued ourselves out of getting suspicious that folk didn't notice."

Unfortunately, she could be right. And perhaps Ellen had made herself so unpopular that nobody had bothered to keep an eye out for her.

Sonia Parsons lived in the last house on Cromwell Road, the one Ben and Robin had passed to access the path to the back of number thirty-nine. Alex Carey hadn't exaggerated about the woman's hair, which was a mass of shocking pink, apart from the obvious pepper-and-salt roots coming through. She welcomed the officers into a house that was as much of a contrast to number thirty-seven as her hair was to Alex Carey's short, blonde locks. The décor might be described as sixties chic and the general appearance as untidy, but it felt like a much-used and much-loved home. Three children, probably aged around ten to fourteen, were sitting around the dining room table, heads coming up from their laptops when Robin and Naomi followed Sonia in and were introduced.

"We're going into the lounge to talk about Ms. Wilkins's death. You can pack up for lunch now. It's all ready in the kitchen." The mouth-watering aroma of some kind of soup gave evidence of that. She turned to the officers. "Would you two like something? There's plenty."

"That's really kind, but we'll have to pass," Robin said, with a pang of regret.

"Oh, yes, sorry. Covid and all that. My great-aunt's recently had her jab. We're so pleased." She led the way to the lounge, settled them on a large sofa, then perched herself on its pair. "What can I tell you?"

"You rang the station to say you'd had an argument with Ellen Wilkins?" Naomi asked, Robin having suggested she start off the interview.

"Yes. This is going to sound silly. Last year the vicar gave a sermon about how we still had to care for our neighbours, even though the restrictions were easing. I felt a bit guilty, because I'd not been doing anything much for other people, what with the children being at home so much of the time, so I decided I should do my good deed for the day and choose a couple of people to at least make the offer to. Mrs. Waverley round the corner in Ireton Avenue was so pleased, and I've been picking up her bits and bobs since the second lockdown happened. Ellen Wilkins was the other." Sonia grimaced.

"How did you choose who you'd offer help to?"

"I know Mrs. Waverley through church. Ms. Wilkins used to play online bridge in the same club as my husband. She put a stop to that sometime around last October, saying she was planning to have a break over the winter and wanted to pick up again in the new year. Harry—my husband—was concerned about her and suggested I drop in and see if she needed any help. I learned my lesson." Sonia had brought a drinks bottle with her and at last took a sip. "I wish this was gin. Just remembering how she excoriated me is a nightmare."

"I can imagine," Robin said. The same story again: Ellen withdrawing from her normal activities with a just-about plausible excuse and putting up barriers to people who wanted to help. "When was this?"

"Sometime around Guy Fawkes night, I think, because I remember the kids and I had been making parkin to eat round the bonfire, and I offered Ellen some, which she refused. I can't give you an exact date. Are you local?"

"I am," Naomi said. "Why?"

"I don't need to explain about the Ramparts's reputation, then. What you might not know is that this corner seems to mark a divide. No, that's too dramatic. It's like a gradient. Ireton Avenue is a normal sort of place, then you come up Rupert Drive and noses start to stick further up in the air. By the time you get into Cromwell Road, community spirit may as well not exist. For most families it's a case of going home, shutting the door, and minding your own business, especially now you haven't got the school-gate or coffee-shop mafias able to operate on their usual patches." She sighed. "Sorry, that sounds very crabby, but it's how I feel."

"When did you last see Ellen alive?" Robin asked.

"In person, that time in November. I know she's been around since Christmas because her bedroom blinds have been open and shut."

Robin glanced at Naomi, who raised an eyebrow at him. "Can you tell us more about that? Fixing dates is going to be vital to us."

"I can fix January the sixteenth for you. It was the day before our Lucy's twelfth birthday, and it's been like a military operation trying to get surprise presents, what with the kids being in all the time and no shops open. I had some deliveries made to a friend's house, and I was nipping along the path at the back to get them. I noticed the blinds were shut in the back bedroom, which was odd as it was only three in the afternoon."

Distinctly odd, as they were now open and that didn't appear to be the room in which Ellen had slept. "Can I ask what made you think of looking up there?"

"Another one of those daft things that happen. I heard a hell of a thump, like somebody had fallen over. I was trying to see what had made the noise, when I saw a big mark on her window, and then a pigeon flew out of her garden, weaving about like it was drunk. It settled on the ground and couldn't walk straight. The stupid creature must have flown straight into the glass. We get them doing that with our windows too. When I went past Ellen's the next day, the blinds were open again, although you could still see the mark clearly. It showed up where the light caught the glass."

That all sounded plausible. Robin had experienced birds concussing themselves on the windows of their previous property and Campbell getting most upset at the sudden noise. "Thanks. Is there anything else you can tell us that might help?"

Sonia, for the first time in the interview, appeared uncertain. Eventually, she said, "I don't like telling tales—live and let live, that's me—but in this instance I can't keep quiet. You must have seen the Carey family next door to Ellen, the other side from the gay couple. I know them because they've got a couple of kids at the same school as mine. He does some charity stuff and she used to like everyone in the school playground to know it. Anyway, I wouldn't necessarily trust anything they say about when she was there and when she wasn't. They wouldn't be able to say for certain."

"Why's that?"

"Because, as I understand it, they're hardly obeying the lockdown rules. Her parents have dropped in several times, and I know for a fact they took themselves and the kids off to his parents' holiday home on the Isle of Wight. Once in the November lockdown and then again at the start of this year."

"How do you know for sure?"

"About her parents, because I saw them, last summer, as Lucy and I were coming down the road. It was when we were allowed to have people round, so Alex introduced them to us. Then I think I saw them walking near here in November and definitely spotted them coming out of her house a few weeks ago. The mother's only recently had *it*, poor thing, which must have been bad because she didn't do any housework and apparently she's very old-guard house-proud *don't you dare drop a crumb* type. Not like us." Sonia glanced round the room, which showed no evidence of tidying and plenty of her children's presence.

"How do you know she's so house-proud? And that she had Covid?" Naomi asked.

"Alex Carey was talking about it on the parents' Facebook group. How her mum was ill and wasn't being a great patient. I assume it was Covid, although I could be getting mixed up. I know, I know"—she flapped her hands—"I sound like a terrible busybody, but I promise I'm not. I have a good memory for faces, and we're friends on Facebook so I see her other posts as well."

Did Sonia make a point of looking for them? "And the holidays?"

"That was because of Facebook too. She likes to post pictures of Carly and Cerys doing stuff, and she put up one of them on the front at Shanklin, at New Year. She soon took it down, but not before some of us had noticed it. One of my mates said she'd heard they'd been away for a long weekend in November too. They'd told the school the kids weren't well. So if the Careys weren't actually here, how could they know what was going on in the house next door to them?"

Robin gave a surprised nod. No wonder Alex had been so keen to keep the policemen sweet, with her offers of coffee and biscuits. If the story of the trips away were true, it explained why the Careys hadn't noticed anything amiss: they hadn't been there to see it. It also explained all the supposed doubts Alex Carey had expressed about whether she'd seen Ellen over Christmas. She wouldn't know if her neighbour had been alive or dead then, so what answer could she give that fitted properly? It also cast doubt on much she'd said about food deliveries and everything else. If she and her husband had been breaking the guidance, they could have been willing to lie to cover up that fact.

Witnesses didn't always tell the whole truth. Would covering over lockdown misdemeanours make that tendency worse? And was breaking the guidance the only thing the Careys were covering up?

Adam had sighed and shaken his head on receiving Robin's reply to his text. It seemed like he'd already been drawn into the case. He'd shot off a quick response.

Only thing I know so far is that she didn't have any close relatives, but you'll know that already. Kelvin says he'll be back here later, so I'll ply him with tea and keep my ears open.

That nearly didn't happen. Kelvin had returned to school at the end of lessons but had headed straight for the toilet, re-emerging minutes later with an ashen face and apologies for puking. Jim had suggested he go home immediately, but Adam had suggested Kelvin needed to get some liquid inside him, especially as he'd been sick at the morgue too. Adam settled him in one of the smaller teaching rooms, then went off to make a brew.

When Adam returned, he laid a mug of hot, sweet tea on the table in front of Kelvin. "Here, get that inside you. Don't want you passing out from dehydration. Want to talk about it?"

"Not really. I want to forget about the whole experience. It's such a shame, because today feels like it'll ruin all my memories of her. I only was shown photographs, but that was bad enough."

Adam took a sip of his own tea, but it was too hot to enjoy yet. "You two were close?"

"Used to be. She'd come up to Manchester once or twice a year when I was small. Always brought me something, like sweets or a water pistol, and she always had time to talk about things that were interesting. She knew about dinosaurs and space travel and stuff little boys like. When I came here, I asked her if she could come and talk to our class, but she said she was getting too old for that malarkey. She did promise to record a talk about dinosaurs and birds which we could show the children, but nothing came of it. I didn't want to press her if she'd forgotten, though. It didn't do to press her." Kelvin grinned. "She and Mum were thick as thieves, like sisters rather than friends, but Mum made sure not to rub Aunty Ellen up the wrong way."

"How did they know each other? School? Work?" Was that leading the witness and would Robin be cross when he heard about Adam's questioning technique?

"No, they met on honeymoon. Mum and Dad's honeymoon, I mean. They'd saved up and gone on a cruise to see the Northern Lights, and they met Ellen through one of the activities. I think they all played bridge together, and when they got chatting, they hit it off so well, they kept in touch afterwards. Mum said she was like the older sister she'd never had, and Dad used to challenge her to number and word puzzles. Which one of them could do the sudoku, or whatever was the fad back then, the quickest. Quicker. Sorry, that 'er' and 'est' thing annoys you, doesn't it?"

"One of my pet hates, alongside 'should of.' 'Quicker' if it's two. 'Quickest' if it's three." Adam waited for Kelvin to continue, but the young man seemed lost in thought. "Go on, if it helps. I like the sound of your godmother."

"It *is* good to talk about her." Kelvin's colour was improving with every sentence. "She was great. Always had time for me, and for my mate Danny when he dropped round. She'd take us down to the corner shop for ice creams or off to the park to collect conkers. There was this one time, I must have been nine or ten. We'd all gone on a conker hunt, and this right bully tried to nick what we'd collected. You should have heard Ellen bawl him out—she said she couldn't bear little 'uns being hurt. Danny made a fuss at being called a little 'un, but he gave her a big hug anyway, because things could have turned nasty. This bloke was twice our size." Kelvin managed half a grin. "I bet she could have beaten him in a fight."

"Good person to have in your corner."

"Yeah. She had muscle as well as brains, and she was determined to keep both of them. You know, Dad was still challenging her at puzzles up until last summer. It took place over Zoom so neither of them could cheat."

"Good idea. You can never trust these old folk." Adam blew on his tea, took a sip, then said airily, "Sounds like the challenges stopped for some reason."

"Yes. She got in touch with Dad to say that she was having a problem with her Zoom app. It had updated and then for some reason it disappeared from her laptop. He offered advice, but she came back to say she'd tried to download it again and couldn't. Dad didn't believe her." Kelvin stared into his mug. "She was really good with technology. Better than me, in a lot of ways. If she'd wanted to sort the programme out, she'd have managed. Or ordered a new laptop from John Lewis or whatever. Her IT going down would have been water off a duck's back, so there must have been another reason but she wouldn't say what. Why are old people so stubborn?"

"They don't want to show weakness." And yes, the story about Zoom didn't ring true on so many counts, including the fact Kelvin's dad and Ellen could have used other methods—Facetime or whatever—to carry on the challenges with.

"That was her, all right. Not wanting to show the slightest chink in her armour. But I still loved her, and now the thought of a postmortem and an inquest, after this morning . . ." Kelvin's hands tightened around his mug.

"Yeah, I know. I also know that this is a cliché, but time's the only healer. At some point you'll be able to think about all the good times you had with her, all the funny occurrences that happened, without feeling sad about it. You can treasure stuff like the last Christmas card from her or whatever." Was that too clunky a way of trying to find out if she'd been alive to send one?

"That's a good point. Funny thing is, I think I still have that card. I'd taken them all down at New Year and was going to go through them. I have a paper address book, believe it or not, and I like to check for changes of address and make sure I have the right names for people's partners or children. It's a bit OCD, I suppose."

"Less OCD than highly organised. I'd show that card to the police, especially if you know roughly when it arrived. They like all the help they can get, no matter how trivial."

"I will do. I'll get Mum onto it as well, because I'm sure she said that Ellen rang her for a chinwag sometime before the big day. If only it had been an odd-numbered year, everything might have been different."

"Eh?"

"Ellen used to come to us for Christmas, every other year. Not sure where she went on even-numbered years—she was quite secretive about it. Mum once teased her about having a fancy man."

"Maybe she did. You know what they say about snow on the roof but a fire in the cellar. Or she might not have wanted to be a burden so pretended she had other commitments."

"That's what Dad suspects. Anyway, this time we made sure we raised a glass of bubbly over Christmas dinner to absent friends. Didn't think she could be in trouble." Kelvin's gaze turned towards the window, where the last rays of afternoon sun were peeping through the clouds. "It felt like the third degree, being asked all the details about when we'd last spoken to her but I guess they're keen to get a fix on the date of death. Hold on." He swung his head round to face Adam again. "Is your bloke involved in investigating this? Is that why you talked about showing the police the Christmas card?"

"Yes, he's in charge. Sorry about that." Adam put his hands up in mock surrender. "You've caught me out. I didn't mean to give you the third degree. Force of habit, because I've ended up involved in several of the cases he deals with. Like the one I told you about, the woman they found dead at the Roman villa site."

"That's okay. I guess I should be angry—I would be if it wasn't you doing the asking. I trust you to do the right thing." That sounded genuine enough. "I didn't think Kinechester was his patch."

"It isn't. He got called across at the last moment because of sickness in the team. A serious case means all hands to the pump."

"Yours included?" Kelvin smiled nervously, a smile that soon vanished. "They reckon it's murder. The young constable told me. He's coming to my flat tonight to get a statement."

"Was that Ben or one of the Kinechester locals?"

"Ben. Nice bloke. Made it as easy as he could."

"He's a good copper, straight as a die. Make sure you tell him everything you can that'll help find the killer."

"I will, Adam. Though I wouldn't want to be in the murderer's shoes if I ever got my hands on him."

Adam nodded. He'd report the conversation back, but maybe he'd leave out the last bit. At least until they had the killer in custody.

By the time Adam had got home, Robin had texted to say he'd be in at a reasonable time. The team had finished work late the night before and were still waiting on information, so a Friday evening off wouldn't do any harm. Adam had shaken his head at that, knowing that while they'd be able to eat together and have a bottle or two of beer, time away from the case would be the last thing that would happen. Robin's mind would be buzzing with it anyway, irrespective of Adam having to report his conversation with Kelvin. Robin swore that when they discussed cases, it often led to a breakthrough of thinking. Sensible spectators like Adam, close to the action on the pitch, often saw more of the game than those playing it.

Campbell greeted him as he always did, as though Adam had been away weeks and he'd been left home alone to both fret and starve. The act fooled nobody.

Sandra, the angel in human form who'd come in every day when they'd lived at Lindenshaw—to ensure the dog had a comfort break and to handle any household jobs—hadn't wanted to travel as far as their new home. They'd anticipated that and had got Adam's mum on backup while they found a new domestic help, but she'd hardly been needed. Sandra had recommended her friend, Kate, who didn't live too far away and might be interested in the job. Kate *had* been interested and was proving every bit as efficient as her predecessor. It was her chicken curry they'd be eating tonight.

The arrangement had been of benefit both ways. Kate had been widowed in her forties, was without children, and desperately in need of a legitimate reason to get out of the house now that her usual charity activities had ground to a halt. The pay was merely a bonus, apparently.

Adam had found a note from her in the hallway when he'd arrived home, saying that she'd taken Campbell for a long walk earlier and not let him chase any squirrels, no matter how much he'd pleaded with her. She'd been baking scones for the old lady who lived next door to her and hoped the lads didn't mind that she'd left a few in a Tupperware container for them.

"They're not for you," he told the dog, who'd been eyeing them. "Your other dad will be in need of one. He'll have had a hard day."

However, when Robin got in, tie already shed, he said his day had been less hard than puzzling. "We're building up a picture of the victim but—unless her death is linked to the case she'd given evidence in—there's no obvious motive or culprit for her killing. I think—" Any attempt to give further details was cut short by his phone sounding.

Adam waved his hand. "You read that, then get changed while I finish making dinner. We can discuss it while we eat. Curry's always good to get the brain cells going."

So it proved. Once the food was served and they were getting stuck into it, Adam started by asking the obvious question, "Who benefits in her will?"

"That's an easy one. The Children's Society. Apart from ten grand to Kelvin's mum and dad so they can treat themselves to another cruise and five grand to the lad himself, the rest goes to what she called her favourite charity. Does Kelvin strike you as desperate for money?"

"No. His partner's an accountant, and his mum and dad are bankrolling his teacher training. He seems genuinely upset at her death." Adam gave an account of the day's two conversations with him.

"That's interesting, her saying she was too old to come and give a talk. That's not a weakness she admitted to the locals. Her excuse for dropping out of things was being too busy."

"Kelvin's family are probably too close to her to use that excuse. The apparent lie about Zoom notwithstanding. Kelvin told me you didn't want to get on her bad side. Did she rub her neighbours up the wrong way?"

"She rubbed everyone up the wrong way." Robin launched into the tale of Ellen's arguments and fallings out. "If you'd wanted to set up a situation where nobody noticed you were dead, you couldn't have done it better."

"Are you any closer to knowing how long she'd been lying there?"

"Nope. We've had a detailed and partly incomprehensible postmortem report, saying at least ten days, but it could possibly be as long as four weeks. Which is no tighter a window than the first guess the doctor made at the scene."

"What else did the PM show?"

"A lack of apparent defensive wounds, for a start, so the killer's likely to be somebody she knew well or in whose company she wasn't on her guard, like a plumber she'd called out. A person she'd get pretty close to without a second thought. One of the wounds appeared different to the others—looked like a scissor blade rather than a knife. Death would have been swift, given the blood loss, and it's highly unlikely the killer wouldn't have been sprayed with it. This is a good curry, I have to say. God bless Sandra's friend network."

"Amen to that." Adam washed down another mouthful with some beer. "You know, if she'd been found dead from natural causes, it would have sounded like she'd been preparing for death. Cutting ties, eliminating commitments, getting her affairs in order. She didn't have a terminal illness, did she?"

Robin's face screamed *What are you on about?* "She was stabbed to death, remember?"

"I'm aware of that, you plonker. I meant, had she been expecting to die anyway? I'm trying to find an explanation for what she'd been doing."

"Sorry. No, the postmortem showed she was very fit for her age. I asked the pathologist about dementia and got a long lecture on cerebrovascular indicators—*brain disease* to you and me—that basically amounted to not being able to tell from the state of the brain how much an older person was affected. I like *your* theory, though. None of us came up with it. And I guess if she believed she was dying or had simply had enough of life, she might have been winding things down."

"Score one for the teacher." Adam chuckled. "If she was stabbed, it must have been a mess. Wasn't the killer spotted, given that he or she must have had blood on them?"

"They could have been drenched in gore and got away down that back path, especially if it was dark. Tell you what, if you fancy a walk round the Ramparts with Campbell, we can meet there tomorrow afternoon. If you see the place, you'll understand the situation."

"You're on. I'm still struggling to get my head round people not noticing something was wrong. The lights were on a timer, you said?"

"Yep. And the gardener used to turn up and do his bit, then go off again. He clearly wasn't paid cash in hand, but I won't know any more than that until Pru reports to the team tomorrow. She's only just tracked him down—that was her texting, earlier."

"What about keys? I can imagine Ellen letting her killer in, but they'd have had to lock up again when they went out."

"The poor dim coppers had worked that out already." Robin grunted. "Trouble is, we don't know how many spare keys she had, so can't tell if one was missing. If the killer had a key already, or kept one afterwards, they could have sneaked in and done stuff to make it appear she was still alive and further obscure the date of death."

"What about the neighbours, though?"

"Hmm. Now there's a thing. Older gay couple to one side, both of whom work in Kinechester General, so they've not exactly been around a lot the last month or so. The other side . . ." Robin laid down his cutlery and had a drink of beer. "I went to see them again this afternoon, acting on information received. Lo and behold, they've been taking trips to his parents' holiday home on the Isle of Wight, all the time they shouldn't have been. They hadn't wanted to admit it, obviously, in case they got fined."

"Hit the buggers in the wallet." Adam had been saying that all the way through the past year. If the consequence of breaking the rules wasn't immediate and sufficiently punitive, they were no disincentive at all. "Although it'll be like term-time holidays. People accept the fine almost as part of the costs. It's still worth it in their eyes."

Robin rubbed his brow. "Probably. Alex Carey—that's the wife—pleaded for another couple of offences to be considered while we were at it. She said her parents had visited a couple of times, because her father's not really coping with lockdown—he's recently been treated for cancer, so it meant he's had to shield—and the mother needed support. Then her mum came down with bronchitis the second week of January, so she went to her parents' house to help look after her. Apparently, her father was so useless it constituted an emergency. That I have a bit of sympathy with, but it all muddies the water about getting a fix on when Ellen was still alive and who's been in and out of the house, especially around the time of death, as Alex Carey could have been away then. She says her parents' neighbours can verify her having gone to stay there, because she saw them. I suppose the best thing about that is it shows old pink-hair Parsons's gossip network doesn't always get their facts right. She'd heard Alex's mum had come down with Covid."

"Did you get any useful information from Ellen's bank or her phone records?"

"We're still waiting on those, not that they'll necessarily mean much. The order for the mirror was placed about ten days ago, and she was definitely dead then, according to the doctor, so somebody has her payment details and was using them."

"Have you got Ben onto getting into her devices? Or has he been too busy dealing with Kelvin? Sorry"—Adam grinned—"I'm starting to sound like your boss, not your husband."

"You're handsomer than any of my bosses have been. Anyway, it turns out Ellen wasn't the type to use her date of birth or anything equally obvious as her password. Which is what we'd suspected from the start, although you can only hope. We've sent them to the specialists, and if they can't get in, then nobody can." Robin scooped up the last bit of curry with a contented sigh, then pushed his plate away. "She worked at GCHQ. Not sure in what capacity, but it's clear she's not made it easy to scrutinise the details of her life. Even down to where she spent every other Christmas. I got your text about that before I left, so Ben's aware of it."

"I doubt Kelvin can help him about that, unless he's more forthcoming in an official interview than he was with me."

"Well, he's not right about her spending the time at home. I rang our Covid rule breakers before I left. They're falling over themselves to be helpful, of course. They said that Ellen was never at home for

Christmas, although they thought she always went to spend the holiday with the Vince family. That's what she'd told them."

"Maybe there'll be something like pictures on those devices that'll help pin it down." Assuming the dead woman had been the kind to document every part of her life on her camera. "Do you think it's significant?"

"I don't know what's significant, to be honest. Except that somebody seems to have made a point of placing the delivery for that day and also opening the blinds so her dead body could be seen. According to the gardener, the blinds in the lounge were often shut when he was due to call and certainly were last time he came to do the garden, which was only last week. Like I said, somebody must have had access to the house to operate those blinds. Despite the fact they hadn't bothered to pick up the post," Robin added, no doubt suddenly struck by that aspect.

Adam had been hit by an idea, as well. "Are they electric blinds or manual?"

"Electric. Like the new ones in your mum's bathroom. Why?"

"Do you have to be in the house to operate them? I don't know the range for the remote control, but would it work from the garden?" Adam warmed to his theme, Robin's stunned expression being a joy to behold. "I can imagine someone taking a spare control and using it from outside the house to confuse the situation."

"I never thought of that. I wonder if Pru has?" Robin eyed his empty glass. "Shame we've had a couple of these or we could go over now and try it."

"Why not do it when we meet up tomorrow? That would make our journey there definitely essential. We don't want to be seen to break the rules."

"Especially not if we're outside number thirty-seven, which is where the holiday-homers live."

A crash resounded outside, making them both jump. Adam went to the window, then flicked back the curtains to see rain starting to lash against them. "The weather doesn't want us to go playing experiments tonight, either. How about snuggling on the settee with another beer and thirty pairs of thighs to admire on the telly?"

"That sounds like bliss." Robin smiled although Adam knew that, despite the multiple attractions of watching Friday night rugby, the case wouldn't be far from his husband's mind.

Chapter Five

There was plenty to discuss when the investigation team met for the Saturday morning briefing. Robin let Naomi present the case of the rule-breaking neighbours and suggested they discount any evidence around the time of death that relied on Alex Carey's testimony. Which led him to the subject of Ellen's blinds being open and shut and his proposal to try operating the things from outside that afternoon.

"Sounds a good idea, sir. Do you also want me to go round and make Alex and the husband give another statement?" Naomi asked.

"Not at the moment. When we've got a clearer idea of exactly when Ellen died, then I think we should get them to focus on those dates, but for the moment I want to keep our powder dry." Robin shook his head. "Pru. The postie."

"I drew a blank there, I'm afraid. She was very helpful but no use, if that makes sense. She hadn't noticed anything peculiar at Ellen's—the woman didn't get a lot of post anyway—and as for noticing a smell, she couldn't. Apparently she has nasal polyps, which she told me all about—" Pru pulled a disgusted face "—which means she has almost no sense of smell and what she does smell isn't necessarily there. Phantosmia, it's called."

"Great." Robin puffed out his cheeks. "Ben, how did you get on with Kelvin?"

"I think he was quite surprised to know that she did go away somewhere the Christmases she didn't spend with them, and wondered if she usually went away to a hotel for a break. Although she couldn't have gone somewhere like that this Christmas just gone, even if she'd wanted to."

Indeed. The particular circumstances of the past year meant that the normal run of assumptions didn't always apply. "Did he have any idea who might have wanted to harm her?"

"No. He'd spoken to his parents too, and they apparently said that other than the people she'd testified against, she didn't appear to have an enemy in the world." Ben shrugged. "It's frustrating, not yet getting into her electronic files or bank records, anything that might give us a clue to where she got to when she wasn't with the Vinces."

"Pru. You and Ashok dealt with the gardener and the paper files. Any luck?"

"Yeah. Ashok, want to talk us through our interview with the 'Man with the Mower'?" Pru gave the constable a nod.

"Of course, ma'am. The gardener's called Tony Yelverton. He'd seen the story about an incident at the Ramparts on his phone when he'd been checking the local newspaper headlines and wondered if it was Miss Wilkins."

"She called herself *Miss*?" Naomi asked. "Sonia Parsons referred to her as *Ms*."

Ashok sniffed. "Maybe that's one of the reasons Ellen had a go at her. Yelverton said he called her that once and she went mental. Apparently, she'd always had a bit of a temper, although he really liked her. Possibly because she paid well and promptly."

"Hold on," Robin said. "Can we scroll back? Why did he wonder if it was her who'd been killed?"

"Because he's a nosy bugger. His words. He was in Kinechester at another job when the story broke, so he took a drive along Cromwell Road. I think we believed him." Ashok glanced at Pru for confirmation.

"He struck me as telling us the truth, sir," the sergeant confirmed.

"Okay." It was plausible: some people couldn't resist rubbernecking where a police car or ambulance were involved. "Carry on, Ashok."

"He said that as a rule he had very little contact with her. He used to let himself in by the back gate, which was never locked but usually bolted. Apparently, he once got accused of being a burglar by a woman with green hair. He's a bit old-fashioned and reckoned that hair colour alone meant she had no right to be accusing anybody of anything. Do you think that could be Sonia Parsons with a previous hairdo?"

"Most likely," Naomi said. "She strikes me as the sort who'd confront him. Well-meaning but overzealous, maybe. I bet Ellen went ballistic when she heard."

"She did. Maybe that's another reason she lost her rag at Sonia." Ashok glanced at his notes. "Ellen paid the gardener by standing order, and he went once a month in the winter. The most recent occasion was two Tuesdays ago. As for garden waste, his arrangement was to take away all the rubbish he generated as she didn't want to pay for a green-bin licence, given that she was paying him and there wasn't much to be disposed of. The lawn's small, and the main bulk of stuff came when he had to trim the hedges."

"What about the wheelie bins?" Naomi asked.

"Apparently she kept them by the door from the kitchen to the garden. He sometimes had to move them when he was dealing with the hedge or weeding in between the slabs. We asked Yelverton if they were there when he last called, but he says he couldn't tell us one way or the other. He did know there were still a few bins out on the back path—there often are, as the bin collection can be late on a Monday and people don't always want to go out there in the dark to get them in." Ashok shrugged. "It has to be yobs who took them, surely. Got into the garden to cause trouble. According to Yelverton, the gate wasn't bolted when he arrived that Tuesday. He made sure he secured it when he left."

"Not bolted?" Robin raised an eyebrow. "So somebody paid a visit to the garden and either forgot or couldn't be bothered to lock up. Although, if you were some scrote wanting to cause trouble, wouldn't you do something worse than nick two bins? Smash windows or rip up plants or an equally unpleasant bit of vandalism?"

"Perhaps they have a better class of scrote in the Ramparts, sir." Ashok consulted his notes again. "Anyway, the only other thing to report is that Yelverton hasn't spoken to her since December, which isn't unusual. He says he's been going there at least three years and if they've chatted above half a dozen times, he'd be surprised."

"November seems to be the last time most people saw her to talk to, doesn't it? Although that would be bursting the envelope for time of death, and December itself would be pushing it," Ben pointed out. "She must have been around to post her Christmas cards, unless she'd written them well in advance and arranged for them to be posted. That would seem a bit extreme, and Kelvin's adamant it's her handwriting, so I don't think it's some elaborate scheme by the killer to make it appear she was still alive."

"Right." Robin studied the pictures of Ellen on the incident board, trying to imagine the lively, smiling woman portrayed in a snap from only eighteen months ago, which Kelvin had provided. Not only a contrast to the horribly disfigured corpse she now was, but seemingly a different person entirely from the bad-tempered hermit she'd become. Was it age alone that had changed her, or had something else happened? People could lose confidence—due to a fall or a burglary, for example—but there was no indication from Ellen's medical records or the police files that either of those had occurred. *Absence of evidence isn't evidence of absence*, he reminded himself. "The last consultation with her GP was two years ago, for BPPV. She was given exercises to do. Can anyone enlighten me on what that is?"

"I bet Google can." Ashok soon flicked up the answer. "Dizziness. Benign paroxysmal positional vertigo. Exercises are the standard treatment."

One of the phones sounded, so Naomi, being closest, picked it up. "Yes, he's here. It's for *you*, Ben."

"Can you transfer it to the desk over there?" Ben gestured towards the other side of the room. "It might be the tech people, and I'll want to make notes."

Once the call had been handed over, Robin resumed the discussion. "Ashok, those two men convicted in the fraud case. Did you get a lead on them?"

"Yes, sir. Can I . . .?" He gestured at the board, evidently seeking permission to update it. On getting a nod from Robin, he crossed to it. "Eric James is currently in hospital in Swindon. He started off with pneumonia and picked up coronavirus along the way. He's been flat on his back for three weeks, apparently, according to his wife whom I spoke to first thing this morning. What's interesting is a story about them I found on the internet on a local news site. Seems that she was one of his victims. She still loved him and got in touch when he left jail. Forgave him everything and let him whisk her down the aisle. The article made it out to be a big romantic story of redemption, but how gullible can some women be?"

Pru glowered at him. "Don't be sexist. Blokes get phished as well. By women or by other blokes."

"Sorry, I didn't mean it like that. I . . . I don't get it. Like women who stand by their men when they've been knocking them or their children around. I know they can be too scared to call us in but it isn't always the case." Ashok had a point, one that had been particularly relevant since lockdowns started happening. Domestic violence had increased, much to Robin's disgust. He and Pru had dealt with a few particularly nasty incidents over on the Abbotston patch, although they hadn't all been female victims.

"It isn't only women who are victims of domestic violence," Robin pointed out. "I've seen two blokes knocked black and blue this past year, one at the hands of his wife and the other by his husband. And you don't know why they don't call us straight away unless you've lived their lives."

"Sorry, sir. I shouldn't have assumed." Hopefully Ashok would remember the lesson.

"Back to the romance scam. Maybe James was genuinely remorseful. It *can* happen. What about Cavendish?" Robin asked, to steer the conversation back to the case in hand.

"In and out of prison like he's been doing the hokey-cokey." Ashok jotted a note on the board next to the fraudster's name. "He apparently kept his nose clean for a few years before he went back to old ways, although he could have been up to no good all the time and didn't get caught. He started committing internet dating fraud again. Using a false name, obviously, given his history, but one of his potential victims remembered the previous case and called the police in. He got a longer sentence, but he was released three years ago. Nothing about him on our files since then apart from a speeding ticket. So, what if he decided to get even with the person who'd helped put him away in the first place? It might have taken him all this time to get an address for her."

"Or maybe he was up to his tricks," Naomi suggested. "Seems like he's a habitual offender, the same way some burglars seem to come straight out of jail and straight back to housebreaking. Ellen got word about it, got back on his trail; he heard about that and decided to put a stop to it before he ended up being put away for a third time."

"Was she involved at all in his second conviction?" Robin asked.

"She doesn't appear to have been," Ashok replied, "although she may have helped out on the quiet."

"We need an address for him, pronto. We *also* need to see what he's been up to since before Christmas." Robin checked a list he'd made earlier. "Filing cabinets. Anything turn up in them?"

"Plenty," Pru said, "although I'm not sure how much is relevant. A file of all the stuff from the fraud trial, for a start, so she must have kept several copies of it if she replaced what the police lost. Nothing for other cases, as far as we could see." Pru's turn to consult her notes. "All the usual kind of stuff you have on paper that you might want to keep. Birth certificate, degree certificate—Cambridge—pictures of her rowing in the college eight. A few bits and bobs of medical and dental stuff."

"Pru looked at those," Ashok said with a shudder. "Ladies' things."

Pru chuckled. "He couldn't face reading the results of her smear test from a few years back. Clear, by the way. Only thing of note among that paperwork was that Ellen had been to see her dentist in November and he'd made a plan of work for her that was due to take place between then and March. Once the surgery is open again on Monday, I'll give them a ring. Might be useful to know if she missed any appointments."

"Agreed." Robin always appreciated his sergeant's thinking processes. "Try them today, though. I'd hate to lose two days for the sake of one call."

"Will do. Apart from that, the files she kept were pretty bog standard, if labelled and sorted more carefully than the average household's. Receipts and guarantees for items she'd bought or work she'd had done. Financial records, statements for tax purposes about her investments, handwritten notes for tax returns over the last few years. She appeared to have gone pretty well paperless. She must have taken an interest in family history at one point, because there was a file about that. A family tree all drawn out. Anything I've missed, Ashok?"

The young constable shook his head. "Not that I'm aware of."

"One last thing." Robin pointed at the picture of the trodden smudge of Ellen's blood, the single trace they'd identified so far that the killer had left. While they had no proof as yet, the forensic gurus had reckoned—going on appearance—it had been made by a stockinged foot. "This is starting to bug me. If this wasn't made by a shoe, and assuming we're not dealing with a one-legged individual who somehow flew in and flew out again, leaving only one mark where they'd alighted, the person must have taken their footwear off before attacking Ellen. Given they wouldn't have said, 'Excuse me while I do my best to leave no evidence behind,' they surely took them off at the door. Okay, but how come we've only that one print? No other blood trail. I mean, if they'd whipped their socks off right there and cleaned their feet with a wet wipe or whatever, surely there'd have been some blood spatter they'd have taken with them as they left the house? I know the carpet was cleaned but not the rest."

"I've got an idea about that," Pru said. "Two actually. Number one, the murder is incredibly well-planned, including the killer working out how to emerge spatter-free. Arriving in a hazmat suit and standing on a plastic sheet to do the deed, all the while Ellen standing meekly there, letting them get on with things. I don't think that remotely likely."

Robin nodded. "I'm sure none of us do. There was no evidence of drugs in her system rendering her incapable of putting up a fight."

"So try this. The killer comes round, takes their shoes off because that's what they normally do in their own house, then gets into an argument with Ellen, subject of which is as yet unknown," Pru said.

Naomi raised her hand. "Sorry to interrupt, but who would Ellen let into the house? Time and again we've been told that she had cut herself off and nobody's told us she's had regular visitors, like someone she bubbles with or whatever."

"Doctor? Cleaner? Gasman or gaswoman?" Ashok suggested. "It doesn't appear she put up a fight, so it surely can't have been an intruder."

"Okay. All suggestions noted and open minds kept all round. Pru, you didn't finish telling us your idea." Robin gave her a wave of encouragement.

"We'd got as far as the argument. The red mist descends, the killer—whoever they are—loses control, takes a knife from their pocket or handbag or grabs one from the kitchen and stabs her. Is horrified at what they've done, and the fact they've got blood on them. Standing in it." Pru jerked her thumb towards the board. "So they get out their mobile phone and call for help. Someone they trust to turn up with a black bag, wipes, change of clothes, carpet cleaner and no questions asked."

"That would work. The fact the doors are on Chubb locks would have made it easy for the clean-up party to get into the house, and fits in with the bins possibly being used." A simple solution, still reliant on luck but likelier to succeed than the killer attempting to extricate themselves single-handed. "It shows remarkable presence of mind, though and suggests they may have been relatively local. It would take a hardened personality—or a psychopathic one—to stand beside a dead body for hours, waiting for someone to leg it along the motorway from London."

"Or waiting for them to fly into Heathrow." Ben, having finished his call and rejoined the group, had an excited glint in his eyes.

"Interesting call?" Robin asked.

"Oh, yes. That was Kelvin's father. He's been thinking about who might have wanted to harm Ellen and decided he had to share a few things she'd told him in confidence. That's why he rang here, now, because Mrs. Vince is out." Ben had edged towards the incident board, where he took up a marker pen. "Ellen's job was research-based. Collation of evidence, wherever it came from, which was increasingly online. She wouldn't tell him exactly what she'd been involved in researching, but he's pretty sure at one point she was helping pin down people dealing with dangerous conspiracy theories, not solely in the UK. That's why she was so good at getting an evidence file together for the fraud case. Mr. Vince says that there may have been other people she was responsible for convicting."

Pru voiced the very concern that had struck Robin. "That gives a potentially huge pool of people. Assuming we could get hold of their names in the first place."

"I'll get Superintendent Denness onto it." Not that Robin held out much hope for success. "Otherwise we carry on with the nuts and bolts. Bank records, fingerprints from the scene, old-fashioned leg work and collating statements."

"We should have the information back from the CSIs, soon," Ashok said.

"Yes, but you'll find that Chief Inspector Bright doesn't think that forensics are the be all and end all of things," Pru said, giving him a smile.

"They have their place, don't get me wrong. But a single fingerprint or a partial DNA profile for someone who's kept their nose clean so isn't in the database doesn't help to put a name to its owner." It was easy to forget that not everything was solved by forensics, nor did such evidence always secure a case. Also, despite what it implied in many television programmes, there wasn't a bottomless budget for utilising lab time and space, nor did results come back as quickly as suggested. "Somebody was in that house, and the chances are they've returned since. Somebody Ellen trusted enough to let them through the front door when the place was off-limits to all the rest. Who has she been in touch with? Did nobody local see anything unusual, like Sonia noticing the blinds? While we wait for everyone else to do their bit, let's focus on the vicinity. If there aren't statements from everyone in Cromwell Road, I want you out there, filling in the gaps."

The Ramparts area looked at its very best in the sunshine that glinted on the smattering of snow they'd had overnight. Not enough for anything truly thrilling, like making a snowman or getting the sledge out, but plenty to excite both children and adults. Campbell gambolled along like a puppy, evidently having a whale of a time.

Adam had met his husband in the car park as agreed, Robin having layered up in the jacket and snow boots he'd taken with him that morning. Adam's parents had always insisted there were few types of weather you couldn't get out in, so long as you had the right clothing. Now, togged up suitably for the Arctic, the pair of them must have seemed for all the world like a couple getting their appointed daily exercise, rather than a policeman and his partner who'd eschewed getting a junior officer to carry out a simple experiment. Adam was pleased Robin had indulged the personal element, grateful for the extra time together but also desperate to know if his idea would prove correct.

They made their way up the path at the back of the Cromwell Road gardens, discussing the mysterious missing bins.

"You know all about children and what they get up to. Is bin nicking a popular pastime?"

Adam shrugged. "Some little tykes can get a kick out of anything. But you'd have thought they'd have made a mess with the contents rather than abscond with the things entirely. Sounds like a murderer's trick rather than a hooligan's. You might use a wheelie bin if you wanted to take something away that was too tricky to carry. That wouldn't explain why two bins had gone, though."

"No, but I like the idea. This was a messy crime. If the murderer put their bloodstained clothes in the bin, then changed, they could transport them somewhere without drawing too much attention to themselves, assuming it was after dark." Robin clapped Adam on the shoulder. "Especially if it was a Sunday night, because anybody hearing them would simply think they were putting the bins out ready for the next day's collection. Right, here we are."

They'd stopped at what must have been Ellen's house. Campbell watched, face a picture of puzzlement, as Robin slipped on plastic gloves, clambered up to loosen the bolt, and then opened the gate.

"You've not got it padlocked?"

"Not yet. I want capacity for my people to get in and out whenever they can over the next few days. The CSIs have given the garden a complete going over, so it's not like there's anything incriminating to remove. We've shut all the blinds so the media can't get pictures of where the body was found, but there's nothing to stop them getting a picture of the back of the house, lock or no lock."

"I suppose there's nothing much to stop *anyone* shinning over this back wall. Especially if they've got a mate to give them a hand up."

"You're right, although I bet the couple next door will be falling over themselves to keep an eye out from now on. Got to redeem themselves somehow for lockdown-breaking. I think she's up there keeping an eye on us." Robin cheerily waved towards the first-floor room of the house to the right. The woman concerned gave a tentative wave in reply, then disappeared.

"I hope she recognised you under that beanie. Or else you'll have Pru coming to arrest you."

With a flippant gesture, Robin headed for the back door, let himself in, before emerging a minute later with a remote control. "We'll try the blinds a set at a time or else I'll get confused about which is which. Help me remember left pocket is upstairs, right pocket is down."

It didn't take long to confirm that anyone in possession of a spare remote control wouldn't have needed to enter the house to create this illusion of occupation. They could have operated the blinds from the back alley, let alone the garden, as both upstairs and downstairs sets responded quickly to the touch of the relevant button.

"Well, you were right." Robin wrinkled his brow. "Can you get your phone out? I want to see if you can work them from the front too."

"Go for it." Adam waited patiently for Robin's call, while Campbell explored the world of new smells that the environs provided. Only one person went past in that time: Adam greeted her with a smile, a nod, and his best attempt at a *nothing to see here, move along* expression. It was a relief when the phone went. "Adam reporting for duty."

"Right. I'm on the pavement. Anything happening?"

"Not a sausage." Adam regretted his choice of words as Campbell nudged his leg.

"I'll try from the front step. I think if I do this . . ."

"That works. The French windows blinds are moving. Ah, no, now they've stopped."

"Okay. I think if you get the correct angle through the front door you can work them, but it's too hit and miss, because I've been pressing all the time, while moving the control around. Let me try the other one."

"That's a definite no."

"Okay. I'm coming back. If somebody had worked them from outside, it would surely have been from that path. And in the dark, at a guess."

"Agreed about the path, although not necessarily about the dark. Those remotes are about the size of a phone. What if you stood pretending you were reading a message or fiddling with your iPod, who would suspect you were making the blinds open or shut? Nobody questions someone fiddling with a device when they're walking along."

"Have I ever told you I admire you for your mind as much as for your body?"

"Not often enough. Hold on." Adam watched as a chap about his age emerged from the property to the left of the dead woman's. He gave Adam a sideways glance, then set off up the path, in the direction Robin had gone, glancing over his shoulder a couple of times. "I bet you get a report rung in this afternoon about a dodgy bloke with a black dog. There's a guy came out of next-door who's just given me a dirty look."

"That must be Greg, the lockdown-breaker."

"No. He came out of the house on the *other* side. The one where you said there were two older guys, so maybe he's the toyboy. Hello? Are you there?"

"Yeah, I'm turning the corner." Robin waved from the distance. "I didn't want to say anything while I walked past *him*. If he's their toyboy, they've done well for themselves."

"Have you actually met—" Adam stopped, as another relatively young man appeared via the same gate.

"Can I help you?" he asked. "What exactly are you doing?"

"Waiting for my partner." Adam gestured up the path with his phone, leaving the call open so that Robin could hear what was going on. "He's the policeman in charge of the murder case. Chief Inspector Bright. I'm helping him with a practical experiment."

"Oh, I see." The man broke into a grin. "*My* partner just rang me to say there was somebody acting peculiarly out the back of Ellen's. I nearly called the police. That would have been awkward. I'm Trevor, by the way and that was Don who thought you were up to no good."

Robin, who'd picked up speed, called out, "It's okay. I'm a police officer," as he took his ID from his pocket.

"I know," Trevor said. "Your chap here's put me straight, at the point I was ready to call 999. A shame I can't invite the pair of you inside for a coffee and cake. It's perishing out here."

Robin halted by them, slightly breathless. "I wouldn't mind the chance of asking you some questions, though. If you could stick on a coat, we could chat in your garden once I've secured the property here." He jabbed his thumb towards Ellen's back door.

"I can do better than that. We've a patio heater I can get going while I tog myself up. Bring the dog into the garden," Trevor told Adam. "We can still be socially distanced and not freeze our nuts off."

The garden at number forty-one was clearly designed for use, more than Ellen's had been. Almost all of it had been covered with decking, with only the borders and a trellised area being arrayed with plants. There was a table, chairs, a heater, and none of it overlooked that much because of the church at the back and tall hedges at the sides.

As Adam waited, discouraging Campbell from following Trevor into the house, he decided that Robin must have made the assumption that the couple were older based on nothing other than their names: Trevor and Don. It wasn't an unreasonable supposition, although probably one Robin would have castigated his constables for. This case must be getting to him already.

Campbell tugged at his lead, clearly hearing Robin emerge from the house next-door before his master did. Adam heard the gate being closed and the bolt shot across, then with a cheery, "Hey, this is nice," Robin entered the garden. "We might get some ideas for our place."

"Campbell would never forgive us if we went for such an expanse of decking. As a seating area, though . . ."

"Glad you like it." Trevor, now swathed in coat, hat, and gloves, came to join them. "A right little sun trap this, even in the winter."

Robin, glancing round, gave it the nod of approval. "Very neatly kept. Do you store your bins behind that trellis?"

"Yes. Bins are quite a sore subject in this road."

"People don't like the wheelie ones?" Robin asked.

"Got it in one. Many years ago, they used to have metal bins that were kept down the area steps, but the binmen got stroppy and refused to lug them up every week. There was quite a standoff, because the residents wouldn't do it, either. Then the council tried sacks, although it didn't take long for everyone to realise those were acting as a magnet for all the urban foxes and gulls. The wheelie bins arrived a few months before we did and are most welcome." Trevor rolled his eyes. "We had them at our last house, and I really like them. Easier to get in and out for one thing, and you can hose them down when they waff a bit."

"Agreed," Adam said, not wanting to simply stand dumb. "Why don't others like them?"

"Storage in between collections. Has to be somewhere out here—in a shed or tucked away like ours are. They ruin the view from the hot tub." Trevor laughed. "And woe betide if you leave them out on the path too long. Hanging offence as far as the Cromwell Road mafia are concerned. Ireton Avenue are really laid back about it, apparently. We expect pistols at dawn on a weekly basis. Sorry, you don't want to hear all about the local dramas."

"Actually, we do." Robin didn't justify the *we* bit. Trevor was evidently expected to treat Adam as part of the team. "Do you get any trouble around here with people nicking bins? Any idea where Ellen's could have got to?"

The witness gave a surprised shrug. "No idea. I'm not aware of hooligans arsing about, either. Wouldn't dare cross the yummy-mummies around here. Although . . ." Trevor rubbed his nose as if in thought. "Don said something about bins. It was over the Christmas holidays, when the schedules all get changed and people are in a state about when to put them out. The Monday before Christmas collection was brought forward to the Saturday, and you'd have thought world war three had begun when some of the households got it wrong. Ellen's were definitely out for collection on the correct day, because Don saw them, so she must have been alive then."

"It appears so. You said she had a food delivery in between Christmas and New Year?"

"Yes. I was coming back off my shift when I saw the van, but I couldn't tell you the company. I was too knackered. Bins, though . . ." Trevor got his phone from his pocket. "There was something else. Let me ring Don and ask him."

Adam, Robin, and an increasingly relaxed Campbell, who had no doubt decided that the patio heater and decking were exactly what any well-ordered household with a Newfoundland needed, listened to Trevor's half of the phone call. Always frustrating not to hear the whole thing, and tempting to fill in the gaps with likely the wrong pieces.

"Right," Trevor said, when he'd finished the call. "Not sure if this helps in any way, but Don saw someone lugging two bins along the path a few weeks ago. Extremely community-minded, is my partner, so he followed this bloke. Turned out he was taking them to his van—one of these bin-sanitation companies—so he must have been cleaning them. Don remembered because he wondered if we should get ours given the once-over, only we've been too busy to follow it up."

Robin nodded. "So we heard. I understand you work at the hospital."

"Yes. Been an interesting time, working hours all over the shop. Anyway, this might have nothing to do with Ellen's bins, but you could give the company a ring. Sparkling Bins, they were called. Very camp, we thought."

"As a row of tents." Adam pointed towards the path. "Has there been anyone lurking about out there over the last few weeks?"

"Not that we'd noticed. And, as you imagine, Don would have mentioned it if he'd seen anybody he felt was acting suspiciously."

"They mightn't have appeared too out of place. Standing like they were fiddling with their phone?"

Trevor threw up his hands. "Nobody would take any notice of that. People around here are welded to their screens. Down by the university you take your life into your hands, with mobs of young people bumping into you because they don't watch where they're going. I had one in casualty last week who'd walked straight into the path of a car because they'd been texting, and don't get me started on drivers using their phones. Sorry, bit of a sore point. I have to deal with the aftermath."

"No need to apologise. Sore point with me too," Robin said. "While I have you, can I ask about the spare key you had? The more we learn about Ellen, the more we're surprised that she'd have given any of her neighbours access to her property."

"As I told your sergeant, it was the previous owners, the Turners, who were given it. I can elaborate, though. We still had contact details for them, because—surprise, surprise—the post office forwarding system doesn't always work as it should. I hope you don't mind, but

I gave them a call. Mainly to tell them what had happened to Ellen because, as you say, it seems odd she gave them a key, and I supposed they might have been closer to her than we've been. They'd seen the news about the murder and had been speculating about who the victim was. At work, I deal with a lot of people in various emotional states and you get an instinct for what's going on below the surface. I'm guessing you're the same, Chief Inspector."

"We call it my rozzer's nose. Go on."

"Well, while they were upset to hear she'd been murdered, I got the impression they weren't surprised. They *had* been pally, because Mr. Turner used to partner Ellen at the local bridge club. He made some remark to me about still waters running deep, then he clammed up. I left things at that, suggesting that if they had anything which could help the police you'd no doubt appreciate them ringing Kinechester station. Do you want the Turners' number?"

"Please."

"I bet they didn't offer Pru that number," Adam said quietly while Trevor was in the house. "They wouldn't have fancied her."

"Behave."

Trevor returned, piece of paper in hand. "While I was getting this, I was thinking about last summer. We had Ellen round for a few drinks, as well as Rose, Craig, and their son Nathan from forty-three. Bit of an impromptu do to celebrate being allowed to socialise again. Ellen was telling Nathan about her old job—he's a real computer nerd and loved every bit of it. She went home early, but he couldn't stop going on about what she'd told him about conspiracy theorists. He thought they'd only cropped up in the last few years. Anyway, Don would tell me to cut to the chase, so I will. Nathan said Ellen was still doing some research and when he started probing about it, all she'd say was she was on the trail of a woman with pink hair and pulling in all her favours to do it."

"Pink hair?" Robin jerked his thumb towards the higher-numbered houses. "Any chance she meant Sonia Parsons?"

"Is that the woman who lives on the corner?"

"Yes."

"I doubt it, then. As far as I know, she only went pink a bit before Christmas. Don would have a better idea exactly when. He likes to guess what colour she'll go next. He'd put money on her queuing up to turn silver as soon as the hairdressers are open again." Trevor shrugged. "Sorry not to be much help."

Once they'd set off again, Robin flashed Adam a grin. "Excellent questioning in there, Constable Matthews. I'll recommend you for promotion."

"Up yours. I didn't want to stand there like a lemon. Or looking like I was your himbo." Adam snorted. "You made the wrong assumption about the age of that pair, Chief Inspector. Did the names throw you?"

"Guilty as charged. Useful witnesses, though. They'd have a note of authority in court. If only we had something for them to be authoritative about. What did you make of the bins story?"

"Entirely plausible. If the killer used the bin to transport their bloody clothes to wherever they ditched them—crammed under a pile of crap in somebody else's skip, maybe—then returned it, they might have been worried afterwards that they'd left blood traces or fibres. If the thing was professionally cleaned, would it take away all the detectable matter?"

"I don't know. Like we don't know if we're talking about the same bins, but it seems huge coincidence if not." Robin held out his hand. "Want me to take the boy while we circle round to the car park? You can weigh up Cromwell Road from the front."

Adam transferred the lead and concentrated on taking in the scene, although by the time they'd passed number thirty-nine, he had little constructive to offer apart from warning Robin to avoid a couple of patches of ice. Despite—or perhaps because of—the snow, plenty of people were out and about, especially on the open space, where children of all ages were constructing small snowballs to hurl at each other. "Like Piccadilly Circus round here."

Robin agreed. "Strikes me that unless it's peeing down with rain or blowing a gale, this is always going to be a busy spot. If you wanted to keep a house under observation, it's ideal."

"You think somebody was observing the property?"

"I have no idea. We don't know the killer's motive or why they seem to have arranged for her body to be found when it was. I get the part about trying to muddy the waters on the exact date and time of death, to give yourself alibi potential, but seeing as the scheme was working so well, why not let it run its course? The longer she wasn't found, the murkier the timeline becomes."

"Perhaps it's about her will. That couldn't go into probate until she was proven dead. If you needed the money, you might want to hasten that process. Although, given how long things take to go through probate, maybe quick money isn't the answer." Adam had nothing else to suggest. "You're going back to the station, now?"

"Yep. I'll see if we can pin down the bin cleaner. Should be home at a reasonable time unless anything startling comes in. You?"

"Got some prep for next week and then I said I'd Facetime Mum. I sometimes think lockdown's busier than nor— other times. Saved myself from a fine, there." Adam, who'd become aware of the slight hesitation in Robin's stride, asked, "What's up?"

"Assumptions, again, like I'd made about Trevor and Don. We've all been assuming we're dealing with an increasingly stubborn and frail woman, one who was making odd excuses for pulling out of commitments and entrenching herself in her home because she was scared of revealing she wasn't as capable as she used to be. We've not explored the obvious."

"Which is?"

"That she was like both of us. Busy. Too busy with something so important—one of her bits of research, maybe—that she didn't want anything extraneous impinging on the time and effort she could devote to it." Robin's face shone, as though the light on the road to Damascus was beaming straight onto it. "Research was part of her job, and when fraudsters impinged on her private life, she amassed enough evidence off her own bat to bring their trial to a successful conclusion. She had a flair for it. Why wouldn't she carry on doing similar investigations in her spare time?"

"You might have something, there." Older people all round the globe had been forced to find new ways to keep body and mind active, this past year. Incentives—seeing grandchildren via Zoom when you couldn't see them any other way, for example—had added impetus to embracing new technology. But Ellen might have fallen back on the familiar, occupying her fallow time doing the research she enjoyed.

"If you have a moment, could you do me a favour?"

"Yep. So long as it's not darning your socks."

Robin made a face. "Can you get in touch with Kelvin and ask him if he has any idea what Ellen might have used as passwords for her various devices? I know it's a long shot, and I doubt she had the same code for everything, but the sooner we can get into her files, the better."

"I'll do that as soon as I'm home."

They'd reached the car park, so shared a hug, then Robin patted Campbell and set off.

Adam got the dog into the car. "What do you make of that, boy? You like playing police dogs, don't you?"

The Newfoundland produced the doggy equivalent of a grin. He'd played his role a bit too enthusiastically in the past, putting both Adam's and Robin's safety above his own.

"No heroics this time, okay? Or I'll confine you to barracks."

Chapter Six

As soon as Robin got back to the station—it was too cold for sitting around in the car fiddling with his phone—he googled *Sparking Bins*. The firm's website stated they weren't open again until Monday, although there was a mobile number where they could be contacted and would get back to the caller as soon as they could. Robin decided not to use it until Monday as he didn't want to risk putting the wind up anyone, and if they'd heard about the murder and were sitting worrying, waiting for the police to be in touch, then it wouldn't hurt to let them stew a bit longer. If they'd had evidence to incriminate themselves, chances were it was already long gone.

The office was quiet, the team either out on enquiries or maybe grabbing a tea before they got together to mop up the day. Some precious time for Robin to get on with the routine stuff that built up during an investigation. He didn't expect to hear from Adam anytime soon, but the man couldn't have been home above ten minutes when he sent a message.

Kelvin says he thinks she used to use rugby players' surnames and their shirt numbers for alphanumeric passwords. Farrell10 or whatever. She was an avid England supporter, although he doesn't know if she followed a club team, because he's a football man. I told him he's a Philistine.

Robin chuckled. *Potentially a helpful Philistine.*

In the room at number thirty-nine with the exercise bike, there'd been a pinboard with various items, including sporting memorabilia, one of which had been a Harlequins pennant.

Robin glanced up as Ben came into the room bearing two mugs. "The very man I wanted to see."

"You're psychic so you knew I was bringing you one of these?" Ben laid a mug down. "I thought I saw your car. Reckoned you could do with a cuppa."

"*You're* the mind reader." Robin took the brew eagerly. "Read this." He passed over his phone.

"Names and numbers. I've come across that before as a way to vary your passwords. She had rugby stuff in the house, didn't she?"

"A Quins pennant. The tech team could start with them, although I'm guessing in a club game it's less likely one player's welded to one shirt number."

"Apart from the hooker or the scrum half." Ben had the common sense of the true rugby fan not to make any snide jokes about the man in the number two shirt. "I'll get onto the tech team now. Actually, have I got time to nip down there and chivvy them?"

"By *chivvy* do you mean help? Go on, it's top priority as far as I'm concerned. Anything you want to feed into the mop up?"

"Not really. I've got a list of local companies who do food deliveries, and I'm halfway down it without having any luck. I thought I'd struck oil with one of them, because they had her listed as a customer, but the last time she ordered was a couple of hampers for Christmas 2019. Maybe to take to Kelvin's family as a present. A follow-up medical report came just as I went off for the drinks. I'll fetch it before I go."

It read as expected. Date of death still couldn't be fixed tighter than January the first through to the seventeenth. A specialist entomologist was working on the flies and what light they could throw on the business.

Robin shuddered. He had a strong stomach, but the lecture he'd attended on forensic entomology had made him squirm. Best to get the gory medical stuff out of the way at the start of the mop up, to lessen the chance of people having it in their minds when they had their evening meal.

When the others had returned and the discussion started, Robin actually began by confessing he'd had an idea earlier. "There's no evidence for it, as yet, so I'll hold fire. Don't want to muddle things with speculation."

"It'll be worth waiting for," Pru assured the two constables. "Mr. Bright's hunches usually are."

"Thanks for the confidence in me. I may fall flat on my face this time. By the way, have any of you come across a mention of somebody with pink hair, other than Sonia Parsons?" No response but blank looks. "Well, if you do, let me know. Ellen might have been on that person's trail. In better news, we've had a bit of a lead on computer passwords, so Ben's gone off to the techies, leaving me to deliver the medical report." Robin launched into a precis of the grizzly details, ending with, "It's still a broad window, but we can hopefully narrow the date of death further. I wouldn't rely on anything to do with the blinds opening and shutting to fix a time. Anybody with a remote control could have operated them from outside. In terms of using the interaction with the delivery company to help us, Ben says he's not had any success pinning that down, yet."

"I've been in touch with the dentist, as you suggested," Pru said. "You were right about giving them a whirl, because they hold a surgery on Saturday mornings. Private practice and they're overrun with work, which is why they were cross that Ellen didn't turn up for her crown prep on January the thirteenth. Not like her to miss an appointment, apparently. In fact, she normally double-checked to make sure she had the right date and time. Clearly she didn't this time and they'd sent her the usual text reminders beforehand, as well as an email with a Covid health assessment form they ask all their patients to fill out. They'd tried to contact her afterwards, to inform her she might be liable for a financial penalty for missing her appointment without giving them notice, but they didn't get through and hadn't followed it up. The practice manager had cut her some slack in case she was laid up in hospital with *it*."

"Whereas she was probably lying dead on her lounge carpet by then." Robin nodded. "Good work. Anything else to report?"

"I have a contact number for Cavendish, sir," Ashok said. "He lives a bit north of Portsmouth, so I've arranged that we'll see him tomorrow."

"Excellent. You and I can take that one. Now, the disappearing dustbins. Somebody from a cleaning company was seen taking a couple of bins off, presumably to fumigate them, during the period we're interested in. Naomi, that's a job for you and me. Don't laugh at the name." Robin wrote the details on the board. "Can you ring them first thing on Monday, please? I don't solely want the particulars of that job—I'd like to get out there and have a nose about."

Naomi made a note. "Okay, sir. You don't want me to check that it *was* Ellen's bins before we make the trek?"

"No. Indulge me. They operate out of a unit on the industrial estate at the back of Kinechester Sainsbury's, so it won't be far to go. And if the lead's a dead end, we can drop in and get sandwiches for lunch." Robin paused as the door opened. A shiver of excitement moved over him as Ben came in, wearing a big grin that suggested he'd made a breakthrough. "The man himself. News?"

"We've got into her phone." Ben held the object concerned aloft, like an Olympic torch bearer. "They're still working on the other devices, so we're not into her files yet, but at least we've got access to messages and emails. I've had a quick scan of what's there, and there's nothing outgoing via text or Google Mail since late afternoon on the eleventh of January."

"That feels like a fix on the date. Well done. What day of the week was the eleventh?"

"I'll check, sir." Naomi picked up a desk calendar. "A Monday. Bin-collection day, if that's significant."

"I hate to be a party pooper, sir," Pru said, "but aren't we forgetting something? I know the eleventh works alongside everything else we have so far; however, given that someone pretending to be her ordered that delivery, it's possible another person had access to her emails so the dating would be useless."

A valid point. Before Robin could respond, Ashok chipped in. "Okay, if that were true, seeing as whoever it was went to such trouble to get that mirror sent on that particular day, wouldn't they have kept up the email pretence up? You could send vague replies saying you weren't well and you'd get round to a proper reply when you felt better."

Another valid point. Working with this team was proving a pleasure. "*Is* there any mail in her inbox about the mirror delivery, Ben?"

"No, although the email address on that was a Hotmail one and the phone is linked to Google Mail. I'll go right through it this evening and let you all know if I dig up treasure. If she had a Hotmail account that she accessed through Safari, it should have an automatic login."

"Right, but in return, get a later start tomorrow to make up. Ashok and I are off to see Cavendish while Pru and Naomi can concentrate on talking to the ex-neighbours, the Turners, and going through the house-to-house stuff, focussing on the few days either side of the eleventh." Robin paused. "Those houses. I know the walls are pretty thick because they were built back when a wall was a wall, but wouldn't somebody have heard something when Ellen was killed? Surely she cried out?"

Pru shrugged. "Trevor and Don at forty-one said they'd not heard anything of note. Mind you, the peak of hospital admissions was around that point and they'd been working their socks off."

"It was pretty noisy when we entered the Careys', as well, sir," Ben said. "Some programme playing upstairs as well as down, so depending on when it happened, the sound may have been drowned out."

"Okay. And if one of them is involved, they're hardly going to admit to hearing her scream. Not when they've gone to such trouble to obscure the date of death. Yes, Pru? Something on your phone?" Not like the sergeant to be checking it during a briefing, so it must be important.

"I was trying to remember why the eleventh struck a chord. Remember that pinboard in Ellen's house? I took a picture of what was on it. That included a Post-it Note with 'Cervical smear, eleventh!!' written on it. I think it was 'cervical', because it read like 'corvical' but I can't imagine her getting the spelling wrong. The handwriting wasn't too neat. Worse than mine." Pru snorted. "Could be referring to the eleventh of next month, but it would be useful to know if it *was* January and whether she turned up. Whatever it was must have been important to get two exclamation marks. Unless she was one of these people who use the things habitually."

"Ellen was sixty-six, wasn't she?" Naomi asked. "I thought smear tests stopped by then. Unless you've got a problem."

"Her last test was clear." Pru made a note. "I'll get onto the surgery."

"Thanks. Ashok will only get upset again if we make him." Robin gave the young man a smile. "You'll have to harden yourself. When I was a constable like you are, I—" He shuddered. "No. Your delicate ears aren't up to that story."

"You can't leave it like that, sir," Ben said. "Our imaginations will run riot and end up with a scenario much worse than the truth."

"Let's just say I opened the door to what I thought was an empty room, to find two senior female officers inside, discussing dainty cervixes. It scarred me for life. Right, back to the case."

"I've got something as well, sir." The professional respect in Ben's voice couldn't hide a puppyish note. Like Campbell when he'd found a Bonio he'd lost. "There's a string of text messages on Ellen's phone from a guy called Jeremy. About some project he and Ellen were working on together. They don't go back that far, and they seem to start in midstream, so either one of them changed their phone or she deleted the earlier string. I get the impression she was the sort who kept her message inbox pretty clear, so there's nothing too suspicious in that."

"When did she stop replying?" Robin asked.

"From the date on that thread, the second week of January. Trouble is, we don't know if she spoke to him via some other means after early on the tenth, which is the time stamp on her last response. Or if somebody else was already replying using her phone. Anyway, this Jeremy might be able to give us a better fix, as he got very agitated about her not responding. At first he only asked if she was okay and wondered whether she'd caught *it*." Ben shrugged. "Easy assumption to make. Kinechester was the county hotspot for a while."

The fact that people had a habit of assuming that every strange event was probably pandemic-related didn't make the police's life any easier.

Naomi clearly felt doubtful about that explanation, given her derisive snort. "Why didn't this Jeremy contact the police if he was concerned at her radio silence? At some point her phone battery must have died so he'd have been told that his messages couldn't be delivered. Wouldn't that make you suspicious?"

"He certainly messaged after the phone went dead, because a flurry of messages came through when I charged it up, including the delivery notification for the mirror, so whoever placed that used her phone number." Ben wrinkled his brow. "There aren't any other personal messages on there and, while I haven't gone all the way through her incoming mail in detail, I didn't spot anything further from him along the 'Are you okay?' lines. She might have used this purely for business type stuff, though, with another address for the personal. And if she had social media, she accessed it through her browser, because there aren't any apps on the phone."

"From the picture we're building up, she doesn't strike me as the Facebook type," Pru remarked. "Maybe Jeremy concluded he'd put his foot in it somehow and she'd given him the cold shoulder like she's been giving everyone else."

"I have a theory about that." Robin moved to the board again, tapping the picture of the victim to emphasise his point. "I said I wouldn't discuss it until I had evidence and that mention of a project is enough. We've been picturing Ellen as a victim of her age, increasingly frail and scared to admit it. What if we're wrong and she actually pulled back from doing other things because she was up to her eyeballs in this project, whatever it is? There may still be an age element, if she felt she had a limited amount of energy to give to things and was putting it all into the one cause."

"I like that idea, sir," Pru said. "My mum's younger than Ellen and she's finding all the extra screen time exhausting. She does work online and then she sometimes plays games for fun and that's quite enough. But then people want her to have Zoom social calls in the evening and they think she's being standoffish when she says she'd rather not. All she wants to do of an evening is power off and sit with a good book or her knitting while her and Dad watch some trashy crime drama."

"What do we think the project might have been?" Ashok asked. "Related to her work history? She used to track down conspiracy theorists, ones who were using the net to spread what we'd now call fake news or misinformation, so she'd have plenty of targets to go after at the moment."

"We need to find Jeremy and ask him. Ben, you can ring him as soon as we're done here. If we can get to see him tomorrow, then Pru and Naomi can take the appointment with Cavendish." Robin glanced at the board again, taking a deep breath. "Not bad progress for a couple of days. Once we've fixed an appointment with Jeremy, we can head home. Except for Ben and his phone."

Ashok raised his hand. "One thing, sir. Your theory about Ellen being totally occupied with this project. It might also go towards explaining why she didn't want people in the house—what if the project was highly sensitive in some way. To do with her old job, maybe. She wouldn't have wanted people seeing any evidence she was building up."

Robin nodded slowly. "Good point, although the search of the house didn't locate anything obvious that she wouldn't have wanted a visitor to spot."

"The killer may have taken it away with him or her."

"Oh, you're quite right, Ashok." Robin gave a sigh. "Possibly in those bloody dustbins."

Robin was home earlier than Adam had expected, so cottage pie for one became cottage pie for two. Campbell had gone through the whole *I haven't seen you for weeks and weeks* thing when he'd arrived. and they'd been curled up on the settee together mostly since dinner. Robin had told him how useful Kelvin's information about the rugby players had been and asked him to pass on the police's thanks. Other than that, he'd not discussed the case much, saying he wanted to clear his mind, so they'd focussed on the latest scandal from Adam's mum, which involved the local Parochial Church Council. There'd been a huge drama when one of the members had had to resign because she'd got an unspent conviction for fraud lurking in her past. As she'd been one of the most vehement voices opposing police checks on PCC members, nobody should have been surprised, but nonetheless, shock waves had shot through the local twinset and pearls mafia.

Discussing this tale had inevitably led onto a discussion about not judging by appearances, and Adam recounting the apprehension of a drug smuggler of unlikely appearance on a reality show he'd been watching that morning.

"So what are your plans for tomorrow?" Adam asked, when Robin had finally come round after forty winks and missing most of the programme he'd said he wanted to watch.

"Portsmouth and interviewing a bloke who likes to make his living via dating agencies. It was supposed to be an interview with Ellen's project coworker, Jeremy, but he's changed his phone number, so Ben's still on his tail."

"Okay, well, I understood all those words individually. Not sure I get the bigger picture. Oi!" Adam fended off a cushion that had come flying from Robin's direction. Campbell raised his head, gave Adam a dirty look at having been awakened, then settled back down again.

"See, you've woken the baby." Robin tittered. "Remember I said that Ellen Wilkins had been a witness in a fraud trial? The bloke in Portsmouth is one of the guys she sent down, and I want at least to eliminate him from enquiries. Better if he pleaded guilty on his doorstep, but miracles like that rarely happen. It also seems I was right about her having been occupied these last few months. Her and this bloke called Jeremy—which is all we know about him—have been doing some venture together, of which we know absolutely nothing. Your mate Kelvin hasn't heard of a Jeremy in connections with her, has he?"

"Not being psychic, I couldn't tell you. Let me message him." Adam shot off the query, apologising for interrupting Kelvin's Saturday night but saying it was fairly urgent so an early response would be appreciated. It came almost immediately.

No worries. I think she used to go out with a Jeremy, but I could of got the name wrong.

Adam winced. He'd be having a word on Monday morning about why it was *have* not *of*.

I'll ring Mum now and see what she says.

"Kelvin thinks he could be an old flame. I guess that might fit with her getting on the trail of the phishing fleet."

"Phishing fleet? I'm stealing that."

"You're allowed to. As payment, you can steal to the kitchen and get us both another beer."

They didn't have to wait long for Kelvin to get back in touch, this time by phone. He explained that he had some information, or rather his mum did, although he hadn't thought it right to give her Adam's phone number. If Robin needed it direct, she was happy to speak to him.

"Thanks." Adam nodded, the sort of thing done habitually despite the caller not being able to see him. "No doubt he'll get onto her, but anything you can tell us now would be great. Let me put you on the speaker."

Robin came over to join him, there not being too much room on the other sofa as it was now pretty full of Newfoundland.

"Okay," Kelvin said. "Ellen used to go out with a bloke called Jeremy when she was in her thirties. He was a colleague at her work. None of us have met him, but Mum heard all about him after Ellen got involved in that dating-agency scam case. I had no idea about half of what went on except that she could have gone to the dating agency on the rebound. Mum's promised me a Facetime call tomorrow to give me all the gruesome details."

"It seems like your mum was Ellen's confidante," Robin said.

"Eh?"

"Somebody she told her secrets to," Adam clarified.

"Yeah, that's probably true, although not very often. But Mum says that when the floodgates opened, they opened." Kelvin snorted. "Seems this Jeremy may have been the love of her life, but it was the usual story. He was married and, while he and his wife didn't have kids, she wouldn't divorce him because she was a Catholic. So Ellen eventually gave him the boot. Which is, I suppose, why she got involved with a dating agency."

"It's possible," Robin said encouragingly. "Did your mum give you his surname?"

"Sefton. Or Seldon. Some name like that."

"Kelvin," Adam said, "you told me that your mum once teased Ellen about the alternate Christmases, asking her whether she had a fancy man she was meeting then. How did Ellen react?"

"She laughed it off, although there was something . . . you know when the children have been a bit naughty and we know they have and they suddenly realise we know? *That* expression."

Adam felt swamped under the weight of *knows* but he got the meaning. "I'm with you. Not quite caught red-handed but wondering how you've managed to read their minds."

"Yeah. Anyway, Mum decided not to talk about that again because she thought she'd hit the truth and if Ellen wanted to tell us, she'd do it in her own good time. Only she never did."

"Thanks, Kelvin. I'll get one of the team to ring your mum tomorrow. It's possible there are things she'll tell us that she wouldn't share with the family." Robin gave Adam the thumbs-up. When the call had been ended with the usual winding-up stuff, he said, "That was a great shout of yours. About Christmas."

"It was based on my understanding of Kelvin's character. He's honest and a pretty bright lad, even if his command of the English language could do with a once-over but he's not got the full range of emotional intelligence, if they're the words I want. What I mean is he gets told something, accepts and remembers it, yet doesn't always catch its significance. It'll be well worth ringing his mum."

"Ben can do that. He's not the kind to miss snatching up an unconsidered trifle." Robin yawned and stretched. "My bed calls. Our bed calls. Unfortunately, I'm not sure I'll be of any use to you romance-wise, although you're welcome to warm your feet on mine. I'll be dead to the world."

"I'll console myself with a book. There'll be other nights."

Time to reflect, yet again, on how lucky they both were to have found *the* one, the person who made life complete. Despite the fact Adam sometimes felt like throttling Robin, he never wanted them to split up.

It seemed that Ellen, like many people, hadn't been so fortunate. Still, there was that old flame. Had he come back into her life on a purely professional basis, maybe picking up some old case they'd worked on together or asking her to help with a new one? Had she been the one to approach him, seeking a person she could trust with work, if not relationships? He'd surely have been somebody she'd have been happy to let into her house, so had that reconnection led to an opening of old wounds, an argument, and a fatal loss of control on Jeremy's part?

Chapter Seven

A shok picked up Robin from a convenient car park off the main road to Portsmouth, which saved the constable coming out of his way. The first ten minutes of the journey suggested he'd be a sensible driver, so Robin sat back and relaxed. He'd had junior officers who fancied themselves as Lewis Hamilton, one of whom he'd refused to travel with unless *he* took the wheel.

Mr. and Mrs. Cavendish lived in a spacious property not far from the A3, with spectacular views out over Portsea Island and the harbours either side of it. Robin knew from the fraud case that Cavendish's wife had been left a lot of money by her first husband and guessed that the house belonged to her. They both came to greet him and Ashok at the doorstep, as if presenting a united front against what they might see as the enemy.

Cavendish, neatly turned out in chinos and a good-quality sweater, hair well-sprinkled with grey, formed a contrast to his wife. While equally elegant, her locks were so strikingly blonde they must have had chemical enhancement to achieve such a colour.

Once they were all seated around a table in what appeared to be a breakfast room, Robin began by simply asking their hosts to account for their movements in the days either side of January the eleventh.

"Our diaries are hardly full to the brim, Chief Inspector Bright," Mrs. Cavendish said, combining a smile with a waspish tone. "We've been here most of the time, when we've not been out walking the dog." A handsome black Labrador, sprawled out on the carpet, gave credence to that assertion. "Poor thing, he's never been so fit as this last year."

"I have a dog too, and he'd agree with you." Robin glanced around the room, spotting a copy of the Sunday telegraph on the windowsill. "But few of us are doing absolutely nothing. We go out to get the newspaper or we're waiting in for a food delivery. We see the dentist or get a jab. I'd like to know, specifically, what you did between the ninth and thirteenth of January. Did you travel to Kinechester at any point?"

"That's not local, is it? I mean the government wouldn't want us doing that." Mrs. Cavendish crossed her arms, clearly daring Robin to argue with her. Cavendish nodded meekly, having said little since an exchange of "Hello" on the doorstep.

It was making a judgement on scant evidence, but suddenly Robin felt a touch sorry for the man. The trapper himself ensnared, only to find that he wasn't going to be top dog in this relationship. "What the government wants doesn't stop people from breaking the rules. I ask you again, and I want the truth, did you go to Kinechester earlier in January? Mr. Cavendish?" he added, before his wife could leap in.

"Yes, I did. I couldn't tell you for certain when. Maybe the ninth or tenth."

Robin pressed him. "We need you to be specific. It's important."

Cavendish sighed. "I'll fetch my diary."

As soon as her husband was out of the room, Mrs. Cavendish said, "Why are you persecuting poor Derek like this? He's done his time and he's turned over a new leaf. I've seen to that."

Robin was sure she believed he had. Maybe it was true. He wondered if "poor Derek" was allowed anywhere near a computer without supervision. "Nonetheless, we're investigating a murder. And the sooner you can satisfy us that you had nothing to do with it, the better." Robin took in the room again. A nice class of watercolours on the walls, although no family photographs. "I believe you had a son from your previous marriage?"

"Yes, William. What's he got to do with it? He lives with his own family, so I hardly see him anyway, let alone when we're locked down." Was there some hint of discontent in those words? Maybe William's partner wasn't keen on their mother-in-law and had encouraged that lack of contact. Or was Robin being too unkind? Plenty of folk had been cut off from their loved ones.

"Here," Cavendish's voice preceded his re-entering the room. He held out the relevant page of his diary for Robin to inspect. "It was the eleventh. We had a grocery delivery on the tenth, which is why I'd got confused."

"Thank you." Robin flicked through the pages for January, trying to appear casual and not get over-excited at the confession. The visit to Kinechester could have been innocent enough. He passed the diary to Ashok, in case he'd missed anything. "All it says in there is *Kinechester, 2 p.m.* What were you doing?"

Cavendish ran his hand over his brow. "Talking to a bloke about a new car for Deborah. He was selling his Avensis. I know, I know, it's probably not allowed but we assumed it would be okay so long as we did it in a socially distanced manner. I wore my mask all the time."

"Did you go too?" Ashok asked Mrs. Cavendish.

The brief glare she gave him, added to the fact she'd not addressed any of her remarks to the constable, screamed to Robin of closeted— or perhaps not so closeted—racism. "My constable asked you a question," he said.

"I heard him perfectly well. Of course I went. I'm not the kind of woman who sits at home while her husband chooses a car for her."

"And did you buy the car?" Ashok continued, seemingly unfazed by her response.

Deborah sneered, although whether at the constable or the car wasn't clear. "No. The paintwork was in a shocking condition. I'd guess it had been driven too close to hedgerows."

"We'll need the name and contact details for the man you saw." Ashok glanced from husband to wife and back again. "Did you visit anyone else when you were in Kinechester?"

"I used the public toilets, if that's what you mean." Mrs. Cavendish sneered. "I'm sorry that I can't find anyone to corroborate that."

"Deborah . . ." Cavendish's tones combined exasperation with a note of warning. He turned to Robin. "Are we supposed to have seen someone else?"

Robin ignored the question. "Were you in Cromwell Road that day?"

"I have no idea where that is so I couldn't tell you." Derek folded his arms across his midriff. "What's all this about, anyway? You said on the telephone your visit concerned a murder, so who died?"

"Ellen Wilkins," Robin said.

Mrs. Cavendish snorted. "That cow who helped put Derek in jail?"

"Miss Wilkins helped to compile a folio of evidence and witness reports that were part of the prosecution's case, yes." Robin, drawing himself up in his seat, employed his most magisterial voice. "Although only the first time he was found guilty. The second occasion he was sent to jail, other people provided the evidence. Mr. Cavendish, you haven't got around to starting up your scheme a third time, have you?"

"No!" Cavendish's expression suggested he wouldn't dare. "I was stupid, Mr. Bright. I wanted to make money the easy way. I've learned my lesson, now. Anyway, we did read about a suspicious death in Kinechester, but I didn't realise it was Ellen Wilkins."

"She played Derek along. Trying to entrap him." Mrs. Cavendish appeared to believe that explanation. Had it come from her husband or had she created the story herself to justify why she had married a man with such a track record?

"I don't think you're being helpful, dear." Cavendish sighed. "Mr. Bright, you clearly think that we visited Miss Wilkins when we went to Kinechester. We didn't. I have no idea where she lives—lived—now. She used to be out in the sticks."

"You never kept in touch?" Robin pressed on. "I know you were quite close at one time."

"I never wanted to keep in touch. I'll put my hand up to what I did, Mr. Bright, but I didn't want to be reminded of it." The statement sounded genuine, as had everything else Cavendish had said.

Ashok, evidently of the same opinion, asked, "Were you together the entire time you were in Kinechester? Apart from your visit to the lavatory, Mrs. Cavendish?"

The couple shared an uneasy glance, before the wife said, "Of course we were. It's not like I could go off round the shops or anything."

"Mr. Cavendish?" Ashok said, with an accomplished mixture of politeness and incision. The lad could go far.

"Yes, we were together."

It struck Robin as such a blatant lie, but he wasn't sure how to expose it. They had no real evidence to the contrary and the "Liar, liar, pants on fire!" approach was hardly professional. He settled for,

"We'll continue to pursue our enquiries, and if we come across any indication that you haven't told us the truth, I'll have you brought to Kinechester for questioning immediately. In the meantime, I'd like your fingerprints, for the purposes of elimination."

Cavendish frowned. "You already have them, Mr. Bright. I'm on your system, remember?"

"I *do* remember. It was yours I wanted, Mrs. Cavendish."

"I don't have to give you them. I'm not under arrest."

"No, you're not." She also wasn't—yet—under suspicion of an offence, apart from lying to the police. Robin hadn't been too hopeful that his appeal to give them voluntarily would succeed, but he found an unexpected ally.

"Just do it, Deborah," Cavendish urged. "You weren't in the dead woman's house, so what have you got to be scared of?"

"I'm not scared. I know my rights, that's all." Mrs. Cavendish crossed her arms again, as though afraid that one of her visitors might grab her hand and force it onto an ink pad.

"I'll jot down that name and number for you." Cavendish fetched a pad of paper and a pen from a little table, pulled off a sheet, copied something onto it from his diary, then passed it to his wife. "I'm going batty in my old age and can't read my writing. Was that his name, dear?"

Mrs. Cavendish huffed. "Give me the pen." She smoothed the paper, pressed it down, then amended the name. "Johnson, not Thomson." She flung the paper across to Ashok.

"Thank you."

Robin rose. "That's all for now. I'm aware that you aren't supposed to be going anywhere, but if you do get the urge to go wandering, let us know." He turned and made his way out of the room, before his hostess could make any final remarks.

"He's not stupid, is he?" Ashok said, as they reached the car. "And she's not as clever as she thinks she is."

"You clearly noticed what I noticed. The fingerprints."

"Yep. That seemed like a fresh piece of paper and, given that we have his dabs and mine, the forensic team can hopefully get a couple of hers. They can compare them to any from the scene. A bit dodgy, PACE-wise, though." Ashok swung onto the road and set off towards Kinechester.

The Police and Criminal Evidence Act, that blueprint for proper conduct. "Technically we haven't taken a set of prints, we're simply comparing two pieces of evidence. You could argue—at a stretch—that we've enough suspicion to warrant doing it formally."

"Why do you think *he* wanted us to have her prints?"

"I have an idea. What's yours?" Good to get into the thinking of a still unfamiliar officer.

"Not sure. They're lying about something but it would be odd if he's trying to stitch her up. Unless he's had enough and wants out."

"Of the relationship? Possibly. If he knew she'd had an involvement with Ellen's death, that might be more than he can take. Villains often have a code of what's acceptable and what's not." Cavendish might wink at fraud but draw the line at physical harm. "I was wondering if it's the reverse. He knows she's innocent and wants to eliminate her from our list of suspects. Although absence of evidence isn't evidence of absence. She could have worn gloves."

Ashok chuckled. "Sergeant Davis said that 'absence' thing was one of your favourite lines. Along with searching for the culprit close to home first off. I guess Cavendish or this Jeremy bloke are as close to home as we're likely to get. What would Mrs. Cavendish's motive be, though? Revenge?"

"She doesn't strike me as being someone who'd forgive and forget that easily. Particularly if she felt he was being threatened again for some reason. Hold that thought while I get Naomi on the trail of the car seller." Robin sent the text, then continued. "I agree they were lying to us about what they were doing and they'd already hoped I'd let them get away with giving us the wrong date. Are they covering up visiting Ellen or something else?"

"It could be as simple as another Covid rule breach, sir. They met up with friends in a house in or near Kinechester. Had lunch in a pub that was open illegally. Went to an over-sixties rave."

"Could be." Robin drummed on the car door. "Talking of lunch, if you see somewhere convenient, stop and we'll get sandwiches. My brain needs feeding."

Adam should have guessed that Kelvin would ring him again about the Ellen Wilkins case. Every time he'd had the most fleeting thought that he was getting away lightly with things, that liaising with Kelvin and helping with experiments at the Ramparts would be the limit of his involvement, he'd given himself a talking to about not tempting fate. Now it appeared fate had decided he hadn't been diligent enough in that department.

Around two o'clock, as Adam stepped through the door from having taken a long walk with the dog, Kelvin rang.

"Adam? I've had a letter from Ellen. It was delivered to number seventy-eight by mistake yesterday and the people who live there only brought it round to my house an hour ago. We're number seventy-three." Kelvin sounded in a right state. "I couldn't discuss it with the other half because she's been in work today, so I tried to ring you earlier but got no reply."

"Calm down, mate, it's okay. Sorry you couldn't get hold of me. Campbell and I were taking our daily exercise, because he likes the mushy snow. I'd left my phone here."

"No need to apologise. I shouldn't be bothering you, but it's like something out of a television show. The letter was with Ellen's solicitors and had to be sent to me in the event of her death. It said she'd sent one to Mum as well, although *she's* not had it yet. Her post is worse than ours, and that's saying something."

"Okay, so is it me you should be ringing or the police? I mean, I don't mind you calling, but if it's relevant to the case, they're the ones who need to know."

"I can't tell if it's relevant or not, and I wouldn't want to waste their time."

"Believe me, you wouldn't be wasting it. What does the letter say?" Adam should really hang up and get Kelvin to call Ben straight away. He told himself he was prolonging the conversation because his colleague needed a sympathetic ear, although the truth was he wanted to know what was so upsetting about the letter, other than it being a voice from beyond the grave.

"Stuff about the will and how she's put money aside to cover her funeral and all the details are with her solicitor. We knew about that because he'd been in touch with Mum to see if she's happy to make arrangements once the inquest and everything is done and the body's released. How we're not to grieve for her but have a big party, once big parties are allowed."

"So, this was written quite recently?"

"It's dated last November. I don't know whether she'd written something like this before and updated it. If she had, she never mentioned it. Like I said, it was a bolt out of the blue."

The solicitor would presumably know if this had been long planned. "Does it say anything else? Any useful leads like the one about rugby players' names used as passwords?"

Kelvin hesitated. "I don't know. Thing is, you get to scrutinising everything, wondering if it could have a double meaning. Maybe it does, maybe it doesn't, and I'd look a right wally handing this over to the cops if basically all it says is, 'Have a party on me and here's what I want played at my funeral.'"

Adam sighed. "Have you got a scanner?"

"Yeah, on my printer. Want me to take a copy of this and mail it over to you?" Kelvin sounded relieved at the prospect of passing on the responsibility. Possibly that was what he'd wanted all along.

"Please. I don't think you should use my school email address, so send it to Adam dot Matthews 3 at Google Mail. Want me to repeat that?"

"No, I've got it. Thank you. Sorry to be such a pain in the arse."

"Apology accepted."

"I guess it comes with the territory, you being hitched to a copper."

"It seems like it, at times. I'll forward it to Robin when it arrives. Anything else?" Adam dreaded opening another can of worms, although the question had to be asked.

"Not at the moment. When Mum's letter comes, do you want me to get her to scan and send as well? Through me, of course. I wouldn't give out your personal details."

"She should send it straight to Ben, or whichever officer she's been dealing with. By tomorrow, he'll be waiting for it."

And the Adam Matthews "post office box for the police" could stand down.

As soon as Robin returned to the office, he convened the team for an exchange of information. This time Ashok was missing, off getting his piece of paper examined for fingerprints, which was the first thing Robin shared with the others, along with an account of what they'd learned about Mr. and Mrs. Cavendish.

"It's as well that you two didn't travel down there," he concluded, waving at Pru and Naomi. "Ashok reckons she wouldn't have let you through the door."

"Why's that?" Pru asked.

"He thinks she's hyper-possessive. Maybe Derek has blotted his copybook too often to be trusted." Robin shrugged. "Jury's out on that, although I'd say she's not the nicest person."

"You're a born diplomat, sir," Naomi said. "She sounds, if I can say so, a right cow."

"You *can* say so, only not to her face. Add her name to the board alongside her husband's, please. Ben, any news on Jeremy?"

"I got a surname for him from Mrs. Vince. Sexton. No nearer to talking to the bloke himself. We still haven't got into her computers, and there's not much on her phone. She must have kept the really important stuff on her other devices. As for emails, the Google Mail account doesn't appear to have been used for anything research related, only everyday stuff, which was labelled for ease of access. Like all the emails for the cruise she had booked for last summer that was shifted to this autumn, that type of thing. She had a Sexton Hotmail address in her contacts, so I've bunged an email off saying that if he's Jeremy, we need to talk to him." Ben glanced up at the board. "Apart from that, Mrs. Vince mainly confirmed what Kelvin said, with further detail. She was surprised that Ellen had been in touch with Jeremy again, as it had all been a bit acrimonious when they'd split. She'd threatened to brain him if he so much as came within five yards of her."

"Real threat or just the usual hot air?" Pru asked.

"Mrs. Vince says she wouldn't have been surprised if Ellen had blacked his eye at any point. She thought she'd still have been capable of it, now."

And yet—if this was the same Jeremy—a working relationship had been reformed that, on the evidence of the messages, appeared to be businesslike.

"Okay. You're getting there, so keep ploughing on. Naomi. The bloke with the car."

"Mr. Johnson. What a nice man. He had the measure of those two." Naomi broke into a grin. "Yes, they'd been to see him on the eleventh of January, and he was fuming because they seemed like time wasters. She took one glance at the car and started complaining. I asked him about the paintwork, as you suggested, and he says there was nothing wrong with it. He's got rid of the Avensis now, but he had some pictures he'd taken and if they're of the vehicle concerned, it seems in good nick."

"We guess the car was an excuse to set up the visit," Pru said. "Mr. Johnson as much as told you that, didn't he?"

"Yeah. He thinks they may have wanted a day's sightseeing and if they got stopped by police, they'd have had a legitimate reason for being in the area." Naomi shrugged. "Did they strike you as the kind of people who'd tell a lie to cover that up?"

"They did," Robin said, "although I'm pretty certain they were covering up more than that. Unless they've already been done for breaking Covid rules so they're at risk of a heftier fine."

"He hasn't." Naomi waved her notes. "I double-checked his record, and there's nothing, apart from the traffic offence, since the fraud stuff."

"I don't suppose anybody in Cromwell Road has reported seeing a couple in their sixties, one of whom would come into the *mutton dressed as lamb* category, lurking about Ellen's house on the eleventh?" Three blank looks greeted the question. "No, well, I didn't think we'd be that lucky. And it's not like the first lockdown, where there were so few cars on the road they'd have stuck out like a sore thumb. Pru. The ex-neighbours."

"The Turners? I spoke to them earlier." Pru glanced at her notes. "Mr. Turner and Ellen used to go to the bridge club in the local secondary school. Mrs. Turner went, too, with a different partner. Didn't want to play with the husband, in case of it leading to marital discord. She has a particularly cautious bidding style compared to him, apparently, so Ellen was a better fit. A tendency to overbid, whatever that is."

"Sounds like going in for a two-footed tackle," Ben said.

"It's like a foreign language." Pru rolled her eyes. "Anyway, the neighbours were originally given the key to the house when Ellen went off on a long holiday. One of these fifty-day cruises halfway round the world. She didn't ask for the key back, so it got mixed up with all the other spares. When the Turners moved, Ellen stopped going to the local club because she couldn't find a partner who suited her. She did carry on pairing with Mr. Turner to play online." The sergeant heaved a sigh. "This morning, I learned more about bridge and bridge sites than any decent human needs to know. Seems like Ellen was still doing that up to last November. Sharp as ever, Mr. Turner said, no sign of her losing her faculties as far as cards were concerned."

Robin nodded. The picture of the victim they'd built up in the first few days continued to shift. "Why did she give up playing in November?"

"She said she wanted a break. The Turners said that wasn't unusual, because she'd done the same thing each Christmas since they started playing online. Sometimes for a few days, sometimes weeks. She then picked up the thread again in January, which is what they were expecting to happen this time. Ellen also mentioned that she was worried she was spending too much time online under artificial light, so it was almost like an early no-screen January. Which *I* find highly unlikely but Mr. Turner accepted it."

"Did she have the Christmas break when they were playing at the local club?" Naomi asked.

"Only if the dates coincided with her being away, staying with her friends—that would be the Vinces—or at a hotel." Pru nodded. "If she was telling the truth, then that's where she spent every other Christmas."

"That would match with something I found in her emails," Ben said. "It wasn't about a booking or anything, only a draft with a series of links to different hotels. I suppose that's a convenient way of bookmarking items, then you can access them from any device."

"My mum has a similar system," Pru said. "Sends emails to herself as well, then archives them for reference."

"Any sign she was planning to do that this year before the new rules came in? I have no idea how far ahead hotels get booked up at Christmas." Not information that Robin would ever need to know, personally. For him, the season had to be spent at home or at the parents'.

"Not among the emails and nothing on her online banking. I managed to get into the app." Ben raised his hands. "Don't get excited, sir. She seemed to use her Barclays account purely for stuff like regular payments. Council tax, the gardener, utilities. Monthly standing orders to The Children's Society and another charity I'd not come across: West London Action for Children. She must have had another account, though. The card number for Barclays doesn't match the card used to order the mirror, so unless there's another Ellen Wilkins involved, I've got to pin that down."

"She didn't have any paper bank statements in her files," Pru confirmed. "In fact, there was hardly any monetary stuff. It might be worth going through it again, though. I can't promise that we didn't miss something. If there was another card, then presumably the killer took it with them?"

"They must have done," Ben said. "It wasn't obvious that anyone had rifled through her bag or purse, but if they slipped it out, then we wouldn't have been any the wiser. I'm on the trail, anyway."

They were on the trail of a lot of things, none of which appeared to be yielding many results. *Early days though*: too early to get despondent. Especially when there were so many odd facts in the case. "Back to the Turners, if we can. Did you get any further with the 'still waters' remark he made about her to the present neighbours?"

"Sort of, sir. Bits of it we knew already—Ellen's career and her involvement in the fraud case—and he backed up what we've suspected about her still doing research. When they were living in Cromwell Road, the Turners were concerned about their nephew and a friendship he'd made on the internet. Sounded a bit off, with this woman telling him she needed money for her sick daughter. Luckily he'd mentioned it to them, given that he hadn't wanted to worry his parents, and before he parted with a single penny, they got Ellen to have a chat with the lad. She warned him what he was probably getting into, giving him lots of similar examples."

Robin could imagine. The cast of characters, the sob story, the apparent plausibility, the all-too-familiar scenario. "He took the advice to heart?"

"Too right he did. Knew he'd had a lucky escape. She didn't leave it there, though. She worked a bit of clever stuff that Ben would understand but that leaves me cold." Pru gave the constable a theatrical wink. "Tracked down the person who was doing the phishing. Lo and behold it was a sixty-year-old woman based in the U.S. She reported her, but I dare say she'll re-emerge with another scam."

Probably as a gay man. "That chimes with something Kelvin told Adam. She really seems to have had a soft spot for protecting youngsters. Did the Turners have any idea what she was working on in the last few months?"

"Not really, although they knew she'd hooked up with an old colleague to do it. They'd had a Christmas card from her, with a line or two of the usual, 'Hope you're bearing up,' stuff. They also think it said she was still busy and that it was a pain she couldn't spend her retirement free of old dogs getting up to their old tricks. Unfortunately the card went in the recycling long ago, so they can't be sure about the exact wording, but the impression they were left with was that she was returning to something she'd been involved with previously." Pru rose, picked up a marker and wrote *old dogs, old tricks* on the board. "Which old dog, though?"

As if he'd been waiting for a cue, and in an action replay of Ben the previous day, Ashok came bounding into the office, evidently bursting with news. The constable looked so much like Campbell when he'd found a bone buried in the garden that Robin had to force himself not to laugh. "Well, we were talking old dogs, but now it's time for cats. Here's the moggy that got the cream."

"Double at that, sir." Ashok waggled a bit of paper. "We got prints for Mrs. Cavendish."

"I don't want to pop your balloon, but are we sure they're hers and not someone else who picked up the pad?" Robin asked, trying not to sound too discouraging,

"Absolutely, sir. She's already on our system, with a conviction for assault. When the prints showed a match, I checked her photo, and she's not changed much in thirty years, apart from her hair colour. She was a brunette back then." Ashok's grin widened. "Her previous husband, the one who left her all the money, had a mistress at one point. Mrs. Cavendish—Mrs. Balshaw she was called then, which is why we hadn't realised she had form—went round and had it out with her. Leave-my-bloke-alone-or-you'll-regret-it kind of thing. They ended up in a fight, during which our Deborah blacked the mistress's eye and generally beat her about. Lucky to escape without a prison sentence, merely a fine and a community order. Probably helped that she had a young child at the time."

"I wonder if Derek Cavendish knows about that? And if he did, whether it was behind him trying to get us her fingerprints." Robin studied the incident board, gathering his thoughts. "I know it's a stretch from punching your husband's fancy piece on her nose to taking a knife to the woman who helped put your next husband away, but she's the first person we've found so far who's connected to the case and has a record of violence. Any of her prints turn up at number thirty-nine?"

"They're on the hunt now, sir. None of *his* match. Still, everybody knows about forensic stuff these days and would have the sense to wear gloves." Ashok frowned. "What's this about dogs?"

Pru gave a summary of what she'd learned from the Turners. "I'd been thinking that Ellen had been referring either to Cavendish or someone she investigated through her job. What if it was *Mrs.* Cavendish, though? Making threats, perhaps."

"That would mean Ellen knew about her criminal record, although if it was in the local newspaper, it wouldn't have been hard to pin down. It may have come up in her research for the fraud trial, if she was looking into the victims as well as the perpetrators," Robin suggested.

"It could be Jeremy she's referring to," Ben said. "If he came back into her life, reigniting the flame and then it turned out he'd been less than honest about his personal circumstances."

"Nicely put, Ben. What you really mean is that he was two timing her again." Pru chortled. "You've read the messages from him. Do they hint at anything other than a working relationship?"

Ben shook his head. "Not unless they used a code that's too obscure to break. Each word having a double meaning that only they'd know. Still, some couples aren't that lovey-dovey in messages, anyway. If you read the texts my girlfriend and I send each other, I doubt you'd think we were other than friends."

Robin smiled. He and Adam had a similar code, which they used when at risk of being overheard. "Don't forget the milk" meant "I love you." Anybody who caught their phone conversations must think they bathed in the stuff, like Cleopatra. "Okay, anything we've missed? Any local CCTV or is that too common for the Ramparts?"

"Nothing useful, sir," Naomi said. "There's a camera on the back of the Methodist church, but it's a dummy. We could try the traffic cameras to see if we can spot the Cavendish's vehicle, although if they took the logical route from Portsmouth to and from where the car was being sold, they'd not pass far from the Ramparts, anyway. All roads seem to lead in and out of the old part of Kinechester."

"It needs a bypass," Ashok said. "I mean, it's got the motorway so the main traffic from London down to the coast doesn't come through, but local journeys are a nightmare. Or they were when we still had proper rush hours."

"There's another good thing about lockdown." Robin did a final review of the incident board. Naomi had pinned up a photo of the smudge of blood they'd found at the scene that wasn't close to the body, the single bit which had evaded cleaning. The forensics on it were meagre, but supported the mark having been made by someone wearing socks, who'd dabbed part of their foot down and just as quickly raised it again. The crime scene investigators had found a few fibres in it that matched fibres taken from other parts of the carpet. However they couldn't say whether those other traces had been there before the attack happened.

Robin would have had his money on the person concerned removing the sock, and then wiping their foot, as there was no evidence of a blood trail out of the door. The makeup of the fibres themselves was a pretty standard mix of polyester and cotton, while the colour—blue—didn't give much help, either. Where was an exotic bamboo blend in shocking pink when you needed it?

They had other samples taken from the scene, which would be useful for comparison purposes once they'd narrowed the field enough to conduct such tests, but none of them were peculiar enough to give the small but vital clue that television programmes were so fond of. And any of the fibres sampled could have been there from before the time of the murder. Fingerprint evidence was scanty, apart from that of the victim herself. The back door handle had been wiped, as had several other surfaces, suggesting that the killer had made sure they covered their tracks.

"Off home, then," Robin told the team. "If you believe in praying, send one up that tomorrow will bring us access to her computer files and contact from Jeremy Sexton. Or a confession from Deborah Cavendish, although that might be a prayer too far."

Chapter Eight

By the time Kelvin's scan of the letter arrived, Robin had already texted to say he was leaving the office, so it didn't seem worth forwarding it to him. Instead, Adam printed off a copy to peruse while he cooked dinner. A couple of pages of handwritten—if a touch untidy—well-crafted text. Ellen would surely never have had to be picked up on her use of the English language, unlike her godson. As the latter had said, it mainly concerned her not wanting anyone to mope at her passing, stating that she'd had a good life and a useful one. She also suggested that the best way for Kelvin to pay tribute to her was making certain he could say the same when he came to the same point.

"Nothing suspicious in that, is there?"

Campbell glanced up from where he was besotted with a dog chew, evidently decided the conversation wasn't important, and returned to the task in hand.

"Please yourself." Adam checked the casserole in the oven, then looked at the second page.

I've always tried my best, despite the fact that sometimes it's led to me biting off more than I can chew. It's a terrible cliché that 2020 has been "interesting" but it really has in my case. You know me and my zeal for getting questions answered, and they don't turn your brain off when you retire, so if something comes up . . . well, it's straight back on the horse.

That backed up what Robin had said about Ellen having been recently involved with a research project.

I know what you're like, Kelvin, so you'll be wondering what I've been up to. If you don't know by now, it means I've popped my clogs before

I had the chance to finish it all, so you'll possibly never know. Suffice to say, play Psalm twenty-three at my funeral and think of me.

That must be the bit Kelvin was puzzling over.

Adam knew the hymn version off by heart but wasn't sure how much it varied from the original. He went to find his grandparents' old King James Bible. The page itself seemed well thumbed, suggesting it was a favourite psalm. Still, the text itself didn't give many clues. A shepherd, still waters, green pastures, anointing with oil, an overflowing cup—all the familiar words and none of them giving him a hint to what Ellen had been working on. Maybe Kelvin had been right and this was what it appeared to be: the choice of hymn to send her off with. Or was the chilling line about walking through the valley of the shadow of death a final cryptic clue, reflecting that Ellen knew herself to be in danger?

Half an hour later, when Robin came through the door with a weary, "Hi! It's me, not a burglar," Campbell bounded off to greet him. The pair came through the kitchen door together, which was a tight squeeze, then Robin gave Adam a hug, which was tighter still.

"Hard day?"

"Not so much hard as frustrating. Lots of little leads. Lack of big chunks of evidence. What's that?" Robin nodded towards the pages.

"It's a present for you. From Kelvin." Adam explained about the phone call, his advice to the young man, the delays in both the post and the arrival of the scan. "I hope you didn't mind me reading it. I wasn't being nosy."

"I believe you." Robin scanned the first page. "Seems innocent enough."

"Yeah, that's one of the reasons I wanted to have a butcher's. I had to decide if I had Kelvin's back or not. On the whole, I can understand why he didn't come straight to you because it's mostly about them not grieving for her although that second page is a bit more interesting."

"That's what I'm thinking." Robin pointed to the line about Psalm twenty-three.

"I've got Gran's old Bible out, if you want to check the words."

"Thanks. Although I know it's got the valley of death bit."

"Valley of the *shadow* of death. You're thinking of 'The Charge of the Light Brigade.'"

"So I am." Robin slowly read the psalm. "She *could* be leaving a clue to her being in danger, although that doesn't seem likely. She knew this letter would only go out after her death, so the recipient would already be aware if she'd met it by foul play."

Adam took the point, but he didn't want to let the potential clue go that easily. "Do you think the timing's important? She wrote this in November, so could something significant have happened to prompt her, something that focussed her mind? I'm not necessarily saying a direct threat to her life—'the valley of the shadow of death' might have been a reference to the soaring Covid rate in Kinechester. I know one of the older support staff at school was so worried about catching it she and her husband drafted their wills. After years of putting the task off."

Robin wrinkled his nose. "Depends if she'd written a similar letter before and this was simply the 2020 version. I'll get Naomi to ask the solicitor. It does strike me as having a significance, though. I'd have a tenner on her leaving a clue in that psalm. What are the modern versions of this like? Are the words very different?"

"Probably. I'll do some digging while you get changed."

"Deal." Robin gave him a peck on the cheek, then headed off to their bedroom while Adam searched for a site where he could compare the different translations of the verses. He was still working through a bewildering array when Robin returned. "There are dozens of versions. Literally. All say basically the same thing, but the individual words are different. Grass instead of pastures. 'Treat me as an honoured guest' instead of anointing heads with oil. If I were you, I'd start with whichever translation Ellen had at her house. You'll have already thought of that, of course."

"Only thirty seconds ago. I'll head there with Ben first thing tomorrow. He's been stuck in front of a screen too much, so a bit of fresh air and an old-fashioned bookshelf will make a change. Can I have a butcher's?" Robin took the iPad, flicking through a variety of translations while Adam carried on cooking dinner. "Some of these are awful. No poetry. No soul."

"You're preaching to the converted on that one. I like the King James or the New English. We used to use newer translations at Lindenshaw, so the children understood the meaning of the Bible verses, but they were really difficult to read aloud. No cadence to the language. This is nearly ready, by the way."

"Magic. I only had service station sandwiches for lunch, and I'm Hank Marvin."

After dinner, they slumped in front of the telly, with Campbell stationed near Robin, perhaps in an effort to ensure he didn't go out again. There was golf from America, which Adam only watched with one eye while he surreptitiously googled some of the words from Psalm twenty-three. He had a couple of ideas developing but didn't want to mention them yet, in case they turned out to be total crap.

"What are you up to?" Robin asked, after quarter of an hour.

"You're too eagle-eyed. I thought I was being subtle." Adam lifted the iPad. "I'm looking up some of the words from the psalm, seeing what other meanings they have. I'm not getting anywhere much. *Still Waters* is the name of a film and a Bee Gees album and a holiday home in Wroxham and that's just for starters."

"Any hotels called that? We're thinking she went to one the years she didn't spend Christmas with the Vinces."

"I think so, although it was a budget type. Hold on." Adam checked again. "Yeah. I'm making an assumption here, but it doesn't seem to be the kind of place she'd have frequented. There were some Green Pastures hotels and similar, but they all seemed to be abroad. You can also find a charity with that name and a play and a kind of omelette amongst other things. Frankly, when you get into charities, there are several with names deriving from this psalm, including Rod and Staff, I Shall Not Want and Still Waters, which seems to win the prize for the most versatile name."

"Any hotels local to Kinechester?"

"I don't think so. Your team might have better luck. I had another idea as well. It may sound silly."

"We may reach the stage where I'll clutch at any straw, silly or not. Go on."

"Over Christmas, I read a novella where they end up hunting out messages hidden within the words of a hymn. It was quite good, to be honest, although don't ask me to explain the plot. Anyway, Ellen was a bright spark. Could she have hidden something in the text?"

"Do people do that in real life?"

"I'm ninety-nine percent sure Wilfred Owen did. Used some secret code that let his mum know where he was located during the war."

"Let's have a gander at it, then."

They scoured the letter, trying all the obvious things like the first word of each line of the last letter of each sentence. After fifteen minutes, two sheets of scribbling and—admittedly—quite a lot of fun, they'd reached the conclusion that if there *was* a secret message, it had eluded their gaze as effectively as Wilfred Owens' had eluded the censor's.

Adam rubbed his head. "That's enough for tonight. My eyes are starting to go in and out."

"Thanks for helping." Robin flashed him a tired but grateful smile. "It was worth a try, even if it feels like nothing in this case will be handed to us on a plate. Apart from a set of fingerprints, and they were on a scrap of paper. You'll appreciate the story of Derek and Deborah."

"Who are this pair? They sound like they've stepped straight out of a sitcom."

"I'd say they'd be at home in a soap opera. The bloke who did the dating-related fraud and his wife, the ones we went to see at Portsmouth. Not the type I'd want to meet down a dark alley." Robin gave an account of the interview, concluding with, "I don't think he did the paper thing by accident. Ashok and I are convinced he wanted us to have her dabs, possibly because she'd got a record for assault. She punched her first husband's mistress."

"There'll be hell to pay when she realises what he's done. You reckon they visited Ellen when they went to Kinechester about the car?"

"Could be. They definitely gave the impression they'd been up to something else. The car vendor felt the same. Exactly what that was . . ." Robin spread his hands.

"What was their hair like?"

"Eh?"

"Derek and Doris or whatever they're called. Did they have lockdown hair? I was wondering if they were illegally getting a cut or a colour. Or whatever else that's not allowed during lockdown and which they're not going to admit to."

Robin narrowed his eyes in thought. "He doesn't have much hair to start with, so a run over with the clippers would work for him. Sort of job anyone could do, me included. *Campbell* included."

On cue, the dog gave Robin such a dirty look they both ended up helpless with laughter.

"I've long suspected he's starting to understand everything we say," Adam said, when he got his breath back. "What about *her* hair. Could 'himself' have styled that?"

"No. Nor me. It seemed dyed, but there are plenty of home-colouring kits available. However, the idea has a lot going for it. Unfortunately." Robin ran his hand over his face. "We could do with a bit of a breakthrough."

"Maybe Trevor or Don will be off shift tomorrow and they'll recognise one of the Cavendishes from their picture."

"And maybe a pig will fly through the window bearing the killer's name on a gilt-edged card. Sorry—" Robin waved his hand "—didn't mean to be snarky. You've done well spotting the potential in this letter. You did well with your idea about the blinds too."

"Apology accepted. Don't get downhearted—you've only had the case a few days and there are none of the usual kinds of suspects to focus on." Somebody was clearly in need of a cuddle. Although before Adam could get there, Campbell had got up and was rubbing his head against Robin's leg. That could tide him over until bedtime, because he was probably in need of something else, as well, something only Adam could provide.

"Maybe we have. There's the ex-boyfriend who's back in her life, for a start. He could be the old dog up to their old tricks. Not *you*." Robin chuckled, as Campbell put on his *Are you talking about me?* expression. "We know all your tricks."

"Don't say that. He'll spend the next week trying to invent some new ones."

"Frankly, if that's the worst that happens in the next few days, I'll be happy."

Please God, that wasn't tempting fate.

Early Monday morning, Ben—carrying the keys to number thirty-nine—met Robin at the property.

"So we're looking for a Bible," he said, with no hint of disbelief.

"Yep. Or anything else that might have a link to this. Read it while I open the door." Robin passed across the copy of the letter that Adam had printed off. "Once inside, we'll split the house—I'll start at the top, you at the bottom, and we'll meet in the middle. Anything we find goes into an evidence bag to inspect back at the station. We can do the filing cabinets together."

"This reads like something out of Poirot, on the telly. The letter from beyond the grave. I get what you mean about the psalm, though. Strikes me as more than a reference to her funeral." Ben halted halfway through into the hall.

"Yep? Out with it."

"I was wondering if this could be another clue to her passwords. Maybe she used *Psalm23*. Or *shepherd23* or whatever. I'm trying to remember the words from when they used it for the *Vicar of Dibley*."

Robin liked that idea. "Ring the tech team now. It won't save us a search, because I'm not leaving any stones unturned, but it may save *them* some work."

"I'll do that from here, sir. No idea what the 4G is like in the basement."

"It's not great anywhere around here. They probably don't want masts spoiling the area." Robin headed up the two flights of stairs, starting with the room containing the exercise bike and the pinboard, although that yielded no clues. He was about to enter the room next to it, when Ben called up, "Bingo!"

"What have you got?" Robin yelled down the stairwell.

"A King James Bible on one of the bookshelves in the dining room. I'll put it in a bag."

"Good. For all we know, the page that has Psalm twenty-three also has a note slipped between the leaves." That was another possibility that had come to him as he'd driven here earlier.

By the time they'd covered everything bar the filing cabinet, their haul was no larger. No other Bibles, religious material or anything that could vaguely refer to any of the Psalms. Not even a painting of a sheep. The files drew a blank too, although Robin was struck by a notable absence. Each hanging divisor was neatly labelled and the material within contained in a cardboard wallet, at least one of which appeared to be missing.

"She's got all the details of her Barclays banking here but nothing for her other card. Not so much as a hint of a note of the sort code and account number." The tab on the file only said, *Banking*, so that provided no clue.

"Let's have a butcher's, sir." Ben inspected the file, then poked about in the cabinet, pushing aside the other items to get a sight of the drawer's base. "My dad has a cabinet like this one, and he's always losing things beneath the files. You'd have thought he'd have learned by now. Ah." Ben triumphantly fished out a thin scrap of paper. "It's an old receipt. Been there years, I'd guess, going on the date."

Robin peered at it. "Probably before we all turned to internet banking as the default. Would you know off the top of your head if those last four card numbers match the one used to pay for the mirror?"

"I think they might. Which presumably means there *was* another file here and it's gone. Taken by the person who took the card?"

"Quite possibly. There are some security details listed in the Barclays wallet, so maybe the other contained similar. Details the killer might have needed so they could use the card. Best to put all of this in another bag—that metal rim seems to be a good place to find prints."

While Ben was dealing with the evidence, Robin had a double-check through the rest of the files. Not that he felt that Pru would have missed anything, but now they had a slightly different emphasis on what to search for.

"Here's a woman who may have carefully compartmentalised her life," Robin observed. "Two different bank accounts for different things. So could there be another set of files that we've missed? Ones that aren't on her laptop?"

"There might have been and the killer took them. No sign of another filing cabinet, though—they tend to leave quite a mark on the carpet where they've been. Would she have left loose files about?"

"If she was working on them at the time she was killed, she might have had them to hand. Although where would she store them otherwise?" Robin rubbed his chin. "Are we being over the top? Just because she had tight security on her tech and used to work for the government doesn't mean she had secret storage places for other stuff. I don't want to go tearing this place apart to search for something that isn't there."

They might be forced to that, though, unless they identified what the hell Ellen had been doing that got her killed.

Maybe the thoughts and prayers directed at getting a breakthrough had worked. When Robin reached the station, he found the other team members in a state of excitement—including Ben, who'd clearly had some news en route.

"Let me get my coat off and we can swop notes."

"I'll get you both a coffee, sir," Pru suggested. "You look half-frozen."

"You're a life saver."

Once he'd got his hand warming round the mug, Robin suggested they go in alphabetical order, for want of another way to decide whose news took priority.

Ashok had taken over the cash-card follow up. It was a Nationwide account, the statements of which he'd got from the bank and had been working through. This had proved to be the account she'd used for personal payments, including online orders for food, toiletries, and clothing.

Robin nodded. "Which makes it odder still that there was nothing about that in the filing cabinet. We suspect the information may have been taken. Perhaps because it contained security details that would help the killer use her card."

"Sorry we didn't spot that," Ashok said. "Although we didn't know that was what we were hunting for." He paused, shoulders hunching. Perhaps he was used to superior officers who hauled their constables over the coals for the least reason.

"These things happen. Pru didn't make the connection, either, and she's usually quicker than I am to spot something amiss. You were talking about bank statements."

Ashok, visibly relieved at not getting a telling off, continued. "A few items jumped out. The payment to Sparkling Bins was there, as was the order for the mirror. They were the last one-off payments that went through, although there was a standing order a couple of days later. Crisis, the charity. She donated every quarter. She also made various payments to Your Fine Foods. They're a local hospitality delivery company that have increased household supplies now restaurants keep opening and shutting."

Ben snorted. "Typical. I only had a few firms left to try from my list and that would have been one of them. I should have started with the end of the alphabet and worked upwards."

"Sods law says in that case they'd have been called *Absolutely Fine Foods*." Robin grinned. "Have you spoken to them?"

"Yes. Her last order was booked and paid for on the twenty-seventh December and delivered on January the second. Since last June, she'd been having them call every two or three weeks. They're going to check with the driver that it was Ellen herself who took the order in. If it was the usual bloke, he'd remember."

"Good. And the other thing that jumped out?"

"That she always went to the same hotel, the Clifton outside Wimborne, for Christmas every other year. Well, that's an assumption going on the dates of the 2018 payment and the deposit she paid them for 2020 that was then refunded. I'm going to ring them and see if they had any other regular guests at the same time, but if they're furloughed, it might take a while."

"I wonder why she didn't have that banking app on her phone?" Ben asked.

"Could be an issue of capacity," Naomi proposed. "Too many apps backing up means you exceed your iCloud storage."

Robin shrugged. Second-guessing rarely got you anywhere. "Ben. You next. Did *Psalm23* work the oracle?"

"No. The tech team are trying some other variations now. Good news is I *have* made contact with Jeremy Sexton, via that Hotmail address. He's not local, but he's available to speak to on Zoom anytime we want. He says he'd like to see our faces." Ben raised an eyebrow. "I suggested twelve noon today."

"Right, anything else?" Robin glanced round the team.

"About the smear," Pru said. "I got hold of Ellen's doctor and she definitely didn't have a test booked, nor was she due to have any more. Too old, as Naomi suggested. Not sure what else that note could mean. Smear campaign?"

"Name of a racehorse and when it was running? Or where it finished last time out? Don't raise a sweat over it—the thing may never make sense. Which forms a corny link into Kelvin's letter." Robin fetched his briefcase, then produced the—by now slightly dog-eared—sheets of paper. "Have a butcher's. You might spot something we've missed. Kelvin's going to give Adam the originals so we'll have them tomorrow."

Ashok, eyes narrowed as he studied the text, said, "Can I ask a stupid question? Is there any chance this could hide a secret message? You know, encoded within it."

"That's not a stupid question at all, unless I'm as daft as you. We checked the first letters and words of each line and they produce gobbledegook. If you're happy to work further at that when you've not got anything else on your plate, then feel free. Can't help feeling the text would read more disjointedly if it did hide a coded message."

And would that actually feel bizarre in this most bizarre of times?

"Hidden messages aren't as silly as what we've got to report," Pru said. "Turnips. Rather, a turnip." She and Naomi both half stifled a giggle.

"I'm dreading further details." Robin folded his arms. "Go on."

"Sparkling Bins. I rang them when their office opened at seven o'clock this morning, then we got there at eight o'clock. Managed to catch the person who'd done the job. Billy Brown. 'Call me Billy the Bins.'" Pru giggled again. "It was all booked online on the morning of the twelfth, and Billy was asked to pick the bins up from number thirty-nine on the fifteenth, which was a Friday. The note on the order specified that the owner would be out that day but they'd leave the back gate open."

"He didn't think that was odd?"

"Nope," Naomi said. "He's got a couple of regular customers in Cromwell Road, so he knows how fussy they can be there about bins left out in the alley when they shouldn't be, and anyway, Ellen was a regular if not frequent customer for his bin cleaning. About once a year. She'd used another company in the past but given them the chop. Shoddy workmanship. This time her instructions to Sparkling Bins were slightly different, though."

"Go on," Robin encouraged her.

"He wasn't asked to clean them. He was told to get rid of the things completely. He said it isn't something they do very often because people then have to pay the council for a new bin, but occasionally he gets folk who want to replace their existing one for whatever reason. Rather than fly tipping it, they want to have it disposed of properly, which is why he offers the service."

That was in line with what Robin had seen on their website: a lot of stuff about environmental responsibility and the company having a proper waste-control licence.

"I'd always assumed that the council took the old bins, but they don't," Pru continued. "Billy showed us all the paperwork. Exactly like the order for the mirror, this was all set up in Ellen's name and, as we've heard, using her cash card. They gave her landline as contact but Billy didn't need to use it. Interestingly, the note on the order also said she was getting new bins because she'd had a dead hedgehog in her garden—she thought an owl or a fox had killed it—and the mess was awful. She'd wrapped the thing in plastic and put it in the bin, but although it had been emptied, every time she'd used the thing, she felt she could still smell it. She'd decided to go for two totally new ones."

"That sounds like a short story rather than a note in a comments box. Isn't that unusual?" Robin asked.

"According to Billy, not necessarily. Especially if people ring in," Naomi explained. "He reckons he has a sympathetic voice because he often gets whole stories from people justifying why their bins need cleaning. As though normal everyday dirt isn't dramatic enough. He confessed it's one of the reasons he likes to do the clean to the best of his ability and then go, especially if the client is a pensioner. He's been to a few jobs where he's left with the impression he was only called in because the customer was lonely and wanted somebody to talk to. Sad, isn't it?"

Robin nodded. Particularly sad in the present circumstances. "Okay, but why get rid of the recycling bin as well as the ordinary rubbish one? I mean, I know from our point of view, because we're surmising that the killer may have used one or other bin to transport stuff from the site, but what excuse did they give Billy the Bins?"

"They didn't. He'd been paid to take both, so he did. His not to reason why and all that." Naomi shrugged. "He opened the lids to make sure they were completely empty and said he'd seen bins in a lot worse condition but he'd also seen them in a lot better. I asked Billy if he could remember if there was any trace of blood in either bin, although I think he assumed I meant the hedgehog, bless him. So, the answer was negative. For blood anyway." Naomi caught Pru's eye and tittered. "There was a turnip in the recycling bin."

"A what?" Robin was sure he must have misheard.

"A turnip. Billy said he's been bingeing on box sets of *Blackadder*, so he thought it was hilarious. We may have shared a few jokes. Turnip for the books and all that."

"I don't want to hear them." Was this another answer to prayer and evidence of the Almighty's sense of humour? "What did he think it was doing in there?"

"He didn't know. He says he's seen too many strange things in his job so this was water off a duck's back." Pru grinned. "Or should I say 'turnips off a duck's back'? If that gate was open, anyone could have lobbed it in there."

"They could, but *really*? If you were a troublemaker, wouldn't you stick something nastier in there? Like an actual dead hedgehog?" Robin suggested. "Or worse."

"Nothing would surprise me at present, sir." Pru's comment seemed to encapsulate the whole case.

Still, the mystery of what had happened to the bins was a mystery no longer, and the explanation had turned out to be both prosaic and in keeping with what they'd surmised.

Pru must have been thinking the same. "It's possible that Ellen herself arranged for those bins to be taken away, of course. If the order was the only thing she did on the Tuesday, before being killed."

"That's possible," Ben conceded, "although it would have meant her doing almost nothing else on her phone between the last email reply, which was about five o'clock in the afternoon, and that next day. It doesn't feel likely."

"So, are we getting a possible picture of that Monday evening? Ellen's going about her business, has a visitor— Hold on." Robin rubbed his head. "Ben, you and I saw the food in the fridge, but I don't remember seeing any evidence of a meal being prepared or having been eaten. Her stomach wasn't full, was it?"

"No. May mean she usually ate later so hadn't started cooking. Not everyone's like my mum and insists people eat at six o'clock." Ben glanced at the incident board, focussing on the victim, the details of whose life kept eluding them. "You know, she might have started preparing her dinner when the killer arrived. They get into an argument, Ellen's killed with her own knife, then the killer stuffs everything—their blood-stained clothes, the half-cooked meal, the weapon—into the newly emptied bins and takes it all away."

"Okay, but it still doesn't make sense," Naomi said. "Why take both bins? It's difficult enough manoeuvring one of those things let alone the pair. And if the killer only took one, how did the other bin end up empty as well? Surely Billy would have found a week's worth of rubbish in it if it got left behind."

"The general rubbish was emptied on the eleventh, the recycling the week before. Ellen lived on her own, so she might not have generated much of either," Ben pointed out. "Easy enough for the killer to slip back once they'd organised for the bins to be disposed of, empty any bits of recycling, and take it away."

"And put it where?" Ashok asked. "That's what keeps bugging me. If you use a bin to take the stuff away, you're hardly likely to be taking it a long distance. And surely you wouldn't bung it straight in your car, leaving her blood all over your boot."

"I've been contacting local skip-hire companies, sir," Naomi said. "They don't tend to get much business on the Ramparts—you can't imagine the complaints about something as small and neat as a Hippo bag being left on the road—but I've had some luck. Got an email this morning from Don't Tip it, Skip it."

Robin rolled his eyes. "Where do these companies get their names? If I didn't know better, I'd think you were winding me up."

"Absolute truth, sir. I think it's a Kinechester thing. Can't call themselves *A1 Skips* or whatever. Anyway, they did have a skip out for hire, delivered the ninth of January and booked for collection on the sixteenth of January. Only it was so full, the minister called from the church and asked the company to collect it early. That would have been on Thursday the fourteenth. And guess where it was? In that Methodist church car park, because they were taking advantage of lockdown to have a total clear out." Naomi wagged a finger at her colleagues, whose ears had pricked up at this news. "Don't get excited. The email said if we wanted evidence, we'd probably be unlucky, as the skip contents would have gone to landfill the day it was picked up."

"Good work, though, Naomi. Can I get you to follow up with the church and with the people on—" Robin checked the map "—Ireton Avenue to see if they saw or heard anyone acting suspiciously near there on the eleventh or twelfth?"

"Could the killer have known about the skip?" Pru asked. "And, come to that, did they know that Monday was bin-collection day so a) the thing would be empty and b) you wouldn't look out of place moving one?"

"Good planning or good luck?" That was a subject for long debate. Had the murderers of the past who'd gone uncaught been masterminds, too clever to be tracked down, or had they merely benefitted from a run of good fortune? "I'd bear local knowledge in mind but don't get too hung up on it. They may have fortuitously spotted the skip when they were driving round trying to find somewhere to park."

Ben raised his hand. "Would this argue against the Cavendishes? Not only the local knowledge argument but all the toing and froing."

Ashok shrugged. "Not necessarily, now we're aware of that skip. I know, I know—I've changed my tune, but I can see how having two people working together would make it possible to do everything in such a small space of time. One of them gets rid of the evidence, say bundling it into a bin bag, taking it round the corner, and slapping it in the bottom of the almost-full skip they clocked earlier. The other one has a hunt through the house, goes in the filing cabinet and takes anything that's relevant, including her bank details. They then nick the cash card to match those details, before having the genius idea of taking the remotes for the blinds as well."

Robin, nodding, stuck out his bottom lip. "Whoever did the murder, whether it was planned or unplanned, I suspect you're right about what happened next in the house and the fact it was all done relatively quickly. Then the killer could go home and decide what to do next, because everything else could be organised from the comfort of their own laptop."

"But it *couldn't*, sir," Pru pointed out. "Ben's right. One of them would have had to travel back here at least once to open the blinds after Sonia Parsons saw them closed."

Of course. "I stand corrected. Still, travelling from Portsmouth to Kinechester isn't too long a journey. Not when you have the incentive of blurring the date of death, and they'd have needed to do that, given we can prove they were in the vicinity on the eleventh."

Pru nodded. "Okay, I'll buy that, but why the mirror delivery? Why decide the body has to be found when you've got away with Ellen lying undiscovered for so long?"

"Stress?" Ashok suggested. "Every day the Cavendishes—or if not them, whoever killed her—would be thinking, 'Will it happen today?' I'd imagine them bricking themselves every time they nipped over to Kinechester to arse about with the blinds, just in case they found us already giving the scene the once-over. Perhaps they got to the point it was better to have her found and then deal with the aftermath."

That seemed a reasonable conclusion. "You could be right. The horrible known versus the potentially worse unknown. Okay, everyone, anything else to add?"

"One other thing, sir," Naomi said. "Local knowledge and local access. The killer doesn't have to live within close driving distance of Cromwell Road. They could have an accomplice in the area. A local, whose face wouldn't seem out of place—excuse the rhyme—if they were taking a walk down that back path. They could have gone past every day, keeping an eye on the house."

"You're quite right." Robin pointed at the board. "There are two distinct elements to this. The murder and the covering up afterwards. If we're searching for the old threesome of means, motive, and opportunity, one person doesn't have to have all of them for both parts."

Which sounded quite profound but got them no closer to a solution.

Chapter Nine

T he word *dapper* could have been invented for Jeremy Sexton. Not for him the state of dishevelment that often typified someone on a Zoom call. His classically handsome features—still handsome despite him being in his late sixties, at a guess—made it plain to Robin why Ellen would have fallen for him. He had a real touch of the James Bond, although his work hadn't been as hands-on as the famous fictional spy's. Aaron, who'd evidently realised he'd rubbed Robin up the wrong way and needed to make amends, had come up trumps, discovering that Sexton's security clearance was at an eye-wateringly high level despite his work being office-based. Aaron's contact had said they should make the most of the bloke's skills, assuming he wasn't the No. 1 suspect.

"Thanks for agreeing to see me rather than use the phone," Sexton said, once introductions had been made and warrant cards held up to the camera. "You can't be too sure who you're dealing with these days."

"Quite." Time to get down to business. "How did you first meet Ellen Wilkins?"

"We were colleagues in the same government department. That must be nigh on forty years ago. We always got on well, then that camaraderie became something else." Jeremy spread his hands. "She was a very lovely woman. Not traditionally beautiful, maybe, and that's not being sexist, because that's how she described herself. She knew she was striking, though. I say there's an aspect to intellect that's highly attractive."

"You had an affair," Ben said.

"Yes. Ellen wanted to, um, regularise things. Which is when I had to confess that my wife would never have granted me a divorce. Ellen was furious, for which I can't blame her. I asked to move departments, and I thought that would be the end of it. Even when my wife died several years later, I didn't want to hurt Ellen by getting back in contact, flaunting my availability." The account came across as genuine.

"But you did get back in contact." Robin made it a statement, not a question.

"Yes. Quite by accident. I've no children and no close family, so I've tended to go away at Christmas. On a cruise or the like. Some hotels specialise in events for singletons like me, and I found one in 2018 that was running a bridge-based seasonal break. Right up my street. Imagine my surprise when Ellen turned up."

"What was the name of the hotel?" Ben asked.

"The Clifton. Near Clapgate, which is an unfortunate name for a place. It's over Wimborne way. It specialises in producing Christmases for people on their own, and I have to say I was impressed. The right mixture of encouraging one to join in and leaving one to one's own devices, which is why it appealed to Ellen. It was the third time she'd gone there. She was fond of good food, was Ellen—a keen cook, herself—and the Clifton measured up to her expectations on the cuisine side."

So far that checked out with what they knew. Robin took a deep breath. "Can I pick up on one thing? I realise it might be painful but it is relevant. You said you have no children and, as far as we know, Ellen didn't, either. But she seems to have been very fond of other folk's kiddies, especially her godson. Is it the case that she regarded those other children almost as surrogate offspring?"

"Possibly. To clarify, I can't sire children, and my wife and I didn't want to adopt. As for Ellen, I'm not sure why she didn't go down the parent route. May have been a case of no opportunity. Though I do have a hypothesis about her and youngsters, based on what she told me about her early life." Jeremy ran his fingers along the table, perhaps buying time to choose his words. "She came from a well-to-do family, only child, wanted for nothing—in theory. But it isn't only poor children who get neglected. She was fobbed off with a string of au pairs, before and after school and often during the holidays, which was one of the reasons she had a smattering of lots of different languages."

Robin wouldn't wish that on anyone. "That sense of emotional inattention stayed with her?"

"Absolutely. She got involved with investigating international child abuse rings at work but had to be taken off it as she struggled to keep a sense of perspective. She hated the thought that any other child would suffer, to the extent of getting prickly if anyone bawled their kids out."

"Does that happen much in Cromwell Road?" Ben asked.

"As much as anywhere, I guess. She told me she'd seen the woman next door bawling her girls out, although Ellen didn't do anything other than give her a dirty look. I can imagine that glare, as it was pretty standard for any behaviour she didn't like."

"Thank you." It all sounded credible. "To get back to the Christmas just gone. What were her plans?"

"*Our* plans were to go there again, although we'd had to book separately. No couples, you see. As it turned out, there were no Christmas hotel breaks whatsoever."

Robin had picked up the key word. "Were you and Ellen a *couple*?"

"You might say so. Not the red-hot passion of youth but the glowing embers of maturity. It didn't happen in Clapgate, though. That sounds like an episode of *Dad's Army*: 'It Didn't Happen in Clapgate.'" Jeremy chuckled. "Sorry. That's one of the things Ellen and I shared, our sense of humour. We took a holiday together in August of 2019. Glorious Devon. That's where we ignited the old flame, if briefly. By the time it got to last spring though, we decided we were better off as friends rather than lovers."

"Did you meet up on Christmas Day 2020?" Ben beat Robin to the question.

"Yes. She came to mine for a few days—that was allowed, as we were in a social bubble at the time."

"If I can digress a moment," Ben said, "we know she had a burglar alarm, but did she do anything else in terms of safety?"

"Oh, yes. She had various devices rigged up to give the impression she was still at home. Lights going on and off, that sort of idea. Why? Ah, you're thinking it might be relevant to her not being found because people thought the house was occupied?"

"It might." Best to stay noncommittal. "Christmas 2020? How long did she stay?"

"Not long. She went home early on Boxing Day—I'm afraid we'd had a bit of a row."

"What was it about?" Robin tried to dampen his enthusiasm. Yes, this was the type of close-to-home suspect that he usually homed in on, but would a guilty man have offered the tale of an argument so readily?

"Nothing. Everything. You know how these things accelerate." Jeremy adjusted his tie. "It started with a difference of opinion on what we'd been working on. I'll explain about that in a minute. Suffice to say, suddenly we found ourselves in the middle of a blazing row, slinging at each other every bit of mud—past or present—we could lay our hands on. She stormed off, but I rang her the next day and we established a truce."

The account had the ring of truth. Robin himself had experienced a similar quarrel with one of his previous boyfriends. The helpless tumbling into the abyss of shouting and hurt, and then the shock of *How the hell did we end up here?*

"When was the last time you spoke to Ellen?" Robin asked.

"Over the phone? I knew you'd ask, so I checked back. I tried her mobile on the ninth of January but couldn't connect, so I gave the landline a go. Turned out her local 4G signal was arsing about."

"How was she? Worried about anything?"

"Not that she said." Jeremy paused, giving the impression—for the first time—that he was on a sticky wicket. "Obviously I was concerned when she stopped returning my messages, and then they weren't being delivered. At first I thought it was the 4G playing up again. I tried ringing the landline but no reply from that, either. I did wonder if she'd come down with Covid. That part of Kinechester was rife with it either side of Christmas. Commuters from London bringing it with them, no doubt."

Robin leaned forward, as he might were they in an actual interview room. "You weren't concerned enough to ring us? Or visit her yourself?"

"I live in Woodhall Spa, Mr. Bright. Kinechester's hardly round the corner."

Robin waited for the witness to continue. Not many people could put up with too long a silence before having to break it. Jeremy clearly fell into the unsettled category.

"The thing is, she hated a fuss being made, and we'd had another little tiff on the phone about what we were working on, so I was treading on eggshells. When she didn't reply, I concluded she'd got the hump on with me, and I wanted to leave her a couple of weeks to cool down. A similar thing happened last October. You just had to give her time and space."

That might be factual, but it didn't sound like the whole truth. Especially given that Jeremy had recently changed his phone.

Robin would come back to that later. "What *were* you working on?"

"Misinformation. I do consultancy work for various organisations—some of which is a bit hush-hush, so I'd rather not provide details over Zoom—but suffice to say it's been a busy few years. Not only tracking down all the nonsense about Covid-19 and vaccines. It's been one field day after another since Trump got elected. The dreaded QAnon and its nasty little tentacles." The renewed confidence in his voice indicated Jeremy was on a flatter pitch when discussing work. "Ellen was helping me—she could never resist the thrill of an intellectual chase, even though she couldn't spend as much time at a screen as she once could because it made her a bit dizzy. BVVP or something?"

"I think that's BPPV. What specifically was she working on with you?" Ben asked.

"People spreading health misinformation within ethnic minority communities, here and abroad. It's an absolute minefield and not simply about the pandemic. You have no idea how much culture affects things we take for granted, like accessing health services. Ellen felt particularly strongly about how some women over here won't visit the doctor about cancer because the disease would signify they have bad karma." Jeremy slowly shook his head. "We've been tracking down sources, trying to counter them, although that part hasn't always been our job. Trouble is, it's like the hydra. Cut off one head and others spring up."

That all sounded plausible to Robin. "And what was your work-related row about?"

"Keeping her on task. She's— She was a bloody good researcher, with a real nose for following up the smallest of clues. Clues I would have scrolled straight past and which led to an unexpected avenue of investigation, for example. But the internet can be a rabbit hole, can't it?"

Robin and Ben both nodded in sympathy. Their own experiences had reinforced that fact.

"So I'd—subtly, I thought—reminded her that as she'd promised to do something, she needed to stick to the task in hand."

"Was this a business arrangement? Were you paying Ellen for her research?"

"No. She didn't need or want money. I wasn't comfortable with that, so we agreed I'd pay a large donation to her favourite charity, one for children. I'll still do that, in her memory. She said it would give her an extra incentive to do a good job. Anyway, I said there was no problem with her going off on a lead, even if it was ultimately proven a dead end, so long as said lead was related to the primary brief. I suggested that she pursue her other quarries in her own time. At which point Vesuvius erupted." Jeremy snorted. "I was reminded that she didn't always have the capacity to spend time in front of a screen when her dizziness was bad. That her own investigations might prove every bit as valuable in the long run as anything she was doing for me. That if she couldn't be allowed a bit of leeway, then I could stick my work somewhere. I won't give the anatomical details."

Robin grinned. "You didn't take her up on the offer?"

"I wouldn't be able to sit comfortably here if I had." Jeremy laughed. "And no, I didn't end our working relationship. As I said, she was too good at her job to lose her. I've been rather assuming she'd decided to lose me."

"What were these side investigations?" Ben asked.

"I'm not entirely sure. Not health-related. Fraud, I think, which was another red rag to her bull."

Robin and Ben exchanged a glance. *Fraud.* Did that point to Cavendish being up to his old tricks? In which case, was the woman with pink hair another potential victim whom Ellen was trying to track down?

Jeremy continued. "Have you got into her computer, yet? The files will all be there or in whatever online storage she used. She'd certainly shared some documents with me on Google Drive, and we used 'meets' to chat about work, so that's another line to follow. There are, however, some highly confidential things . . . and I'd rather not give the details on how we exchanged those. I'm not sure if any of this is helpful."

"Believe me it *is*, Mr. Sexton. It would be a further help if you could give us a clue on getting into her devices. We've only managed to access her phone, and that was by a bit of a fluke." Robin surreptitiously crossed his fingers beneath the desk.

"Well done, Ellen. She always felt she could baffle anyone. The phone didn't worry her too much as she wouldn't use it for confidential matters. Anyway, you're in luck, because I have some notes she sent me about how to access her files, should I need to."

The finger crossing had worked. "That was prescient of her. Was she particularly worried for her safety?"

"Only from the bloody rona. It's focussed a lot of minds. Can I make a hell of a request? Can you stop your people from trying to crack her devices? I'll get myself down to you tomorrow—maybe you could suggest a local hotel that's still open for necessary journeys, where I can put up overnight? I'd like to be there in case you turn up anything that's relevant to my work. It really is highly secret, and I wouldn't want your constables, no matter how good they are, seeing something they shouldn't."

"It's a deal, but only on the understanding that we have to keep copies of everything, whether we open the files or not. And if they seem like they're relevant to the case, one of the senior officers will need access of some kind."

Sexton wasn't happy about that, although he gave a reluctant agreement. As Robin pointed out, they couldn't yet eliminate him from their enquiries and while they could give him twenty-four hours grace—assuming the devices hadn't already been accessed—unless orders came from a higher authority, those files would be fair game.

"I'll get one of the local constables to make you a hotel reservation and will send the details via the email address Ben has."

"Fine."

"Unless you'd like to give us your new phone number?" Ben evidently had the same thought in mind as Robin. "Why did you change it, by the way?"

"Oh, bog standard reasons." Jeremy waved his hand. "Been wanting a new one for ages and took advantage of a great deal online."

"You didn't bother to change your old number across at the same time?"

A distinct touch of sheepishness. "Ah. You've caught me telling only half the truth. You see, I have a couple of ex-girlfriends who had my old number and whom I didn't want anything more to do with. It seemed an ideal opportunity to break off all ties."

"Did that include Ellen?" Ben pressed him.

"No. I'd never have wanted to lose contact with her."

"But you didn't message her from your new phone, did you? It would have come through when we got the thing charged up."

Ben's words hit home, the vagaries of Zoom not hiding Jeremy's flinch. "No, I didn't. I *had* been in contact, I promise you, on a closed messaging system we used for work. I gave her my new number and asked her to drop me a note on it. When she didn't, I assumed she was either under the weather or still cross with me."

That probably wasn't the entire tale, but they could probe further when they had the man in a room with them. The subtle facial clues, the nuances of body language, those helped to build up an impression of the veracity of a statement but were eroded when using a screen to communicate. "One last question, and you'll appreciate that we have to ask this of everybody," Robin added, pleasantly. "What were you doing on the tenth through to the twelfth of January?"

"I couldn't tell you without checking my calendar. Hold on." He must have been looking at an online diary, given the way his eyes flicked over the screen. "The tenth was a Sunday, so I have sod all appointments listed here. I probably went for a walk and watched rugby on the telly, assuming there was any on. The eleventh I was in a Zoom meeting from ten in the morning to a little after noon, then another one from four in the afternoon until half past seven—the joys of different time zones. The twelfth I was delivering training online. I can have all that verified if need be."

"We'll no doubt take you up on that later." Robin sat back in his chair. "Let's call it a day. We'll speak again tomorrow."

"Yes. Fine. See you then." Jeremy's expression suggested he wasn't exactly relishing the encounter.

"What did you make of that?" Robin asked, when the call ended.

"At a guess, he told us some truth, but not all of it. His information fills in a few of the blanks and confirms some of our ideas, although it leaves other stuff unanswered. I think I believe him about his relationship with Ellen."

"I do too. Now we've got plenty of reasons why she might not have had time for other things—a new research project and an old flame rekindled." Robin cupped his hands, then blew into them. "He was lying about the new phone, though. He didn't like discussing that."

Ben nodded. "Agreed, sir. He mentioned fraud. Could that be circling round to Derek Cavendish?"

"That did cross my mind. Either involved with his dating scams again or turning his talents to another scheme. Although we can't jump to conclusions. It could be that American woman who did the phishing, for all we know. By the way, did I see you and Aaron in conflab?"

"Yeah. He's been doing a lot of useful work on people's backgrounds. He's got a chip on his shoulder the size of Belgium about not getting into the force, of course. Blames it on his dad having got a record. Done for racist chanting at a football match." Ben rolled his eyes. "Not the greatest family background, if what he says is true."

"Apple doesn't fall far from the tree, then, does it?" Robin could imagine Aaron's attitudes being ingrained early on in life.

"That's what they say. Anyway, I can't wait to start poking through those files. Good foresight from Ellen to give Sexton the access details and a stroke of luck that he's willing to share them."

"Hmm. It strikes me that if she provided him with her passcodes and whatnot, maybe he also had access to her email account. You can sign into Google Mail from any browser. And when you get the alert to say your accounts been accessed from a new device, you can simply delete it. If you know the account holder is dead, there's no risk that they'll spot you're hacking them."

"Yah. You could also delete any messages that related to you and dump them out of trash while you're at it." Ben pursed his lips. "There are ways to get into permanently deleted emails, but if you didn't know about those, you might assume they were gone forever. That shouldn't apply to Jeremy, of course."

"I wasn't so much thinking that as wondering if it would be a clever way to cover up the date of death. We've settled on it being the eleventh because that's when the last emails went out, but what if it was the tenth, or late on the ninth, assuming Jeremy's telling us the truth about speaking to her then and that should be easily checked on phone records so he'd be stupid to lie."

"So he knows he'll have a stone-cold alibi for the eleventh and twelfth but can't prove where he was on the tenth? You could be onto something, sir. Although if that's what happened, he's not necessarily being as clever as he thinks. You can take a Zoom call from anywhere. Horrible thought that you'd do it from the same house that a fresh corpse was lying in, though." Ben shuddered. "The only proof he'd have is if the meetings were recorded and he could show he was in his own house."

"Adds a whole new dimension to alibi checking. Now"—Robin tapped the desk—"I'm on a roll. Fixing time of death. Did Ellen have a health app? I know not everyone carries their phone around all the time, but there should be a record of any steps she took with it in her hand or her bag."

"I forgot to look at that. I'll do it right now. Although that would be easier to fake than accessing her emails, because you wouldn't need any password, would you?" Ben pointed out. "Assuming the killer took the phone, then carried it around for a few days—in a plastic bag to avoid accumulating fibres or whatever—before returning the thing, then that would obscure the date of death as well. If they had a key to get into Ellen's house, they could return it easily enough. It was found in the kitchen, wasn't it?"

"Yes. She may have had it with her if she was cooking, although on the other hand it might have been the place she habitually left it. Not everyone wants to be at the beck and call of their mobile."

"That's what my girlfriend says. She sometimes gives me an ultimatum—the phone or her."

"She's very wise."

Adam hadn't quite gone as far as that, but there had been some occasions on holidays where it had come damn close.

Adam hadn't been home longer than a few minutes when he heard Robin come through the front door. They went through the whole "You're early, have they had enough of you?" banter routine, punctuated by Campbell sticking his wet nose everywhere he could, before Robin set off for a shower while Adam attended to dinner.

"Feeling better?" he asked when Robin appeared in the kitchen.

"Miles. I didn't manage one this morning. Too tempted by the extra fifteen minutes in bed. Here, let me make that sauce. Not been taking my fair share of domestic work recently."

"I won't argue." Adam knew that Robin sometimes found cooking a useful way to de-stress and clear his mind. An easy dish like puttanesca sauce to go with pasta would be fiddly enough to do the trick.

"How's Kelvin? There's no hidden agenda in the question, by the way."

"He's okay, on the whole. He was saying today he gets the odd flashback to identifying the body. I feel sorry for the lad as I think he's never had to deal with anything really challenging before. He asked if that letter was any help."

"We're not sure. We found her Bible in her house—King James version—but there wasn't a note stuck in there or words underlined or anything obvious. Maybe there was no message intended and it's a red herring. Don't tell him that, though. Not until we're absolutely sure." Robin bashed the wooden spoon against the side of the pan, perhaps taking out his frustrations.

"Are you any further forward?"

"I think we are, although who knows. I'm aware it's still early on, but I always want to solve the case yesterday. The longer it takes, the more I worry that this will be the dreaded murder that lies unsolved for years. The sort of case that gets resurrected in ten years' time and you have people going through our every move and decision, trying to work out what wrong steps we made and whether we missed the bleeding obvious." Robin suddenly broke into a happy grin. "Actually, I got one up on Ben tech-wise today. *He'd* missed something which was bleeding obvious to anyone with a mind to apps."

"Well done." That would have been a feather in his husband's cap.

"I thought so. We're trying to pin down the time and date of death as closely as we can, and Ben hadn't tried the health app on her phone. I suggested he do it."

"Great idea. Did it help?"

"It told us that phone hadn't moved since half past six on the eleventh of January, which is the day we think she died, but we didn't have a fix on the time previously, as there were no message responses or outgoing mail since late afternoon. The killer might have moved the phone themselves, of course, but they didn't leave their fingerprints on it. Everything points to that day, unless the killer has set up a very clever suite of evidence to create the illusion that she was still alive when she wasn't. As they did to a lesser extent with the blinds. Still, we've got someone coming down tomorrow who's confident they can get into her files, so that might move us forward." Robin licked the spoon. "This is going to be tasty."

"It smells excellent. Any news on the mysterious disappearing bins, by the way?"

"Yes. Somebody using Ellen's debit card arranged for them to be taken away and disposed of. Probably, we're speculating, to hide any evidence one of them had been used to carry off bloody clothes and the murder weapon." Robin paused, wagging the wooden spoon. "What do you know about turnips?"

"Hate the buggers, which is why we never have them. *Pourquoi*?"

"*Parce que* Billy the Bins—don't ask—checked they were empty before he took them away. In the brown recycling bin, he found a turnip. No *Blackadder* jokes, please. Although if you've got any bright suggestions about why anyone would have put a turnip there, I'm willing to hear them."

"No bloody idea. Was the lid open, meaning it could have been lobbed in there by someone arsing about?" That hardly counted as a sensible theory. "Had Ellen herself put it there in a moment of forgetfulness? Like the time you once put the ice cream in the cupboard and the spare plate in the freezer?"

"That's my only offence, and I soon realised what I'd done. It's as good a theory as any, though. She puts the recycling in the general waste and the turnip in the brown bin because she's thinking of something else. Like I was thinking of what to get you for your birthday when I had the ice cream aberration." Robin tasted the sauce. "This isn't far off. Let's get the pasta on and change the subject. For example, what we can do in the garden over half-term. Fancy decking like Trevor's?"

The subject of garden redevelopment—ideas, likely costs; timescale of when they should get quotes; and who from—occupied them while the pasta cooked and while they started eating it. However, Adam had only taken a few forkfuls when he halted.

"My cooking not up to snuff?" Robin asked.

"Your cooking's probably fine." Adam raised his fork again, looked at the food, then shivered. "Does it taste okay to you?"

"Yes. I . . . No." Robin turned pale, the implication of Adam's question no doubt hitting home. "You've got to be kidding."

"Afraid I'm not. This tastes a bit like how petrol smells. I'm going to have to self-isolate while I get a test for *it*, aren't I?" Adam pushed his plate away, feeling too sick and worried to eat, even if the food had been the best a Michelin-starred restaurant could turn out. "You carry on with yours while I get my iPad and check what I'm supposed to do."

"I think I've lost my appetite."

Several minutes, a handful of internet pages, and a lot of concern from Robin later, Adam had his answers. They were what he should have expected and what neither of them wanted. He'd have to book a test as soon as possible; luckily, they lived only ten minutes' drive from one of the testing centres, so that should be straightforward. As far as they could see, Robin could still go to work, although they'd have to self-isolate from each other at home until they knew the test result. That would mean making up the spare bed, one of them using the little shower room downstairs rather than the main bathroom, and definitely no snogging.

Robin got onto the business with sheets and towels—aided by Campbell, who must have known something odd was afoot—while Adam booked his test and then rang Kate to ask her not to come over to do any housework until he advised her further. She offered to come and walk the dog every day, which Adam immediately agreed to, having forgotten that angle. He also got on the blower to Jim Rashford to tell him he'd be without his deputy's services for at least a few days and possibly longer. Adam had imagined the bloke getting straight into planning mode, not just to cover one post but to deal with any self-isolation among other staff that would have to follow a positive test.

As it turned out, he was already on the case.

"I was about to ring *you*. I've had Avril on the phone, in a flood of tears." Avril was one of the learning-support assistants who worked with the Reception class and who'd been doing sterling work with the younger children over the last few weeks. "She's distraught. Turns out her sister has tested positive for Covid—the stupid woman has been working as a hairdresser in people's homes and she's picked it up. Avril hadn't realised any of it had been going on until she asked how the hell her sister had caught it, because *she's* always going on about how she's been obeying the rules. Avril's dobbed her in to the police now and hopes she'll get slapped with a hefty fine to teach her a lesson. Anyway, the pair of them were chatting at the weekend, when the sister dropped off a birthday card and must have been infectious. They were out the front of Avril's house, but it was for a good quarter of an hour, so she's isolating and getting a test tomorrow. I'll be warning all the staff to be on the lookout for symptoms."

As soon as the call had finished, Adam gave Robin the bad news. "We've all been careful in the staffroom not to be in each other's pockets, but you never know."

"I'm so sorry." Robin grimaced. "For all I know, I've picked the virus up at Kinechester station and brought it back with me. I'd give you a hug, but that's probably not a great idea."

"No. It's going to be *No touch, Dettol wipe city* here until we know one way or another. I'm not telling Mum, though. She'll be down here like a shot, treating me like I'm six, irrespective of the fact she's more at risk than me if she catches it." What a pain. Although they'd been fortunate, given the nature of their jobs, not having had to self-isolate up until now. Robin's Aunt Clare had only recently completed her second batch of "house arrest," as she'd elegantly described it.

Robin gave him a smile. "It'll be fine, you know. This too shall pass."

"That's what I'm trying to tell myself." They'd experienced worse. What was a swab stuck up your nose and the prospect of a few days confined to barracks compared to having a gun or a knife waved at you? "Fancy a beer?"

"On a week night? Things must be bad. Yeah, only the one, for a nightcap. See me off to sleep."

Unfortunately, given the circumstances, they wouldn't be enjoying any particularly pleasurable ways of ensuring a good night's sleep anytime soon.

Chapter Ten

Tuesday morning, Robin turned in the bed to give Adam a hug, then remembered the funny-tasting pasta sauce and the spare room. Oh, joy. He pulled on a sweatshirt over his pyjamas before braving a peep out of the window. The weather forecast was cold, foggy, and generally miserable, a typical January day laden with the annual post-Christmas depression. He couldn't hear any coughing coming from the direction of the spare bed, which was one good sign, so decided to go down and get a brew going. Adam would appreciate a mug of tea in bed, and Campbell would welcome being let out for his morning comfort break in the garden.

A few minutes later, and not a touch too soon given how the dog dashed out of the door, Robin watched Campbell bound about, clearly not bothered about the inclement conditions. Hardy souls, Newfoundlands. Hopefully Adam would be as hardy if he *had* picked up the dreaded virus. All the demographic factors were in his favour, so he should be able to fight it off, but Robin was well aware of fit blokes, younger than them, who'd been absolutely floored by Covid and who were still not right months afterwards. He shot up one of his infrequent prayers, putting in a word for the love of his life and asking that Adam would get through this sticky patch okay. That they'd *both* get through it okay.

"How did you sleep?" Adam's voice sounded from behind Robin.

"Not bad, considering. You?"

"Took me a while to drop off. Mind going ten to the dozen, of course. I'll be pleased when we know one way or the other."

Campbell, whose super-efficient hearing had clearly detected the presence of his other master, came haring towards the house, bounding through the door as Robin opened it. "He knows something's not right. He's been eyeing you suspiciously ever since you gave him that extra biscuit last night."

"He probably thinks we're buttering him up because we're about to go on holiday. He's going to be very confused at me lurking around here and not taking him for walks."

"He'll forget that as soon as Kate arrives. Memory span of a goldfish, when the subject matter isn't food."

"Your dad's being so rude about you, boy." Adam rubbed the dog's ears. "As soon as he's out the house, we can swop stories about him. But *you'll* have to give him his goodbye kiss this morning, because I'm not allowed to. Make it nice and slobbery."

"You bugger. I'll *nice and slobbery* you when this is all done."

"Promises, promises." Adam jerked his thumb over his shoulder. "Go and get washed and dressed and I'll make you a proper breakfast. Do you fancy pancakes? A sausage sandwich?"

"Are you supposed to be doing that? Shouldn't we be handling all our food separately?"

"Probably, but given that I've been cooking for you the last few days—let alone the hugs and kisses—I dare say another meal won't make much of a difference. I'll wash my hands and not cough on the plate."

"You're most likely right." Robin rubbed his face. "Nightmare, this. If you've got it, I'm guessing I'll have got it, so part of me says I should stay at home. But in the circumstances, I'd hate to let the team down if you've got nothing worse than a tummy bug or something."

"I know. Your boss said stick to the government website rules, didn't he?"

"Yeah." Robin had been in text contact with Denness the previous evening, and the bloke was happy to do nothing other than be extra cautious at the moment. "Surprise me with breakfast. It'll be great whatever it is."

So long as it didn't taste of petrol.

As soon as he was in the office, Robin called the team together and gave them the heads-up concerning the situation in the Bright-Matthews household. He suggested they should all take additional care, if such a thing were possible, and reassured them that, if the worst came to the worst, he'd still be involved with the investigation while he was in the isolation period. Denness had already approved a plan that saw Pru take over control at the coal face while Robin would retain overall charge. Assuming matters came to that point. If Robin himself ended up flat on his back, then Denness would take the reins until he could get hold of another body.

"I feel sorry for him," Robin concluded. "He reckons at this rate, we could be sending the police dogs out to interview witnesses up on Cromwell Road. On a brighter note, he's so pleased with the work Aaron's done on this case, he's seconded him onto another one that needs similar research undertaken. Win-win."

"Too many cooks spoiling the broth? Especially ones who can't keep an open mind." Pru clearly spoke for everyone present. They were quickly gelling into a close-knit team. "I didn't like to mention it, but he was grilling me about you and your partner. Were you married? Is Adam called Mr. Bright now as well or did he have a double-barrelled name, like Bright-Smith or whatever?"

Robin had been asked the question before and not always in so polite a fashion. *Which one of you is the wife?* had been a particularly offensive variation, met with the contempt it deserved. Maybe Pru had made Aaron's rendering of it politer than it had really been. "Did you tell him where to get off?"

"I did. Remained as professional as I could when I wanted to punch his nose. I said you'd decided it was easier to stay with your original names, given that's what people at work know you by. He nodded and said it was like actresses, when they get married." Pru rolled her eyes. "He couldn't be more offensive if he tried. I told him it wasn't just actresses. I have a pal who's a consultant anaesthetist and she stuck with her maiden name. She isn't defined by her husband."

"He's either going out of his way to be as nasty as he can get away with or he's completely oblivious. Whichever, he's going to have to start growing up in terms of his attitudes. That's enough of Aaron."

Robin waved him away with a flick of his hand. "Naomi, skips and their contents. You were on the trail yesterday afternoon."

"Not sure I have anything good to share. No real luck with the Methodists," the constable said. "I spoke to the minister, the steward, and a couple of parishioners. They're a nice bunch, very keen to be helpful, very keen to show that they've been obeying all the lockdown rules. Masks, fresh air, enough hand sanitiser to float the Titanic—I had all the details."

"No holding midnight raves in the aisles?" Robin chuckled.

"Not that they're admitting to. For the clear out, they worked in small groups, one lot sorting the crap, another lot shifting it into the skip. They did a few hours on the Saturday—that was the ninth— then another couple on Monday, before finishing the job on Tuesday. It wasn't the same group of volunteers each time, so if someone had sneaked a bag of rubbish into the skip on Monday evening, nobody was likely to have noticed, especially if they stuffed it down the side."

"Why have various groups of people involved?" Ben asked. "Sounds like a recipe for disaster. Wasn't there someone supervising it?"

"The minister, Gary Rose, nominally. He was around most days, although he said he was really there supporting his flock and to make any decisions on whether a particular item should stay or go. He fell over on the ice at the New Year and still has his arm in plaster, so he was no use for shinning up into lofts or lugging bags of crap. His word, not mine." Naomi chuckled. "The practical side of things was under control of the steward, Ray. *He* told me he'd been forced to have different teams of volunteers or a fist fight could have broken out. They had to be fair to everyone who wanted to take part, despite some of them regarding it as a bit of a jolly—anything to get out of the house and do something different."

Robin resisted a comment along the lines of asking what the world had come to. He could understand people clinging to whatever would bring a bit of variety to their day. "What kind of crap did they generate?"

"Any and everything." Naomi consulted her notes. "Broken toys and sports equipment from the children's and youth groups, a tatty plastic Christmas tree, a few rotten old display boards. Much as you'd imagine it. The minister says they recycled as much as they could, although that was mainly paper and cardboard. Most of the rubbish was beyond hope, so they put it into big plastic bags for ease of transportation from the church to the skip. That included a series of dead bats, rats, and one squirrel from around the building and once they'd been lobbed in the skip, nobody wanted to go treading in there. Not even to tamp the crap down. If an extra bag of stuff had been sneaked amongst the other stuff, Ray says it would have seemed like everything else. He and Gary were both sorry they couldn't help further. They had nothing to say about Ellen, either, except that she had occasionally attended services in the past, although not for a couple of years. Gary had been round to see her the summer before last to check that she was okay. You can imagine the reception he got."

"Excoriation?" Ben suggested.

"Pretty much. She said that if and when she was ready to return, she'd be back. Then she shut the door on him." Naomi shrugged. "I'm not victim shaming, much, but she doesn't seem to have been very good at keeping people sweet."

That was an understatement.

Pru cut in. "Maybe that's understandable, given what happened in her love life. Two blokes let her down, one of them—literally—criminally. Perhaps there were other folk, friends or lovers, who led her on. It could leave anyone with a chip on their shoulder and a determination not to let people get too close ever again."

"She let Jeremy Sexton get close. Despite him hurting her before," Ben pointed out. "Although that could be a case of *the devil you know*. She could go into that relationship with her eyes open. Same as if she got involved with Cavendish."

Robin, whose mind had wandered off to Adam and his virus test, which was imminent, threw Ben a sharp glance. "We've not considered that. Do you think that's a genuine possibility?"

"I don't know, sir. I'd not thought about it until it was out of my mouth."

"It's worth considering, surely," Pru said. "If she was investigating him again, it would be to her advantage to get close to him, either in person or online. You two spoke to Cavendish—is the idea a goer?"

Robin rubbed his chin. "Ashok, what do you think?"

Ashok, clearly chuffed at being given the opportunity to air his thoughts before Robin did, said, "I think that if she'd had any sense, Ellen wouldn't have touched him with a bargepole, but if she had an ulterior motive, I could understand her taking the chance. I came away with the impression that things weren't going well in the Cavendish household, so he might have welcomed the chance of taking comfort elsewhere."

"I got that impression too. If he was having a fling with Ellen, that would also give Deborah Cavendish a motive to eliminate her rival, like she's dealt with rivals before. Goes to Ellen's house, confronts her, the argument gets out of hand, Deborah grabs a knife . . ." Robin exhaled loudly. "It feels a much likelier scenario than a random conspiracy theorist that Ellen's been investigating getting hold of her address and deciding to kill her."

"We know that Deborah was in the area on the day," Ashok reminded them. "*And* Derek Cavendish seemed keen for us to have her fingerprints. Perhaps he's too scared to tell us direct in case she goes for him, as well."

"Possibly. We still need to account for the one distinct wound, though. The one that looked like it had been done with scissors. I suppose Deborah might carry them in her handbag. Any luck with people living near the church seeing somebody chucking stuff away?" Robin asked.

"Not really," Pru, said. "People remember the work going on at the church—the Browns, a retired couple who live opposite, said it was the best entertainment they'd had in ages. Not quite the picture of harmony and cooperation that the minister told Naomi about."

"Really?" Robin's copper's nose had twitched at the mention of discord.

"Yes. Fred Karno's Army, Mr. Brown called it. Whatever that is. Probably what my dad would call a shite show. The Saturday morning was shambolic, tempers fraying all round, until Gary Rose came and got a system organised. Boringly straightforward after that. Monday morning, they had new volunteers on, and one of them wanted to rearrange the system. He said the skip needed reorganising to begin with, then started to take stuff out. The minister had to talk him out of it and prevent a pitched battle." Pru giggled. "Mr. Brown quite unashamedly admits to lurking in his front garden for an hour, ostensibly touching up the pointing on his front garden wall, but in reality listening in. Mrs. Brown had to keep fetching him coffee and tools and anything else she could think of so she could watch the show."

A shame, if their theory was correct, that hadn't happened on the next morning. The skip unpacker might have turned out more than he bargained for. "What about the Tuesday?"

"The Browns decided to clean their windows to get a grandstand view, although they said there were no further arguments. Only a lot of hilarity when the volunteers were trying to load the last bits into the skip and not disturb what was already there. So yes, bloody chaos all round, which supports the view that someone could have slipped a bag into the skip and not been noticed. As does this . . ." Pru paused, a touch dramatically; if people's attention had wandered during the tale of the unrepentantly nosy neighbours, she'd recaptured it now. "I've left what might be the best part to last. Mr. Brown says he heard somebody wheeling a bin along their bit of the road about eight o'clock on the evening of the eleventh of January. He knows it was around then because he and his wife were in between programmes on BBC two and he'd gone upstairs to their bedroom to get a cardigan. He thought it might be another outbreak of shenanigans at the church, but he couldn't see anybody around. The skip was located well away from the road, so if somebody had been there, he'd not necessarily have been able to see them. Anyway, he went to the loo, then looked out again, up and down the road, and someone seemed to be hauling a bin towards Rupert Drive."

"No chance of an identification?" Robin guessed what the answer would be; he wasn't wrong.

"Nope. He'd discussed it with his wife, and she put it down to a yob having a lark with one of the bins which hadn't been taken in. They'd not thought about it until I mentioned it, and all they could recall was the person was on the tall side. They didn't recognise either of the Cavendishes, either. No matter how many pairs of glasses they used to study the photograph."

Robin peered at his sergeant, recognising the little twinkle in her eye, suggestive of more revelations to come. "And the rest of the story, please."

The sergeant's eyes glinted again. "Remember the picture of the Cavendishes that Ashok found on Facebook?"

"The anniversary one on their friend's page?" Robin gave Ashok a nod in appreciation of a good piece of work.

"Yep. I hawked it around Ireton Avenue without luck, then I trotted round to Cromwell Road with it. Showed the picture to as many neighbours as I could catch. The Careys *umm*ed and *ahh*ed, before coming to the conclusion that they couldn't say if they'd seen the pair or not. It could have been another case of them not knowing what had gone on while they'd been away illegally and not wanting to let slip the fact. I kept deadpan about it." Pru had an efficient poker face when such a thing was needed. "Don at number forty-one was really helpful. He recognised the photo straight away. Derek's one of the patients on his private list."

Robin snorted. "Small world. What's his speciality, where does he practice, and what day does he do his private work?"

Pru checked her notes. "Ear, Nose and Throat, the Nuffield Hospital in Kinechester, and Fridays. Why do you ask?"

"I was wondering if it linked to the Cavendishes visiting Kinechester and if his clinic was on a Monday. And whether he dealt with venereal problems or something equally embarrassing that neither Derek nor his wife would have wanted to admit. I'm determined to get that loose end tied."

"Don didn't tell me what he saw Derek about, obviously, although he did say that it was pretty routine. Thing is, he didn't only remember them from the hospital. He'd seen them both in Cromwell Road and they'd blanked him."

"What? When?"

"He isn't sure, sir. Sometime this side of Christmas. He particularly remembered because it's usually the other way round. Patients recognise him and he has to apologise for not identifying them out of context, but he said in this case there was no way he'd forget the couple. *She* came into the consultations with her husband. Like he was a little boy." Pru pulled a disapproving face. "Apparently she justified it by saying that Derek was extremely nervous in hospitals, but Don's sure she was keeping him under her thumb. The patient certainly appeared embarrassed by the whole situation. Anyway, Don says that was maybe why Derek blanked him when he said hello. Hashtag awkward."

"Deborah wouldn't be embarrassed, though, which suggests it was a deliberate act. Hashtag extremely awkward if they were heading to Ellen's." Robin rubbed his hands together. "We need to pin down the date if we can. Did you ask him if it could have been the eleventh?"

"I did and it could have been, given his commitments on the eleventh, but it could equally have been four or five other days this month, according to his diary. He knows he was on his way to work and is sure it was a late-start day. It's been all hands to the pump the last couple of months, and he's been doing some later clinics for patients who have to be seen." Pru checked her notes again. "He saw them as he was getting into his car and knows he wouldn't have parked more than a few doors away from his house."

"Great to have them spotted almost outside Ellen's door, but it's a shame Don can't pin them down to the right day," Ashok said.

"Naomi and I aren't sure they need to have been seen on the eleventh to take this further." In a typically considerate manner, Pru waved a hand in her junior colleague's direction, to let her take up the story.

"We know whoever's responsible for the killing would have had to come back again, to operate the blinds for a start. *Any* proven visit would show they'd lied," Naomi pointed out. "They told you they'd not been in Cromwell Road, didn't they?"

"Not quite. I suspect he was being quite clever. Hold on." Robin racked his brains to think of the exact words Derek had used. "As I recall, he said he didn't know where Cromwell Road was so couldn't tell if he'd been there or not. Is that right, Ashok?"

"Yes, sir. As if he was setting up his excuse in advance." Ashok pulled at his chin. "It might be better for us if they *were* there another day. That would be dodgier than them going for a stroll after they'd been to see the Avensis. That's another positive about lockdown— people have to justify their travel."

"But only to yourself if you're the Careys," Ben muttered, to the team's amusement.

"Shall I arrange for us to talk to the Cavendishes again?" Ashok asked, clearly chomping at the bit to get his teeth into them.

"Not yet. Much as I'd like to make them squirm, I want to see the files on Ellen's laptop first. We need all the ammunition we can get. He's been convicted twice, and she had been once, so they know the ropes. I'd be surprised if they haven't learned how to cover their trail more efficiently than when they strayed off the beaten track in the past." Robin consulted his checklist, making sure that everyone had plenty to keep them busy. There were still threads to follow—like whether there had been other regulars at the hotel with Ellen at Christmas and if any of those friendships had become romances.

And, of course, there was the most annoying thing of all. The turnip in the bin, which probably didn't mean anything whatsoever but would nag away at Robin until he knew what it was doing there. *Possibly for the rest of my life.*

Jeremy arrived a little before lunchtime. Ben had nabbed one of the interview rooms so they could work on Ellen's devices—which he'd retrieved from a rather miffed tech expert, who had sworn he was on the verge of breaking into them when the moratorium was introduced—in peace.

Robin thanked Jeremy for coming, told him that Ashok had gone out to get sandwiches in for them both, then left the pair to it, with a simple, "Call me in when you find something you think's relevant. I trust both your judgements." He also trusted Ben to pick up any underlying hints about why Jeremy had changed his phone. Matters had been slightly complicated owing to a message from Denness that said he'd been told from on high—which presumably was a governmental source rather than God himself—that Sexton was a person in whom absolute trust could be placed and the work he was involved in made a vital contribution to the nation's welfare. It meant they couldn't quite treat him like the average suspect in terms of his access to what was on Ellen's computer, although Ben was under instruction to watch him like a hawk and not let anything get deleted.

Time to find a quiet corner and check if Adam had been in touch. He would have had his test by now and would have a clearer idea of how long it would take for a result to come. One to three days, according to the NHS site: the sooner the better as far as Robin was concerned.

Adam: *Been swabbed. Thought it was going to go all the way through and come out of my ear.*

Robin squirmed. He had a pretty strong stomach but that was definitely *TMI.*

Adam: *Results might be back tomorrow—no guarantee, though. Still got an odd taste in my mouth. Made the mistake of googling what else could cause it. Think Covid might be one of the better options. Love you.*

Love you too. Keep me posted, Robin replied, curious as to what worse options there could be but determined not to venture into the symptom-researching minefield. *Keep off Google. That's an order.*

Barely an hour, and a ton of boring but essential admin, later, Robin's phone went.

"Ben here, sir. Can you come down now? Jeremy's gone to the loo, and then he intends on having a fag or two outside, so we can have a quick chat before he returns."

"Got something?"

"Got plenty. You'll like it."

When Robin entered the interview room, Ben couldn't hide the triumphant look on his face.

"You're like a dog with two tails." Robin plonked himself in a chair.

"I'm a constable who's got two leads. Neither concerns the stuff she was working on with Jeremy, which he's been talking me through. That's mainly targeted at people abroad, so I'd be inclined to discount it for the moment, until we've explored closer to home." Ben's expression turned unusually serious. "She's been keeping an eye on Cavendish for years, it seems. Odds and sods of irregularities turning up, although they're not anything he'd need to get agitated over, even if she confronted him about them. Unless I've not found the smoking gun yet. As you can imagine, there's a hell of a lot of stuff to go through."

"I'm sure there is, like I'm sure you're the right officer to take charge of it. I'll put Ashok or Naomi to work with you, so you can share the load."

"I'd appreciate that, sir."

"And what's the other lead, then?" Robin felt like a straight man, supplying the cue for the punchline.

"Greg Carey. She's been investigating her own neighbour for fraud."

Robin shot out of his chair, almost upsetting the coffee he'd brought with him. "This I have to see."

"Before we do that, sir . . ." Ben glanced over his shoulder towards the door. "Jeremy seemed particularly interested in the Cavendish files, over and above what I expected. He was trying to hide his interest, too."

"Any idea why?"

"Nope. He said that the Carey case must have been what he and Ellen argued about. You know, her spending her time on it, although he didn't know the name of the person involved up until now. When I asked, in that case, if he could be absolutely sure it wasn't *Cavendish* she'd been focussing on, he laughed the question off. Said that Ellen wouldn't have been wasting her time on small fry."

Did that imply Ellen had regarded the fraud as a big fish? "Hmm. We'll add that to the list of things to ask him about."

Ben nodded, then brought a file up on the screen. "He'll be back in a minute, so we should discuss Carey now. I've been wondering if this was the real reason why Ellen didn't want to do the bloke's taxes. Because it might incriminate her if she got embroiled with him?"

"That wouldn't surprise me. Or she was concerned that she wouldn't be able to keep a straight face. Maybe it was something she'd spotted in his previous return that made her suspicious in the first place."

"And *there's* the Psalm twenty-three link." Ben tapped the screen.

According to Ellen's notes, Greg had been doing work for the charity I Shall Not Want, whose mission statement—according to the information that Ellen must have screen-capped from their website—

was helping families who were on the cusp of struggling, the sort who don't always get help because the kids aren't eligible for free school meals and they don't fall into any particular categories. Adam had mentioned some of the pupils at his school who struggled to make the progress their peers did, white boys from working-class families who didn't attract any extra support or funding.

"So she was getting together a file of evidence about the charity's accounts?" Robin asked. No wonder she'd been distancing herself from the Careys.

"Yes, sir. I've not been into it in any detail, but her master sheet of notes suggests she went back as far as she could, looking specifically at payments to directors and level of expenses paid to volunteers. One of the things that may have alerted her is the relatively small percentage of income that ends up directly benefitting the people the charity is supposed to be helping."

"Siphoning off of funds to people who shouldn't be getting them?"

"That's what she suspected, although it's complicated. She's got screen grabs of the charity website, which implies that many of the volunteers themselves might have children who fall into the 'client' category, so their families are also being helped indirectly. Gaining work experience and upskilling to increase their employability and self-esteem. On the surface that seems fine, but for some reason she smelled a rat. That's led her to talk to ex-volunteers." Ben pointed at the screen. "There are several statements in here I'd need to go through."

"You do that. It's time we talked to Mr. Carey, so get yourself up to speed and then brief me as soon as you can. I'm going to call the bloke right now."

"You'll get him in here today?"

"If I can. A trip to the station might rattle him a bit."

"Rattle who?" Jeremy asked, coming through the door with a noticeable waft of cigarette smoke hanging about him.

"Someone Ellen was investigating." Robin wasn't going to provide further details until he'd asked Jeremy those questions he had lined up. He also couldn't see how charity fraud could be in any way linked to the welfare-of-the-nation aspect of Sexton's work, which the big-wig had emphasised to Denness. "Thanks for doing this. Ben will have his work cut out for days, going through these files, and he's very good at making sure he forgets anything he sees which isn't relevant to our enquiries. If it's not linked to Ellen's death, it won't be used."

"I expect nothing less. It's been a pleasure working with you." Jeremy began to clear away his things.

"Actually, could you leave off packing up for a moment? We've not quite finished," Robin said.

"Of course. Other files of Ellen's you want help to get into?"

"Not quite. I wanted to ask about you changing your phone."

Again, that distinctive change in Jeremy's demeanour, noticeable even though the bloke was wearing a mask. "I thought we'd discussed that. Time for a new one."

"And a new number to get the exes off your back. So you said." Robin wagged his finger. "Trouble is, I don't believe that's the whole story. You've been pretty upfront with us, much more helpful than perhaps we could have hoped for. And all the time you've spoken about your work and your research, I've not doubted a word. Then we mention your phone and the shutters come down. You don't play poker, by any chance?"

"No. Why? Ah." Jeremy shook his head. "No poker face. Ellen always used to say it was just as well I never got involved with field work. I'm not cut out for lying. Perhaps my love life would have been better if I was."

"No details in front of Ben. He's a delicate soul." Robin gave Ben a smile, but the constable was already deeply ensconced in perusing Ellen's files. Or pretending to be, in a more convincing manner than Jeremy might have managed. "So give us the truth."

"This is going to sound stupid." Jeremy shook his head sheepishly. "I received a threatening message from an unknown number. I ignored it, thinking it might have come to the wrong phone. It happens. A couple of years back I went through a phase of getting calls for a catering firm whose number was one digit different to mine. Eventually they must have changed theirs because the calls to me stopped. I thought it was something similar happening again."

Robin believed the business with the misdirected calls for the catering firm had happened, although he felt it was being used as a convenient—and not particularly convincing—excuse. Still, he'd keep his powder dry at present. "How many messages did you get altogether?"

"Three. All of them telling me to stop poking my nose in their business or I'd get a punch up the bracket. Not those exact words, obviously. A nonspecific threat of violence. Can you blame me for changing my number?"

"No. But I can blame you for not telling us the truth straight away. I'm not sure you're being frank with us now. You're an intelligent man, so if you really did believe it was a wrong number, why not reply and tell them they had the wrong person? Or call us."

Jeremy paled again. "I did. Reply, I mean. They said it was definitely me they meant to talk to. They knew my name."

"'They'?" Ben asked. "Two people? Three?"

"No. I mean I don't know. I'm using the word *they* because I don't know their gender. You can't tell from a text. Sorry, I didn't mean to sound so snarky. I was extremely concerned at the time." Jeremy passed his hand over his face. "I'd never been threatened before. Not in that way. Had one or two ex-girlfriends threatening to cut off my nads with a pair of scissors, but this was different. Very unsettling, especially when you have no idea who it comes from. Thank God they've not got hold of my new number."

Which suggested that *they* might have found it through one of his old contacts, one whom he'd not informed of the number change. "Did you have your old number listed somewhere? A website you use to advertise your business?"

"Nope. I do it all by email or messages on the site. No threatening ones there."

"So, why not contact us?" Robin asked.

"Because I was all Billy Big Bollocks and thought I could handle it myself."

That wasn't unknown among blokes who were used to relying on their own resources, but it probably wasn't the whole truth. "And you changed your mind on that?"

"To an extent." Jeremy opened his briefcase, fishing out a piece of paper, which he passed to Robin. "I decided if it came up today and seemed relevant, then I'd come clean. Dates of messages and what they said. I think the first was the thirteenth of January. I made a note when

I got the second one, which came two days after the first. I've had to guess at the exact words as I'd deleted it, but you get the gist."

Robin had read plenty of threatening messages during his career, and these didn't quite measure up. As though the person writing them had been trying to work out how a genuine piece of intimidation might be phrased. *We know what you're doing. If you don't stop, you'll regret it,* hardly measured up to a graphic threat, although it would have been enough to shake anyone. Especially if it arrived out of the blue and as part of a series.

Jeremy continued. "I wanted to ask Ellen if she'd had anything similar, but by then she wasn't answering her messages. And yes, I was worried, more so than I confessed to yesterday. I didn't lie to you, although I did tell half the truth. I actually wondered if she'd also changed her phone, and was waiting for her to message me with her new number."

This was beginning to sound like the truth. "What else have you only told us half the truth about? Did Ellen mention any concerns for her own safety, apart from Covid?"

"No, I swear. Not that I think she would have told *me*, because that would have offended her pride. She was the sort to shake off most things, and if she'd become genuinely fearful, she'd have contacted you. And kept a baseball bat at her side."

No baseball bat or similar means of self-defence had shown up at number thirty-nine, although Robin couldn't help but think of the knife that had killed her and that had still not been found. Had it been her own, one she'd carried around to protect herself?

"Sir." Ben pointed to some figures at the bottom of the sheet. "Is that the number the messages came from, Jeremy?"

"Yes. It's not one that I've run across in connection with my work. Do you recognise it?" The number was certainly distinctive, consisting of a small selection of digits.

"I might. It's all the sevens and threes that ring a bell. Hang on while I ring upstairs to the office and get them on the hunt."

While they waited for a response, Robin asked Jeremy why, given his penchant for investigation, he hadn't tried to identify the owner of the number himself. His sheepish response, that he'd had his legs slapped in the past for using official channels to check private matters, seemed to ring true. There also could be an element of male bravado in why he hadn't reported the threats to the police, the old story of "I can handle this myself." And the equally old story of not wanting to look a wally if it was one of the exes winding him up.

Robin also asked Jeremy to brief him about what he and Ellen had been working on. His conclusion was much the same as Ben's—better to concentrate nearer to home and pray that was where the answer lay, because if it was connected to the vipers' nest of conspiracy theorists, the case was likely to become impenetrable.

After five minutes, Pru rang back to say that they'd drawn a blank. The number he had given didn't match any of the details listed for the witnesses or suspects they'd questioned, nor any of the contacts on Ellen's phone. She'd get Ashok to bring the latter down to the interview room when he had the chance.

"But I've seen that number somewhere recently," Ben insisted, once the call had ended.

"Is there a list of numbers stored on here?" Robin pointed to the iPad. "No, they would be the same as the contacts on the iPhone, wouldn't they?"

"They would, but I think you've cracked it, sir. I think she had a file on here"—Ben indicated the laptop—"with names and addresses to do with the various things she'd been investigating. I flicked through it but—" He stopped. "Here."

Robin picked up the paper. The number Jeremy had written matched one on the list. Cavendish, but not Derek. *Deborah*.

"I have no idea who she is. I've heard of *him*, of course. Ellen told me how she'd helped to get him banged up, although I already knew the tale. It made the national news at the time, and I've always been a fan of reading the court reports. It didn't surprise me when her name cropped up among those giving testimony." Jeremy studied the messages again. "It still makes no sense. Why on earth should his wife be giving me grief?"

And why in such an ineffective way? Robin couldn't help but reflect on the wording of those texts and how they weren't that specific. Unless that had been a deliberate ploy: the messages being able to be explained away as something else if Deborah was confronted with them.

"Maybe the messages came from him," Ben suggested, "using his wife's phone if there was a chance that you'd tell Ellen about the threats and she'd recognise the incoming number. Maybe he habitually used his wife's phone in his frauds, which was why Ellen had the number on her list."

"Maybe," Jeremy conceded, "but the same question applies. Unless they've assumed Ellen and I were working together to catch him out. She clearly thinks—sorry, thought, can't get used to her being gone—that he's up to his old tricks."

"Did you ever help her gather information for the original fraud prosecution?" Robin had been struck by the unpleasant thought, for which he had no evidence other than disliking the woman, that Deborah might think it unlikely that Ellen could have accumulated the evidence without male help.

"No. Ellen and I weren't in touch at that point in our lives."

A sharp knock heralded Ashok's head peering round the door. "I brought Ellen's phone."

"Thanks." Ben took it from him. "I want to check her incoming calls and messages against these numbers."

"Join us," Robin told the constable. "You'll want to hear this about our favourite couple."

"I knew they couldn't be trusted," Ashok said, when he was up to speed.

He seemed on the verge of adding to that when Ben punched the air. "Yes. She got a message from Derek's number, spring of last year. Said he was getting a new phone and could she contact him on that one going forward."

"Unlike you not to have already spotted that, Benjamin." Robin grinned.

"There was no contact name with it, Mr. Bright." Ben returned the grin. "It could have come from anyone. Actually, Ellen didn't keep the sort of contacts list on her phone that most of us do. No names against any of the numbers apart from standard ones like her dentist and doctor."

"She wouldn't necessarily have needed to. A remarkable memory for numbers," Jeremy said.

Ben scanned the phone again. "There's no evidence of another message thread using the new number. Ashok, I bet you'll want to check whether that's the contact he gave you, because if it isn't, he may have two lines."

"You're right I'll check. And *you* were right, sir. If we'd hared down to see them today, we wouldn't have known any of this."

"Call it experience, Ashok. When you're as old and wise as I am, making the right call comes as second nature." Robin eased back his chair. "Jeremy, you've played a blinder. We'll obviously need to talk again once we've spoken to the Cavendishes, but if there's anything else about those messages that springs to mind, let us know. Or about Greg Carey too."

"Carey?" Ashok asked.

"We'll update everyone now. Ashok, if you could see Mr. Sexton out, then we'll reconvene in the incident room." With some bombshells to lob in the water and see what got thrown up. Things were moving, at last.

Chapter Eleven

The briefing was pretty upbeat, compared to previous ones, possibly because of Robin's positive mood. He'd dropped into Denness's office en route to update him on the day's developments and had been encouraged by the confidence his superior officer had expressed in him.

Robin let Ben detail the things they'd found on Ellen's laptop, while Naomi made relevant notes on the incident board.

"I've rung Greg Carey as requested, sir," Ben concluded, "and he's not happy at the prospect of missing his usual mealtime. He kept asking why he couldn't be spoken to in his own home, so I suggested he wouldn't want his family to overhear the questions we'd like to ask. That made him change his tune. He'll be here at six this evening."

"Good. That'll give us time to get a full grip on what's in those files." Robin jabbed his finger at the laptop. "Pru. Would you and Naomi like to visit Alex Carey at the same time as we see Greg? I know they've had weeks to get their stories straight, but they don't yet know how much *we* know, so it's a good moment to catch any disparities about who was doing what around the eleventh as well as this fraud business."

"Before he gets home tonight and they seal up any potential gaps between accounts?" Pru nodded. "I'll be ready for her if she plays the family-care card when I ring. I've seen the children, and they're quite old enough to entertain themselves in their rooms for half an hour. Naomi can watch a Disney film with them."

Naomi snorted. "Star Wars is more my style, but I'll take one for the cause."

"Ben's in with me to see Mr. Carey, given that he was there when we interviewed Alex the first time so he's got experience of the family. You'll get your turn in the limelight tomorrow, Ashok, when we leg it down to Portsmouth." Robin gave the constable an encouraging smile.

"Will you need to go there, sir, if Carey confesses?" Naomi asked.

"Yes. For a start, I doubt we'll be lucky enough to get him to confess to murder—it's not like we've got incontrovertible witness or forensic evidence to confront him with—but that's by-the-by. Even if we get the murder wrapped up, there's still *his* possible new fraud offences, and I want to know what they were doing in Kinechester when Don saw them. And there's the matter of threats made to Jeremy Sexton."

"I bet those threats are why he was so keen to come down and help us get into Ellen's files," Ben said. "I got the impression he was searching for something in particular and trying to hide the fact. He probably can't turn the researcher mode off."

"I guess he's found what he wanted, now. I think his surprise at who was behind the threats was genuine. Maybe he *was* expecting one of these QAnon types—passionate but pretty clueless—to be behind it and ended up finding out it was only . . ." Robin tried to find a comparison to use. Howard and Hilda from the sitcom he used to watch reruns of with his parents was an example likely to go straight over his team's heads.

"Dolly from *Dinnerladies*?" Ashok suggested. "I wish the rest of the team could have met this pair, because it really feels like they've stepped out of a TV show. You know, I've an idea about how they could have come across Jeremy's name. Back in the dating agency days, before Ellen started to suspect things weren't as they appeared, she may well have opened her heart to Derek Cavendish, telling him the story of her doomed affair. He might have made a note of it—if he was running an efficient scam, he'd have surely kept records of what conversations he'd had with who."

With whom. Robin could imagine Adam itching to correct the grammar. He resisted glancing at his phone to see if any updates had come through from home since the earlier text that had stated: *Feeling grotty, having an afternoon on the sofa. Can't decide if it's psychosomatic.*

It was always easy to think oneself into displaying symptoms. *He'd* not been feeling great on and off all morning, but was ninety percent certain it was all in his mind. Or, if real, most likely due to pressure of the case and long hours taking their toll.

"You reckon they got Sexton's number from Ellen's phone after she was killed?" Naomi asked.

"It's possible," Ashok said. "Although if she's been in contact with Cavendish, he might have obtained it before that. They meet, she goes to the loo, leaving her phone on the table, unlocked, he has a nose around . . ."

"Or he accesses the phone while she's asleep in the bed next to him," Pru suggested. "Sex doesn't stop when you pass sixty. Maybe the Sexton angle provided a cover story for him to tell Deborah. 'Where do you keep going, Derek?' 'Oh, I'm meeting this guy who threatens to expose my past.' 'Leave him to me, I'll sort him.' Does that sound plausible?"

"It does, although I have to say it doesn't feel likely. I could be wrong, because we know that Derek and Ellen were back in contact and that she suspected him of being up to his old tricks." Robin pointed to where *Old dog, old tricks* was written on the incident board. "I'd put money on him not wanting Deborah to know about him and Ellen meeting up. Explains the different number to contact him on. A cheap little pay-as-you-go for his liaisons."

"It's possible their meeting up again goes back further than last year," Ashok said. "Ten minutes before I came down with the phone, I was talking to someone at the Clifton hotel. The one Ellen used to go to at Christmas. They checked their records and gave me a list of people who'd been there for the same break as Ellen in 2016 and 2018. At first the names meant nothing, apart from Sexton's, then I remembered that Deborah's previous name was Balshaw. A Mr. and Mrs. D. Balshaw spent Christmas at the Clifton in 2018. I've sent the Cavendishes' picture to the woman I spoke to, although I'm not convinced she'll remember them and most of the other staff are on furlough. I hope she'll be able to ask around, though. I've also requested details of the card used to pay for the Balshaws' break."

"So, why didn't Sexton recognise them?" Naomi asked. "Surely it wasn't such a large group that he didn't run across them at the hotel."

Robin shut his eyes, exhaling furiously. Was losing the plot an early symptom of Covid? "Sorry, my fault. I never showed him their photo. Because he didn't recognise the names, it never occurred to me he might know them as somebody else."

"It's all three of our faults, sir," Ben said. "None of us thought to do that. For all we know, they used false Christian names at the hotel, as well. David and Dora or whatever."

Ashok made a note. "I'll get the hotel to check that too. Although the names they registered with may not have been the ones they used among the other guests."

Everyone was being kind to him regarding his mistake. Either because he didn't haul them up over their own oversights—unless they were completely stupid ones—or because they felt concerned for him.

"I'll get the picture to Sexton as soon as we finish. Do we have one of Carey we could share with him while we're at it?" Ben asked.

"I'll rustle one up off Carey's Facebook," Pru said. "Naomi and I perused it earlier, in case he'd made the mistake of putting up pictures of his holiday. He hadn't." She turned to Robin. "Carey being involved would potentially tie up a lot of loose ends, wouldn't it? He'd know about bin-collection days, likely saw that convenient skip when he went running locally, and possibly knew which bin-cleaning company serviced the Ramparts area. Most damning, he could have gone in and out of Ellen's house without much chance of being seen. Especially if he simply slipped out of their back gate and into her garden. In the event of him being spotted and challenged, he could play the 'I was worried about her welfare because she'd not been seen around' card. Then he and whoever challenged him could *happen* to find the body. He'd also have an excuse if there was forensic evidence of his presence. He dropped in to pick her brains about his accounts, and he swears she was still alive when he left her."

"Agreed on all points." Did it feel a touch too convenient, though?

"You've clearly got your doubts, sir," Pru said. "It's written on your face."

"You know me too well. I couldn't say why I'm dubious, though. On the face of things, it fits my favourite 'most at risk from your friends and family' theory." Robin shrugged. Why should he feel such uncertainty? Perhaps it was a matter of coping with the great leap that had happened with the case, their going from having no clarity on motives or opportunity to having two separate viable strands to investigate. Or perhaps it was the worry about Adam that kept nagging quietly in the back of his mind. There was nothing as unsettling as uncertainty, and the sooner they had the test result, the better. He took a deep breath and gave the team a smile. "Ignore me. Go and give Alex Carey your kindest third degree."

Carey arrived for his interview promptly at six o'clock. He was tall, lean, and gave the impression of wiry strength. Perhaps the build of a typical middle- or long-distance runner, which accorded with what his wife had said about him liking to keep fit. The musky scent of whatever aftershave of cologne he wore was strong, although not unpleasant, and must have been the aroma Robin had detected in number thirty-seven.

Carey didn't like it when Ben made it clear they'd be taking notes of the interview, although Robin smoothed things over by saying that such a process protected both parties. There could be no dispute about what had or hadn't been said. He reminded Carey that he wasn't under caution and that they were routinely checking facts in the light of new information received.

"But I've already told your officers everything I know about Ellen's movements over the last few months," Carey said, drumming his fingers on the table of the interview room.

"You've not told us about your own movements, though. The Isle of Wight."

"Oh, is *that* what this is about?" Carey crossed his arms defensively, although he appeared instantly less tense. "Okay, we broke the rules, but the kids were going stir-crazy, cooped up at home and not seeing their grandparents."

"Plenty of people are in the same boat, and they haven't done what they shouldn't. Anyway, that's a matter for another day and another officer. It's not why I called you in. I've got a murder to deal with."

Carey's shoulders tensed again, suggesting he was back on the defensive. "Alex and I have told you all we know. Isn't it obvious now why we wouldn't have noticed much about what's been going on next door?"

"When did you get back from the Isle of Wight?" Ben asked.

"On the fifth of January. Why?"

The constable ignored the question. "What were you doing on the following Monday, the eleventh?"

"What I've been doing the last few Mondays: helping Alex with the kids and their schoolwork while I try to do my job. Actually, that Monday I'd have been doing it all on my own because Alex was still away helping to care for her mother." Carey's aggressive reply suggested he was squeezing as much of the truth as he could manage into his answer. *Bamboozle the coppers with facts and hope they don't probe the bits in between.*

Robin, who'd heard similar testimony innumerable times, was certain Carey *had* done all those things, but was the list exhaustive? Carey didn't strike him as a stupid man, and if he *was* involved in defrauding either the charity or its donors, then he was executing the con in a very clever way. Ellen's notes gave him that amount of credit. So, he must surely have come to the interview ready with what he was prepared to admit and what he'd want to hide. "Did you see Ellen at all that day?"

"If I had, wouldn't I have told you?"

"Answer the question, please. Did you see her?"

"I think she'd already put her black bin out when I hauled mine onto the path." Carey avoided Robin's gaze, concentrating on the door.

Robin closed his eyes, shook his head, and said, "If you keep evading the direct question, you're going to make us more suspicious than we already are. If you've got nothing to hide, then the truth can't hurt you."

"I saw her that morning," Carey conceded. "I'd gone out for a run, quite early and when I got back, she was cleaning the inside of her upstairs windows. It was one of my usual routes, finishing with coming up the path from town that leads to the open area opposite us, then across the grass to get home. I shouldn't have done the last bit, because I got my trainers covered in dirt. Ellen must have seen me go splashing in a big puddle of mud, because she was killing herself laughing. Sorry, poor choice of words."

"Did you tell my officer that when they took your statement?" Robin was pretty sure it had been Naomi who'd spoken to the man and doubted that she'd not have pressed him about it.

"I don't think so, because I've literally just remembered while you've been questioning me." Carey, tight-lipped, didn't seem likely to budge on that point.

"Tell us about I Shall Not Want," Ben said.

The question's impact on Carey was like something from a silent film. He turned white, opening his mouth, then clamping it shut again. The silence in the room—one of Robin's favourite tactics for getting an answer—prolonged itself, to the point he must have felt compelled to respond. "They're a charity. A bloody good one, doing a lot of much-needed work. Particularly needed at the moment, when kids are stuck at home instead of in school. Not everyone has an iPad or internet access."

Robin couldn't resist saying, "That may be so, and I applaud those who are giving that practical help. Some might say that not every school has been pulling its weight."

"Indeed not." Carey, relaxing slightly, launched into a diatribe against his children's own school, which had been far too reliant on worksheets rather than online lessons during the first lockdown.

Robin allowed him a couple of minutes ranting and the lowering of defences it might produce, before launching in with, "When you look at the charity's accounts, there doesn't appear to be a lot going out compared to what's coming in. Not going out in the right direction, anyway."

Carey waved the question away, although it seemed to have riled him. "You have no idea what overheads are like these days. Office rent, salaries of full-time staff—because we can't run with volunteers alone. Costs of PPE for one thing."

Robin noted the *we*, how Carey was automatically aligning himself with the charity. And, again, there was a hint of relief that he was being asked about this rather than anything else.

"But these discrepancies were happening before the pandemic," Ben pointed out. "There must be at least three years of a disparity between income and legitimate outgoings."

"Where are you getting this from? Sounds like a load of cobblers. Why is somebody trying to make trouble for an organisation that's doing so much good?"

Robin always appreciated hearing a suspect fall back on what he thought of as "the Lance Armstrong defence": accusing other people of telling lies about you and causing trouble for somebody who had done nothing wrong. On most occasions it meant said suspect was guilty as sin.

Ben produced a sheet of paper from the file he'd brought with him. "Charity accounts are available to the public. These are the ones for 2018 to 2019, and they make interesting reading alongside your annual report. Especially interesting when you start to pick them apart and realise the level of so-called expenses given to a select number of volunteers at the charity. Like yourself."

"All those expenses are entirely legitimate."

"I wonder if your supporters would think that once this hits the news?" Ben said. "Those annual reports are at best misleading."

Carey pointed at the papers, evidently reluctant to touch them, as though that might in itself incriminate him. "Is this your work?"

"No. It's Ellen Wilkins's research. It seems like she was on the verge of handing it all over to both the police and the charity commission. Her murder prevented her."

The implication of Ben's words clearly hit home. "I didn't kill her," Carey blustered. "I've done nothing wrong. Are you going to charge me with false accounting? Go ahead and do it, then we can fight it out in court."

"That's not going to be my team's case," Robin said calmly, collecting the papers together, to illustrate that they may have served their purpose during this interview. "That's a specialist crime, so we'll be turning everything over to the proper department, and they can pursue it. I'm interested because this gives you—and anyone else who's been fiddling the charity funds—a motive for silencing Ellen Wilkins. You live next door, so you have one of the other parts of the famous trio, as well. Opportunity. Not only do you have a grandstand seat to see who's entering or leaving her house, you're the person who can most easily enter it yourself."

"I didn't kill her," Carey reiterated.

"Did you know that she was investigating you? Is that why she said she couldn't help you with your last tax return?"

"No and no. She told me she was too busy. Why should I think any different?" Carey shook his head. "Maybe that was it; I don't know. She might have had suspicions—unfounded ones—which could mean she didn't want to be dragged in. Perhaps that's why it felt like she was avoiding us."

That part sounded true, unlike much of what Carey had said.

"Right. I'm going to get my constable to caution you with regard to the fraud allegations." That might not be Robin's area of expertise, but a quick phone call earlier to his mate Henry, in fraud, had assured him they'd collected enough evidence to launch an investigation. Especially as Henry had already heard unsubstantiated rumours about some Kinechester charities and had a feeling they could be opening a proper can of worms. Ben had been busy sending all of Ellen's relevant files across since this part of the story broke. "You'll be asked to make a statement about that by the officers handling that case." He sat back while Ben issued the caution, before resuming. "So, returning to Ellen. I'm going to ask you again to tell me the truth. Was the last time you saw her *really* when you were coming home from your run?"

"Yes. I swear." Something seemed to have changed in Carey's attitude, though. Robin's long experience made him ninety percent certain of that fact given the flicker of resolution in the witness's eyes, which usually preceded a revelation, great or small. "Okay, I should have told your officer this when she took my statement but I'd forgotten, simple as. When I was getting my bins in that Monday, I thought I heard voices coming from Ellen's garden. It would have been about seven o'clock, give or take a bit either side."

How convenient to have "remembered" that now, when they'd identified a motive for him to kill her. "Why the hell didn't you mention that earlier? Can you see how suspicious it appears?"

"Of course I can. It's a hell of a shock, discovering you've been living next door to a dead body. So, a couple of days after I made my statement, when I remembered hearing those voices, I thought exactly what you've said. That it would look bad for me." Carey put his head in his hands. "Alex told me I should give you a ring but, like a total pillock, I persuaded myself that it wouldn't be any help to you. I could never have identified who was speaking, and anyway, it might have been coming from Trevor and Don's garden. They sit out there in all weathers, with their chimenea going."

As an explanation, it landed slightly on the right side of believable—people did end up not mentioning something because time had elapsed. The longer they didn't speak up, the harder it became to break the silence. Still, Robin found it hard to keep the sarcasm out of his voice. "Tell us about these people you heard. And anything else you've conveniently forgotten about."

"One was male, definitely. Quite a deep voice, like Trevor's. The other may have been a woman. I didn't hear it enough to be sure."

"Doesn't that argue against it being Trevor and Don?" Robin pointed out.

"Gay men *do* have female visitors. I think Trevor's sister might bubble with them. She's divorced."

Robin pressed on. "Did you hear what they were talking about? Were there any other noises?"

Carey shrugged. "No details of the conversation that I can recall, so neither of them could have mentioned a dead body or I'd have been on the alert. I may have heard a bin lid slamming down, but I won't swear to that. I might be retrospectively putting it into my memory."

Robin had known witnesses to do that too, sometimes in a genuine attempt to be helpful. Ben had asked him about dustbins, what seemed like weeks ago now, so Carey would be aware that they were on the police radar. "Anything else you can tell us about that day? Cars parked nearby that aren't any of the usual ones, for example? The more helpful you can be, the likelier it'll help you regarding the other charge you're going to be facing."

"Don't you think I know that already? I can't make up stuff just to please you."

"I wouldn't expect you to." This was going nowhere fast. They'd reached an impasse, the lack of concrete evidence linking Carey to the murder giving them no lever to get to the truth with. In a last-ditch effort to make progress, Robin produced the picture of the Cavendishes that he'd been touting about. "Have you seen this couple before?"

The effect on Carey was electric. Literally, given the way he started in his chair, before making a noticeable effort to compose his face. "I think I've seen them around, yes. I don't believe they live in Cromwell Road."

"But you've seen them there?" Ben asked.

"I believe so. I couldn't tell you when."

Obviously Carey had recognised the couple, and Robin would bet that it wasn't from having seen them lurking outside. He must have particular cause to remember them. Surely this was a case of playing the *What am I supposed to have seen and when?* game. "You know them from somewhere else, though. Is it through your charity?"

Rarely had a shot in the dark produced such a good result. Carey slumped back in his seat. "How the hell did you know that? Are they named on that stuff?" He jabbed a finger at the accounts.

"He's been on Ellen's radar, same as you." If she'd made the same connection between this pair, though, why hadn't Ben found it? Everything he'd turned up in the files about Derek Cavendish related to a possible resumption of the man's old wrongdoings. "Tell us in your own words."

"Deborah Cavendish used to hold fundraising events for us. Pre-Covid times. Big, glitzy things."

"Did she do that under her married name?" Ben's tone wasn't his usual confident one. Something had unsettled him.

"No. She wanted to retain some anonymity, she said. No virtue signalling. Not that I believed that for one moment, because she's too fond of playing Lady Bountiful." Carey sniffed. "Anyway, in the annual report, where we list supporters, I think we always used her previous name."

"Balshaw?" Ben asked, voice still a touch shaky.

"Yes. Like the rugby player."

"So, when you 'saw them around'"—Robin made a quotation-mark gesture—"was that in Cromwell Road? We have another witness who puts them there."

Carey nodded.

"Had they come to visit *you*?"

"Yes. But it wasn't on the eleventh, if that's what you're thinking. It was the fourteenth because that's my parents' wedding anniversary and I told Deborah if she wanted to see me, it had to be late morning because I was seeing them in the afternoon. And no, we weren't having an illegal party with Mum and Dad, only a chat with tea and cakes over Zoom. Alex had recently got back, so even if we'd wanted to nip up there, which we didn't, she was too tired." As with earlier in the interview, Carey was giving as much detail of what was probably the truth as he could afford to.

"What was so urgent that she insisted on meeting you?"

"She was getting twitchy about her past fundraising events. Wanted me to help her cover her trail." Carey sat forward. "I'm not going to pretend that things are all as they should be at the charity. I've been working hard myself to get people to act in a way that will bear scrutiny."

Robin and Ben shared a knowing glance. Had Carey realised at last that the police weren't going to stop digging into the charity's business until they knew exactly what had gone on? If so, it would be in his interest to start presenting himself as the voice of reason and to sell his fellow swindlers down the river.

Robin asked, "Are you saying that Deborah Cavendish's actions are among those that wouldn't bear scrutiny?"

"You could say so. There was a disparity four or five years back between the money she'd apparently raised, with her ticket charges and raffle proceeds, and the money which got sent to the charity. Hostess's expenses that were probably exaggerated. A possible mismatch between the reports of what was raised and the reality. Everything hidden away in some carefully presented figures." Carey sighed. "Nobody challenged her, so it carried on."

"With the connivance of those running the charity and handling its accounting?"

"Yes, Mr. Bright. I admit it's all a bloody mess, but my involvement is at the milder end, I swear."

"We'll wait for the official verdict on that, shall we?" Robin picked up the photograph. "This pair were in Kinechester on the eleventh, looking at a car for sale which they were supposedly interested in. We suspect they had other business too. You say they didn't call on you, so can you tell us what they were up to?"

Carey shook his head. "I have no idea. They didn't mention they'd been up here only a few days before. Are you thinking they'd been to see Ellen?"

"Why not? Did you know that she'd been friendly with Derek Cavendish years ago?" Ben asked. "That she was crucial in getting him sent to jail?"

"Bloody hell." If Carey had already been aware of the fact, he was putting on a damned good act. "She never told me. What was he in for?"

"Dating fraud. Obtaining money by false pretences from innocent women. He's been sent down for it twice. She was trying to find out if he was at it a third time."

"With that dragon of a wife on his case? He wouldn't dare." Carey paused, brow creased in thought. "Unless she knew about it, egging him on in order to get a share of the proceeds. When they visited me, she made some remark about how the last year had been a challenge and needing to find different sources of income. He changed the subject, and I assumed it was because he didn't like her implying that the charity dos had provided a nice little earner for them."

Robin made a note, one of many he'd generated during this discussion. He was going to have plenty to brief Ashok with the next morning on the way to what increasingly appeared to be a crucial interview. "Mr. Carey, I think we'll leave it there. We *do* need to take your fingerprints. I won't say it's mainly for elimination purposes because we both know my team will be scrutinising them against all the significant prints we've lifted from Ellen's house." Not that there were many of those, but Carey wouldn't know that. "One final question, and you'll need to bear with it, because it does make sense. Does your family eat turnips?"

"Turnips?" Wide-eyed, Carey shook his head. "I can't stand the things. My grandfather grew them in his garden and inflicted them on us every time we went there for Sunday lunch. I think Ellen liked them, though. You'd need to ask Alex. We get one of these fruit and veg delivery services, and sometimes it has stuff in we're not keen on. I can remember last summer we gave her a couple of turnips, because she made the inevitable *Blackadder* and Baldrick comments about them."

"Thanks." Maybe, just maybe, Ellen had been about to prepare a turnip, large knife in hand, when she'd got into an argument with her killer. Had only a few minutes previously cut off any sprouting tops with her kitchen scissors. Which, if they existed, weren't now in the kitchen.

Robin gathered all his papers together. "Ben, could you get a uniformed officer to take Mr. Carey to be fingerprinted?"

"I'll do that now."

When Ben had left the room, Carey said, "If I promise to give you all the assistance I can, will it help my situation?"

"With the fraud case, probably. If it turns out you killed Ellen Wilkins, then it'll be irrelevant how much help you've been about other people cooking the books. You've got yourself into murky waters, not being honest with us from the start."

"Don't I know that?" Carey put his head in his hands again, where it remained until Ben returned with one of the duty officers.

Almost as soon as the door shut behind Carey, Ben said, "I'm *so* sorry, sir. I scanned the annual reports for I Shall Not Want and I saw a mention of a Ms.—not Mrs.—Balshaw who'd fundraised for them over several years, up to 2019, but I never made the connection."

"No harm done. We're all tired and all making mistakes." How many was Robin making? "We can probe the links tomorrow, unless Henry's beaten us to it."

"Do you think that likely?"

"I wouldn't be surprised. He's always been a workaholic, and he was like a dog with two tails when he heard we had solid evidence for him. I'm guessing this is the tip of some iceberg he's been waiting to ram." Robin checked his phone, not solely for work matters. "No news from Pru yet, so it doesn't seem like she's found out anything as significant as we have. I hope she'll have the sense to go home before reporting in." He stifled a yawn. "We need to be heading off too. My brain's got to the point where it's ceasing to function as efficiently as it should. I can't decide if Greg Carey's a believable liar or an honest but fallible man. Only time will tell."

"Are you all right, sir?" Ben asked. "You don't quite seem yourself. Not like you to be always reaching for your phone and then stopping."

Had he been doing that? "I'm okay." Robin spoke the lie automatically, before remembering that his constable would know him too well to believe that. "A touch worried about Adam, that's all. Part of my mind keeps coming back to how we'll organise things here and at home, if he and I have to isolate ourselves for a fortnight or however long it is."

"We'll all cope, we'll have to." Ben nodded. "It'll be better when he's got the test result back."

"You're telling me." Come to think of it, wasn't Ben's chair farther away from his than when they'd started the interview? They'd been properly socially distanced then, but now it might be called socially remote. Had Ben been edging away, suspecting something wasn't right with Robin medically? If so, Robin couldn't blame him.

Adam's test result was due the next day; what with that and the interview with Derek and Deborah Cavendish, it could end up being quite a Wednesday.

Chapter Twelve

Adam woke, aware of two things. That the large canine lump that had been on the sofa with him was no longer present and that someone was coming through the front door. Given that Campbell wasn't barking furiously, the person must be Robin, rather than a burglar, although he could never tell with that dog. There'd been one occasion at their previous house when Campbell had quite happily sat in the garden alongside a gun-toting intruder, although in that instance his assessment of character had proven to be fairly accurate.

"How are we doing?" Robin asked, as he came in the room and then halted, a good couple of metres away.

"Tired, mainly, which is why I've been having a kip. Not developed a cough or a temperature, yet, but I've got a bit of a headache. All in all, I really don't feel well." Adam hated sounding so whiny, probably more than he hated being ill. "How are you?"

"Not feeling great, although I can't decide if that's mainly tiredness and stress from late nights and working all weekend or psychologically induced. What my mum would call 'coming out in sympathy' with you. I guess we won't know until you get your test result. Shall I nip to the chippy? I can't face making a proper dinner, and sandwiches don't appeal."

"No need. Kate had today's catering already planned, so she brought us some salad when she came to exercise his lordship, and you can have that with the pizza I defrosted. I'll get it on now." Adam pushed himself out of the comfy nest he'd made, heading for the kitchen. "She's offered to get in groceries or cook meals for us and bring them round if we both end up flat on our backs. I said how grateful I was and asked her to be on standby."

"You *must* be feeling off colour."

Indeed. Neither of them ever wanted to feel they were imposing on someone else's goodwill. "Well, as *my* mum would say, I'm not at my Mae West. I compensated for my guilt by making Kate promise to let us settle up for anything she bought, as I don't want her being out of pocket. I also said she was doing us a favour as, if it did turn out that I've got the rona, she's younger than our mothers and it's safer for her to drop stuff off than either of them. Not that I'd tell *them* I'd said that."

"You'd end up feeling worse than you do now. That's fighting talk, and I bet they're both handy with a rolling pin." Robin suddenly shuddered.

"Are you all right?"

"You're the second person who's asked me that in the last few hours. I must look like I'm at death's door."

"A bit, although no different than after any hard day's work." Adam gave him a smile. "You shivered, that was all."

"Association of ideas. You in the kitchen making dinner and me making jokes about a rolling pin used as a weapon. I've a feeling our victim was killed with her own knife while she was preparing her own meal." Robin's phone ringing cut off conversation, as so often when a case was in progress. "Pru," he said, before moving into the hall to answer the call.

Adam hoped this wouldn't turn out to be bad news that would mean Robin having to go into work again. Usually he wasn't so selfish but despite his husband's explanation about why he'd shuddered—which didn't appear to be the whole truth—the bloke *did* appear off colour. He no doubt needed a good night's sleep and maybe a later start in the morning.

By the time the call had finished, the food was ready, so Adam put cutlery and plates on the lap trays Aunt Clare had given them as a house-warming present and encouraged Robin into the lounge, where he could get stuck into his dinner while sitting comfortably. Albeit at a distance.

"Want to talk about your day?" Adam said, once Robin had got a hefty amount of his meal inside him. "Opportunity, not obligation, as they say."

Robin raised an eyebrow. "Do you really want to hear about it? On top of feeling grotty?"

"Of course I do. I'm already bored, so I'm up for anything that's not Netflix or the Puzzle Page app."

Robin gave a wince of sympathy. "I wouldn't mind, actually. You know it helps me to see things clearer. And it'll be better than having them whizzing round my head. Not till I've finished this, though."

Once the meal was done, Adam took the trays to the kitchen— no point in leading Campbell into the doggy temptation of surreptitiously licking the plates. He brought them both back a cuppa, then put his feet up on his own sofa, matching Robin's relaxed position on the other one. Talking would also have the advantage of helping to keep the bloke awake: if Robin dozed off on a full stomach, he always woke up groggy and irritated.

"We've gone in one bound from having no tangible leads and plenty of unexplained facts, to having two credible threads to follow." Robin frowned. "At least, that's how it appeared until about half past six this evening."

"What changed?"

"We spoke to someone whom Ellen was about to shop to us. I'd better rewind. When we got into Ellen's computer files, we discovered that she's been doing research for pleasure—I think you'd call it that— as well as for work. She put together a dossier about her next-door neighbour, who's almost certainly been involved in charity fraud."

"Not the fragrant Trevor?" That would put the tin lid on a grotty day. Adam had already got cross at a television drama where the murderer had turned out to be the only gay suspect, which was a cliché he'd hoped was long gone, alongside the once-inevitable killing off of any gay or lesbian characters.

"Nope. Greg Carey, one half of the lockdown breakers on the other side. I saw him while Pru was talking to his wife. At first she denied all knowledge of him doing anything dodgy. Swore they're not that kind of a couple. That got punctured as soon as Pru reminded her we knew the full extent to which they'd been breaking lockdown. After that, she was all tears and apologies again and giving a dozen reasons why it was okay for them to do it."

"I can imagine." Adam had heard it all before, the innumerable excuses about why it was perfectly safe for somebody to do what they were doing, despite it not being allowed.

"At the end of it, she was still sticking to her story that she knew nothing about what her husband was doing with the charity. Her only involvement, she swore, was helping to source books and other presents to give out at Christmas."

"So long as my new mate Trevor's in the clear."

"He is. He and his partner are on the nice list, because Don's given us half of the other lead. He saw the Cavendishes—the couple I went to see in Portsmouth on Sunday—near the victim's house, sometime during the last few weeks. Which, of course, they didn't tell me about. Turns out *he's* one of Don's patients." Robin took a sip of tea. "If Don's like Trevor, he'll make a good witness. I can't imagine a defence counsel getting under their skin."

Adam agreed. He also, albeit based on what he'd heard about Mr. and Mrs. Cavendish, wasn't surprised that they mightn't have been telling the truth. "Do you think they were calling on Ellen the day she was killed?"

"I had that in mind until this evening, when it turned out my two leads might cancel each other out. Carey admitted that the Cavendishes had been to see him, because Mrs. C. is also up to her eyeballs in siphoning off funds. So that might have been when Don saw them and, according to Carey, that wasn't on the day of the murder. I can't see why he would lie about the day, especially as it would be to his advantage to be able to point the finger elsewhere."

"Unless they're colluding," Adam pointed out. "He alibis them for when they've actually come to Cromwell Road to dick about with those blinds."

"I was thinking about that on the way home, but I'm not sure what he would get out of it." Robin rubbed his head. "I was pretty confident that all Ellen was investigating Cavendish for was a possible resumption of his old dating-fraud business, but now I wonder if it went further. It certainly appears that he and she had been back in communication, maybe as a result of them meeting up again at one of her Christmas hotel trips. Whether that meeting was accidental or planned, I don't know. Maybe there was a touch of hanky-panky thrown in, given that the messages could be read as flirtatious."

"Flirtatious?"

"Him calling her a cheeky little monkey. Her saying he'd be getting his legs slapped if he wasn't careful. Sort of thing that if a bloke said to me, I'd be giving him the whole 'Nay, Sir Jasper, I'm a married man' bit." Robin chuckled. "I need to interview Cavendish on his own to try and get some clarity on all of this. I doubt he'll be completely honest in front of the wife."

"What's he got that all these women fall for him, some of them knowing his record? Is he a silver fox?"

"If he is, I don't see it." Robin shook his head. "I can understand Ellen perhaps wanting to get close to him in order to gather the information she needed to report him to us again, but why Deborah married him when she'd been one of his victims beats me."

"Love's blind. Or maybe she wants a bloke she can control completely—you know, if he misbehaves, she can dob him in to the police, so he has to be at her beck and call." Adam wrinkled his nose. "Nah, that sounds too far-fetched. Like something out of a bad film."

"You say that, but I've met them and came away with the impression that he wanted us to have her fingerprints, which is why he set up the palaver with the paper that I told you about. That's how we knew she had a police record, although we've not found her prints at the murder scene. Not yet, anyway. He might have known there was a chance they were there, though. If she confronted Ellen and killed her."

"Which would mean a custodial sentence and Derek would be free. Free of his wife, at least. Here, when did Ellen start investigating this charity business? Could he have given her the tip off?"

"Genius boy." Robin gave Adam the thumbs-up. Not as good as a hug or even a fist bump, but Adam knew that was the best they could do. "One step ahead of the rozzers again. That's a great theory, because Derek would know from bitter experience how efficient she was at finding the truth, and it would make a better explanation of why she kept in touch with him. He might have offered the information as a sop for having tried to con her the first time."

"She saw through him, then, if she still thought he was up to his old tricks. Had she found any evidence for that, by the way?"

"Nothing concrete, according to Ben, other than Derek having adopted a new persona online which he was using to chat up women. He'd not yet got any dosh from them, as far as she could tell. Not the ones she'd spoken to, anyway." Robin yawned and stretched. "We'll find out more tomorrow. Assuming my mate Henry from fraud and I don't end up tripping over each other's feet."

"Henry? Thin bloke, glasses, fit in a David Tennant-doctor way?" Adam had been introduced to the officer one day the previous summer, when they'd bumped into him while walking along one of the local towpaths.

"I knew you'd remember him." Robin snickered. "According to Pru, he arrived with a search warrant when she was leaving the Careys' house, wanting to locate anything to do with the fraud case before they had the chance to shred or burn it."

"Ooh. Curtains will have been twitching all up and down the road. The Ramparts are turning into East Enders. I'm glad we didn't move there. Hotbed of crime." Adam rubbed his head, which was starting to hurt again, as was his left shoulder, perhaps from where he'd been lying asleep on the sofa. "Henry's quick out of the blocks. I thought these fraud cases took forever?"

"Putting the evidence together and getting it through court, yes, but Henry's like Usain Bolt once he gets on the trail. Like Campbell in pursuit of a biscuit." Robin eased off the sofa. "I'm heading to bed. Got a headache brewing and I hope it's nothing more. I'll wash up in the morning before I leave."

"You will not. I'll load the dishwasher now and handle the rest tomorrow. I need to stave off the boredom."

"Are you sure?" From Robin's tone and the concerned expression he couldn't hide, he must have been worried.

"I'm not at death's door yet. Off you go. I can have a lie-in tomorrow."

Not that Adam thought he'd get much of one, or even a half-decent night's sleep, given how grotty he felt.

His prediction proved correct. Not really able to settle, Adam dozed fitfully until half past one, at which point he gave up trying and headed downstairs, where he could stretch out on the sofa and watch an old war film. One he knew so well that it wouldn't matter if he did get some kip halfway through it.

In the morning, while he couldn't hide the fact he'd decamped to sleep in the lounge, Adam did put on a brave face about the state of his health. Robin had enough on his plate without worrying that Adam was feeling like death warmed up. Whether he actually convinced him there was nothing to worry about was a moot point, especially as Robin said that while his headache had cleared, he still had some muscle aches.

Once Robin had left for work and Campbell was settled with *his* breakfast, Adam had a quick once-over of a few websites about whether his symptoms matched with Covid but soon gave up. It seemed like almost anything might or might not be *it* and there was too great a risk of him seeing some other condition—inevitably extremely serious—that might explain how he felt.

He'd clean his teeth, in an effort to stop his mouth tasting how a wrestler's jockstrap might, then go back to bed and await his test result. All the while feeling sorry for himself and trying to forget his attempts at self-diagnosis.

Chapter Thirteen

The journey to Portsmouth didn't seem to take as long as it had previously, despite the traffic volume appearing similar. Robin supposed it was the well-known phenomenon of a first trip anywhere different always seeming to take forever. He couldn't shake off his concerns about Adam, who was as unwell as Robin had ever seen him, definitely worse this morning than he'd been the previous day, although Ashok's chirpy presence helped focus his mind elsewhere. The constable wore his emotions on his face, specifically the bit that could be seen above his mask, which went through a pantomime of expressions as Robin brought him up-to-date with the revelations from Carey's interview. Revelations that Ben would be sharing with the rest of the team around the same time, probably.

Denness was going to be present too, wanting to get a handle on the details, Robin only having given him the headlines so far. And that had been on Tuesday evening, when Robin had been at his least coherent. Fronting a briefing might be a daunting prospect for Ben, but it would do him no harm to gain some experience of speaking in front of superior officers.

"I'm a rookie in terms of murder cases, sir," Ashok said when Robin had concluded. "Do you often run across coincidences like this? Carey knowing the Cavendishes and Ellen investigating them both at the same time but for different things?"

"We don't know for certain she hadn't already made the connection between the two lots of people. Or had the connection made for her, if it came from Derek Cavendish. Just because there's nothing about Deborah in her files—that we're aware of yet, anyway—doesn't mean it wasn't in Ellen's head."

"It didn't have to be Derek snitching on Deborah. Ellen might have seen the pair with Carey and it started to make her suspicious, knowing Derek's track record, albeit for a different variety of fraud."

"Possibly. Or she was quicker than we were at making the link to the name Balshaw in the annual report, and it was *that* which got her thinking. As for coincidences, I've seen some that if they featured in a telly programme you'd be shouting at the screen about it being an unbelievable storyline. It's a cliché that it's a small world, but like many clichés, it's true." Robin noted the constable's expression, one screaming that he had an idea. "Have you got another theory?"

"I don't know, sir. My thinking's been more along the lines of how Carey lived next-door to her and was involved in the same organisation as her old adversary's wife. Could there be a connection there? I can't imagine a situation where she would have been willing to introduce him to them."

"Exactly. Ben says Carey and Deborah Cavendish have both been involved with the charity for years, since before she married Derek, so that must surely predate Ellen's path crossing Derek's again, given the dating of those messages between them."

"It has to go back at least to 2018. It probably *was* the Cavendishes at the hotel using the name Balshaw. My contact there is only eighty percent sure she recognised the couple in the photo, but the address they gave is the one we're going to right now, so unless somebody else was impersonating *them* . . ." Ashok shrugged.

"If they are, then I'm resigning. It's complicated enough." Complicated on the one hand, yet blindingly obvious on the other. As Adam pointed out, it would have been easy for the Cavendishes and Careys to be in cahoots, each with motive for silencing Ellen and each with the opportunity to do so. And yet it felt like there was a hole in the case. Maybe a turnip-shaped one—Robin pulled himself together, aware that he wasn't thinking clearly. "It could be pretty busy when we get to the Cavendishes' house. Henry's got a warrant to search the property, and depending how quickly he got his skates on this morning, he might have beaten us to it." The bloke had texted earlier to say thanks again for the information, which was a gold mine.

"He must know from experience there's a risk that evidence will have been destroyed if Carey's been having a word with the others. Doesn't he have the resources to visit them all at the same time?"

"Unfortunately not. We're not in county-lines territory."

"How late did he get away from Carey's if he was pitching up when Sergeant Davis left?"

"I dread to think. He said Carey arrived home while his officers were going through all his files and about to confiscate any tech they could locate. He got such a shock that Henry reckons he'll roll over like a puppy. Couldn't do enough to help them last night, apparently. He'll be trying to reduce his sentence."

"There'll probably be a rush to throw each other under the bus. I don't know much about fraud, but I can't believe Greg Carey and Deborah Cavendish were acting without anyone else helping to cover things up." Ashok negotiated a tricky bit of overtaking, getting past a meandering lorry where the dual carriageway was particularly wide and straight. "That thing about the hotel, sir. Have we heard yet from Jeremy Sexton whether he recognised them as being there when he and Ellen were?"

"Yes, I got a text from Ben about it last evening. Don't get excited because it's a resounding 'maybe.' Jeremy thinks there were thirty or forty guests present, and he only really remembers the ones he saw a lot of, which he doesn't think was this pair. On the other hand, he can't swear that they weren't there, although he thinks he'd have remembered such a platinum blonde."

"It might have been how they got his phone number, though. If they engineered access to the hotel records."

"I suppose that's possible. One of them may have exercised his or her charms on the person manning the reception desk." Possible but not at all likely. Very few places had an old-fashioned signing-in book. "That would suggest they had suspicions about him two years ago, which—as far as we know—predates any investigation into the charity."

"You're right." Poor Ashok. Disappointment writ large all over his face. "Fast forward to 2020, then. For whatever reason, Ellen becomes unhappy about I Shall Not Want's activities. Starts to dig. Derek Cavendish has either been the catalyst or finds out anyway, because Ellen mentions it to him, not realising that his wife's involved."

"Why should she do that?" Robin asked. "Why trust him?"

Disappointment turned to devastation. Still, Ashok fought his corner. "Bear with me, sir. I know it's unlikely, but we've both come across people who do things that don't bear logical scrutiny. Especially if they're tanked up or in bed."

"Okay. We'll assume this long shot applies and Ellen let her guard slip. Carry on."

"Derek knows, because Ellen's also spoken—off her guard—about her 'official' research, that she's working in tandem with Jeremy. Derek spills the beans to Deborah, who suspects that the pair of them are investigating the fraud. Or both frauds. Is it always this confusing with a murder case?"

"Sometimes." Life was itself confusing; people weren't straightforward and they got themselves into terrible muddles. Still, spilling the beans to an old adversary didn't sound like the sort of thing the Ellen they'd come to know would have done. "We start by asking about the Carey connection. Then we mention the hotel. Keep in our pockets the fact that Derek and Ellen had been in touch. We may need a grenade to drop in the pool."

When they arrived at the Cavendishes' house, it was clear that a grenade had already been dropped there, courtesy of a tired yet satisfied-looking Henry, who came out to meet them.

"Robin. Sorry to beat you to it but we're onto something big here and I needed to get my paws on the evidence before it went through the shredder or the hard drives got hammered." Henry pointed over his shoulder. "Possibly this is the tip of a nasty iceberg, linking to another couple of charities in other parts of the country. Your victim was several steps ahead of us."

"She was a smart woman. Shame she couldn't keep several steps ahead of her killer."

Henry lowered his voice, tipping his head towards the house. "One of that pair?"

"Not sure. If it isn't connected to them or to Greg Carey, then that's all my active leads wiped out." Robin surreptitiously crossed and uncrossed his fingers. Fate not to be tempted. "Have you questioned them yet?"

"No. I was hoping I could sit in with you while we cover joint ground. Then maybe we could get them apart and compare notes afterwards? I've cautioned them over the fraud charge."

"Sounds like a plan. I suspect mister may have things to tell us that he doesn't want missus to hear."

The atmosphere in the house would have taken an electric saw to cut through. Deborah shot Robin a deathly glance as he came into the conservatory, where the pair had been asked to wait, although Derek merely appeared sheepish.

Robin began by saying they'd been seen in Cromwell Road and asked what they'd been doing there. He deliberately didn't mention a date.

"We went to see Greg Carey. I wanted his advice, professionally," Deborah said.

"When was this?"

"When was it, Derek? You've got the diary." Deborah drummed on the chair arm, immaculate fingernails beating an irritating tattoo.

"The fourteenth of January," Derek confirmed, after a glance in the diary. "Because it was annoying he couldn't see us on the eleventh, when we were visiting there anyway."

That would need following up: Carey had been adamant he had no knowledge of the previous visit.

"Maybe we weren't socially distanced, sitting in his house, but this was a matter of business, not socialising." Deborah went onto the front foot. "They're not the type of people we'd have as friends." The supercilious sneer might have been comical in other circumstances.

"Not likely to buy enough raffle tickets at your charity dinners? Which would mean less profit in your pockets?" Henry suggested.

"How dare you say such a thing. I don't have to sit and listen to this, do I, Derek?"

Before either of the policemen could assure her that she did, Derek said, "I think it's best we cooperate, dear. It will only appear suspicious if we don't."

"I'm not that interested in the details of what happened to the money you raised," Robin said. "That's my colleague's concern, and he'll be following up every single detail. Probably at the police station. I'm particularly interested in the fact that you were in the house next-door to where a murder had occurred, discussing a matter that the dead woman had been investigating, a dossier about which she was readying to present to us."

"The cow never could keep her nose out of other people's business." Deborah shook off her husband's hand. "No, Derek, I'm going to speak my mind. She's had it in for you for years, ever since she couldn't have you. She's a jealous troublemaker. *Was* a troublemaker."

"Is that why you threatened her colleague, Jeremy Sexton?"

The name took the wind out of Deborah's sails, but only for a moment. "Who?"

"The man you sent threatening messages from your mobile." Robin half expected her to say something like, *Derek, have you been using my phone?*

Instead, she crossed her arms with a curt "I have nothing to say about that."

"You'll have to answer the question at some point, Mrs. Cavendish, and were I you, I'd be thinking 'the sooner I did it, the better for me.'" Robin glanced at Henry. "You'll be accessing the phone records as part of your enquiry?"

"Absolutely. Those records don't lie, not like people do, and you'd be amazed what gets let slip in a text message."

Still no response from Deborah. Robin gave Ashok a nod.

The constable took his cue. "Christmas 2018. You both stayed at the Clifton Hotel, near Wimborne. Using an assumed name."

"Ah, technically it isn't quite an assumed name. Not in the sense of being plucked out of the air." Derek cleared his throat. "Deborah's previous husband was a Balshaw, so we sometimes use his name. My suggestion, because I'd hate anyone who knew about my previous life to see the name Cavendish and make a connection. Embarrassing for Deborah."

"Is that why you use the name Balshaw when you're doing your charity stuff? Covering the fact you have a prior association with fraudulent practices?" Henry raised his hand. "Sorry, we'll explore that later. Constable, the floor is yours."

"Thank you, sir. Both Ellen Wilkins and Jeremy Sexton were staying at the same hotel at the same time. Let's take him first, as we've mentioned the hostile messages." Ashok's tones grew harsher. "Did you spend time with him then?"

"There were lots of people staying at the hotel. We were hardly going to all become firm friends," Derek replied, not unpleasantly.

"Please answer the question."

"Yes, Constable, we did spend some time with him," Deborah suddenly chipped in. "We were put on the same table one evening for dinner. A dozen or so of us. He drank too much and made a pass at me. As you can imagine, I told him where to go. Obnoxious man."

Obnoxious wasn't a word Robin would have used to describe the Jeremy he had met, although he'd not seen him "with drink taken," which was what Granny Bright used to call *roaring drunk*. They certainly knew he had an eye for women and that might have been amplified by alcohol. If true, it could indicate that the man had lied to them when he said he didn't recognise the couple, although if he had been drunk, he might simply not remember that evening.

"So we return to the phone messages you sent him," Ashok said. "How did you get his number?"

"He insisted I have it. Said if I changed my mind about his suggestion, all I'd have to do was get in touch. Didn't he, Derek?" Deborah's appeal for confirmation didn't appear to be spontaneous. Part, perhaps, of an explanation planned in advance should these questions come up. As Henry had said, phone records didn't lie and would have to be accounted for. Robin could guess where this was all leading.

"Yes." Derek nodded, a touch too vigorously. "I told Deborah to keep it, in case he had somehow found *her* number and got in touch. So she'd know."

"Really?" Robin shook his head. "That beggars belief."

"It may beggar your belief, but it's true. And he *did* get in touch, although not until this Christmas just gone, so it was a good thing I kept a note of his number. He said he was sad not to be going to the Clifton again and how he wished that I was going to be there with him." Deborah rolled her eyes. "I didn't reply."

"How did he get your mobile number?" Robin asked. Pursuing the part about Jeremy's number would get them nowhere.

"He didn't. Not until I messaged him and told him to lay off."

Robin glanced at his colleagues, but they appeared as bewildered as he was. "I don't follow."

"He *emailed* me. He could have got that address easily enough, you see. One of the entertainers the hotel laid on was an excellent pianist, and I rather fancied seeing if he'd perform at one of my black-tie dos. He had a piece of paper where one could sign up for his mailing list."

A reasonably credible story. "How many emails did Sexton send? Did you keep any of them?"

"Of course not. I deleted them from my inbox and then from the trash." Deborah shuddered. "Invading my personal space."

"But you messaged him from your phone," Robin pointed out. "Isn't that more personal? Couldn't you have bought and used a cheap mobile if it was so important to you?"

"That would never have occurred to me—we don't all live in a world of burning phones or whatever they call them on the telly." Deborah snorted her contempt at the idea. "I'd planned to change my phone in the new year, so it seemed an ideal opportunity to contact him from it. I'd have got a new number with the new phone, and he'd have been unable to contact me on it. I'd have done that already had you not insisted I keep the number for the time being so you could keep in contact."

Again, plausible, especially as getting a new number may have avoided some awkward phone calls once the shite hit the fan about her charity work. "Constable Mankad, could you show a copy of those messages to Mrs. Cavendish, please?"

"Yes, sir." Ashok produced them from his file. "We don't have the first one and the second is how Sexton remembered the wording but the third is verbatim."

You'll regret it if you don't stop. Easy enough to get your address and send a friend around.

Outside of the interview room and in the setting of a domestic conservatory, the message read exactly like something copied from an eighties' television show.

"You sent these?" Robin asked.

"Yes. The second message isn't quite word for word but the gist is there." Deborah waved her hand. "I didn't really mean I'd send anyone round. Some people only get the point if you act tough. He stopped bothering me so it must have succeeded."

Robin glanced at Derek, but the man's blank expression suggested neither support nor denial of what his wife had said. No matter how long Robin's career had been, or how much experience he'd had within interviews, he still had to fight the entirely human inclination to trust the person he liked—Jeremy Sexton—and disbelieve the one he disliked. Who was sitting facing him now, drumming her nails on her chair arm. "When did you send the first one?"

"I-I don't know. Couldn't tell you the date off the top of my head, and I've deleted the message thread. Derek, can you remember?"

"No. You know what my memory's like." The feeble response fooled nobody.

"Let me tell you, then," Robin said with a smile. "The thirteenth of January, which is a long time after Christmas, if that's when he's supposed to have emailed you."

"It was after I decided to change my phone. Lots of good deals around," Deborah blustered.

"Was he still emailing you then, well into the new year? It'll come up when we access your account."

Deborah pressed her fingers to her forehead, clearly flustered. Was this one little part of their story they'd omitted to plan in advance or had they not accounted for how thorough an investigation would be? "No, he'd stopped. I suppose I was getting my own back. Hell hath no fury like a woman's scorn."

"The quote is 'a woman scorned,' actually," Henry said. "Only, you say you scorned him. Was it really a case of him rejecting your advances and you made it out to be the other way round to get your own back?"

If that was a bow drawn at a venture—to quote another often-misquoted phrase—it appeared to have come pretty close to the target. Whatever else was going on, the fleeting horror on Deborah's face and the guilty look she gave her husband suggested she'd at least considered a fling with Sexton.

Before she could regather her composure, Robin pressed on. "Irrespective of who wanted to seduce whom, what exactly did you mean by asking Sexton not to poke his nose into your business?

That doesn't read like it's a woman telling a man where to stick the unwanted pass he'd made at her. It *does* sound like warning off somebody who's investigating your dodgy fundraising."

"No. How dare you come into my house and tell a pack of lies."

"Mrs. Cavendish, Ellen Wilkins being murdered—probably on the eleventh of January—is a fact. We know she was investigating both you and Greg Carey for financial misconduct and that some of her files were taken." The police had no record of what should be in that filing cabinet so who knew if and what charity files were missing? "We also know, because you've admitted it, that you started sending threatening messages to her colleague on the thirteenth of January, the day before you went to see Carey himself. No lies anywhere. Not on our part, anyway. So, I study that sequence of events and ask myself if they're related. You or Carey discover she's been *poking her nose in* as you might put it. One of you kills her, deliberately or in an argument that turned violent. You all get involved in covering your tracks, including trying to scare off somebody else who may be investigating you. That's how it appears."

"It appears wrong, then." Deborah crossed her arms again.

Derek wasn't quite as defiant now, and had been squirming in his seat as Robin had laid out the theory. It was time to get this pair split up.

Henry clearly felt the same, suggesting that he take Deborah into another room, where he and one of his officers could concentrate on their case. "I know Detective Chief Inspector Bright has some further points he wants to discuss with you, Mr. Cavendish."

Derek appeared horrified at that prospect, although Deborah went quietly enough. Robin would have put a tenner on her old fire returning soon: Henry was going to be in for an interesting time.

"Now, Mr. Cavendish. I'm pleased we've got the chance to talk to you on your own. Can you tell me when you first got back in touch with Ellen Wilkins?"

Derek flashed a terrified glance in the direction his wife had gone. "She doesn't know, Deborah. She'd kill me if she found out." He put his hand over his mouth. "No, I didn't mean that. It's what you say, isn't it?"

"Although not everybody says that about someone who has a conviction for assault."

"I suppose not." Derek shut his eyes and took a deep breath before continuing. "Deborah's always had a temper, but she'd only attack me with words, not her fists. Make my life hell."

"Is that why you made sure we had her fingerprints? So we'd know she was the Deborah Balshaw who'd attacked her husband's mistress?"

Despite the situation, Derek suddenly appeared pleased with himself. "You realised I'd deliberately done that business with the sheet of paper? Deborah would never have admitted that to you, but I felt we had to be upfront."

Hardly upfront, messing around with fingerprints. Couldn't Derek have rung the station and tipped them the wink? Deborah surely didn't keep an eye on him every moment of the day or he wouldn't have had the opportunity of reacquainting himself with his old flame. "When did you first contact Ellen again?"

"At that hotel, although I didn't contact her." Derek rubbed his forehead. "This is coming out all wrong. Let's start years ago. The last time I'd seen her was when she was in court giving evidence against us. Imagine my shock when we turned up at the hotel and she was there. She'd hardly changed in appearance, apart from some grey hairs and wrinkles, although in terms of personality I'd say she'd mellowed. I expected her to blank me, but she didn't. She made a point of getting me on my own later that evening and saying that she wouldn't let slip who I was. That was a great relief."

"Did you see much of her over those few days?"

"Not really. We were at the same table for that one dinner, as Deborah told you."

"The one where Sexton made a pass at her?"

"Ye-es. Although I was the other side and it was a large group, so I wasn't aware of what had gone on at the time or I'd have said something." Maybe he hadn't been aware of it until they'd been getting their stories aligned over the past few days.

"Didn't Deborah react?" Ashok asked. "If my girlfriend had been in a similar situation, she'd have raised hell."

The question appeared to flummox Derek. Perhaps that detail hadn't been worked out in advance. Maybe a glimpse of the truth might emerge. "Well, now you come to mention it, I do recall her and him leaning quite close. So they could hear each other, I thought, because the room was getting rather noisy. Then she got a bit flustered at whatever he said."

"Did you sit next to Ellen at the dinner?" Ashok asked.

"Yes. It could have been rather awkward, but actually we found plenty to talk about."

"And you started messaging her not long after?"

"No. She got in touch with me the following Christmas, wishing us both the compliments of the season. I'd given her my number, you see. To prove that I'd gone straight, or whatever it is you want to call it."

Robin would have called it bullshit, although he could understand why Ellen might have been happy to have a number for him if she believed he was likely to start up his dating scams a third time. All the better to investigate him, perhaps.

Ashok continued his questioning, tone polite but serious. "What did you talk about?"

"Oh, this and that. Just chatting, as you do. She was a very clever woman, the sort who could hold a conversation about anything. We both liked puzzles. The logic type, like this." Derek reached under the coffee table, fetching out a book.

The GCHQ Puzzle Book. Robin and Adam had flicked through that the Christmas before last, trying to find a present for Aunt Clare. He remembered, because it had appeared scarily challenging. The thought of Adam made him itch to look at his phone. How was Adam doing and had he received the result of the test yet? Resisting the temptation to get the thing out, Robin concentrated on the interview. "I take my hat off to you if you can solve these."

"I try my best. Ellen used to give me clues. I miss that."

It hardly seemed like Deborah would be any help solving them, although that was making assumptions. Robin wouldn't have credited Derek being capable of working them out.

"Did you meet up again in person?" Ashok asked. "To do your puzzles or whatever?"

"She suggested it but then lockdown happened. We kept messaging each other, talking about how we were coping with being cooped up at home. I'd have liked to have chatted on Zoom, but . . ." Another flick of the eyes in Deborah's direction. "We never did get to meet up. Ellen changed her mind and then stopped messaging entirely."

"Did she say why?"

"Not really, Constable Mankad. She pleaded that she was too busy." Derek shrugged. "I don't think that was true."

Ashok pressed on. "What do you think happened, then?"

Derek paused, clearly weighing his words. "I'm not sure. I wondered if she thought I was up to my old tricks. You see, she saw me in Southampton with another woman. Please don't tell Deborah that, because the meeting was entirely innocent. An old friend I was catching up with."

Entirely innocent my arse. "If it's not relevant to Ellen Wilkins's murder, your wife won't need to know," Robin assured him. "If it's the reason you decided to silence her . . ."

Derek's flushed face turned white. "I swear I didn't. I may have been a rogue, but I'm not a killer. I'm not stupid, either. This was back in August, so if I'd been scared that she'd tell Deborah and wanted Ellen silenced, surely I'd have done it months ago."

That sounded like the truth, although not the whole of it. Rather like his story of the old friend he'd been seen with in Southampton. "Okay, scroll back. You wondered if that was what Ellen thought, but you weren't convinced. Tell us the rest."

"You're quite scary, Mr. Bright. Can you always see through people so easily?"

"Only sometimes. Go on."

"Please don't tell my wife you heard this from me." Derek lowered his voice, even though Deborah and Henry couldn't have been within earshot. "Greg Carey. Somehow last summer he managed to get into Ellen's house. I don't know whether he got hold of a spare key or she'd lent him one to keep an eye on her property while she was on holiday. I knew about her going away because she mentioned it while we were chatting, that time she saw me in Southampton. I had to pass the time of day or it would have seemed like I had something to hide."

"And how do you know that Carey had got in?"

"He told us, when we went to his house a few weeks back. He'd become suspicious that *she'd* become suspicious, if you get my drift. It started when she said she wouldn't do his taxes. Too busy, she said, same as she'd told me. Carey didn't believe that any more than I did. After that, she started getting reclusive, which wasn't like her at all, and then she became downright abusive to them."

"Abusive?" That hadn't come up, unless telling people to leave her alone counted as out of order. "When was that?"

"I couldn't tell you. All I know is that Carey said Ellen had got shirty. He and his wife knew she had a track record for gathering evidence of wrongdoing, because she'd told them about her life and . . . and giving evidence against me. They became convinced she was hiding a project and that it probably concerned them."

Robin raised an eyebrow at Ashok, who appeared equally shocked at the revelations. "They unlawfully entered her house to have a nose around?"

"Yes. Not the pair of them, though, only Carey. *She'd* taken the children out so they wouldn't know what their dad was up to."

"What did he find?"

"A file. Ellen had a locked cabinet, upstairs, but she'd left the key in a drawer, meaning he could find it easily. Apparently it contained nothing incriminating, just background information about I Shall Not Want, although that was enough to make him twitchy." Derek shrugged.

"Did she know he'd broken in?" Robin asked.

"Possibly. I mean, I couldn't tell you for sure one way or the other, so it all depends on how clever he was at covering his traces and how easily she'd have noticed if something was moved. As long as he didn't take anything, it wouldn't be that obvious, although in a battle of wits, I'd say she'd always come out on top compared to him, therefore it wouldn't surprise me if she knew."

Robin gathered his thoughts. Ellen's habitually unlocked back gate would have worked in Carey's favour, making it simple enough to get in and out of the house if he had a key. She couldn't keep both doors to her property bolted on the inside while she was away. But there was a burglar alarm, as well. Surely she'd have set it, assuming it had already been installed and hadn't been a reaction to unwanted intrusion.

"It's all a matter of timing," Derek continued. "Did she cut off communication with me because she'd made the link between us and the charity?"

The story certainly had an internal logic and could slot another piece into the incomplete jigsaw of Ellen's life in the past few months.

"Not because you've started your dating fraud antics again?"

"No, Mr. Bright. Ellen may have had her suspicions on that front, as I said, but I promise I've learned my lesson. I'm too old to want to spend further time in a jail."

Especially, perhaps, if he found himself imprisoned in a marriage that he now regretted. How awful to have turned your back on crime only to find yourself hitched to somebody who was embroiled in it.

Once outside, Ashok said, "How the hell did Greg Carey get hold of a key to Ellen's house, sir? Do you think he sneaked a spare out somehow and got it copied?"

"Possibly. It's equally possible that she gave the Careys a key so they could access the house while she was on holiday, then asked for it back when she realised what had gone on. They wouldn't have told us, would they? I'd say all that stuff Alex Carey told me and Ben about getting a cheery wave from Ellen when she got back off holiday was another lie." It would be interesting to go over the Careys' statements again in the light of Derek's allegation.

"This will sound really stupid, but it's a shame we can't interview victims before they die. Otherwise it's all second-hand."

"That's not stupid at all. Particularly in a case like this where the dead person doesn't have social media or anything else where we can get a handle on them in their own words. All we've got for Ellen is the letter she sent after she died." Robin sighed. "I'll check my messages before I get in the car, and then I want to ring Sexton before we hit the road." He wasn't going to drive all the way to Kinechester before checking if there was another part of the story that people had kept from the police, a part that might need putting to the Cavendishes.

"Good idea, sir. I mean, it's possible Jeremy was so rat-arsed that he's forgotten all about trying his luck with Deborah, but on the other hand, he might be as big a liar as the rest of them seem to be." Ashok got into the car, perhaps having worked out exactly why Robin was so keen to look at his phone.

The important message was there, having come through not ten minutes previously.

Great news. I think. The test's come back negative.

Robin immediately felt better than he had done in days and not solely in terms of his stress levels. He would swear that the tickle in his throat and aches in his legs had suddenly almost disappeared. *Glad to hear it. Is Kate coming today?*

If she wasn't, then maybe Mrs. Matthews should be summoned to come and fuss over her boy, because if he didn't have Covid, could it be something worse? Robin mouthed, *Five minutes,* at Ashok, getting a thumbs-up in return.

Kate's walking Campbell now. She's brought cottage pie for dinner so we're catered for. For about a week, given the size of the thing.

While that was bound to be delicious, the state of the cuisine in the Bright-Matthews household was less important than the state of health.

Can you get an e-consultation with the doctor's surgery? You need to be checked over.

Already left a request for one, Mother.

That action showed how ill Adam was feeling: normally he had to be dragged to the doctor kicking and screaming.

Keep me updated. I hope your diagnosis turns out to be straightforward, compared to my case. I'll tell you all about it tonight. Speak later.

Robin got into the car. "Adam's Covid test is all clear."

"That's good news, sir. Naomi and I are enjoying working with you. Not that Pru wouldn't be a good team leader, but . . ." Ashok paused, clearly as self-conscious at making such a very un-British outpouring as Robin was at receiving it.

"You're a pleasure to work with. Always keeping an open mind—don't ever lose that ability. Right, Jeremy Sexton."

Jeremy's response on hearing Deborah's assertion about him making a pass was unexpected. "Oh hell. Not her. Was she the woman in the photograph you asked me if I'd seen?"

"Yes. The one you said you didn't think you recognised."

"I didn't. He's rather nondescript and she's changed her hair, because it used to be bright pink."

"Pink?"

Robin had the call on the speakerphone so that Ashok could hear it. The constable mouthed, *The woman with pink hair*, at which Robin nodded. Very likely that was whom Ellen had meant when she'd spoken to Nathan from number forty-three.

"She might have been wearing a wig, I suppose," Jeremy continued. "I wasn't so close that I could tell for certain. I didn't make a pass at her, though. *Au contraire.* She put her hand on *my* leg."

Well done, Henry. Robin was inclined to think this was the real account of events. Sparse at it was, Derek's story about what he remembered of the dinner would fit with this version. "Did you give her your number?"

"No way, Mr. Bright. I know I'm one for the ladies but grant me some discrimination. I like brains, and while I felt the lady in question was possessed of plenty of low cunning, I don't think she was really the intellectual type. More physically attractive than Ellen, maybe, but any man of sense would have preferred to spend his time with *her*."

Rather a spiteful assessment although possibly accurate.

"Was Ellen investigating her too?" Jeremy continued. "In connection with hubby's dating scams?"

"It appears he wasn't the only one committing frauds. The wife was at it too, with the same charity Ellen was investigating."

"Well, well. I had no idea." Sexton paused, clearly waiting for Robin to elaborate, then realising he'd have a long wait. "I don't remember seeing that on Ellen's laptop when we got into it."

"Neither do we, although we may not have found the files as yet." Robin had to weigh up carefully how much to reveal. If the fraud was linked to the messages Sexton had received, they needed to know that. "Did Ellen use memory sticks or other backup?"

"Not memory sticks. She hated the things because she'd had a bad experience with files being corrupted on them."

"I'd understand that." Back in the early days, when the things had carried around five hundred megabytes, Robin's Aunt Clare had lost weeks' worth of research into family history because she'd transferred them onto a stick, mistakenly thinking they'd be safer, only to find that the documents had turned to gobbledegook. "What about online storage she could access from all her devices?"

"That's highly likely. She didn't appear to have anything like One Drive installed but she may have used Google Drive for storage as well as sharing. She also sometimes used old-fashioned paper records."

"Like the ones in her filing cabinet?"

"Yes. I used to tease her, but she said they could be equally safe, if not safer, because you couldn't hack into a filing cabinet from halfway across the world. As long as nobody broke into her house, she'd be safe." A sharp intake of breath. "Do you think somebody took the files after she was killed?"

"Perhaps. We also think someone got into her house and accessed them before that, while she was on holiday."

"May I ask a question, sir?" Ashok whispered.

"Constable Mankad wants a word, Jeremy."

"Of course. How can I help?"

"Did Ellen store her paperwork anywhere else than the usual places like that filing cabinet?"

"Quite possibly. Not the secret safe set into the wall behind the Rubens, so beloved of a country house drama, but something more prosaic. I know she once bought a thousand euros for a holiday abroad and kept them in her kitchen cupboard in a box of Bran Flakes, tucked under the inner packet. On the principle that a burglar wouldn't look there."

"Good thinking. In our experience, they do tend to go for the standard, like bedside cabinets." And knicker drawers, which had become too obvious a hiding place.

"If she suspected somebody had been in her house, she could have got spooked and moved whatever she felt they were after. Sorry not to have anything really concrete to offer."

"The cereal box idea is concrete enough. One last question and it's back to Deborah Cavendish. Any idea how she might have got your contact details? She says you emailed her, by the way, early last year."

"Bloody cow. What a liar. Actually, I think *she* may have emailed me. I've been thinking about why that charity rang a vague bell, and I remember I was contacted by someone from them sometime last spring. If it wasn't I Shall Not Want, it was a jolly similar charity, and they were asking if I'd like to support one of their dos by sponsoring the entertainment or providing a raffle prize. I contacted the charity to say there wasn't any way I'd be supporting them, as I'd not consented to my data being used for that purpose. I'd assumed they bought my name off a list, but it might have been Pink-rinse who got her paws on it. Hold on, hold on." Jeremy *umm*ed in thought. "Ellen told me she'd had a similar begging letter. She'd wondered if the hotel had sold our data. It would have been premium stuff—nobody there was short of a bob or two. Reminds me of those competitions they have in the Telegraph that seem to be primarily a way of data farming."

"Did she follow that up with the hotel?" Ellen didn't sound like someone who'd ignore such an invasion of her privacy.

"No. I rather talked her out of it. Said if somebody at the Clifton had sold the list, then surely we would have been bothered by other organisations and long before this charity bothered us, neither of which happened. It was a one-off and I forgot about it. Clearly Ellen didn't."

"So, considering those threatening messages Deborah sent you— or her husband sent from her phone—in the context of what you now know, do they make any more sense?"

"Not on a personal level. I mean if I *had* been bothering her, then she would have had every right to tell me where to stick it, but those texts make no sense given it was the other way round. I can only think that she must have suspected I was involved with this charity investigation. Which I wasn't. That was purely Ellen's baby, and if it got her killed, I'll— Sorry. Was about to say things I shouldn't. Please get whoever did this, Mr. Bright. I'll do anything I can to help."

The offer sounded as heartfelt as any Robin had come across. "Thank you. We'll do our level best."

"Want to go back in and grill her?" Ashok asked, when the call had ended.

"Nah. We'll just get into a game of *he said, she said*. I'll text Henry about the emails and he can follow it up. It wouldn't surprise me at all if La Cavendish has been obtaining lists of contact details on the sly. A photo of a register here and there. Not everyone who received a begging letter would be so concerned about their data being protected as Ellen was."

Ashok started the car, then pulled smoothly away. One of the better drivers Robin had been chauffeured by. "I agree about Deborah being the sort who'd not be too picky about obeying the GDPR rules, sir, although I can't work out why she'd have sat on them for so long."

"Perhaps she was hoping that a delay would mean people wouldn't associate their stay at the hotel with getting the mailing. Or she had other lists she was working through first. When the new rules came in, some mailing company users were getting twitchy about their providers sanctioning them if they got too many unsubscribes and 'I didn't sign up for this list' complaints, so I can imagine they'd space out sending begging letters to new contacts. First-world problems, I know." Robin sighed. "I'll text Ben to get him poking in Google Drives or whatever, if he hasn't already. See if we can find anything about Ellen's research into Deborah. That thing Derek said about it being a matter of timing . . . I'll get Naomi started on working out a timeline and, when we get back, you can help her."

"I thought we already had a timeline for January, sir. What little we know about who was where and when."

"And a fat lot of good it's done us so far. No, I mean going back over the last two years. When people met, who contacted whom and about what, the exact time Ellen was on holiday so Carey could get into the house. At what point she started cutting off contact and whether there's a sequence to all of that. Marked up with what's corroborated and what's based on one person reporting it. We're struggling with getting any solid forensics and no two people are telling the same story, so we need to start from scratch, maybe find a logical order of events before we get Carey back in for questioning."

"Sounds good, sir." Ashok nodded. "What about you and Sergeant Davis?"

Robin gave him a sidelong glance. "If you were us, what would you be doing?"

"Going back to number thirty-nine to see if we missed any paper files that could be the solid evidence we need."

"Bang on target, Constable." Robin noticed the fleeting discomfort writ large on Ashok's face. "I'm not blaming you or Pru, because you were focussed on that filing cabinet and we're sure at least one file has been taken from there, so perhaps the other stuff was too. Don't forget, Ben and I went over that house and neither of us spotted any obvious hiding place, but then we weren't looking for one. We certainly didn't shake out any boxes of Bran Flakes."

"You think it's possible she realised Carey had been in the house?"

"It would make sense if she had. Assuming the timeline works and we're not wrongly connecting cause and effect." Robin remembered the distinctive aroma when Carey had been interviewed. "Carey reeks of aftershave or cologne. Now, when I was a callow constable, much the same age as you, a burglar's aftershave helped track him down. Smelled like a tart's hanky when we arrested him. A woman whose house he'd broken into had an acute sense of smell and both noticed—and could name—the brand as soon as she entered her house after the robbery. Never burgle someone who works in the perfume industry."

"Ellen may have smelled that when she came back off holiday?"

"It's possible." What a shame she hadn't called the police in then. There was a chance it could have prevented her murder. "In which case, why the hell didn't she report it?"

"I've an idea about that. It's a bit of a coverall." Ashok blew out his cheeks. "At first we explained Ellen's actions by her failing mental facilities. Then we veered away from that. What if there's an element of truth in the idea, though? She was still able to do her research, but she was losing the ability to make logical judgements. You know, retreating into her shell and relying only on herself?"

Such a theory could be used to explain any aspect of Ellen's behaviour that didn't make sense. Was it really what had happened or a convenient straw to clutch at?

Chapter Fourteen

When Robin and Ashok got back to the office, the air of excitement was almost palpable. Naomi, bouncing about like Tigger, seemed fit to explode.

"Sir, I've started on that timeline like you asked, but I think you're going to want to hear this." She was clearly about to unveil unexpected yet vital information. Such enthusiasm was a joy to behold.

"I'm all ears."

"Deborah Cavendish was married before she became Mrs. Balshaw. We only found out because Pru had the bright idea of seeing if she'd been DBS checked for her charity work. That can turn up all sorts of odds and ends."

"Not entirely *my* bright idea, sir," Pru said, with typical modesty. "I was browsing through that charity's website, and they were really bigging up their safeguarding stuff. I said it was a shame her charity work wasn't directly with the children as she'd have had to be cleared and it would have showed up her assault charge. Then they might have thought twice about having her involved. Naomi was the one who said the charity DBS would be worth a follow up as she would have to enter any other names she'd used."

"It was her son, sir. I wondered if there was an angle there that we'd missed." Naomi walked over to the board, pointing to Deborah's picture. "She used to be Mrs. Brown. The funny thing is she was also *Miss* Brown, before she married."

Ashok grinned. "Bet she wasn't. Married to a bloke with the same surname as hers had been, I mean. If she found herself up the duff, she might have wanted to cover up the fact she wasn't wed. Understandable, given the situation."

"That's possible. You've met her, so you've probably got a better idea of her personality." Naomi nodded. "Although it's not an unusual name, so the story might be true. Remember, Brown's a name we've come across twice in this investigation."

Robin rubbed his forehead, trying to think what those two instances might be but could only remember one. "The couple across from the Methodist Church? The ones who were so helpful about the skip and the person with the bin?"

"Exactly. In the prime spot to divert our attention with a misleading description of who'd been dragging that bin and when. As well as to advise the killer when and where they could dispose of evidence and keep an eye on it until it was safely collected by the skip hire company. They'd been carefully watching what was happening with that skip and maybe it wasn't only nosiness," Naomi suggested.

"You know, when I showed them the picture, there was a whole palaver about finding the right glasses to study it. That could easily have been to distract me," Pru said. "It's possible Mr. Brown could be Deborah's brother, given their ages. It would be worth finding out."

"It would indeed," Robin agreed. "Who's the second one with the same name?"

"Billy the Bins," Naomi said. "From the cleaning company."

"He's bound to be in a position to know the Cromwell Road collection day," Ben pointed out. "Easier for him to dispose of evidence, because nobody would question if they saw him taking a bin anywhere, any time. Simple for him to help his mum out if she needed. What was Deborah's son's name, Ashok?"

"William, which would accord with Billy," Ashok confirmed. "But he was paid for doing that, out of Ellen's account. Why link yourself or your family to the crime if you didn't need to? He'd have expected that we'd tracked him down, in which case he could have told us he was paid cash and given a false description of the person who was supposed to have paid him."

"People have been known to do some pretty stupid things while trying to cover their tracks. They think they're being clever. And maybe Billy *did* act cleverly, if she was one of his regulars. She'd be expected to pay by card if she'd done so in the past." Robin tapped the desk where he'd perched himself. "Hold your horses. There's a third Brown. Wasn't that the name of the constable on duty at the house?"

"It was, sir," Ben replied. "The one who might have been there on his own at some point because his colleague got called away, remember?"

"Exactly. Anybody know if his first name is William or Bill?"

"Couldn't tell you, sir," Naomi said. "But if we're talking about who had access to removing evidence, one of us would always be in the frame, particularly if we were the first officer on the scene."

Robin found his eyes drawn to the picture of Ellen that graced the incident board. The net around her killer must be drawing in, surely? "Enough speculation. We need to do some digging and see if any of these three—four—people have a connection to Deborah Cavendish. Ideally, we do that without talking to them, because I don't want the wind put up anybody. Better they think they're above suspicion for another twenty-four hours."

"Should we add all the Browns to the timeline? The Ireton Avenue couple, Billy the Bins, our PC and all?" Ben asked.

"Absolutely. If nothing else, they're all key witnesses, with backgrounds that need investigating. You three can split them between you. Start on their social media, because we know Deborah's on Facebook. Sorry." Robin raised a hand in apology. "You all know where to go to find connections."

"I've already gone through Ellen's laptop files," Ben said, "but no mention of a Brown there."

"Okay. Pru, while we're at Cromwell Road hunting down paper, we should look out for a mention of anyone called Brown, as well as Balshaw and Carey. Oh, to hell with it, let's load up with evidence bags and bring back every paper file we can lay our hands on."

"That works for me, sir. Very seventies." Pru grimaced. "What about PC Brown? Will we be seeing if *he's* connected?"

"Yes, we'd better handle him, although not before I speak to Denness. If he's Deborah's son, this could get messy."

"And if he's involved somehow, he'll be shitting bricks. You've got a bit of a reputation for smoking out bent coppers, sir," Ashok said, voice full of admiration.

Robin sniffed. "Then let's hope he doesn't do a runner."

Before either talking to Denness or heading to the murder scene, Robin checked his phone, having felt the rumble of an incoming message as the discussion wound up.

Adam: *I've got a phone consultation late this afternoon. I have to send pictures of my shoulder for some reason.*

Was getting an appointment so quickly a bad sign, indicating the doctor thought there must be something serious going on? Didn't meningitis start as a headache? Robin hid his concern behind a humorous reply.

Robin: *So long as that's all you have to send photos of. Didn't your mother warn you about doing that?*

Adam: *You're just envious that I don't send them to you. It's only my shoulder. If she asks for pictures of anything from below the waistline, I'll refuse. Anyway, don't panic. They haven't dragged me in to the surgery now or suggested I go to hospital, so it can't be that bad, can it?*

Robin hoped not. Now to resist googling any serious illnesses connected to shoulders.

Adam finished the telephone consultation with the doctor wearing a big grin and feeling fifty percent better than he had over the previous forty-eight hours, despite nothing having changed symptom-wise. Funny how a definitive diagnosis made such a difference to your well-being.

Shingles. That's what the doctor had diagnosed. Not the most pleasant disease to have, especially now that Adam had developed an uncomfortable rash—about the size of Belgium—all over his left shoulder and front of his chest. However, as a diagnosis, it was a damn sight better than many of the alternatives that he'd found earlier, when googling his symptoms. The doctor had given him plenty of guidance on what to do, had told him who to avoid contact with, and had signed him off work for a few days until he'd be feeling human again. She'd also advised—didn't doctors always do this?—to get back in touch if the situation got worse or if he was worried.

Adam decided not to call Robin, as the bloke was already on the way home and even though he had hands-free, the news might still be distracting. The doctor had assured him that shingles wasn't contagious, although she'd stated that it was best for Adam not to be in contact with anybody who hadn't had chicken pox. If Robin couldn't say whether he fell into that category, they'd have to consult Mrs. Bright and hope the answer was yes, or they'd be spending time in separate beds until he was no longer infectious.

Adam was putting the final touches to dinner when he heard Robin coming through the front door.

"I'm in the kitchen. Rapidly turning into a nineteen seventies housewife."

"Don't you dare. Househusband, maybe," Robin said as he entered the kitchen, Campbell entwining himself joyfully around his other dad's legs. "Am I allowed to kiss you?"

"Depends if you'd had chicken pox. I've got shingles."

"Shingles?" The wave of relief on Robin's face was a joy to behold.

"Yep. Want to see my spots?"

"Not particularly. Do you want me to see them?"

"Only to get sympathy. They're pretty horrible and really painful. It'll be the spare bed for me again tonight, given that I can't get comfortably settled."

"You have my every sympathy already." Robin paused, frowning. "Are you contagious?"

"Doctor reckons not, unless people never had chicken pox. Hence the question."

"I had it when I was nine." Robin's smile shone out again, then disappeared. "The spots literally appeared during the course of a school day, so you can imagine what the other boys said."

"Come here." Adam drew him into a hug. Robin had suffered a lot of bullying when a pupil, and while he'd got over much of it—with Adam's help—flashbacks still occurred, leaving him anxious. Especially when he was tired and under stress as he was now, under the twin onslaughts of a case and possible contact with Covid. A cuddle and a kiss would make everything better.

"That feels good. I hadn't realised how much I missed it. As has someone else."

"Campbell!" Adam extricated the dog from the two-way hug that was threatening to turn three-way. "You can have him all to yourself later. He's mine now."

When they'd caught up on enough cuddles to keep them going, Robin pulled back, peering into Adam's face. "Does shingles explain *everything*? The headaches and the peculiar taste in your mouth?"

"Apparently so. I told Dr. Powney about all the symptoms I've had, and she said that headaches and generally feeling yukky is par for the course. *And* she told me she's come across at least one other case of shingles where the patient's sense of taste went tits up, although in that instance the rash was on his face. There's an outside chance I have that joy to come, so this could be the last kiss you get for a while."

"Believe me, the prospect of a week without kisses is far better than the thought of you ending up on a ventilator or being flat on your back for months. It calls for a beer, I think."

"So do I. Get changed and I'll have everything on the table ready."

"Including you in a frilly apron? Ow!" Robin retreated, grinning, as Adam flicked him with the end of a tea towel. Normal service was at long last resuming in the Matthews-Bright household.

Over dinner, Adam encouraged his husband to discuss his day at work, if he wished. He was delighted when the offer was taken up, especially given the air of optimism about Robin, not entirely explained by the medical news, that hinted at progress in the case. Adam always took an interest in his partner's work, as Robin did in *his*, but this time his enforced days at home—being under house arrest, he'd described it to Kate—made him especially eager to pit his own wits against Ellen Wilkins's killer.

"It's been one of those days where you turn up a sack load of new leads," Robin said. "Greg Carey, the nasty neighbour as opposed to Trevor the nice one, may have gone into her house when she was on holiday, looking for whatever Ellen had on him and his pals' dodgy practices."

"No wonder she started to cut herself off from people. I bet she knew."

"That's what we're going on. Henry from the fraud team is giving them all a hard time, which is working in our favour, because they're fighting on two fronts. At some point, somebody will forget what's supposed to have happened and when. There's already a crack or two showing on the Cavendish domestic front." Robin launched into the story of Derek being seen in Southampton with his supposed old friend, interspersing it with mouthfuls of the excellent cottage pie.

"There's an incentive to tell the truth. Easier to keep track."

"Yep. Then there's the case of the multiple Browns." Robin scooped up the last of his dinner. "Can you tell Kate that I'm forever in her debt for how she's helped over the last few days.?"

"I will, although only if you tell me what the hell you're on about with this Browns business. The colour? A regimental nickname?"

"Deborah Cavendish's maiden name and the surname of her son. Also allegedly the name of her first husband, but we can't find any evidence of that marriage. It may have taken place abroad but more likely the 'Mrs.' was a matter of convenience. Attitudes were surprisingly old-fashioned thirty-odd years ago."

"Still are. In some families. Where does the multiple bit come in?"

"We've got three lots of them in the case. The people who live opposite the church with the convenient skip, the ones who heard somebody trundling a bin there the evening we believe Ellen was killed. Then there's the guy who took the bins to dispose of them—the one Don saw. He has the right Christian name to be the son but if he's involved, why tell us that Ellen arranged it all and used her cash card to pay?"

"Because you'd know from her bank records that she'd paid him?"

"Yes, but why put it through as a real transaction at all? Why not take the bins and if challenged, tell us he was paid cash? Less chance of him being tracked down that way."

"He might think it would appear suspicious if it was all supposed to be dodgy-dealing cash in hand from someone who had no connection to the property. Sort of job a responsible bin-cleaner should refuse." Not that Adam had any knowledge of bin-cleaners or the job they performed. Nor did he understand the criminal mind. "Irrespective of how the disposal of the bins was arranged, isn't it about the *when*? Obscuring the date of her death?"

"I'm not sure I know."

"Come on, let's head for the sofa and continue the conversation there."

Once in the lounge, together, with Campbell happily ensconced on the floor beside them—clearly delighted that his two dads were sprawled all over each other again—Adam asked who the third Brown was.

"Ah. This is the angle that's going to be trickier. He's the constable who first attended the scene."

"Blimey. I hope he's not involved, for all your sakes."

"So do I. We've been wondering why the mirror delivery was arranged for that particular day and time, and I guess it's possible that PC Brown could have organised it so that the body would be discovered when he was on shift and likely to be given the call. I'll have to tread carefully though. I wasn't able to see Denness this afternoon because he's been in a meeting about local policing priorities, and I'm not willing to discuss anything that delicate over messaging. It might be different if I was at my own nick, but when you're not entirely sure of the lie of the land..." Robin shrugged. "I've told the rest of the team not to ask anyone what the bloke's Christian name is, because you know how speculation spreads. Especially when it's based on fact. I'm not sure what's better—dealing with a potential conflict of interests or sitting in the kind of meeting Denness has been attending."

"I know which one you'd prefer." Adam snorted in amusement. While Robin wasn't lacking in ambition, the non-investigational side of the job was a distinct downer for him as far as being promoted was concerned. He'd always told Adam he wanted the thrill of the chase, no matter how complicated or frustrating that chase could be. "Although maybe you won't feel that way when you're fifty and getting short of breath every time you run down the road after villains."

"I can't recall the last time I ran after a villain. That's what constables are for. I get your drift, though." Robin stroked Adam's head. "I can't imagine I'd ever lose the intellectual desire to solve cases, no matter how out of condition I get. Like I can't imagine you ever wanting a desk role. You'd always want to do some teaching, wouldn't you?"

"Probably. I don't fancy one of these headships in a tiny school where you're forced to teach as well as do everything else, but I'd always want to provide a bit of classroom cover. For one thing, it's the only way to find out what's going on."

"The children snitching on the staff?"

"Something like that. They can be incredibly candid when it's not about what *they've* been up to. Get them onto that subject and it must be like you trying to pick out the truth from what your suspects have said. Hold on, while I make myself comfy." Adam re-settled his shoulder, which was starting to become sore again. "Are you getting a feel for who did it or is it still *keep an open mind* time?"

"It's never *not* time to keep an open mind. Back in the Stone Age when I was in training, I heard about cases where the investigating officers were quite convinced they had the culprit bang to rights, yet they had to change tack at the eleventh hour. Maybe they'd gone in with a fixed idea, like some of the cops on the TV shows, although in one case it was a single, crucial, new bit of evidence that changed the perspective on things." Robin snuggled closer. "Chances are that Carey and the Cavendishes are working together to cover up their dodgy dealings. They knew Ellen was onto them. However, apart from a motive and the obvious opportunity, I've got no forensics or witness statements or basically anything of use in a courtroom that links them to the murder. One bloody footprint from a sock, where the killer must have stepped in the blood, but unless they teleported out of the room, they must have removed said sock and cleaned their foot, so that's a dead end. So, unless we're barking up the wrong tree, it's less a case of whodunnit as how do we *prove* they did it?"

Adam rubbed the top of Robin's head, which hopefully would prove soothing for both of them. "I know I normally try to steer well clear of your cases, admittedly not always with success, and I know you've got your team and all the technical stuff at your fingertips, but if there's anything a reasonably intelligent deputy headteacher can do. One who's pretty well confined to barracks and by tomorrow afternoon will be climbing the walls with boredom because doing school stuff makes his head ache like mad . . . well, let me know."

"I appreciate the offer. Not sure what I can ask you to do that we can't. Unless you want to pick your mate Kelvin's brains about whether Ellen ever mentioned anyone called either Brown or Balshaw. Or had threatening texts telling her to stop nosing about in other people's business or suspected her neighbour had been poking about in her house, although unless Kelvin's a total wally, he'd have told us that already."

"Yeah, he would. Brown and Balshaw bit would be worth following up, though. I said I'd ring him first thing tomorrow to discuss some school stuff, so I can slip the question in."

"Thanks. Not that I'm holding out much hope, but you never know. Key pieces of information come in odd ways, and they aren't always obvious at first sight."

Adam's vicarious experience of murder cases had already taught him that. "I'll tell Kelvin what you said. He'll like that. He keeps telling me that he and his family want to help in any way they can, so I'll give them a few things to mull over. Can I tell him the psalm twenty-three connection to the charity name?"

"I'd rather you didn't. You can tell him it's given us a significant clue, which is almost the truth, because even if we hadn't found Ellen's computer files, we would have got round to looking at I Shall Not Want eventually. Probably. Once we'd eliminated all the other options and turned totally grey." Robin fingered the hair at his temples. "I found a slightly grey one here, this morning."

"Only the one?" Adam ran his hand through the rest of Robin's still dark thatch. "When I'm better, I volunteer to check you all over for any others. May have to be a thorough search."

"I'll hold you to that." Robin stretched. "Sorry to break up such a tender moment but I need my bed. If I fall asleep on this sofa, I'll wake feeling like crap."

"Off you pop, then. I'll tidy up and give himself a turn round the garden. Not like I have many other calls on my time at present." Adam gave his husband a goodnight kiss, then nudged Campbell in the direction of the back door. Thank God it *was* only shingles. He hadn't let himself speculate too much, while he was waiting for his test results, but now that he allowed himself to think of the worst, coming so close potentially to spending weeks flat on his back in a hospital—or at best in his own bed—let alone the worst that could happen, made him literally shudder.

A cold nose in his hand brought his thoughts to pleasanter things. "Sorry boy, not attending to my duty."

Campbell, maybe sensing that his dad needed love, raised himself on his hind legs, put his paws on Adam's chest and gave him a bit of a slobber. Adam gently pushed him away, patting and making a fuss of him in the process. "Much appreciated, but maybe not at the moment. *You* don't want to get chicken pox, believe me. Now, go and do your stuff and you can have a dog biscuit afterwards. Don't tell your other dad, though."

The Newfoundland produced what seemed suspiciously like a conspiratorial grin, then bounded off into the garden, leaving Adam to count his blessings. In the greater scheme of things, an itchy shoulder was no great shakes.

He wasn't so sure of that next day. At six o'clock, he woke up feeling like he wanted to scratch himself all over. Worse than Campbell when he'd caught a flea. Dr. Powney had recommended calamine lotion as the best thing for his rash: the old methods were sometimes the best. Adam had checked the medicine cupboard the previous day but, as he'd expected, there was none in stock. He thought about asking Kate to pick some up on her way over, but a trip to the nearest chemist later that morning wouldn't hurt.

He went through the usual routine, determined not to simply slob around, then got on the phone to Kelvin. Once the school bits were dealt with, Kelvin himself provided the cue for further questions.

"Any news about Ellen? There's not much on the local paper website, but I don't know if that's normal."

"It's still early days. Robin reckons they've picked up some useful leads and wanted me to thank you and your family for the help you've given so far. He's got a couple of things he wants me to run past you if you've got five minutes."

"I'll always have time to help catch her killer. I got to the school car park even earlier than I meant to, so fire ahead."

Fire away? Go ahead? Kelvin really did struggle with getting his English right.

"Did Ellen ever mention the names Brown or Balshaw?" Adam idly patted Campbell, who had come to offer his canine brains to the situation.

"Not that I can recall. I'll ask Mum and Dad, obviously, but don't get your hopes up." Kelvin sniffed. "Are these Robin's chief suspects, then?"

"I can't say. That's not me being cagey, by the way. I genuinely don't know much one way or the other." Which wasn't quite the truth but as close as Adam was prepared to get. "One other thing. Did Ellen ever say how she got on with her present neighbours? Anything mentioned from over the past year?"

"I can give you her opinion on them. There's a gay couple she liked a lot. They made good cocktails, apparently. Industrial strength." Kelvin chuckled. "The other side there's a couple with children. The woman Ellen described as nice but dim and as for the husband, she used to trust him then changed her mind. That turnabout in opinion must have been relatively recent, because I remember she told us over a Zoom call and we wouldn't have used that before Covid. I'm guessing it would have been for Mum's birthday."

"Which was when?"

"September the fifth, which was a Saturday or Sunday, so we could all meet up virtually on the day itself."

Adam made a note. Whether that would help Robin or hinder the timeline his team had been working on. "She didn't happen to say what had prompted her to change her view of him?"

"No and Mum gave her the third degree about it, all right. Never likes half a story, my mum. All Ellen would say was that once life was back to normal and she was able to go away again, she'd be changing her locks." Kelvin paused. "Was she worried that this Brown or Baldock person was going to break in?"

"Balshaw, not Baldock. Like the rugby player. And I can't answer the question. Robin might be able to, but he's not here to ask."

He'd be getting sent a message imminently, though.

After the call, as Adam was keying in a summary of what Kelvin had told him, he remembered Robin mentioning that Ellen Wilkins had been away for Christmas. Presumably she hadn't had her locks changed before doing so or how would the old key have opened the front door for the police? Robin and his team would have to put that on their timeline and contemplate it.

Another morning, another visit to number thirty-nine in search of the elusive evidence that Robin so desperately needed. He and Pru were prepared for a long haul, starting at the top and moving down to the basement: not usually a job that an officer of Robin's rank would be involved in but on this occasion he didn't want to delegate. He had to walk out of the house knowing that—short of tearing the place apart brick by brick—they'd explored all the hiding places it had to offer and had squeezed every piece of useful information from it.

An unpleasant aroma still hung about the house, despite the fact that every time the police had made a visit they'd opened the windows to let air in. While the house might eventually lose that smell, would it ever be free of the association with violent death or would that sense of something wrong still linger?

They'd got no further than the hallway when a message alert made Robin fish out his phone. There was a text from Adam, reporting what Kelvin had told him about Ellen's intention to change her locks. He passed it to Pru. "Read this and tell me what your first thought is."

"That it's bloody peculiar, sir. I can understand why she might delay getting them done if she didn't expect to be travelling immediately, but she had that hotel booking for Christmas, which was only cancelled because of lockdown happening again. She must have thought there was a good chance she'd be on away over Christmas."

"Agreed. Actually, she strikes me as the kind of woman who'd have got a locksmith booked in as soon as she could, and there was nothing to stop you getting workmen in during the autumn lockdowns, so it can't be that. But then, she did get a burglar alarm fitted."

"I wonder how new the system is? Maybe she opted for that because it would protect her against a wider range of potential intruders." Pru jerked her thumb in the direction of number thirty-seven. "If so, I bet she made sure Carey knew all about it."

Robin snorted. "I bet she *didn't*. She probably enjoyed the thought of him getting a shock if he tried his tricks again. The control panel has to be around somewhere."

"Under the stairs, I think. I saw it last time I was here."

"Okay, so get any details from it, then ask Ben to get on the trail. I know it's not high priority, but it's part of the jigsaw and part of the timeline."

"I agree. I wish we had some of the significant pieces, though. At present it seems like all edge and sky."

And a ruddy great blank in the middle.

"Ask him if he knows the burglar alarm code, as well. We should reset it when we leave so that Carey or anybody else is less likely to get in here."

Once Ben had been set to work, the first room they visited was the kitchen, ostensibly to see if there was any evidence of something being been taken. The drawer where the cooking utensils had been kept contained several knives, although no large ones, as might be expected in the kitchen of any keen cook, which was how Jeremy had described her. Robin sneaked a peek in the fridge, immediately remembering why he'd regretted it before.

"Trying to find a turnip, sir?" Pru asked.

"Yes. There aren't any." Robin swiftly shut the door. "We need to get this fridge cleared. It's disgusting."

"I'll organise it. I can't imagine there's anything in there that'll end up needing analysis. Like a turnip might."

"What's your view on that bloody vegetable? I think I'm getting a complex about it."

Pru shrugged. "It's a loose end, and neither of us like those. I can't imagine why anyone would put it in there deliberately, unless it was solely to give the poor old PC Plods something to vex them."

"Hmmm. I'm wondering if it existed at all. If Billy the Bins turns out to be involved in the disposal of evidence, then maybe he simply spun you a line about what he found. Come on, let's do what we came to do. Beginning with the boxes and packets in here. Given that she once hid euros in a packet of Bran Flakes, they're as good a place as any to start."

Ten minutes later, they'd found a hundred quid stuffed away in an old Alpen packet—a touch more upmarket than bran cereal—but nothing else.

"Log the money to take back to the station, please, Pru."

"Will do." Pru stuck out her bottom lip. "Is it usual for people to have stashes of cash?"

Robin shrugged. "My mum got out a hundred and fifty in cash at the start of the first lockdown, not wanting to be using cash machines, only to find that almost everywhere went cashless. She ended up paying most of it back in. Ellen may have done the same. Another little mystery."

He headed for the staircase and the basement. What a pain it would be to live in a house that sprawled across so many levels.

"Where would you hide something in a place like this?" Pru asked when she'd come down the flight.

"I'm not sure. I'm trying to think like Ellen might and failing miserably."

"My mum always used to hide stuff at a height or down low, on the basis that people don't tend to look at a level much different to their eyeline. It worked with my dad. Talk about hide in plain sight—he could never believe he'd walked right past things. Not sure that would have been Ellen's style, though. Nothing on the top of those kitchen cupboards, for a start."

"Quite."

This was going to be a long morning.

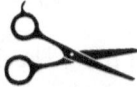

Cranshaw had a small but well-stocked pharmacy in what constituted the main shopping area. Albeit that was some dozen assorted shops, mainly suited to the slightly aging population the area was known for. Adam had never had cause to use the pharmacy before, getting any general medical odds and ends when he or Robin went to the supermarket and not needing anything specialised since they'd moved there. In fact, he'd not had prescription medicine for years, the last time being when he'd developed a sinus infection that wouldn't shift.

As he came out, a vaguely familiar bloke gave him a wave and a bright "Hello!" Adam returned them both, hoping he might be given a clue to the other guy's identity.

"You don't remember me, do you? Trevor. You admired my decking while your partner was doing his detecting."

"Oh, of course. Sorry. Brain not working at its best. I've got shingles." Adam waggled his bottle of calamine in evidence. That should save the long explanation he felt obliged to give anybody he met about why he wasn't at work.

"Ooh, nasty. I won't ask to see your rash or I'd have to charge a consultation fee." Just a touch of flirtation. "I didn't realise you lived around here."

"We've not been in the area that long. Previous neighbours must have got sick of having a cop in the road. We had the occasional unwanted visitor." Adam realised he was gabbling on more than he normally might, but Trevor was an agreeable sort and, frankly, anything different was welcome at present.

"That'll be a novelty here. My father says it's so genteel that a Macdonald's cup in the road creates a major scandal."

"He lives here?"

"Yes. On his own since my mother died, although he won't move. Too stubborn and independent. Except for now, when he's laid up with a broken foot and confined to barracks." Trevor grinned, waving a piece of paper as Adam had waved his bottle. "He has a home help who comes in but some things he doesn't want her to buy for him. Athlete's foot cream is hardly Viagra, though, is it? How's your handsome policeman?"

Adam wondered whether there'd been any connection in Trevor's head between Viagra and Robin. "Busy with the Ellen Wilkins case. We're like ships that pass in the night at present."

Trevor nodded. "Don and I are like that when our shifts get out of synch. I wish Robin luck with finding the killer, though. I know people think that Ellen was becoming increasingly difficult to deal with, but she always had a smile for us. And however antisocial someone is, they don't deserve to be murdered and certainly not to have their body left in such a callous way."

"Very true." This murder did come across as particularly calculated, considering—if that business with the blinds was any indication—how the killer had taken such pains afterwards to cover up the crime, without any regard to how long the victim was lying unburied and prey to nature taking its course.

"I hope you weren't offended when I called your chap 'handsome,' by the way. Don says I read too many old-fashioned mysteries—golden-age stories they call them and quite right, too, because people don't write them like that anymore. When I first saw you two, I thought of Ngaio Marsh's 'Handsome Alleyn.' Not that you're anything like Agatha Troy," Trevor added, with a smile that might count as flirting.

"Maybe I should call him Handsome Bright to wind him up." Adam was about to say his goodbyes when a change in Trevor's expression gave him pause. Like the face of one of the Culdover pupils when they were desperate to speak but didn't know whether they should wait to be asked. "You and Don must be taking a close interest in the case."

"I'm ashamed to say we are. I've come up with half a dozen different scenarios, all of which are far better suited to *Midsomer Murders* than to real life. I won't bore you with them because I hardly think it likely that she was killed by Sonia Parsons for putting poison in her hair dye. It's silly, really but it's been helping us to cope with the shock. Keeping reality at bay, I guess." Trevor grinned sheepishly.

"If you come up with anything that might be helpful—like if you know that Ellen did try to poison someone—he'd be pleased to know."

That gave an open enough cue for Trevor to pick up. "Has he been questioning the Careys, do you know? The people at number thirty-seven."

"I believe so." How much to say? "I clearly don't know too much about it, except that they're believed to have broken lockdown."

Trevor nodded. "We could have told you that. They didn't have the wit to leave lights on a timer or some other thing to make it seem like they were still at home. I suppose we should have mentioned it, although it didn't seem important enough."

So what *was* important that he still wanted to disclose? "Trevor, stop me if I'm barking up the wrong tree, but is there something you want me to pass on to Robin?"

"There is. It's too vague, perhaps too silly, for us to have told the police direct. Could be slanderous, for all we know." Trevor glanced around him, then encouraged Adam to come closer to the kerb, where the few customers using the shops couldn't overhear. "Alex Carey, the woman at number thirty-seven. Don and I think she looks like Olivia Mears. Or how Olivia Mears would be as a woman of thirty-odd."

"Olivia Mears?" The name rang a dim bell. "Sorry, you'll have to elaborate."

"Fifteen, twenty years ago? A teenager and her mate beat up an old woman for her pension money. The woman died a few days later, possibly as a result of the attack. Shock and effect on the heart."

"I remember now. The other girl's back in prison, isn't she? Murdered her husband a couple of years ago." Adam and Robin had discussed the case at the time, not long after they'd met, which was several years previously. While they both believed in the sanctity of "innocent until proven guilty" they knew how hard it would have been for people to consider the case separately from the previous one, which had made national headlines time and again. Reporting restrictions had been imposed and only lifted after the verdict, the story having competed with the Olympics for front page space. At least one of the tabloids had made sporting puns in their headlines about it.

"She pleaded she'd been a victim of domestic violence. She wasn't believed."

On the contrary, the prosecution had produced witnesses to show that the dead man had been the person being abused. "What happened to the other one, this Olivia woman?"

"No idea. The internet says she served her time in youth custody as a model inmate, then was probably given a new identity, like Suzie Banks was. *Her* real name only came out after the murder trial. That was when the papers featured pictures of Olivia Mears again, and Don thought they reminded him of Alex Carey. It's the nose and the ears you see." Trevor, maybe by reflex, tapped those parts of his own face. "Ears, noses, and throats are Don's line of work, so he tends to notice them. I have to say, they're pretty similar, hers and Alex's, going by the pictures. We thought if the two women are the same person, that would have shown up on the police system, but then I wondered if it's a case of not finding what you're not looking for. They wouldn't routinely take Alex's fingerprints, would they? They didn't take ours."

"I don't think they're allowed to unless they have good reason." The police would now, though. "Trevor, I'm going to call Robin straight away to tell him what you've said. It'll be easy enough for them to check, although I doubt he can let you know the outcome. Unless she ends up being charged and going to trial, because in that case the whole world will know who you've got living on your road. I can guess that he'll want to know if you mentioned your suspicions to Ellen. If you're not happy to tell me, then can you or Don ring the station about it?"

"Oh, I trust you enough to tell you, especially as the answer's no. It wouldn't be responsible, would it?"

"No. I didn't think you were the sort to spread tittle-tattle."

Trevor gave him a wink.

It felt like they were almost heading down the flirtation road again, so time to make an escape. "I'll let Robin know. I hope your dad makes a good recovery."

"Thanks. I hope your spots get less itchy."

As soon as he was back in his car, Adam got out his phone. What had Robin said about information coming in odd ways? It certainly had this time.

Chapter Fifteen

A s Robin had suspected, hiding things in plain sight didn't appear to be Ellen's style, given the results of searching the cellar and the ground floor of her house. They hunted in the obvious places, including ones they'd covered before, then the less obvious places, but all to no avail. No sign of a safe disguised as something else, unless the disguise was so good it defied all location, rather than being the usual false electric socket or food tin. No evidence of a carpet being taken up in order to hide things underneath. Perhaps Ellen hadn't had a hidey hole and this was a complete waste of time. Or perhaps she did and they'd locate it only to discover Carey—or the killer if they were two different people—had already raided it.

They were en route to the attic rooms when Robin's phone sounded again, this time with an incoming call. Not like Adam to ring him at work, so this must be important.

"Hello. Are you okay?"

"Itchy but fine. I ran across Trevor outside Cranshaw pharmacy, though. You'd better hold on to your hat."

"Hat held. This sounds like a bombshell."

"Either that or a damp squib." Adam snorted. "He and Don think Alex Carey might be Olivia Mears. The teenager who was all over the papers when she and her mate beat up an old woman."

"Blimey. I'll put you on the speaker so Pru can hear. Would you repeat that?"

Adam did so, adding, "Remember when the other girl was jailed for murder and Olivia's photo was all over the papers again? It reminded Don of Alex Carey. Something to do with the nose and the ears."

"He's an ENT specialist, so that makes sense." And, as Robin had felt from the start, the man was likely a reliable witness. "Anything else?"

"Only that they didn't mention their suspicions to anyone, let alone Ellen. The ball's in your court, now."

"It is. Thanks for this. See you later."

"Yeah. Don't forget the milk."

"Don't forget it yourself, you spotty bugger," Robin said, with a grin.

Pru was already on her phone finding an image of Olivia, although it didn't give them as much help as it had given Don. "Could be, I suppose. Only way we'll know is from fingerprints. Still, she's got an alibi for the eleventh of January and either side of it."

"Has she? We've not asked her parents to confirm that." Robin paused. "No, she said their neighbours could back that up too, so she must have been confident about the alibi. Unless the neighbours are thick as thieves with the parents and as likely to cover for her as they would be. If you recall the original case, Mr. and Mrs. Mears were adamant that their daughter had been led astray by the other girl. The court didn't believe them, but it might have been true. Could have been the other way around, as well."

"Or a case of a nasty pair of teenagers egging each other on?" Pru scrolled through an online account of the crime.

"Much as I hate the thought, we could ask the children. They'll say whether Mummy had to go and take care of Granny."

"Unless they've been drilled to lie. Oh, wait." Pru turned her phone screen for Robin to see. "Here's a colour picture of teenaged Olivia. Are those pink streaks in her hair?"

"Looks like it. You're thinking of Ellen being on the trail of a woman with pink hair?" Robin recalled Sexton's remark about Ellen not wasting her time on small fry: had Olivia Mears been the large fish she'd been angling for?

"Yes. Although that makes two of them involved in this case, doesn't it? Three if you include Sonia Parsons. Hmm." Pru put her phone back in her pocket. "I'd ask if we wanted to go and see Alex Carey now, but I don't think she's in. I saw her go out with her shopping bag over her arm while I was by the front room window."

"She's waited all this while, so she can wait a bit longer. Let's finish this job first."

By the time they'd reached the front attic room, the hunt had still drawn a blank. Not wanting to give up, because sod's law would make sure that any place left unsearched would hold a treasure trove, Robin stood by the tiny window to get a cheering view of Kinechester's rooftops. Life going on as normal—or as close to normal as the pandemic allowed—in hundreds and thousands of houses. Were people wondering whether a killer stalked their city or had Ellen Wilkin's death already become old news for everyone except those living in the Ramparts? What would those locals think if they knew their quiet, overpriced, residential road possibly harboured both a fraudster and a notorious juvenile offender, either of whom could have killed their neighbour?

The sight of the access hatch to the tiny loft brought to mind Ben saying the space wasn't big enough to hold anything other than the header tank. They hadn't checked it, though. "Did you take a shufti in there?"

"Nope. I'll do it now." Pru produced a torch that she used to peer into just about every crevice. "Can't see anything, unless it's been put in a waterproof container and hidden in the tank, which I doubt because from the cobwebs it doesn't look as though anyone's been in here for ages. It was a good idea to check, though."

"Thanks. I shouldn't have expected us to be successful so easily." Robin gazed around the room, seeking inspiration: the strategy appeared to work. "I've had an idea. Imagine you're a nineteenth-century maid and this is your bedroom. Where would you hide anything you wouldn't want your mistress to see?"

"Like a letter from my sweetheart the coalman? Or a note from the son of the house who's desperate to get his leg over?" Pru removed a piece of cobweb from her hand. "I'd use that old standby of fiction, a cache under a loose floorboard. There's no fitted carpet in here, only the rug, so it'd be easy enough for such a hidey-hole to still be used nowadays."

"Okay, well, you start under the window and I'll begin working my way across from the other side. If that doesn't produce results, we'll check the other room at the back of the house." Robin dragged the rug out of the door, then set to work.

"Bingo!" Pru exclaimed barely a minute later. "Got the bugger."

Robin turned to see his sergeant kneeling in the middle of the room grinning, with a piece of floorboard in one hand and a large envelope in the other.

"That's cheating. You were supposed to start at the edge of the room."

"That's using my brains, sir. When you took the rug away, I noticed a length of floorboard that appeared to have been repaired at some point. Seemed obvious to start there." Pru waved the item in question before replacing it. "The nails don't go all the way down so it's easy enough to hook in and out. Sits nicely too."

"Thank God Carey didn't use his brains like you did. What's in the envelope?"

"Two further envelopes." Pru pulled them out. "One labelled 'Carey,' the other labelled 'Carey and Cavendish.'"

"Let's have a gander."

Pru opened the Carey and Cavendish one, drawing out various bits of paper that they pored over together. "Well. No wonder she wanted to keep this hidden."

"Yes. Not the kind of stuff the average punter can get their hands on legally."

This was rather different to what Ben had found on the laptop. Copies of bank statements, some phone records, information about Deborah Cavendish's conviction that didn't appear to have come from the public domain.

"How the hell did she get this stuff?" Pru asked. "Was she a hacker?"

"I'll have to ask Jeremy. Unless *he* got hold of them for her." Robin scanned the sheets again. "If Carey managed to get his eyes on this, he'd have been shitting bricks."

"In which case, Ellen must have hidden it here after she suspected him of getting in."

"Quite possibly. It might also explain why she hadn't yet come to us with her suspicions. She'd have needed to assemble and put forward a portfolio of evidence that she'd acquired legitimately. Want to guess what's in the other envelope before we do the big reveal?"

"Got to be about Alex Carey's identity. Unless it's about a totally different Carey and we end up with three of them, like we've got three lots of Browns. Only joking." Pru gave him a sympathetic smile. "What's your guess?"

"Before you opened the first one, I'd have said it would be pictures, newspaper reports and the like. Now I'm thinking it might be stuff she's hacked. How easy would it be to find a change of name by deed poll? Or get access to our systems?"

"Only one way to find out." Pru tipped out a sheaf of papers. As predicted, they were pictures of Olivia and a few of Alex. Artists' sketches from the court, one each of Suzie and Olivia, another of their parents: Carl and Geraldine Banks, Victor and Carol Mears, all of them looking shell-shocked at the situation they found themselves in. There was a much more recent photo that might have been taken at a school fundraising event, with Alex among other members of the school playground mafia, although the image was so vague, she could have been almost anybody. "If that's all Ellen could find online, then Alex has done a pretty good job of keeping herself below the parapet."

"Sonia Parsons said she puts pictures of her children and her trips on social media. Good way to avoid posting ones of yourself. I bet Alex knew nothing about these." Robin pointed to a couple of snaps that appeared to have been taken through a window, zooming in on the back of the Careys' garden. "She must have been trying to compare them. Old and new."

"She didn't have Don's ENT expertise to help her, though. I can see a resemblance, although it's a bit like when you see a newborn baby and are trying to spot the mother or father's face in the little sprog. You see what you want to see."

"What made her first think of a possible connection? Surely it can't date back to the Suzie Banks trial and she's been trying to prove the link all that time. Five years, nearly." It was hard to credit her level of efficiency was that low or that she hadn't been able to access favours back then.

"Unless the Careys were living elsewhere in 2016. Moved to Kinechester because somebody had identified her at their old house?"

"No, that wouldn't work. Alex told me they moved here nine years ago and, given that's something we can easily check, I don't think she'd have lied about it." Robin perused the other documents in the envelope, without much luck. There were only the anticipated newspaper stories, plus another couple of bank statements for *her* account, not highlighted like Greg's had been. Whatever Ellen had been searching for, she'd not located it. Or somebody had removed it from a different hiding place. "Let's finish checking this room and the other one. I don't think she's got another hidey hole, but I'm leaving no stone—or floorboard—unturned."

By the time they'd established that if there was anything else to be found, it was beyond their ability to do so, Pru had spotted Alex returning to her house.

"That's her coming up the road now," the sergeant confirmed.

"Let her get settled indoors, and then we can nab her. Can you call Ashok or one of the others to bring out a fingerprinting kit? She'll either confirm or deny being Olivia Mears and, given that I'm struggling to believe what anybody in that household says, I'd like some objective proof of identity. We'll take her NI number, for a start."

"Good shout, as it's possible her prints have altered slightly. I know they're supposed to be fixed at about twelve, but it says here that Olivia had only just turned thirteen when she was arrested." Pru shrugged. "I suppose they might have changed enough not to match up with some of the partials the CSIs found."

"Agreed." Both means of identification would help to move this investigation to the next phase. Unless, of course, it turned out that the NI number proved that both Trevor and Ellen had been mistaken. "Get one of the team looking for any record in our files about Olivia Mears's change of name. She would probably have had to let us know about it. Although that doesn't guarantee that she or her family did."

The minute Alex Carey opened the door to them, her face dropped. "Haven't you caused enough trouble for us? Greg's had to borrow an old laptop from his brother so he can do his work. I thought they were going to take the kids' iPads, which would have meant they'd be unable to complete their schoolwork. It's so embarrassing."

"If you've got issues with the way the fraud enquiry is being conducted, I suggest you talk to that unit. If they haven't given you a contact number, I'll find one for you. Or you can contact your family liaison." Robin smiled sweetly. "I'm only interested in what Greg did or didn't do if it touches on Ellen's murder. I need to talk to him as well, but we'd like to start with you. I've an officer coming out later to take your fingerprints for both elimination and identification purposes."

All the colour drained from Alex's face. "Can we discuss this somewhere the children won't be able to hear?"

It seemed like she was willing to cooperate. "Of course. Grab your coat and we can go out the back and into Ellen's garden. You can tell them you're doing what all good citizens do: helping the police. Greg's here to keep an eye on them, isn't he?"

Alex nodded, ushered them in, then went off to deliver whatever whispered message she'd see fit to give the girls. They were busy with brushes and paints, wearing smart matching plastic aprons that might have been Christmas gifts, so new did they appear. Robin supposed that art and craft lessons still had to go on, as part of home learning or for fun. Whatever they were up to, they were enjoying themselves.

Once in the garden of number thirty-nine, Robin asked Alex, "Have you always been known by the name Alex?"

"No. I was born Olivia Mears, and then I was known as Alex Odell. My parents and I changed our names by deed poll. We kept the police informed at all stages. I'm so pleased we did opt for the change, when everything came out about Suzie murdering her husband and my picture was all over the papers again. Awful."

Was it the murder that had been awful or being in the press?

"Does Greg know?"

"Yes, Mr. Bright. And he also knows that I was simply a stupid teenage girl caught up in doing what she shouldn't. I could have told Suzie where to stuff her ideas, but I was too weak. Too easily led. If I could go back and change everything, I would." That sounded genuine enough, but maybe there were multiple things Alex regretted doing.

"Who else knows? Or knew," Pru asked, emphasising the past tense.

"Nobody round here, I hope. Nobody at all, apart from Greg and his parents, who've been most understanding." Alex glanced up and down the row of houses, as though afraid the bricks had ears. "I want to keep it that way, Mr. Bright. Not only for me, but for my children and for my parents. *They* only live a couple of hours' drive away, near Oxford, and they like to visit when they're allowed. They've house sat for us in the past, and I'd hate to think they couldn't do that in the future because of tongues wagging and curtains twitching. Sorry, I'm going off on one of my tangents again, but I find this very stressful."

Robin couldn't help giving her a sympathetic nod. Maybe she *had* been led astray by Suzie Banks and found herself potentially paying all through her life for a youthful mistake. "Did Ellen say anything to you about your background?"

The colour had returned to Alex's cheeks but now it drained again. Guilt or shock? Robin couldn't tell. "No, she did not. How horrible that she could have suspected me."

"But it wasn't merely suspicion, was it?" Pru said. "She'd realised the truth."

"And what was she going to do with it?" Alex stuck out her jaw. "Cause trouble for me like she'd caused trouble for Greg?"

"I have no idea what her intentions were. It might have been merely satisfying her curiosity." Unlikely as it was, they couldn't eliminate that as a possibility. Ellen had probably had enough information on Greg already to have come to the police with her suspicions, so there must have been something holding her back. Robin wouldn't have been surprised to find that she'd wanted to do as much of the work herself as she could.

"As if. She got Derek Cavendish convicted years ago, didn't she?"

"I think you'll find that Derek Cavendish got himself convicted— twice over—by trying to fleece innocent women out of their money. He made a mistake by picking on Ellen as a potential victim."

"Oh." That was evidently not the version of the story Alex had heard. "Well, you'd have thought she could have found a better use of her time than poking and prying. She was a really clever woman. Couldn't she have turned those brains to doing good?"

"I would think Derek Cavendish's victims would say that helping put him behind bars was a very good use of her talents." Robin sniffed. "We'll need to talk again, obviously. I've got an officer coming out to take your fingerprints. It's possible they've changed slightly since you were arrested back then."

"You're welcome to them. They won't do you any good." That sounded depressingly like she was telling the truth.

Time to return to the house and tackle the other half of the partnership.

Alex took over keeping an eye on the children, giving Greg a brief nod and mouthing, *You next*, as she did so. Had they been expecting the conversation that had just happened ever since the police turned up at the house next-door? Even if innocent of any involvement in the murder, they surely hadn't expected their luck to hold on the new identity front.

"Let's talk in here." Greg took them into the kitchen, shutting the door behind him. "What now? Come to take the rest of my stuff?"

"Not this time. We know that Alex is Olivia Mears." Robin raised his hand, forestalling comment for the moment. "Frankly, I'm not concerned who she is, as long as she's kept her nose clean all these years. I genuinely do believe that people can turn over a new leaf, and if I had no evidence that this was in any way linked to Ellen's death, I'd pass it over as coincidence."

Voice constrained, Greg said, "So what evidence is this that you've got? Alex didn't kill the woman."

"Ellen had begun to suspect Alex's true identity. She was actively researching it around the time she died. In the same way as she was looking into your activities—and Deborah Cavendish's—with the charity. It had always been her job to get to the truth, as mine is." Robin glanced at Pru, but she'd already got her pen and notebook poised. "Remember, Greg, you're still under caution. Last year, when Ellen was away on holiday, did you enter her house?"

Greg's jaw dropped, although he quickly recovered his composure. "Yes. We had a spare key which she'd given us years ago in the event of emergencies. I was worried because I thought I could smell gas coming from her house and I didn't want to risk an explosion."

"Why didn't you turn off the supply and call out British Gas?" Pru asked. "You could have let them into the property."

"Because it was the afternoon, we were due to go off on holiday ourselves the next day, and I had no idea how long they'd take to attend. It was simpler to investigate for myself. It turned out there was no smell in the house, only in the garden. The gas meter's at the front, so I guessed it had to be something else." Greg rolled his eyes. "Bloody bins, stinking in the sunshine. I lifted the lid of the black one and immediately wished I hadn't."

That could all have been true, except that it came so glibly and easily, as though well-rehearsed.

"What did Ellen say when you told her what you'd done?"

"We didn't see her until we returned. As I said, we were due to fly off ourselves."

"Did you leave her a note to say what had happened? Or drop her a text?" Pru's tones matched Robin's level of incredulity.

"No. I mean, there was nothing to report, and the bin would have been emptied the following Monday so it didn't seem relevant." Greg tugged at his hair. "Why don't you believe me?"

"Because we've been told you entered her house to find out what she'd been researching." Robin wasn't surprised at the flinch his statement caused. "Specifically whether she'd been investigating you."

"Who told you that?"

Robin ignored the question. "Is it true? Did you have a snoop around and discover her file about the charity?"

"I—I noticed a folder when I was in there checking for gas. It had *I Shall Not Want* on the front, so I couldn't resist opening it. I'm only human."

"Where was the file? We'd been told she kept it in a locked cabinet."

"She may have done, but she'd left it out on her desk."

"Which is upstairs," Pru pointed out.

"Yes. I wanted to check the whole house." Greg appeared to relax slightly, perhaps confident they had no solid evidence to disprove his version of the tale. If his fingerprints were found on Ellen's paperwork—or at any part of her house—he'd provided an explanation. They also couldn't discount the possibility that Derek Cavendish had embroidered the story.

"What exactly did you find?" Pru asked.

"Stuff about the charity and how she thought some of the people involved might be a bit dodgy. Deborah, for example."

"Anything personal?"

"About me? No. What had she found?" For the first time in the interview, Greg came across as being genuinely curious.

Maybe time to give him something to think about. He'd find out soon enough when his case came to trial. "Your bank statements, for a start."

"How the hell did she get hold of those?" Greg flicked a glance at the closed door, then lowered his voice. "She had no right to access them."

Robin nodded. "Quite correct. Unless you or Alex gave her copies, which I'm sure you didn't."

"We did no such thing. Why would we get involved with helping people stir up trouble? Haven't we got enough on our plates, what with trying to work and help the kids with their school stuff, and Alex's dad not being well?"

"I thought it was Mrs. Mears—Mrs. Odell as she is now—who'd been unwell," Pru said.

"Yes, she had a nasty bout of bronchitis, but it's Victor we're anxious about. You know he's battled cancer once? Well, he thinks it might be back. Brain tumour this time, and we're not sure yet if it's malignant or benign. It's a hell of a strain, and we hate loading worry on them."

"I am sorry to hear that." Robin spoke the truth. "My dad died of cancer, so you really do have my every sympathy. I still have my job to do, though. That will mean talking to them."

"But they don't know anything about this fraud allegation, and I'd rather they didn't at the moment, given their situation." Greg heaved a sigh. "Look, I have less of an issue with you guys doing what you have to do than coming to terms with a nosy neighbour who hacked into my stuff. Was it that bloke of Ellen's got his hands on my accounts? Sefton. No, Sexton, like the rugby player. Derek said he's a nosy bastard."

Robin ignored that jibe and the question. "Did you find anything in Ellen's house last summer to make you suspect she was investigating the Olivia Mears link?"

"No. We'd have been devastated if we'd realised." Greg tugged at his hair again. "I promise I didn't kill Ellen and neither did Alex."

"Then who did?" Robin asked. "Derek Cavendish?"

Greg hesitated. "I don't know, Mr. Bright. That's all I can say."

"But he *was* in Kinechester on the eleventh, which is when we believe Ellen died. He said they'd asked to visit you then, rather than come back again, but you refused. Why was that?"

"I had my hands full with the children. Alex had gone to her parents, remember?"

"Okay, well, we'll leave it there. For the moment." Robin held out his hand. "Can I have that spare key, please?"

"I don't have it anymore. I gave it to the copper on duty here the night her body was found. You'd better ask him what he's done with it."

The doorbell ringing, apparently heralding the arrival of Ashok with his fingerprinting gear given the familiar voice they could hear booming in the hall, brought the interview to a natural pause. While they waited for him to do his stuff, Pru drew Robin out into the hallway and murmured, "Gave the key to PC Brown? *He* didn't mention it that night."

"To give Brown the benefit of the doubt, it may have been after we left the scene because he was still there. He may have given it in when he got back to the station—no need to report that to us, so long as there was an evidence trail."

"Or he could have had a copy made. As could Carey I suppose. Hand in one and keep another for accessing the property on the quiet."

"If he did, he missed those bank statements, though." And had he perhaps left something behind, other than a waft of the distinctive cologne? Ellen had evidently been like Campbell with a bone, continuing to gnaw at it until satisfied. At what point had she bitten off more than she could chew?

"You know what, sir?" Pru said, once they'd left the Careys' house, having waited for Ashok to finish his fingerprinting. The constable could take on the new task of following up on the house key once they were back at base. "It felt like Carey was telling the truth when he said neither he nor Alex killed Ellen."

"I got that impression too. He was lying when he said he didn't know about whether Derek Cavendish had done it, though." All three were keeping up a brisk pace along the road, guarding against the extreme cold of the morning.

"Maybe he knows Derek *didn't* do it, but he didn't want to say that," Ashok suggested. "Wants to keep your attention focused away from Cromwell Road. Not that I was there, so tell me to shut up if you want."

"Feel free to chip in." Robin thought of all the times Adam had made an important point based on nothing stronger than reported testimony. The outsider's view sometimes cut through all the extraneous stuff to the heart of the matter. "Did you notice a couple of things in that conversation with Alex, Pru? The assumption that Ellen must have suspected her and was going to use that information. Surely that didn't all come into Alex's head as a result of your question."

"I agree, sir. She may not have mentioned it to hubby, though. And it's clear she's another person who's been fed a tale by Derek Cavendish. I'm sure she didn't know what had really happened with his dating frauds."

"Yes. She also appeared to feel on solid ground about her fingerprints being taken. She's either not directly involved with the killing or is sure she cleaned away any evidence she'd left."

"They're a shoes-in-the-house family too. All of them were wearing them, kids as well," Ashok pointed out.

"Eh? Oh, back to the bloody sock print. I keep forgetting about that." And yet, there was something buzzing in the back of Robin's brain that wouldn't make itself known—like the tiny flies that sometimes got themselves into his car and that evaded all efforts at being swotted.

They'd almost reached the car park when Robin paused to give the other two a sidelong glance. "Ellen liked puzzles, didn't she?"

"Yes. Sudokus and other things. Why?"

"*Smear* is an anagram of *Mears*. What if that note you saw on the pinboard was a message hidden in plain sight?"

"But what about the eleventh? How does that relate to Alex?" Pru shrugged and then suggested, "maybe it's a reminder that she had a call due with one of her dodgy contacts on the eleventh of January or upcoming in February. To discuss them hacking into whatever would prove Alex used to be Olivia."

"Perhaps. But why leave a note like that there? Nothing else like it on the board. Unless . . ." Robin snapped his fingers. "What if the eleventh refers to the day she died? She made the note, pinned it up when she went to exercise, with the intention of using it in some way. But she didn't, because she was killed."

"What do you think she intended to do?" Ashok asked. "What possible action could she have been considering taking, short of blackmail?"

It was as much of a mystery as the bloody turnip.

Chapter Sixteen

Back at the station, Robin left Pru to brief the team on the latest developments while he spoke to Denness and brought him up-to-date.

The chief superintendent rolled his eyes at the news. "I had no idea Olivia Mears was on our patch. Not that we're made aware of every person who's served their time and changed their name, but when it's someone so high-profile, I'd have expected a word in the ear."

"Her change of name is on file, although not her most recent address, so I'm double-checking everything, because I don't trust any of the witnesses to tell me the truth at the moment. Or that they won't deny it all down the line, so we get egg on our faces for not checking properly at the time. The fingerprint scanner threw a wobbly, so we've had to go old-fashioned ink. Ashok's putting them through the system, but we can conclude there are none of hers at the crime scene, or they'd have already showed up."

"I was going to ask if that was suspicious, then realised it would be very unlikely you'd find my fingerprints in my neighbours' houses." Denness grinned. "If the killer wiped down, as they appear to have, then everyone's dabs will have gone, innocent and guilty. That rings a bell. You'll have to double-check but I've a feeling Mr. and Mrs. Mears were suspected of helping get rid of what their daughter had been wearing at the time of the attack, although it was never proven. The Careys have children themselves?"

"Yes. Aged seven and nine, I believe. Ashok was brilliant at their house, by the way. He took the children's thumbprints too—made it all into a bit of a game so they'd be the same as their mum. I don't think the parents liked that, but they didn't kick up a fuss, and the girls got to keep them, anyway. I hate the thought of what would happen if both parents end up being jailed. The children have got their grandparents, of course, but it leaves me with a bad taste in my mouth."

"Not your responsibility, Robin, even if it feels like it might be. *The parents* are the ones who chose to commit a crime." Denness spread his hands.

"Anything about PC Brown yet?"

"He's a Sam not a William, for a start, and nothing else is showing. He's off work at the moment, though—went arse over tip while chasing a mugger round the back of the high street. Damage to his ankle and to his pride, because Jane Hazel caught the lad while Brown was sprawled on his backside. You're not thinking that's suspicious in itself?"

"Not unless there's a key not where it should be." Robin grinned. "I'll only bother to explain that if it comes about."

"Please do." Denness laughed. "So now we have a surfeit of suspects. Are we any closer to knowing which of them dealt the fatal blow or are they all in it together?"

Robin shrugged. "I'm not sure of that or who my money's on. Two women, both with a record of violence, two men, one a convicted swindler and the other probably going in the same direction. I'm not yet suspecting Brown of anything, but I need—for my own peace of mind at the very least—to know if he's linked to Deborah Cavendish, despite the name."

Denness nodded. "His family background should have shown up when he applied to join the force, although people do find a way round these things, so I'll do some further digging. We don't want another Abbotston happening here."

"Absolutely." Robin leaned forward, edging out of his chair. "I think that's all for the moment."

"Okay. I'm giving a media briefing later today and I'll give them something about pursuing new leads. Somehow the local rag has got hold on the fact Ellen worked for the government, so that might be all over the national press tomorrow and I'm bound to get grilled on it. I never thought I'd be grateful for animal mutilations."

Ellen's death had coincided with an outbreak of horrific injuries being inflicted on sheep and other livestock down in Wales. The media had been full of it, including interviews with so-called experts on feral big cats. Sad that it took precedence over the death of a human in terms of newsworthiness, if a blessing for the police.

"If it turns out this Welsh business is connected to this case, I'm resigning."

"Me too." Denness rubbed his forehead. "I've often wondered how people afford the properties in the Ramparts. If anybody mentions Brink's-Mat, Robin, do let me know."

With a snort, Robin made his getaway.

Next official job was to ring Jeremy, to see if he knew how Ellen had got her hands on confidential information, but before that he'd touch base with Adam. A medical update, saying thanks for the Olivia Mears tip, and a bit of mutual support was worth taking a few minutes for.

"So, all in all, your shingles has been useful," Robin said, after he'd given a summary of the morning.

"I'll remember that when I want to scratch myself to pieces."

"The Mears element seems to have partly solved another mystery. We were wondering why Ellen had a Post-it Note with 'Cervical smear eleventh!!' on it. *Smear* could be an anagram of *Mears*."

"Could be. I don't think eleventh is an anagram, though. The elven? That sounds like *Lord of the Rings* territory. Vet Helen? Does that ring a bell?"

"Not the slightest tinkle. Keep working at it, though. Right, I have another call to make. Milk thing. You know."

"Yeah, I know."

One call ended, Robin got onto the next one. Jeremy Sexton's reaction at hearing about the stash was an awestruck "She had been busy, hadn't she? I'm aware of the charity business, but am I allowed to know what else she was digging up?"

"Not at present. If it results in a prosecution, you'll know soon enough." Jeremy wasn't stupid and would be able to fill in some of the blanks that the media wouldn't be able to access when—if—this case came to court. Better not to count his chickens yet. "I don't want to compromise either what you do now or what you did for the government in the past, but I need to know whether Ellen was capable of hacking into company or other files. Through a ton of security."

"I doubt it, unless she'd acquired the skill recently and kept the fact to herself. Beyond both our capabilities, which is a bit of a shame as it might have proved useful. I will deny saying that, by the way, Mr. Bright." Jeremy chuckled. "She did, however, know people who were both capable and unscrupulous enough to hack into almost any site or system they wanted to, given time. Again, without compromising security, I think I can tell you she'd have had contacts who'd have done it for her, quid pro quo."

Robin remembered what Trevor had said about the conversation in his garden. Ellen being on the trail of a woman with pink hair and calling in favours in the process. "One last thing. Did Ellen mention what happened five years or so ago that raised her suspicions about somebody she knew? Sorry to be vague again."

"I understand perfectly. Five years ago we hadn't got back in touch, so all I can think of that happened that year was one of her cruises. I know she was on the high seas during the summer of 2016, because it was the Olympics and the internet was so poor she couldn't keep up with events."

"I'd heard she liked her athletics." She'd no doubt have fumed at the postponement of the 2020 Olympiad. "Did anything recent get her thinking?"

"I do remember a conversation when we went on holiday last August, but I doubt it's what you want, because it had to do with this Carey bloke again."

"I'd still like to hear it. Might be useful for my mate in fraud."

"Cross all the *i*'s and dot all the *t*'s type, is he?" Jeremy quipped. "Then tell him Ellen mentioned the neighbours' children and how they'd had their grandparents dropping in. She said that may not have turned out to be their wisest move. She wouldn't tell me exactly what she meant, which I'm afraid led to another row. She may have been talking about them breaking Covid rules—she complained about that a few times—but I suppose she could have recognised his parents from one of her fraud or other investigations and suspected the son of also being involved. Coincidences do happen."

"They do indeed. I'll pass that on." Robin would also bear the fact in mind. Yes, it might have been exactly as Jeremy theorised, but it could have been Alex's parents who'd visited. If the couple's faces had rung a bell, or a conversation overheard in the garden had raised suspicions, that might have been the catalyst for Ellen to get her research claws into a new topic.

Robin entered the briefing room to find everyone still discussing developments, some of which were new to him. The Browns of Ireton Avenue had been eliminated from their enquiries. Pru had recalled that they'd been keen on family history, telling her how researching their family trees on a certain internet site had kept them sane over the last year. Using that information, Naomi had soon located their page and found no mention of a Deborah, nor indeed any woman of the right age among the various Browns listed.

"I'm quite pleased about that as I'd taken quite a shine to them and their unashamed nosiness." Pru chuckled.

"I'm pleased too. We've enough tangled lines to untangle." Robin turned to Ashok. "What about the spare key?"

"Safe with all the other evidence," the constable confirmed. "Logged in when PC Brown came off duty. Are we still thinking he's connected?"

"Denness thinks not. Wrong name for the son, no obvious links, although if he was a more distant relative, they might not show up. I'm inclined to do nothing other than keep him at the back of our minds for the moment. Two Browns down, one to go," Robin added, with a rueful smile.

"Third time lucky. Chances are Billy the Bins *is* Deborah's son," Naomi said. "I found old pictures of him on social media. There was a meme doing the rounds a while back about posting snaps of yourself when you were younger. There he was with his mum. We all reckon it's Deborah."

"Good work. Do we have anyone called Helen involved with the case, by the way? Or a vet?" Blank looks greeted Robin's question. "I've had a thought. If *smear* is an anagram of *Mears*, then maybe *eleventh* is an anagram too. Or we're reading too much into it and it simply means the eleventh."

"It would have been a lot easier if Ellen hadn't been so fond of puzzles and hiding things," Pru said. "I'm starting to think everything has a hidden meaning."

Too easy to get distracted by hidden files, word games, and the like. In the end, this would come down to the basics—who was where and when, who had the motive, and who was able to get out of that house without leaving a trail.

"Sorry to have to muck up your timeline with new information." Robin cast an eye at the display on the board. "Hey, you've not hung around."

"Naomi's been all over it since we heard the latest," Ben said.

"Well, get your marker, because I've something else to add." Robin pointed at the early end of the timeline, where the date of the Suzie Banks trial had already been added. "According to Jeremy, Ellen was on a cruise during the 2016 Olympics, which is when this all hit the news, so it's possible she didn't see the flurry of interest about Olivia. Pru and I were wondering why she'd not got on the trail back then."

"So what did set her off?" Ashok asked.

"Jeremy said something about the grandparents visiting, which he took to mean Greg's mum and dad, because they're the ones with the holiday home and I think Ellen had been complaining about their lockdown breaking, which must have been going on during that first clampdown, as well. The grandparents' visit must have been before Ellen went on holiday with him in August because that's when she mentioned it to him. She said . . ." Robin consulted his notes. "She said it may not have been their wisest move."

"If it ultimately led to her death, it may not have been her wisest move, either. Investigating the family Mears, I mean," Pru said. "We'll put that conversation on the timeline too. It's all starting to make sense in terms of explaining her behaviour."

"How's this for an explanation," Naomi chipped in. "Alex Carey wasn't already at her parents' house on the eleventh. She was here and she saw Ellen. Maybe putting those bloody bins out. Ellen says something about her former identity that made Alex see red. Perhaps the children were with her and she was worried they'd find out if Ellen kept mentioning it."

"But she habitually kept shtum about everything," Ashok pointed out. "It wasn't Ellen's style to blab, so why risk dropping a hint?"

"Maybe it was nothing intentional on Ellen's part," Ben said. "Alex misunderstood and thought it was a dig at her."

Robin wanted to avoid going down another line, especially as Naomi's theory felt plausible so far. "That happens. Go on, Naomi."

"Alex broods on that all day. Goes round to see Ellen later that evening, maybe taking her bin in for her as an excuse. Ellen comes out from the kitchen into the garden, tells her to naff off—'I can take my own bin in, thanks, I'm not that useless'"—as an impersonation of a crabitty old woman, it was spot on—"then turns on her heels. Alex follows her into the house, has a 'What's the big idea?' type of confrontation, grabs a knife—or scissors, or both—and does the deed. Realises what she's done and knows that with her history, any story about an accident or self-defence—even if it were true—is unlikely to be believed."

"So she panics?" Ashok asked.

Naomi shook her head. "No. That's exactly what she doesn't do. Calmly, she rings Greg to bring her a change of clothes and some wet wipes or whatever. Which he does and they dispose of the evidence. Into the bins, which they then get taken away and chucked, care of Billy the Bins, whose mother is coerced into making it happen on the principle that Greg will grass her up if she doesn't. Hence the visit to his place later that week."

"But the bins were empty," Ben said. "Didn't the stuff go into the church skip?"

"We have no proof of either of those things. Only Billy's statement and he could have been lying. The skip and the person with the bin in Ireton Avenue were red herrings." Naomi sat back, evidently delighted with herself.

"Two points," Robin said. "The Careys could easily have picked up the remote control for the blinds and would be likelier to know about how they operated than a stranger to the house, but what about the missing bank card?"

"Same applies." Naomi moved to the incident board, pointing at the timeline. "If Greg had been through her files, he could have known about the two accounts. Easy enough for the Careys to go in and out of number thirty-nine time and again, as their plan developed, picking up what they needed to keep up the pretence of her being alive."

"That could also explain why they wanted to create that uncertainty about the date of death. Pack Alex off to her parents' house to 'care for her mother'"—Pru did the speech marks things with her fingers—"and then she gets her alibi because she makes sure the neighbours can vouch for her too. Just not on the right day. She was back on the fourteenth, because they had the Zoom party for *his* parents, although we only have his word for that. She could have logged in from any device, anywhere and pretended to be at home. Later, the Careys arrange for the body to be found because the longer they appear not to notice anything wrong, the dodgier it looks for them."

Robin was beginning to like the sound of this, although niggling doubts remained. "What about the bloody sock print? This scenario doesn't really work with the *take your shoes off at the door* one."

"No, but have you tried taking your shoes off while you're standing, especially if they've got laces?" Naomi grinned triumphantly. "Every chance you'd put your foot down where you shouldn't. You realise you've got blood on your sole, and then you put the thing down again. Until your helper helps you out of the room, you hopping and them taking the weight, like a footballer coming off the pitch."

How simple and how neat an explanation. Remembering getting changed on the beach, carefully cleaning one foot only to put it down in the sand again, Robin could imagine that happening. And while he couldn't "see" the killer yet, he could envisage exactly that scenario playing out.

"Greg Carey would have to organise all the cover up on his own, then, if she'd gone to the parents the next morning," Ben said.

"With the help of Derek and Deborah," Naomi said. "That's one of the reasons they were there on the fourteenth. He'd been in touch with them, threatening all sorts if they didn't help out."

"Maybe that's why they started texting Jeremy Sexton," Ashok suggested. "We don't know what Ellen had left lying around, ready to hide away later that evening. If Greg had found something implicating Deborah Cavendish, perhaps something with Jeremy's name on it, he'd have used it as leverage and they'd have been spurred into action on two fronts."

"But the timeline doesn't work for that," Ben pointed out. "They met on the fourteenth. Those texts started on the thirteenth."

"Carey told them over the phone. Sent them a picture of what he had." Ashok shrugged. "We shouldn't play down Derek's possible role in any cover up. He's a convicted conman, don't forget, good at creating a believable story."

"We're going to have to get statements from the children, aren't we?" Pru said.

Robin shuddered. "Yep. I hate having to do that, but it may be the only way to get to the truth of who was where and when. We better be damn sure we're right before we go in mob handed. So far, the only hard evidence we have linking the Careys to the killing is the key to Ellen's house and Billy the Bins—and he's at one step removed."

"They're bright kids, sir," Ashok said. "They were asking me lots of questions about what's going on. They said their grandad lets them watch old episodes of *Midsomer Murders* with him and they're keeping him up-to-date with everything that's been going on, especially as he's not been well, so he likes the gossip. I get the impression that pair see themselves as the hub of local knowledge."

"Sonia Parsons won't be happy—she'll think that's her role." Naomi chuckled.

"It might mean Greg's plans not to let the grandparents know anything about the fraud case are pointless," Pru said. "I wonder if the girls have been telling their grandad about the raid on their house? So, what next, sir? Billy the Bins?"

Robin, closing his eyes for a moment, rubbed his forehead. He had to find a logical way forward. "Not yet. If we show our hand too soon, he'll be giving his mum the heads-up, then she'll get on to Carey. At present, they don't know we've made that connection and they may be hoping we never work it out. I'm inclined to get all of them in here at the same time so they can't collude any further, but I can't do it on what little I have. We must be still missing something we could use. Traffic cameras helped cracked the last murder case we tackled, Pru, so what's the equivalent this time?"

"Phone records of where people were and when?" the sergeant suggested. "I can apply to get a fix on the Careys and the Cavendishes, although it won't pin down exactly which house they were in."

"It would tell us if Alex was away or not on the eleventh itself and if Derek and Deborah were in Cromwell Road that day." Small pieces of the jigsaw were slotting in, yet Robin still had no clear depiction of the whole scene.

He'd always dreaded being in charge of a case that defied adequate solution, where suspicions could never be backed up with enough evidence of a quality to convince a jury. A case that slowly fizzled out, added to the file of cold cases that might get revived if new facts emerged. A blot on his record, perhaps, although that was less of a worry than the impact a lack of resolution would have on those affected. The constant niggle of going about your daily business, meeting other people and thinking, *Was it him? Was it her? Am I really safe?*

The briefing came to an end in a sombre mood. There were plenty of jobs still to do, including liaison with Henry's team to find out if they'd turned up anything relevant, but it all felt like nibbling round the edges. At least Robin and Pru had a clear focus for the next few hours. They rarely tackled a case where a statement had to be taken from a child or other vulnerable person, so reading through all the legal guidance on interviewing in such a situation would be vital before putting together a plan of action. Neither thing would be enjoyable, but while the reading couldn't be avoided in the short term, hopefully they'd get a breakthrough that would make talking to the children unnecessary.

Chapter Seventeen

A dam had got to the point all he could smell was calamine lotion. Not an unpleasant aroma, but you could soon tire of it. Even dinner—homemade soup that he'd found the strength to whip up, which suggested he was on the road to recovery—bore a vague hint of lotion. Hopefully the soup wouldn't taste of the stuff.

Robin had arrived home earlier than expected, saying that he needed to think so was going for a run. When he got back, he showered while Adam prepared their meal, emerging clean, fragrant, and frustratingly seductive. While Adam's physical well-being was on the up, those spots and the wretched calamine they were daubed with both acted as passion killers. A brief cuddle and a snog while the soup finished heating was all they could manage comfortably.

"That's good," Robin said, as they broke the clinch. "I wish I felt as happy with the case."

"Still none the wiser? I guess you didn't discover that the murderer was a vet called Helen?" Adam asked, as they headed to the table with soup, cheese, and crusty bread.

"Eh? Oh, the anagram. No. No vets, no Helens. Although Ellen is quite like Helen isn't it, but there's not enough *l*'s to make her name out of it."

"You've clearly been mulling it over like I have. It's addictive once you start. Very soothing while you're making soup."

"Yeah. Same when you're driving. Or not driving, as the case may be." Robin cut himself a piece of bread, loading it with brie. "I got stuck behind a broken-down car at the Cranshaw lights on the way home, and my mind went off on a tangent. I tried mashing eleventh and Mears together but got nothing meaningful."

"Same here. In light of what Trevor told me, I read up about the Olivia Mears case. It's a shame there's no *o* in 'cervical.'"

Adam hadn't expected quite such a dramatic response to his words. Robin, eyebrows raised, had put down his bread and cheese, when it had been halfway to his mouth. That showed the importance of whatever it was.

"Can you say that again, please?"

"You could do with an *o* in 'cervical,' instead of the *e*. Then you get *Vic* and *Carol*. That's the names of Olivia Mears's parents. Otherwise you get *Vic* and *Carel*, which doesn't quite work. What is it? What have I said?"

"If I wasn't all soupy and cheesy, I'd kiss you." Robin grinned. "Victor and Carol Mears. That's either the coincidence of the century or Ellen playing word games again. Pru and I both saw the Post-it Note, and it did look like an *o* in what she'd written—'corvical' rather than 'cervical'—but we assumed it was nothing more than her handwriting being unclear."

"Is it possible Ellen saw them in Alex's garden or going into her house on the eleventh and made a note of the fact for future reference? A note that only she'd understand, if anyone came into the house snooping?"

"It could have been a reminder to try and compare them to the drawing she had from the original trial. Then she died before she could act on it and then take the note down."

"Why was Ellen doing all this? I mean, I get the bits you've mentioned about exposing fraud, but what I can't see her motive for wanting to know about Alex, apart from bloody nosiness. Unless she thought the woman was breaking some law." Adam could see why his husband found this all so frustrating. New questions cropping up that defied answers.

"Perhaps she wanted to know for self-satisfaction. In the same way that she enjoyed doing puzzles, to find the solution." Robin waved his spoon. "Maybe she couldn't help herself, either through some variety of neurodiversity or because she was so used to doing it. When you've spent all your life researching other people's secrets and lies, it must be difficult to get out of the habit."

"I doubt her victims—if I can call them that—would have appreciated the thrill of solving the riddle. They'd have assumed she was out to get them, so maybe they thought they'd better get her first before the shit hit the fan. What do you call it? *Cui bono*? No, not Bonio." The last remark was addressed to Campbell, who had been lying quietly in the corner until he'd heard what he'd evidently thought was a reference to his favourite biscuit. "Solve your dad's case and you can have a whole bag of them. You fancy yourself as a police dog, but this time it's brains that's needed, not brawn."

"Yeah. I'm not sure I'd want him on my quiz night team."

"Unless they had a round all about d-o-g b-i-s-c-u-i-t-s. Or how to defend your masters from attack. He's good at that. I've said something else, haven't I?"

Robin's eyes glinted. "You have. You need to come into the station and give us all the shingles if this is the effect it has on thinking processes. Campbell's put his life on the line for us before. Who else would?"

Adam, still not sure why he'd merited such compliments, took his cue to play along. "Who'd put their life on the line for me personally or a person generically?"

"Start with you. Who'd risk everything for Adam Matthews?"

"Robin Bright, I'd hope. My mum. My dad when he was still alive— Oh, I see. I was being thick. Vic and Carol Mears, they of the anagram."

"They of the 'our daughter's a good sort who got led astray' defence." Robin picked up his spoon. "Let's finish this, by which time I might have a murder theory to get your opinion on."

"You certainly know how to give a boy a good time."

Once they'd finished eating, Robin insisted on giving the dog his reward as he might, inadvertently, have helped them make progress. "We'd have got here eventually, I'm sure, because it feels bleeding obvious now. I won't suggest a beer for us because that might be tempting fate to celebrate prematurely, but a cup of tea wouldn't go amiss."

"You feed himself and I'll get the kettle on."

Mugs in hand, they plonked themselves either end of a sofa, legs meeting in the middle. A self-satisfied Newfoundland lay on the floor between them, evidently hoping another biscuit might come his way if he played his doggy cards right.

"Listen to this and tell me what you think. Mr. and Mrs. Mears, or whatever they call themselves now, come down to Kinechester to visit their grandchildren. It's not allowed, but they don't care. Greg Carey tells them he's found out that Ellen's been trying to discover if Alex is really Olivia. One or both of them goes ballistic, because we know how protective they are of their daughter. 'How dare anyone interfere with Olivia's new life?'" Robin's impression of elderly outrage was spot on. "Does that work so far?"

"All apart from one point. You told me that Carey had got into Ellen's house last summer. If that's when he discovered what Ellen was up to, why not tell the grandparents before?"

"Either because he didn't know at that point, which is what he alleges or he *did* know but didn't want to mention anything because Mr. Mears has been unwell. We've been told he's not coping with lockdown and his cancer may have returned, so they might have wanted to protect him."

"Bad people still do good things. And vice versa." Adam nodded. "So why change their minds and tell him now?"

Robin shrugged. "It slips out by mistake, perhaps. I can imagine the children saying something about the time their dad had been investigating a gas leak next door, and Mr. Mears smells a rat. Excuse pun. Anyway, people do let things slip if they're taken off guard. You seem less than impressed with that as a theory."

"That's because I *am* less than impressed. Not up to your usual standard. Yes, people do let things slip, but that pair must be used to guarding their tongues."

"Okay, let's go with the second option. I'm thinking that over Christmas, while Ellen was away, Carey discovered his wife was under investigation too. He swore to us he'd not discovered anything along those lines the previous summer, which could have been perfectly true. Serves me right for not asking open questions." Robin grimaced. "So, somehow he obtained the code for Ellen's alarm and he got into her house for another poke around. Maybe he found the same stash we did or something she'd left lying about because she thought the place was impregnable."

Adam had been struck with an idea. "Kelvin said how well he got on with her when he was a youngster. That she always had time for him and his mate—stuck up for them against bullies too. How friendly was she with the Carey children?"

"Probably friendlier than she was with the parents. Bought them chocolates and things. Why?"

"Just thinking of the security keypads we have at school. We have to change the code regularly because the children have eyes like hawks and can work out the number sequence straight away if they see an adult tapping it out. If the Carey children happened to drop round when she was turning the alarm off, if they helped her in with her shopping or whatever . . ."

"Or went round to get their Advent calendars." Robin affectionately poked Adam's ankle. "Have I ever told you how much it helps having an outsider's perspective?"

"Yes, but not often enough." Adam returned the prod. "I hardly feel like an outsider, though. Kelvin. Flirty Trevor. They treat me like one of the team."

"Trevor's been flirting with you, has he? I'll have to watch out."

"Get back to your theory. So far, we have the Mears parents suddenly finding out Ellen's snooping on their daughter. What then?"

"Well, originally I was going to say that Mr. Mears goes round to confront her. Through the unlocked back garden gate and into the house. Bold as brass. To the extent of taking his shoes off." Robin wagged his finger. "No, I haven't gone loopy. We've been trying to explain the bloody sock print on the carpet, and I knew that at some point one of the witnesses mentioned someone else being house-proud. Only tonight have I remembered it was the local gossip, Sonia Parsons, who told me and Naomi that Alex's mum was a *no mess on the carpet* type. Words to that effect."

"I'm going to be devil's advocate again. If Vic Mears had been her bosom friend and Ellen wasn't that concerned about her privacy, then I might buy it, but he wasn't, she was, and I don't." Adam grinned.

"Note the 'originally.' You bringing the children into it gave me a new idea. What if he—or Mrs. Mears, although I've two particular reasons for focussing on him—decides to be sneaky? Takes the girls round with, say, a homemade thank-you card or whatever. Then he sends the children back next-door because he says he wants a grown-up word with Ellen. They get into an argument."

"That works in terms of getting him into the house, with his shoes off because it's habitual for him to shed them at the door. You wouldn't find the card they'd brought because it would be taken in the general tidying up, either on the day or later. Thing is, I seem to remember you saying she didn't have defensive wounds and was happy to turn her back on the killer. That doesn't sound like she was in a raging argument. Don't be disappointed." Adam gave his partner's toes an affectionate squeeze. "I hope you don't wear your emotions on your face when you're interviewing suspects."

"Never. I only let my guard drop with you. Always have done."

"Even when you had me on your suspect list for killing Ian Youngs?"

"You have no idea how much a fight every interview with you was. Kept telling myself not to flirt. You're very distracting." Robin rubbed his hands along Adam's foot.

"Hold those thoughts for when I'm less itchy. Nothing doing bed-wise until that point."

"We'd better get back to discussing the case, then. That's usually a passion killer." Robin put his hands behind his head, perhaps not trusting them to behave themselves. "Can we put the argument bit to one side? Let's see if there are any plot holes in the rest of my shiny new theory."

"Hole-picking device ready and waiting. I'm really quite enjoying the mental challenge. Let's start with why Mr. Mears and not Mrs.?"

"For a start, because we've been told he has a brain tumour, which may or may not be malignant. That might affect his behaviour. It might also make him reckless if he thinks he's coming to the end of his time. Secondly, those girls are keeping him updated on all the developments in the case. All they know about, anyway. That might be innocent, of course, but it's grist to the mill." Robin shrugged. "Right, Mr. Mears is in Ellen's house and for whatever reason, she turns her back. Maybe to go and put that card in another room. In the kitchen, he spots a knife and a pair of scissors and the red mist descends, because he instantly sees a way of stopping her prying. He goes after her and kills her, then he comes to his sense and realises he's up shit creek. This is where his being a fan of crime shows comes in. He knows he has to minimise what traces he leaves at the scene, so he gets out his phone, calls Alex, and says, 'Help!' She and Mrs. Mears come to the rescue. There's some suspicion Mr. and Mrs. Mears helped get rid of the evidence when Olivia attacked that pensioner, so they might have experience of it."

Adam considered that for a moment. Unlikely as it seemed, he could imagine such a thing happening, from what he'd seen at school. "Actually, that's one of the most convincing bits of your theory. I can see them telling him not to move, then stripping him of his clothes, putting them straight into a bin bag, maybe making him stand on a plastic sheet while they did so."

"It sounds like you were there."

"Almost. If you've never seen a female learning-support assistant mopping up a child who's covered themselves, the desk, and the floor with projectile vomit, you wouldn't credit it. They leave barely any evidence of what's happened. Lads like Kelvin try their best but something's missing. Lack of practice, probably. Male LSAs with kids of their own are fine. But"—Adam prodded Robin's leg—"there'd be an awful lot of going in and out between the two houses involved. Admittedly it would be dark and so there'd be less chance of them being spotted, but wouldn't the girls be suspicious? They'd wonder what was going on."

Robin grinned. "See how convincing this is. Whoever's looking after them—and I'm guessing that would be Greg—simply tells them that Grandad's been taken ill and that he needs to be cared for. Maybe Greg takes them to the local McDonald's drive-through or whatever, saying that Grandad wants them to have a treat, although it's really to get them out of the way. If they realise that's what's happening, Greg says that was Grandad's plan, because he doesn't want them to see him unwell, but they mustn't let on that they know what the old man's done. Alex drives her parents home and stays with them for a few days, not only establishing a potential alibi, but helping manage the cover up from their end of things. Including all the stuff with blinds and what have you, to obscure the date Ellen was killed."

Adam nodded slowly. "Has it occurred to you there's another reason for pretending Ellen was still alive when she wasn't? Those two children. If they're as bright as they sound and take that much interest in what's going on, then if I was in their parents and grandparents' place, I'd be doing everything I could to make them think Ellen didn't die the night Grandad was taken ill and they were whipped off for a takeaway Happy Meal."

Robin's eyes narrowed in thought. "She said something about the girls, Alex Carey did. That they liked to see Ellen's lights shining from the hallway onto the pavement because it was pretty. It *is* nice, where some of the houses have what must be the original stained glass above their front doors. I can see the area's appeal."

"Are you still glad we didn't move there?"

"What do you think, given the last few weeks? I've never had to investigate my neighbours, and I hope I never will. I could plead that I was only doing my job, but it would put you in an awkward position, wouldn't it?" The distress Robin felt at the notion couldn't be hidden. "Especially given the way every murder case seems to decide you need to be involved at one step removed."

"The first one dragged me in directly, remember? I mean, I should be grateful for it having brought us together, but being part of a group under suspicion isn't an experience I want to repeat anytime soon." There were worse memories from that time: the sight of a dead man in the little school kitchen, the knowledge that someone he knew was likely responsible, a stand-off that had taken place in his own home. But none of them gave Adam quite the frisson that being a suspect had. "Is that how the Careys must be feeling? And the other pair? Like they've got a weight on their shoulders that only the police can shift."

"I guess so. Even if they're all involved in the cover-up, it could be that only one of them did the deed and unless someone breaks ranks and tells us who it was, they're all equally tainted. Assuming it's any of them to start with and this isn't some random act by a lunatic or a carefully devised assassination by one of the groups Ellen has been officially investigating. In which case, we haven't realistically got a snowball in hell's chance of identifying them, not in the short term. And everyone lives with carrying that weight."

That was too gloomy a note to end the evening with. Adam knew how much his husband worried that he'd be landed with an unsolvable case, and he didn't want Robin dwelling on it. He wasn't going to give bland reassurances—*You know you'll get the person who did it, you always do*—so settled for, "We'll cross that bridge if and when we come to it. You've got a shiny new theory to test, remember?"

"I do. I'd really like a few solid bits of evidence to back it up, though." Robin patted Adam's leg. "When you say your prayers tonight, could you ask for a nice fingerprint or deleted email conversation or anything else that might impress a jury?"

"I'll do my best." Adam ran his fingers through his hair, unsettled. Could Robin really fail this time? "Although I suspect God would say that's your job, not His."

Adam woke dripping with sweat. Why was it that when he roused before the alarm sounded, then went back to sleep again, he had such vivid dreams, in which time was either hugely elongated or compacted and everything felt so real?

He and Campbell had been running around the Ramparts, when Trevor had come out to join them. So far, so normal dream fodder, including Campbell having turned a peculiar shade of pink. Trevor had been chatting him up, as usual, although Adam had known from the start that his flirtation had an ulterior motive. He was trying to prove that Robin was in fact Lord Lucan, and when he'd tried to entice Adam into his house so they could carry on the conversation, Campbell had taken a chunk out of the bloke's leg.

All very peculiar, but it had left him with the germ of an idea, one he wanted to put to Robin before the bloke left for work.

"Good morning, gorgeous," Adam said, as he entered the kitchen. "Good morning, Robin, as well."

"You can get your own tea, for that. Campbell can't manage to pour it, without thumbs." Robin cracked a smile. Perched on a kitchen stool, with the dog sitting patiently at his side in case a piece of toast fell to the floor unheeded, he gave the impression of a man who'd had a good night's sleep and was significantly less stressed than when he'd arrived home the previous day. The discussion they'd had the evening before had clearly helped. "How are the spots?"

"In need of calamine but not as bad as yesterday. I'm gradually clawing my way back to humanity."

"That's a weight off my mind. A few days back I'd convinced myself you were going to be really ill. You *do* look a lot better this morning."

"Probably because I've got another idea. About your case. Feel free to ignore it because it's based on the weird dream I had in which Campbell was protecting me from Trevor. Don't ask." Adam leaned against the sink as he waited for the kettle to re-boil. "How far would Ellen have gone to get to the truth?"

Robin shrugged. "As far as hacking into—or getting someone else to hack into—computer files, for a start. Why?"

"I was getting round your 'What's Vic Mears doing in the house?' problem. This idea doesn't need thank-you cards or people taking their shoes off despite the fact they've come to have a blazing row."

"If you can sort that out, you have my full attention."

"What if she invited him? Or both of them? She wants to put some questions to them, not realising for a moment that her life might be at risk if she does so."

"Which could explain that bloody Post-it Note. If it was about an appointment." Robin idly rubbed the dog's head, clearly using the soothing activity as an aid to thought. "It would also fit in with the Careys *not* having told the Mearses what Ellen was up to. Otherwise they might have refused to go, suspecting a trap. They must have had experience from dealing with the media back when Olivia's trial was happening."

"Have either of the children got birthdays around now? It would be a great pretext for getting the grandparents round strictly on the quiet. 'Don't tell Alex and Greg but I'm planning a surprise for little Sophie' or whatever she's called."

"Carly. Or Cerys."

"I've got two Carlys in my class. Cerys is a bit of a different name. Anyway, Ellen seems to have liked kids, so might have said something like, 'I don't have any children or grandchildren of my own, so I enjoy treating them.'"

"I don't know about the children, but Greg's got a significant birthday coming up. Ellen could have played exactly the same card about him. This is all circumstantial, of course, but it makes as much sense as any other theory we've had." Robin took out his phone, then stuffed it back into his pocket. "I've been sitting here *umm*ing and *ah*ing about whether to text Pru to tell her my idea, and that nearly swung it for me. I think I'll wait, though, and think it through again. If it all still hangs together when I get into work, then I'll put it to the team."

"And if it doesn't?"

"Then I'll be asking you to have a little kip and see if you get another useful dream."

A quick kiss and a pat for the dog, then Robin was gone, leaving a faint hint of aftershave and a scattering of crumbs on the floor, which Campbell began to hoover up gleefully.

"I hope your dad's on the last leg of this investigation and we can soon get back to normal," Adam told the dog, who ignored him in favour of locating the last remnants of toast.

Chapter Eighteen

Despite being held up by roadworks on the way to the station, increasing both his stress and available thinking time, Robin hadn't thought of any new objections to his theory. In fact, he was becoming increasingly convinced that they were at last getting closer to the truth. He tried to rein in his enthusiasm, not wanting to let himself in for a fall, but it was difficult when his much-vaunted copper's nose was telling him he was on track. The one degree of caution he *would* exercise was not mentioning any of this to Denness until the idea had passed the rigorous appraisal of his team and, hopefully, got some concrete facts to support it.

"You're chipper, sir," Pru greeted him as he entered the office. "I thought when you texted to say you were stuck in traffic you'd be steaming at the ears when you arrived."

"It gave me time to think." Robin did a quick head count, finding all his core team present, as well as the key admin support but without Aaron, who was still on secondment. Aaron. Robin had a half-formed idea prompted by the bloke that needed to coalesce into something tangible. He didn't have time to consider that now, though. "I've got a theory and I'd like to talk you through it. Adam's already picked holes in it and I've had to sew it together again but feel free to pull it apart."

"We've had a couple of developments here," Pru said, "although we'll hold fire on them for the moment. They'll either support your idea or blow it out of the water."

That sounded ominous. "Are you sure you shouldn't fire them at me first?"

"Nope." Pru crossed her arms, settling back to listen. "I, for one, want to hear what you have to say unimpeded by any new information."

"No pressure, then. Let me get my coat off and I'll start." Robin ditched his outer layers, then went to peruse the incident board, in case there was an obvious point he'd missed. Ben appeared at his shoulder, bearing a mug of coffee. "Thanks." Robin grabbed it happily. "I need that."

"Pleasure, sir. I'm looking forward to hearing you too. I'll have a fiver on my new evidence helping rather than hindering." With that enigmatic remark, the constable took his seat again.

Robin knocked back a deep draught of coffee, then said, "Okay. This takes everything we know and shakes it about a bit. It's got some huge-arse assumptions, including one that reverses our understanding of how Ellen ended up with a killer in her house. I want to explain why I think one—or both—of Alex Carey's parents is the killer. I know they're now called Odell, but for my sanity, I'll stick to the old surname, and while I'm going to refer to Vic Mears as the murderer, for reasons I'll go into, it's possible it was Carol Mears who did the deed. And the first clue is the word 'corvical,' which was on that Post-it Note and which we read as 'cervical,' as in smear. It's an anagram of the names 'Vic' and 'Carol.' 'Corvical smear' equals 'Vic and Carol Mears.'"

He took another drink, then launched into an account of the last few months as seen through this different perspective. The Carey girls getting the code to Ellen's alarm, Greg making another entry into the house, at which point he discovered that both he and Alex were under investigation. Ellen meanwhile secretly contacting Mr. and Mrs. Mears, probably on one of the occasions when they were visiting, and arranging a meeting with them on the eleventh. The couple realising they'd been contacted under false pretences. An act of violence, arising from an argument or a cold-blooded attack to protect a loved one. The rest of the family rallying round, clearing up and covering up. False alibis created, waters muddied, statements to police that told sufficient truth to make them convincing.

"So," Robin said finally, and before he finished off his much-needed coffee, "does your new information mean this is a load of tripe?"

"Far from it, sir." Pru brandished some sheets of paper. "First thing today I went back through the details of Ellen's phone calls, matching them to our timeline. It gives us proof that she was in touch with Derek when he said she was, but the relevant point is a series of calls either side of Christmas. One to the Vinces, which we already know about, and several others that we've assumed were also to spread the old seasons' greetings. Once we fixed the date of death around the eleventh, we'd not followed them up. Things is, there are ones to and from a Mrs. Carol Odell. It could be the mother."

Robin restrained his excitement. This could still be coincidental—although Odell wasn't a common surname. "Can you verify that in your best subtle manner? If it *is* them, then get the details onto the timeline and check Ellen's message records for anything from the same number. Ben, are you about to explode?"

The constable nodded, then glanced around the team. "I stayed late last night— I know, we were supposed to go home and get a break, but you'll be pleased I did. We'd already studied her browsing history for the weeks up to her death, but there was nothing in there that didn't link up with what we knew about or seemed particularly suspicious. So I went further back, into last year. She'd been doing a lot of research into the Olivia Mears case but not only that. She was taking an interest in people who'd committed violent crimes as youngsters and whether they went on to do the same as adults. Specifically if they'd gone on to harm their own children. If she found anything of note, she hadn't made a file of it, like she did with the fraud stuff, but maybe that's because she had very little to show that specifically linked to her next-door neighbours. Or maybe her years of training had taught her to take them with a pinch of salt. Some of these sites she went on are pretty lurid, and I'm not convinced they're totally reliable. So yes, I'd say that also backs up your idea, because it shifts Ellen's motive for digging into Alex's past from nosiness to child protection, at least in her own mind."

"So far, so good, then." Robin gave his team a nod of encouragement. "Now, shoot me down in flames. I want any loopholes in this identified by us, not by some smarty-pants solicitor."

Ashok raised his hand tentatively. "One thing. How did she physically get in contact with Vic and Carol Mears in the first place? Without Alex, Greg, or the girls finding out?"

"She could have slipped them a note," Naomi suggested, "if she saw them around and about."

"They used to come and house sit," Pru said. "Alex told us that. What if they house sat last summer? If Ellen was already on the trail then—and was bloody furious about Greg having got into the house, which she suspects because someone's been touching that file—she might have wanted to get her own back. Sets up contact with Mr. And Mrs. Mears on the off-chance it would be useful, playing the 'organising a special surprise' card or whatever."

"Okay, but here's the second bit. How did they manage a visit to Ellen on the eleventh of January without any of the Careys realising what was going on?" Ashok asked.

"They lied. Told the others they were nipping out for fags or chocolate for the girls or going to the cash machine to stock up on cash," Naomi said. "It's easy enough to make an excuse and if only one of them visited Ellen, it would look less suspicious."

"Any other major objections before we put this to the ultimate test?" Robin gave his officers time, but they didn't appear to have any other queries. Yet. Pru seemed unusually pensive, obviously mulling something over, although she didn't raise it. Robin tapped the desk. "The rest of this morning, I want you to put together every bit of concrete evidence we've got and look for any new stuff. Traffic camera footage from the ones nearest Cromwell Road that Alex Carey could have passed on the evening of the eleventh, when travelling to her parents' house. I'd be keeping an eye out for two cars, possibly travelling in convoy—the ones the Mearses came down in and Alex's own. She'd have had to get back a couple of days later. Is there anything significant from Ellen's bank records after her death apart from the bins and the mirror?"

Ashok shook his head. "I bet the card's long gone, cut up and disposed of. Same with the spare remote for the blinds. You don't want us to go sifting through the stuff at the tip, do you?"

"Not at this precise moment. It's human fragments I want examined. I want you and Ben to contact both Jeremy Sexton and the Vinces, because they seem to be the people who knew Ellen best. Find out if she ever mentioned Olivia Mears or her parents. Or if she showed any signs of obsession." Robin moved to the board, pointing at the victim's picture. "Right from the start, we've had people telling us that they thought Ellen might be losing her faculties and beginning to act oddly. Not only the Careys, who'd admittedly have a motive to lie so we've tended to discard what they've said. We've been trying to rationalise that testimony away, linking Ellen's behaviour to her wanting to spend time researching and her wish to cut herself off from Greg Carey because of his fraud. What if it's got an element of truth, though? One of the signs of dementia can be aggression—hence the arguments with Jeremy and telling people to naff off—and it can also lead to irrational behaviour. What if she fixated on the Careys: his fraud and her identity? Saw both of those elements as a threat to the children, whom she clearly liked."

"There's nothing in her medical records," Pru said, "but she'd likely be in denial. I might talk to her dental surgery again, given that they'd seen her relatively recently. Remember they said she used to contact them to double-check her appointment details? They might have a gut feeling for any changes in her behaviour, such as signs of forgetfulness."

"Great. Any other bright ideas, feel free to pursue them if they'll help get the two outcomes I want. The first is not to have to take evidence from the Carey children, although I'm increasingly convinced that unless we get a confession, they're going to be our key witnesses. The second is for Pru and I to have enough of a case for when we head up to Oxford later today."

"Oxford? To interview Vic and Carol Mears?"

"Yep. Although you and I are going to have to remember to call them Odell. I'll contact their local nick and arrange an interview room. Finding themselves being formally spoken to, recording and all, might have the desired effect."

By the time they were ready to head off in the direction of Oxford, they'd accrued some new but potentially vital evidence. The traffic cameras nearest the Odell home had come up trumps, as had the calls to those who had known Ellen best. Naomi had also discovered that the Odells had received a lecture from their local police—and a warning—about lockdown breaking, based on a report from the people across the road who'd said they had family members staying with them in the run up to Christmas. Dobbing in your neighbours had been an aspect of alibi creation during lockdown whose usefulness Robin hadn't yet considered: Would Alex and her family have been banking on getting reported again?

Ben had persuaded Jeremy to admit that the Boxing Day argument he'd had with Ellen had begun because she'd suspected he'd been eyeing up another woman when they'd been out on a walk. It had blown up out of all proportion to the offence, and Ellen had said some peculiar things, including that leopards never changed their spots. He'd taken the leopards remark as referring to *him* but then—with the typically baffling non sequitur that can happen in an argument—she'd said she had children to protect back on her home turf. He could only think it referred to her other research. He'd also conceded that, with the benefit of hindsight, there might have been signs of Ellen not being quite as mentally stable as she had been in the past, although he swore that her brain—when focussed on work—was as sharp as ever.

Mrs. Vince couldn't offer Ashok anything about Ellen's recent state of mind but confirmed Jeremy's assertion that the woman had always felt strongly about protecting children from harm. "I wouldn't say it was obsessional, although it wasn't a subject you wanted to get her started on, because she wouldn't stop. I put it down to her having no children of her own, so she enjoyed fussing over other people's. There was something bugging her about her own childhood too, because it hadn't been all that happy. That, combined with not having kids, meant she was lacking a bit of healthy perspective."

Another part of the picture of a woman who cared—perhaps too much—for youngsters and their welfare.

Pru offered to do the driving, which suited Robin. He wouldn't have to spend some of the journey gripping his seat or the door handle, as he'd had to do at times when Anderson had been his sergeant.

She still seemed to be brooding over something and concentrating harder on driving than the road and traffic conditions dictated.

"Penny for them?"

Unusually solemn, the sergeant said, "My thoughts? Do you really want to hear?"

"Too right I do, now you've said that." Robin studied her sidelong. Not like Pru to be so reticent; this had to be both serious and important.

"I'm hoping that we can *prove* it was Vic or Carol Mears. Or anyone else who puts their hands up to the crime."

So did Robin, but he still wasn't getting what this was about. "Okay. Is that because you think they might change their plea when it comes to court?"

"No. Look, I didn't want to say this in front of the others, and I've been debating whether to say it to you because it's not easy. In fact, it's horrible." Pru, eyes fixed firmly on the road, took a deep breath. "There's another possible explanation for what happened at Ellen's that day. Keep the killer's cry for practical help and the subsequent cover-up in mind but go down a generation, instead of up. I don't know if you can inherit a tendency to violence, yet traits do run in families."

"I . . . Oh, dear God. You're thinking there's a chance one of the children did it." That's why Robin had thought about Aaron—the offhand remark to Ben about apples not falling far from the tree. Like mother, like child?

Pru nodded, gulping hard before she replied. "It's awful, I know, but I can't get the scenario out of my head. Who would you move heaven and earth to protect above all others? Your children. Who would Ellen have let into her house without a second thought? Those girls. Both of whom watch *Midsomer Murders*, which is hardly full of blood and gore but which still might put ideas into their heads."

Robin heaved a sigh. They couldn't dismiss the notion out of hand, no matter how far-fetched or unpalatable it appeared to be. *Test every theory; don't jump to conclusions and pursue only what you think is the right solution.* Some of the key elements of modern policing as it should be, despite what many television shows implied. "Let's examine the idea. Means—yes, they could have grabbed a kitchen knife as easily as anyone. Opportunity—possibly better than anyone else we have in the frame, certainly in terms of putting Ellen off her guard. What's their motive, though?"

"What if they'd overheard their dad talking about what Ellen had been researching and how it could mean prison for him? Combine it with them hearing that their mum might have her identity exposed and how that could mean moving to a completely new area, away from their friends. In a child's mind that could be enough to want to take action." Pru shot him a worried glance. "Especially if there's an unstable streak in them. You don't need me to name cases where children have committed the most despicable acts."

"I don't." Almost anybody in Britain could give an example and in the most infamous recent case, at least one of the perpetrators had been in and out of the media several times, mainly related to new offences. To be on the fringes of such notoriety, even on the right side of the law, wouldn't be comfortable for any of the team. "We need to take all emotion out of this at the moment. Treat it like we'd do if our suspects were adult. So, if one or both of the girls did it and their mum and granny dash to the rescue, why did Alex then drive to her parents' house that evening, leaving the girls behind?"

"Maybe she didn't. I mean, we know she went because we've got the traffic camera images, but what if she took the girls with her? It wouldn't matter where they did their schoolwork from so long as they logged in, so the school wouldn't be suspicious. In the process, Alex sets up an alibi for both herself and them. They return to a situation where Greg's dealing with some of the practicalities and then carry on as if nothing happened until they get to the point they need the body found."

Pru's logic was, as always, persuasive.

"But those girls have given no hint. Wouldn't they be having nightmares, or somehow showing a change of personality that would make their teachers raise concerns?"

"Would their teachers spot that if they're being taught online? Assuming they *are* getting proper teaching rather than only being sent worksheets." Pru pulled a face. There had been plenty of stories about schools delivering little in the way of learning during the first lockdown.

"Greg did mention a lack of proper online learning first time around, so the situation may not have changed."

"Ashok says they were asking him all about our investigations. It might be nothing other than curiosity, of course . . ."

"Hm." Robin stared through the windscreen, thoughts troubled. Could they have reached the kernel of the case now, or was this a red herring, a plausible theory that fitted the facts but wasn't what had happened? The sort of thing you'd get in fiction, rather than in real life. "If there's any chance of this being true, we're going to need a tighter case than the one we're making against the Mearses. Sorry, the Odells. The case we're probably both thinking of featured CCTV footage that put the culprits and victims together. We've got absolutely nothing."

"Don't I know that, sir?" Pru set her gaze firmly on the road, and the next twenty minutes passed in silence between them. Robin took the opportunity to ring Ben, to get someone to keep an eye on the Careys, in case they decided to do a runner to that holiday home or another bolt hole. Maybe he should have had the foresight to do that already but hindsight was always the clearest sight.

As they gradually neared their destination, discussion started up again, the normal planning that would go into the upcoming interview. Still, what had been said couldn't now be unsaid, so the discussion would have to have cognisance of the possibility that *any* of the three generations could have struck the final blow.

Carol Odell—a well-dressed woman, as facially like her daughter as two bees—appeared composed but under strain. They'd separated her from her husband to get one point of view at a time, although no doubt their stories had been practiced in advance. She'd come with her solicitor, probably as a result of having gone through this kind of experience before.

Once the preliminaries had been gone through, Robin said, "Can I take you back to the eleventh of January? You were in Kinechester that day."

The witness shook her head. "I'm afraid we weren't. That was when I had bronchitis and was flat on my back. Alex had come up to nurse me."

Robin tried to appear perturbed at the information. "When *did* she come?"

"The Sunday morning, I think. I really was quite out of it and Vic's about as much use as a chocolate teapot when anyone's ill."

Robin nodded. "And were you sufficiently recovered by Monday the eleventh to vouch for where your daughter was that evening?"

"Yes. She was still looking after me. She'd made some soup for me, but I couldn't swear to exactly when I ate it. Six-ish, maybe." Mrs. Odell shrugged. "It all rather ran together."

"May I remind you that this is a formal interview and you'd be as well to tell us the truth?" Robin detailed for the recording that he was showing the witness a photograph. "This was taken from the traffic camera on the road leading off the dual carriageway. The way anyone would come to visit you if they were driving from Kinechester. At ten o'clock that night, Alex was driving past that camera in her car, towards your house."

The witness glanced at her solicitor, then said, "I would have been asleep by then. Perhaps she went out to get some milk in or other supplies."

"At that time of night?" Pru shook her head. "Here's another photo taken from the same camera a few seconds later. *Your* car. Following Alex's. Although the image isn't clear, there's both a driver and a passenger in yours. Is that you?"

"No comment." That response, so beloved of those with something to hide.

Pru pressed on. "I'd suggest that you and your husband are the people in the image, on your way back from Kinechester, where you'd been earlier that day. We're in the process of verifying both cars' locations along the route, and we can apply to get your phone's positions, so it would simply be easier for all concerned if you told us the truth now."

"No comment."

Time for Robin to up the stakes. "Although we can't be certain from the images, we suspect that Alex has your grandchildren in the car with her."

That hit home. Mrs. Odell turned white, glancing at her solicitor again before saying, "Why are you bringing them into it? They've done nothing."

"Did Alex bring them here on the evening of the eleventh of January?"

"No comment."

"I'm going to suspend the interview now." Robin rose from his seat. "I'll be back after I've spoken to your husband. One of you needs to tell me the truth, because at the very least you're both facing a charge of obstructing us in our duty. Maybe you'll be charged with shielding an offender and we could add in preventing the lawful burial of a body, although your solicitor might feel that would be stretching it. The Crown Prosecution Service might feel differently. Of course, there's murder to add into the mix. We've enough evidence to reasonably suspect one of your family members did it."

That might have been an exaggeration on the evidence front, but it had the desired effect.

"I shall take this opportunity to speak to my solicitor, then," Mrs. Odell said, with great dignity. She'd clearly been shaken, though. Hopefully those offhand remarks about Mr. Odell's ability to cope with crises would turn out to be true and he'd be an easier nut to crack.

The first part of the interview with Victor Odell was almost a rerun of his wife's, even to the matter of the soup, which was supposedly leek and potato. The only difference appeared to be that he had a Mr. Cooke with him, while his wife's solicitor bore the impressive surname of Tattersall. Mr. Odell was equally perturbed by the traffic photos and reverted, like Carol, to saying, "No comment." His reaction to Robin's belief that the young Careys were in the car brought the first note of difference.

Mr. Odell shot out of his chair, leaning on the table and pushing his face nearer Robin's. "How dare you? How *dare* you? What are you trying to say—that because Alex got led astray when she was younger, somehow that's been passed on to Cerys and Carly?"

And funny how nobody had mentioned either of the girls' names in these most recent interviews, up until now. As though there'd been a concerted effort to somehow distance them from the case. Robin tapped the table. "I've said no such thing. I only wanted to establish whether Alex brought them to your house on the eleventh of January. Are you telling me that she or the girls have something to hide?"

That seemed to sober Mr. Odell up. He sat down again. "No, why should they? Okay, we'd been down to see the family when we shouldn't and we've been caught lying about it, but you can't lock us up for that. We came back all together, because my wife wasn't feeling well and, frankly, I'm useless at the domestic stuff if she comes down with anything. Couldn't boil an egg."

That sounded entirely plausible, given that there were still men around, particularly older ones, who refused to lift a hand when it came to household tasks and had all their lives been waited on hand and foot. Although it begged the question of why Mrs. Odell hadn't given that simple explanation. Which of the pair had gone off script?

"Cerys and Carly came with you?" Pru asked.

Mr. Odell paused before answering, perhaps weighing up how much evidence the police had about what had gone on. "Yes. Greg's a nice chap, and while he's fine with rustling up a meal, he's pretty useless at all the school stuff, so the girls came with Alex. I was able to help them with their school science project." He spoke the last part with evident pride. "Lockdown breaking again, although I understand that emergency situations take precedence and this was an emergency."

"Why did Alex tell us that she was already at your house on the eleventh?"

Mr. Odell shrugged. "You'll have to ask her that, Sergeant. Maybe she got confused. All the days do seem to melt together during lockdown."

Robin pushed back his chair. "Interview suspended at 10:55. I'm going to verify what you've said. While I'm away, you can solidify all the days out from each other again, especially the eleventh. When I come back, I want some answers about what went on in Kinechester."

Back in the other interview room, Mrs. Odell had appeared to have had a change of heart. Once the recording had begun again, she said, "I didn't tell you the truth, earlier. It was very bad of me, but I didn't want to get into trouble for lockdown breaking. We'd already had a warning last year, when the family came up to exchange Christmas presents. Eric has advised me to come clean." She gave the solicitor a smile.

"Let's have the truth, then. The evening of the eleventh of January." Robin sat back.

"We'd been down to Kinechester. I began to feel unwell, and we all drove back here together. All bar Greg, I mean."

"And why didn't you and your husband return alone?" No doubt the answer would stick to the party line. Perhaps the initial divergence had been a simple ploy to make it seem like they hadn't rehearsed their responses.

"As I said, Vic's useless. That was no word of a lie. Greg can rustle up a meal, but the schoolwork isn't his scene, so Alex brought the girls along so she and Vic could make sure they didn't fall behind."

Did the use of exactly the same turn of phrase about Greg— *rustling up a meal*—confirm the setting of a script for what had supposedly happened? Best to stick to events. "Okay, so at last we have what happened late that Monday clear. Let's go earlier in the day. In fact, let's go back to last year, when you were in phone contact with Ellen Wilkins, Alex's neighbour. Alex's now-dead neighbour."

If the Odells had planned this in advance, they'd surely taken account of the police having phone records. While Carol Odell appeared surprised, she clearly wasn't as alarmed as she'd been when Robin mentioned her granddaughters. "That's entirely innocent, Mr. Bright. It's Greg's fortieth later this year, and she wanted to organise a surprise for him. They'd been very good friends in the past, and she said she wanted to make amends for letting their friendship wither. I told her that these things happen and that he'd no doubt appreciate the gesture. Although she wasn't to go to too much trouble. He's not keen on fuss."

Robin nodded, pretty certain he'd been told the truth on that score. "So she arranged to see you on the eleventh? We have found a note of hers which we believe refers to such an appointment."

The mention of the note had evidently been unexpected, but Mrs. Odell, eyes briefly registering what might have been panic, soon rallied. "Well, I suppose she might have expected us. We'd left it that one of us would drop in when we were next down, assuming we could get away without Greg suspecting we were on a secret mission. If she'd heard we were coming . . ."

"Mrs. Odell, we believe that either you or your husband *did* get away, late afternoon on the eleventh. That you went to see Ellen Wilkins."

Carol Odell opened her mouth, paused, and tersely said, "No comment."

Given they'd obviously reached the part of the pre-determined plan where the suspect was to revert to that line, Pru—clearly chomping at the bit—brought out the big guns. "Was it you or your husband who called in on her? And which of your granddaughters went with you?"

It took Mrs. Odell a good ten seconds to get to the point she could force out the words, "No comment."

"You'll have to tell us the truth at some point," Robin said, as sympathetically as he could manage. "As you've already found out, it's so much easier if you tell us it in the first place, rather than covering up. We'll get there in the end, believe me. Maybe the girls themselves will tell us the truth."

Mrs. Odell flinched, then glanced at her solicitor, who shook his head. Addressing the table, she said, "No comment."

Time to go see if Vic Odell would be an easier egg to crack.

Between interview rooms, Pru pulled Robin to one side. "They're very cagey about the girls, aren't they? You know how I stand on this—I'm convinced one or both of the girls is involved in the attack, so I might be biased. You've got more of an objective view."

"I have. If we'd not had that conversation in the car, I'd still have made a note of their reactions. I don't have kids, but I understand how people who do wouldn't want them dragged into this ghastly mess. Except we know that they already have been dragged in if they're keeping Grandad abreast of developments." Robin glanced up and down the corridor, at both doors. Behind them lay the people who knew exactly what had happened at Ellen's house the day she died and subsequently. He had little doubt of that. "We keep on doing what we're doing until we have enough to charge them."

Pru pulled a disdainful face. "Or their solicitors force us to let them go."

Robin blew out his cheeks. "We've got to believe we can get enough evidence one way or another to settle this case. Even if that feels as likely as Elvis charging down this corridor on Shergar."

As Robin and Pru re-entered the interview room, Vic Odell was standing by the window and Cooke, the solicitor, appeared unnaturally absorbed in reading his paperwork. At a guess, they'd been involved in a crucial discussion—what a shame that the recording equipment couldn't have been surreptitiously left running, despite the legal complications that would have entailed.

"Mr. Odell, can we recommence, please?" Pru got the recording restarted, then said, "Your wife has confirmed that you all came back from Kinechester on the evening of the eleventh. She also confirms that Ellen Wilkins had been in contact with you since last year, as we already knew from her phone records. What was that about?"

Vic Odell waved his hand. "A surprise present for Greg, or something. Again, not my department. Carol always knows what to get people and what we've given in the past."

"Then she arranged to meet you when you were next in Kinechester to discuss this surprise? We have a note to that effect." Pru waited for Mr. Odell to exchange glances with Cooke and then nod. "That would be the eleventh. Quite a busy day."

"Yes, it was."

Mr. Odell flinched, evidently realising what might be inferred from that.

Robin swiftly cut in, "So which of you two went to see Ellen that day? Was that when she told you she was investigating Alex's previous identity?"

"I . . . No comment."

Perhaps the expected response, given how these interviews were proceeding, but not the strong protest one might have expected. It was becoming clear that Vic Odell wasn't as accomplished a stonewaller or liar as his wife. Since hearing Robin's question, his face might as well have had *Help me, please!* written on it.

"Mr. Odell, we'll get to the truth sooner or later," Robin said. "I'd prefer sooner, and I'm sure both you and your solicitor would, as well. Did you know that Ellen had discovered Alex was Olivia Mears?"

"Oh, yes." Mr. Odell studied his hands. "Greg had found out somehow. They hadn't told us until that day. Probably protecting me, given my medical history. They treat me like a child sometimes. Not Cerys and Carly—they're my par—" He stopped.

"They're your what?" Pru asked gently.

"They're my pals. They don't judge or fuss when I have a funny five minutes." That much was clearly true, the affection he had for his granddaughters unmistakable. Robin was pretty sure he'd been going to call them his *partners in crime*, though. "We watch the telly together, and they never complain if I lose track of the plot."

"They're certainly intelligent girls," Robin said. "My constable, Ashok, was very impressed with them."

Mr. Odell nodded, beaming with pride. "Yes. They've told me all about it. They were so excited when he took their fingerprints."

"Fingerprints?" The solicitor tapped the table. "I must protest most firmly. What authorisation did you have to do that?"

"Let me clarify," said Robin. "He had come to take their mother's fingerprints and to put the girls at ease, he let them each make their thumbprints. Which they both got to keep, so we couldn't have used them for comparison purposes, irrespective of whether we wanted to. Which, as you pointed out, would have been irregular. I observed the whole process and am quite happy that everything proceeded correctly."

Cooke harrumphed but made no further complaint.

"Now, hold on. Mr. Cooke here's quite correct. You shouldn't have taken the girls' prints at all." The sudden aggression in Mr. Odell's voice, especially when the matter of correct procedure had been cleared up, would have been baffling, had they not some idea of the context. A brain tumour and the man's devotion to his granddaughters. "If you use them for comparison or whatever you call it, that's inadmissible evidence. Anyway, the girls used to visit Ellen, so their prints are bound to be in her house."

"Like when they went into Ellen's house on the eleventh?" Pru asked. "Was it both of them? Were they with *you*?"

"I . . . I . . . We went to thank Ellen for a present she'd put through the door for them at Christmas. A voucher for Amazon. The girls had made a card—they love doing that sort of thing. I believe in proper manners." Mr. Odell, calm again, wiped his hand across his brow.

"Did proper manners include taking your shoes off at the door?"

"Of course. I hope your parents taught you the same, miss. Anyway, Ellen must have been frustrated that she couldn't discuss this present-for-Greg nonsense. She suggested that Car—" Odell stopped, mid-word, laying his hands on the desk like a child who wanted their cleanliness inspected. "I refuse to say anything else. You can't make me. No comment."

Cooke, giving Robin a warning glance, touched his client's arm. "Chief Inspector, I must make you aware that my client has a medical condition which sometimes affects his ability to answer questions as clearly as you and I would wish him to. I don't need to remind you of your responsibilities under the Police and Criminal Evidence Act."

"You don't. Sergeant Davis and I were doing our homework earlier today. We're well aware of our obligations if we have to interview children too." With that parting shot, Robin suspended the interview and advised the two men they were free to take a break, stretch their legs or get a drink but that they shouldn't leave just yet.

"I'm sure he was going to say the girls were his partners in crime rather than his pals," Pru remarked, as they headed to get some fresh air and thinking time before tackling Mrs. Odell again. "Then he thought better of it."

"You could be right. He seems to flit between knowing exactly what he's saying, then having—what did he call it—a funny five minutes. I don't think he's a good enough actor to be putting it on." Which wasn't helping them to get closer to the truth.

"I think we're being set up, sir. Have been from the start. They've been banking on us not pinning down the exact date of the murder, who was where and when, but they also have a backup plan to explain what went on if they needed to. As much of it based in truth as they could manage, like the reason Ellen contacted them." They'd reached the rear entrance of the station: even the cold air of the car park felt refreshing after the last few hours. Pru glanced around, no doubt working out if they could be overheard. "They've got the ideal fall guy in Mr. Odell. Unwell, perhaps terminally ill for all we know. Possibly unfit to stand trial if he makes it that far. Anything he says to be taken with a pinch of salt."

"Yes. Notice how the story about discussing the present for Greg morphed into delivering a thank-you card? Maybe he's getting the official line confused."

"Perhaps the thank-you card did happen and he wasn't supposed to mention it."

"Do you really think they'd throw him under the bus to save the actual culprit? I'm tending to agree, especially as I don't think he'd have gone to see Ellen about a surprise present. That would have been Carol. And I bet she'd have kept her head in a crisis better than he would." Back to Adam and his example of the female learning assistants. Adam, whom Robin had barely had time to think of today, apart from exchanging a few texts on the journey, asking how the shingles were progressing and advising that he'd be home late. The response had been positive on the illness front and understanding on the work one.

Stay out as late as you want, so long as you get this case solved. I'll sleep in the spare bed tonight so you don't need to worry about waking me. Campbell sends his love. Or maybe he's angling for a biscuit. You can never tell.

Robin checked his phone again now, having had it in silent mode during the interviews. There was a message, although not from home. Henry from fraud had turned up something, which he said he'd put in an email because it might be important.

"Henry's got a lead. Cross your fingers while I open the file." A frisson of excitement shot up Robin's spine as he scanned what he'd been sent.

We've been going through Greg's browsing history. There's a lot of bookmarked pages about juvenile culpability under English law. I don't think it's to do with his wife's past—this isn't looking at twenty years ago—it's about the law as it stands now. Not sure if that helps with your case?

"What a beauty," Pru said. "No wonder Greg was cross when they took his laptop: because he'd not deleted them. A stupid oversight."

"It's the stupid oversights that help us catch people. Maybe the list of unsolved cases is full of people who managed to avoid them." Or were simply lucky.

"I wonder if they've got a potential explanation for this in their party manifesto? You know, like him saying he was only idly speculating what would have happened to his wife if she'd assaulted that pensioner today. We can't prove what was in his mind when he made the searches."

"No, but proving that he did it might be enough to rattle his mother-in-law."

Back in the room with Mrs. Odell, who was showing significant signs of impatience, not least drumming on the table. They formally recommenced the interview, Robin slowly laying down his phone in her sight, trying to indicate it held something of importance. "Mrs. Odell, your husband verifies that Ellen Wilkins got in touch with you about a present for Greg. He also stated that you were both aware that she had been researching your daughter's past."

"Yes. We were horrified when we discovered that."

"When *did* you discover it, by the way?"

A brief flicker of panic as Pru's question caught Mrs. Odell on the hop. "I don't remember. All the days roll into one with this wretched lockdown."

"We don't need a specific day." Pru smiled. "Before Christmas? In the new year?"

"New Year, definitely. What did Vic say?"

Robin ignored the query, changing tack to wrong-foot her. "He confirmed our belief that you were due to see Ellen on the eleventh. He says that he and your granddaughters went to her house. We don't believe that's true."

The suspect couldn't hide the pantomime of emotions crossing her face: horror at the mention of the girls, relief at Robin's doubt.

"What *really* happened that day?" he asked.

"My husband went to see her on his own, because it would have seemed odd to Greg if we'd both sneaked out. Vic told Greg he was going to get a magazine as he was short of reading material and he doesn't do books. I'm not sure Alex believed him, but she didn't make a fuss. As for the girls being with him, he does get rather muddled."

Mrs. Odell shook her head. "He's got a tumour on his brain, you see. It means that sometimes he gets mixed up between what happened and his imagination."

"Why would *he* have gone, though?" Pru said. "He admits that presents aren't his scene, so he'd not have been much use to Ellen, and it would have been easy enough for *you* to slip out, saying you were picking up his magazine for him. In fact, if he is losing his faculties a bit, that would have been a likelier scenario."

"Likelier, maybe, but not the actual one. Vic dropped in there, on his own, told Ellen he was sorry *I* couldn't get away. She was alive when he left. Unless . . ." Mrs. Odell stared at her solicitor. The performance seemed to have reached the next act: melodrama at its least convincing. "No, it couldn't be. Eric, is it possible he killed her and then forgot he'd done it?"

Before Eric Tattersall could reply, Robin cut in, "I don't believe you, Mrs. Odell. If that had happened, your husband would have had bloodstains on him when he returned to Alex's house. That crime scene was cleaned and the killer—or their accomplices—have been working hard ever since to cover up the date of death. So, if you're trying to pin the crime on Vic because he's unlikely to face trial, you'll have a lot of explaining to do. For example, why your husband was so adamant that there'd be nothing suspicious if we found your granddaughters' fingerprints at the scene. He told us he'd gone to Ellen's to deliver a thank-you card from the girls and one of them had gone with him. Most likely Carly."

Carol Odell's face was a picture of stifled anger. She was clearly torn between the standard *No comment* line and making a protest, which would risk letting a kitten or two out of the bag. She opted for silence.

"You see, Mrs. Odell, everything in this case revolves around your family and their connections," Pru said. "Ellen was very good at her job, which was researching and compiling evidence of wrongdoing. She'd helped put people in prison, one of whom—Derek Cavendish—was in your daughter's house not a few days after the murder; we think he and his wife were involved with helping to cover up the crime. We both know that Ellen was also investigating Greg's financial probity regarding the charity he helps. It wasn't only him under her microscope, but Mrs. Cavendish too, which Greg knew because he went into Ellen's house when she was away and found some of her files. The fraud thing must have been bad enough but to then find out that she posed a risk to your daughter's reputation . . . I can imagine the tongues wagging on Cromwell Road when they discovered Olivia Mears was living there."

"Spiteful bitches with not enough to do other than gossip on social media." Mrs. Odell rolled her eyes. "What you'd call 'fur coats and no knickers.'"

In any other circumstances that would have raised a smile. In that room, the effect was sickening. "She'd also been researching whether juveniles who'd committed a violent crime went on to do so as adults. Specifically if they hurt their children."

"Had she? What a cow. My Alex would never hurt the girls. She wouldn't have hurt *anyone* had it not been for Suzie Banks."

"Let's not bring Suzie into this. I think you already knew about Ellen's research, Mrs. Odell." Robin sat back in his chair. "Let me put this scenario to you, so both you and Mr. Tattersall can see where our thoughts have got to from what we know. The eleventh of January. You're at your daughter's house. You nip round to Ellen's without telling Alex. We can guess that because chances are she'd have stopped you if she'd realised your intention. You take one of the girls with you because you want them to be in on the big surprise for Daddy. Carly—she's the elder, isn't she?"

"She is," Mrs. Odell said begrudgingly.

"When you get there, Ellen's not happy that you're not on your own. She wants to talk about who your daughter really is and the threat she thinks Alex poses to the girls or to other people. She doesn't want to waste this chance, so she occupies Carly with something while she has a little word."

"Craft in the kitchen. Cutting out paper dolls or something else she'd like," Pru chipped in.

Robin wondered where that had come from, then remembered the snippets of coloured paper on the kitchen floor, which Pru must have clocked—as he had—on one of her visits to the property. If someone had cleared the worktop, they'd missed those. Mrs. Odell's ashen face suggested Robin was getting very near the truth. "She tells you she knows who Alex is, maybe threatens to report her to social services or otherwise kick up a stink. You get into a row. Carly comes in to see what the noise is about. She's upset."

"She's carrying the scissors she's been using," Pru said.

"No!" Mrs. Odell thumped the table. "Carly had nothing to do with it. Okay, I'll fess up or whatever it is they call it." She shook her solicitor's hand from her arm. "Yes, it was exactly as you said, although I've nobody to vouch for that, because I was on my own. Ellen suddenly flipped. Started ranting about Alex. I could put up with that—my God, I've done so often enough—but when she started on about the girls and how they were at risk, *I* flipped. In the cold light of day, I now see there was little risk of social services taking my granddaughters away from us, but at the time all I could think of was some officious social worker overreacting because they'd been in trouble previously for not coming down quickly and hard enough. Panic set in."

"What happened next?" And how much would this be based on what the suspect had witnessed another member of their family do?

"She'd turned round to get something—she said it would prove how at risk the girls were. There were some scissors on the side table, so I grabbed them, and when she turned back again I stabbed her. Here." Mrs. Odell indicated a place just under the rib cage, exactly where the postmortem put the rogue wound. "She went down like a ton of bricks, clutching her chest, so I thought, 'Finish her off, Carol. You'll be hung for a sheep as much as for a lamb.' I used the knife, because I thought that would be quicker."

"Which knife?" Pru asked.

"The knife that . . . Ellen had brought in from the kitchen with her. She was busy in the kitchen when we arrived." Mrs. Odell flushed at her obvious mistake.

Robin pounced. "*We?*"

"I meant me. I was on my own. I'm prepared to swear to that."

"She didn't try to defend herself from you?"

The suspect paused, clearly wrong-footed by the question. "No. She'd flopped onto the floor, clearly in shock or too focussed on trying to stem the flow from the first wound."

"She might well have been in shock and not just at the wound. If it was someone she knew and trusted who attacked her," Robin suggested. "Or two people were working together, one of whom was either holding her arms or distracting her so she couldn't defend herself."

"No! It wasn't like that. I was on my own."

Pru said, "Then what happened, after you'd killed her?"

"I felt remarkably calm. It sounds callous, but I went into dealing-with-an-emergency mode. I had the sense to stand still, fished my phone out of my pocket, called Alex, and pleaded with her not to ask questions but to get round and bring something with her to help clean up. She got a hell of a shock when she saw what had happened, but when she understood the situation I'd found myself in, she got stuck in. We cleared up everything, all apart from one smudge on the floor where I'd obviously stepped forward and then back again. I wanted to scrub it up, but we decided it wasn't worth the extra time it would take. Would you like the details of me stripping off completely and putting my clothes with the knife and scissors in a black bag?" Mrs. Odell smirked.

Robin ignored the sarcasm. "Yes, please. I'd also like to know why one of you didn't return later to clean up the footprint."

"Because I was concerned that every visit would increase the chance of leaving evidence to link me to that house. Alex put everything I'd been wearing in the dustbin, saying that she knew how to get rid of it. The rest of the business, like the blinds and the cash card, got planned and executed afterwards. I think we did quite well."

She could be right, if they managed to get away with covering up the involvement of the children.

"Mrs. Odell," Robin said, "you've produced a convincing description of Ellen Wilkins's murder. I have little doubt that you know exactly what went on, at the time and afterwards. However, I have serious concerns about whether you've told us the whole truth. You see, if nothing happened which involved either Carly or Cerys, why has Greg been doing a lot of online searches about what happens nowadays to children who are accused of serious crimes? Like manslaughter."

"I . . . I . . . No comment. You have my confession. I refuse to say another word."

Which was exactly what she did, despite anything that Pru or Robin put to her.

Out in the corridor again, between interview rooms. Pru, clearly tired and leaning against the wall, said, "We're still being set up, aren't we? Wouldn't accept it was him so maybe we'll believe it was her."

"They've played both their last cards, though. Nowhere new to go if we can prove they've lied." Robin leaned back on the opposite wall, eyes closed. "Right. Where did we make Carol Odell uncomfortable? The knife and the defensive wounds. She didn't seem to have her story off pat for them. Flaky on the scissors too." He opened his eyes. "We'll have one more crack at Vic and maybe another at her if we make progress. We've got nothing to lose."

As soon as they re-entered the other interview room, Cooke said, "I hope you haven't come to question my client again."

"I've actually come to update you both, as there's been a development. I'd like Mr. Odell's view on it." Once the recording equipment had started up, Robin continued. "Your wife has given us an entirely different account of the events on the eleventh. She says *she* went to see Ellen, alone."

"Oh. I was rather hoping she'd keep quiet about that. I suppose I watch too many TV dramas—doesn't someone always confess to protect their loved ones?" Odell turned to his solicitor, who appeared completely bewildered. "I thought I was doing the right thing."

"I completely understand the desire to shield those near to us," Robin said softly, "which is why I think Carol is playing the same hand, at least to some extent. I have no doubt she was there when all this unfolded and played a significant part. Trouble is, she says neither of the girls went with her. That's the bit I don't believe. She as good as let slip that Cerys was with her."

"Not Cerys. It was—" Mr. Odell stopped. Time appeared to stop, as well, everyone in the room frozen.

"Mr. Odell, we don't at present think Carly *meant* to hurt anyone." Robin, who could now see the scenario clear as day, picked his next words with extreme care. "She hears the argument between Ellen and Carol growing worse. She maybe hears her own name mentioned, so she rushes into the lounge. Lunges at Ellen, punching and screaming, like children do."

"Why should she get angry? She's hardly a two-year-old having a tantrum." It sounded like a last-ditch attempt at defence on Mr. Odell's part, though. The aged fighter on the ropes.

"Because Ellen had threatened to contact the authorities, to get them to take her and Cerys away from Alex and Greg. Away from you and Carol." Robin could see from Mr. Odell's flinch how the words had hit home. "Carly's got those scissors in her hand, and in blind anger, she stabs at this woman who's trying to ruin her life."

Robin waited—they all waited—for the witness's response.

Suddenly, Odell visibly crumpled, sobbing with his head in his hands. "Poor thing. Such a shock. We've had to get them both new aprons, you know. Carly's was covered in blood."

Robin and Cooke exchanged a glance and a nod. The solicitor said, "I think that's enough, Mr. Bright."

"I think so too." Robin sighed. He'd always dreaded having an unsolved case, but now he knew that a resolution could actually be worse. Facing Carly, the likely killer, would be the stuff of nightmares.

The late afternoon and early evening in Kinechester saw Robin undergoing an experience he never wanted to repeat. Root canal treatment would have been more comfortable; in fact, anything would have been preferable to an hour spent interviewing Carly Carey.

The specialist officer who helped Robin and Pru through the interview with Carly was totally professional and totally efficient. It soon became plain what had happened that fateful afternoon when Carly and her grandmother had visited Ellen Wilkins. The girl explained how she'd left her boots at the door, so as not to get mud on Ellen's "nice carpet." That's why she'd only been wearing her favourite blue socks around the house. And, irrespective of the Odells' supposed confessions, Carly didn't hide the fact that she'd inflicted the first wound.

"I was in a paddy at Ellen," she freely admitted, "because she said she'd have us all split up."

The rest of the girl's testimony showed that she and Cerys had subsequently been told that Ellen had only been slightly hurt and had actually been killed at least a week later.

As the interview finished, Carly blew her nose and asked, "Can you let me know the name of the murderer when you find out? I always liked Ellen. Even if she did go a bit funny in lockdown."

Robin left the interview room and headed straight for the toilets, where he could splash his face with cold water, grateful that he hadn't had much for lunch or it might be coming back up. Pru could well be in a similar state.

Back in the incident room, the team were quietly considerate.

"How did it go?" Naomi asked. "Or would you prefer a cuppa before you answer?"

"I'm not sure either of us could face food or drink. I'll give you a summary of what happened." When he'd outlined the main points, Robin finished with, "Carly says she didn't realise the scissors would hurt Ellen but was adamant the woman was alive when she left to get help."

"How did they manage to make so little mess?" Ashok asked.

"As we understand it, straight after the stabbing, Carly stepped back in shock. Carol Odell scooped her up, then whipped her socks off so she wouldn't get blood on Ellen's 'nice carpet.'" Pru grimaced as she made speech-mark signs. "Immediately after that, Carly ran home to get help from her mum while her gran was supposed to be ringing 999."

"That step back explains the smudge on the carpet," Robin said. "The one they missed in the big cleanup."

Ashok nodded. "Why didn't they tackle the hall and kitchen as well in case they'd left anything there? Were they interrupted?"

"I think they had to weigh up their chances. The longer spent cleaning, the more chance of being caught at it." Pru frowned. "She said that. Carol Odell. 'I wanted to scrub it all up, but we decided it wasn't worth the extra time it would take.'"

"They were lucky things went so well. Or had they planned it, cleaning and all?" Ben asked the question Robin had also wrestled with.

"I don't think anything specific was planned, ahead of them visiting Ellen, or I genuinely think Carol wouldn't have taken Carly with her." Robin took a look at the incident board—all those suspects who had worked together, almost in a *Murder on the Orient Express* style. "The family made up a really convincing story to tell the girls, and Carly was certain Ellen was still alive for the next week or so, although too unwell to have visitors. Not because of what had happened with the scissors, but some nasty illness like her granddad has. Carly and Cerys had made her a card, which Alex put through the door and must have nipped in and removed when the girls were in bed. Carly told us all about how her granny had given Ellen first aid and called an ambulance to take her to hospital to be checked over. Carly didn't see the ambulance, she says, as they'd already left for the grandparents' house, because Granddad had been taken ill again. She's really worried about her grandad."

"Poor kid." Pru, who rarely showed any hint of sentimentality, appeared to be on the verge of tears. "Maybe if Carly's mum wasn't Olivia Mears, then her granny mightn't have reacted in such a way. Carol Odell's first reaction might have been to call an ambulance and everything would have been regarded as a terrible accident. The sins of the parent falling on the child's shoulders."

Robin nodded. "Do you know what's the saddest thing? Carly says she and her granddad have been sharing theories about what happened, and they both suspect it was something to do with Ellen's old job. I actually think Vic Odell believes that, at times. I wonder what a jury will make of him? What they'll make of the whole case, given the lack of the stuff they might expect from the television. DNA and the like." For all that he liked witness evidence, statements might be challenged in court and portrayed as being made under coercion, especially where the person concerned was clearly ill. Or a child who loved watching *Midsomer Murders*. Forensic evidence could be portrayed as more robust . . . and juries liked it.

"Would an explanation about the turnip cheer you up, sir? Billy the Bins has confirmed that the dustbins weren't empty when he came to pick them up and that he faked the story about a turnip because he wanted to be clever." Naomi's sneer spoke volumes. "He'd been asked not to open the dustbins, but he was determined to have a gander. The recycling one had the usual bottles and newspapers plus what appeared to be cut-up Christmas cards, so he didn't take much notice of that. But the black bin had bloodied clothing and a plastic apron. A mixture of child and adult sizes, he says, and he should know because he stuck it all in a plastic bag and put it in store."

"Stored it?" Robin's hopes sailed higher than they had all day.

"Yep. He wanted to cover his back in case he and his mother were being shafted. The CSIs are picking it up today." Naomi shrugged. "He swears his mother was forced into making him help and that the Careys were behind everything. He's willing to make a full statement if we go lenient on him—and her."

"That's a decision for tomorrow. And for discussing with the Crown Prosecution Service. They can have the final say on the matter." Robin yawned and stretched, desperately weary. "Home, all of you. Lots of *t*'s to cross and *i*'s to dot in the morning."

Chapter Nineteen

Adam woke early, with no idea what time his husband had come in the night before. *He'd* been dead to the world, having got an early night, and Campbell mustn't have stirred, either. He sneaked a peek around their bedroom door, to find Robin out like a light. Clearly it wasn't going to be an early start, which might indicate he'd had a very late return home and—hopefully—a significant breakthrough. Whichever way, the bloke was going to be treated to one of his favourite breakfasts, a mushroom omelette with toast, which Adam could quickly put together.

The sound of the toilet flushing upstairs gave the first hint.

"Your other dad's up and about." Adam gave the dog a pat. "You make sure you give him a good fussing over."

When Robin entered the kitchen, he was greeted with a cold, wet nose in his hand and then a hug from Adam. "What have I done to deserve this? It looks amazing."

"Working too hard, for a start. Rare for you to have a lie in."

"I needed it. I got home at half past stupid o'clock." Robin grabbed the coffee Adam had already poured.

"Progress in the case?"

"Yes. Leaves a nasty taste in the mouth, though. Hello, boy." Campbell, evidently remembering the instruction about fuss, rubbed against Robin's leg. "Grandmother Odell completed what her granddaughter had started by inflicting the first wound." He launched into a story of cover-ups and people being thrown under the bus.

"That's awful," Adam said, when the whole tale had been told. He could envisage it, though. Children *did* lose control and do things without thinking. And parents told all sorts of lies to make their own lives easier as much as to protect their children. "I have to ask. Are you convinced there was no premeditation on Carly's part?"

"As convinced as I can be. The girl appears remarkably honest. About what she believes to be true, anyway." Robin had another swig of coffee and a pat of the dog, clearly needing both. "We're getting some other evidence together today, then I'll be interviewing the Careys and the Cavendishes again. I expect the latter will be doing some under-bus-shoving too."

"That's good. About the evidence, I mean." Adam squeezed his husband's hand. "It'll be okay. I know everything feels like a ton of shite now, with a child involved, but these things happen and someone has to deal with them. Better somebody like you, who's going to act with integrity."

"I guess so. I've got you and himself to come home to, as well. Thank God I didn't have a case like this before we met."

Adam thanked God for it too.

They'd both put in an effort to make the evening special. Adam had promised his husband a takeaway, a bottle of wine and—later—a nice, not-too-spotty deputy headteacher in a big, warm bed. Chicken tikka masala and all the trimmings for dinner with a decent Chablis to wash it down and both candles and flowers on the table would make the meal something of a celebration.

As he laid the table, Adam watched a flurry of snowflakes dance in the street lamps' soft glow outside the window. It was going to be another bitter night, and Robin would be finding cold comfort in his job over the next few days and weeks. It would be Adam's job to provide the warmth of affection and a place where the man could be at ease.

A wet nose nudging his trouser cuffs reminded him that job wasn't his exclusive preserve.

"Yes, you help take care of Robin as well. But there are some things only I can do. And if you don't know what they are, I'm not sullying your tender ears with an explanation."

The dog had consented to being washed, so a fragrant hound greeted his master at the front door at half past five, although the Newfoundland had been waiting there for ten minutes. He got the first hug, although the one Adam received was longer and more emotionally charged.

"I needed that," Robin said when he finally loosened the clinch. "Can I put in an order for another hug, later?"

"Order as many as you like. You've limitless credit at the bank of Matthews. And the Campbell building society," Adam added, at the arrival of a wet nose. "Go and get changed and I'll have a glass of white waiting."

"My hero." Robin gave him a kiss, then trudged wearily towards the stairs. Maybe their big, warm bed wouldn't be seeing anything other than a prolonged snoring session that evening, but that didn't matter. Sex, good as it was, wasn't the be all and end all of things. Love and comfort and all the other timeless values were the rocks on which the Matthews-Bright relationship were built.

Adam glanced down to see two dark eyes peering up at him. "Yes, I know. Your dads are turning into an old married couple. What are you going to do about it?"

The swift application of the dog's tongue to Adam's hand felt like the seal of approval.

Explore more of
The Lindenshaw Mysteries series:
riptidepublishing.com/collections/lindenshaw-mysteries

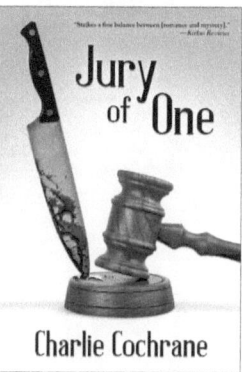

Dear Reader,

Thank you for reading Charlie Cochrane's *Lock, Stock and Peril*!

We know your time is precious and you have many, many entertainment options, so it means a lot that you've chosen to spend your time reading. We really hope you enjoyed it.

We'd be honored if you'd consider posting a review—good or bad—on sites like **Amazon, Barnes & Noble, Kobo, Goodreads, Twitter, Facebook, Tumblr,** and your blog or website. We'd also be honored if you told your friends and family about this book. Word of mouth is a book's lifeblood!

For more information on upcoming releases, author interviews, blog tours, contests, giveaways, and more, please sign up for our weekly, spam-free newsletter and visit us around the web:

Newsletter: riptidepublishing.com/newsletter
Twitter: twitter.com/RiptideBooks
Facebook: facebook.com/RiptidePublishing
Goodreads: tinyurl.com/RiptideOnGoodreads
Tumblr: riptidepublishing.tumblr.com

Thank you so much for Reading the Rainbow!

RiptidePublishing.com

Also by
Charlie Cochrane

Novels:
Best Corpse for the Job
Jury of One
Two Feet Under
Old Sins
A Carriage of Misjustice
Lessons in Love
Lessons in Desire
Lessons in Discovery
Lessons in Power
Lessons in Temptation
Lessons in Seduction
Lessons in Trust
All Lessons Learned
Lessons for Survivors
Lessons for Suspicious Minds
Lessons for Idle Tongues
Lessons for Sleeping Dogs
Broke Deep
Count the Shells
The Case of the Grey Assassin

Novellas:
Lessons in Loving thy
Murderous Neighbour
Lessons in Chasing the Wild
Goose
Lessons in Cracking the Deadly
Code

Lessons in Playing a Murderous
Tune
Lessons in Following a
Poisonous Trail
Lessons in Solving the Wrong
Problem
Lessons in Keeping a Dangerous
Promise

Collected novellas:
An Act of Detection
Pack Up Your Troubles
Wild Bells
Love in Every Season
In the Spotlight

*Standalone novellas and short
stories:*
Second Helpings
Awfully Glad
Don't Kiss the Vicar
Promises Made Under Fire

Anthologies (contributing author)
Given in Evidence
Capital Crimes
Lashings of Sauce
Tea and Crumpet
British Flash

About the Author

Because Charlie Cochrane couldn't be trusted to do any of her jobs of choice—like managing a rugby team—she writes. Her mystery novels include the Edwardian era Cambridge Fellows series, and the contemporary Lindenshaw Mysteries. Multipublished, she has titles with Riptide, Carina, Lume, and Bold Strokes, among others.

A member of the Romantic Novelists' Association, Mystery People, and International Thriller Writers Inc, Charlie regularly appears at literary festivals and at reader and author conferences.

Where to find her:
Website: charliecochrane.wordpress.com
Facebook: facebook.com/charlie.cochrane.18
Twitter: twitter.com/charliecochrane
Instagram: instagram.com/cochrane.charlie2

Enjoy more stories like
Lock, Stock and Peril
at RiptidePublishing.com!

www.ingramcontent.com/pod-product-compliance
Lightning Source LLC
Chambersburg PA
CBHW030642020726
47493CB00006B/1826